kop killer

BOOKS BY WARREN HAMMOND

KOP
Ex-KOP
KOP Killer

Available from Tor Books

kop
killer

WARREN HAMMOND

TOR®

A TOM DOHERTY ASSOCIATES BOOK
NEW YORK

KOP KILLER

Copyright © 2012 by Warren Hammon[

All rights reserved.

Edited by James Frenkel

A Tor Book
Published by Tom Doherty Associates,
175 Fifth Avenue
New York, NY 10010

www.tor-forge.com

Tor® is a registered trademark of Tom Doherty Associates, LLC.

Library of Congress Cataloging-in-Publication Data

Hammond, Warren.
    KOP killer / Warren Hammond.—1st ed.
        p. cm.
    "A Tom Doherty Associates book."
    ISBN 978-0-7653-2827-4 (hardcover)
    ISBN 978-1-4299-4283-6 (e-book)
    1. Ex-police officers—Fiction.   I. Title.
PS3608.A69585K69 2012
813'.6—dc23
                            2012011471

First Edition: June 2012

Printed in the United States of America

0 9 8 7 6 5 4 3 2 1

For Roger, a good man

acknowledgments

FOR believing in this novel, a hearty thank-you to Jim Frenkel and Richard Curtis.

For their unwavering support, advice, and friendship, my deepest thanks to the Pearl Street Grill critique group: Mario Acevedo, Margie Lawson, Tom Lawson, Tamra Monahan, Jeanne Stein, and Terry Wright.

And for her love, my undying thanks to my wife, Kathy.

kop killer

one

THIS was my turf now. Mine.

I stood at the head of the alley. Smoke billowed from fire pits, the flames licking at slow-turning 'guanas on spits. Neon signs blinked overhead. Hookers danced in the street, their eyes hidden behind lizard masks, their tits bouncing free. A five-piece band at the far end pounded out a heavy beat beneath a BIG SLEEP '89 banner. Offworld teens drank and groped and drank some more. I breathed deep of air scented with perspiration and opium.

Mine. Nobody could stop me.

I weaved into the rollicking crowd, sliding past sweat-slick flesh, my face whipped by hair from dancing hookers. Some whore tried to shove a mask in my face. I pushed her away.

Every door in the alley was propped open for the steady stream of mostly male offworlders. On a day like today, a hooker could score a new trick every ten minutes. The Big Sleep was a hot time for offworld kids on their school breaks to come down to Lagarto's surface with their bottomless pockets and insatiable libidos.

I looked up at the ash gray sky. Weak light trickled down. The darkness would be upon us soon.

I navigated past tubs full of shine, through a floating set of fornicating holograms, up a short set of well-worn steps, and found myself stuck at the end of a line of kids jamming the door. One yelled over the music, "Let's get up to the roof. The sun's about to drop."

His buddy shook his masked head. "You go. I'll come up later."

The first one stepped out of line and tossed his drink to the ground. He kicked off his sandals, and just like that he was on the wall, crawling upward, gecko style. I stared while he picked his way through a tangle of power cords above the door. He cleared the last of the pulsing neon and quickly scurried up three stories, past clotheslines and patches of creeping vines, finally disappearing over the top.

Fucking offworlders. How do they do that shit?

I bulled my way inside, ignoring the protests. The foyer was packed with disrobing offworlders. Seeing their impossibly perfect bods, a chill came over me. There was something creepy about these kids, how they looked too perfect to be real, like a room full of mannequins come to life. Not an ounce of flab. Not a single strand of back hair. Not one pimple-plagued ass.

The teens at the head of the line were completely naked. They waited patiently with projection units pressed against their temples, pornographic imagery beaming directly into their brains. Every minute or so, a whore would come by and grab one of the erect from the front of the line. The limpers had to wait. No time for foreplay. Not today. Today, the whores would keep the johns moving in and out as fast as possible . . . in more ways than one.

Time to reclaim my turf. I turned left and stomped through a pile of clothes. A lizard mask crunched under my right heel, glittery scales popping free from the plaster. I pushed through a curtain made of strands of strung monitor teeth that clacked and chattered at my entrance.

Chicho sat at his desk. It had been almost two years since I'd seen this pimp. He hadn't changed. He had the same pinched lips, the same sharp nose, the same rodent eyes peering through a pair of wire-rims.

"Juno?" he asked. "What are you doing here?"

"I'm back."

"What do you mean, you're back?"

I stepped up to his desk, piled with holographic ledger sheets. "It means from now on, you pay me. Just like the old days."

"This isn't a good time." He looked down to read a ledger.

I gave his desk a swift boot, startling the glasses right off his face. "I'm talking to you."

His eyes had opened so wide that white showed all around the black beads at their centers. "What's your problem?"

Had the holo-ledgers been made of actual paper, I would've swiped them to the floor. Instead, I settled for pressing my fists into the desktop and leaning way down to get in his rat face. "You pay me now."

"You can't boss me around. You're not a cop anymore."

"No?" I lifted my right knuckles off the desk, and my hand immediately started to shake like it always did. Nerve damage from an old run-in with an offworlder. Using my bobbing index finger, I drew an imaginary shield over my heart. "What do you see right here?"

"I don't know. A badge?"

I grinned wolfishly, showing molars and everything. "That's right, Chicho. A badge. You want KOP to leave you alone, you pay me every month. I don't get my money, and we'll shut this shithole down. Got me?"

"What's wrong with your hand?"

The question took me aback—not the question itself, but the fact that he was asking it in the middle of a fucking shakedown. As if he had no fear.

Puzzled, I stayed silent, letting my scowl do the talking.

When it became clear I had no intention of answering, he

exhaled like he was trying to find the patience. "Listen, I pay
Captain Mota for protection now. What do you expect me to
tell him next time he comes to collect?"

"You let me take care of that pretty boy."

"Um, okay. Whatever you say."

I didn't like his sarcastic tone. This was going all wrong. He
should be scared. I caught his eyes flicking to the right and
back. He'd just looked past me to the door, like he was expecting somebody. The bastard could have a panic button somewhere under his desk. My skin prickled.

I rushed to the door, arriving just as the lizard-tooth curtain
began to part. I threw a right at what I guessed to be a face. The
impact was painful—a monitor's incisor got caught between
my knuckles and my target. Whoever the bastard was, he disappeared behind the rattling strands of teeth. I reached for
my piece but my shaky right failed to grab hold. The muzzle
of a lase-pistol came through the curtain while I continued to
fumble for my weapon, hopelessly incapable of a quick draw.
Fucking hand. I backed up, hands raised, my right bobbing out
of control.

Following the lase-pistol through the curtain came a slight
wrist, then a forearm, and then came the rest of her. Fuck me.
A woman. *You don't hit women, asshole.* Hitting women was for
cowards like my wife-beater father.

A thin red mark underscored her left eye. A crimson drop
broke free and trickled down like a tear. The left side of her
face was visibly reddening, quite a feat considering how overly
rouged her cheeks already were. "What the fuck?"

Dammit, Juno, what did you do? "Sorry," I said lamely. "I didn't
know."

"What didn't you know?" She held the weapon firm in one
hand, like this wasn't her first time. With her other hand, she
swiped at the blood, painting the back of her hand with a broad

red smear. She made like she was going to wipe it on her skirt, a number so skimpy that it barely qualified as a mini, but she thought better of it and let her hand hang by her side.

"I didn't expect a woman."

"So what?" Her eyes creased at the corners, her forehead wrinkled in anger. She stepped up and jabbed the lase-pistol into my ribs. She was short, and looking down at her, she was nothing but hair and cleavage. A toxic mix of hair spray and perfume assaulted my nostrils, and I had to turn my head to find clean air. Without warning, she rammed a knee into my crotch.

I doubled over, my lungs heaving, my face burning, my forehead breaking out in an instant sweat. There's nothing like nut pain.

I dropped to my knees, and she pulled my weapon from my waistband at the small of my back.

Chicho must've been staring at me, his rodent eyes delighting at seeing me down. How many times had he fantasized about this? Month after month, year after year, I'd taken his money, and there was nothing he could do. Fuck with me, and the Koba Office of Police would've put him out of business. I used to run that place, me and Paul Chang. I was the chief's right hand, his enforcer. It had been my job to keep the money coming in, and to do that I had to keep everybody on the far side of the law in line—pimps, pushers, smugglers, gene-traders, bookies, bootleggers, fences . . .

And cops. Especially the cops.

I was the strongest of the strong-arms, a heavy-fisted, skull-cracking beat-down artist with a mean streak. The most ruthless enforcer KOP ever saw. But I'd fallen a long way since Paul was killed by rivals. I'd lost my badge. I'd lost my wife. And here I was, doubled over and blowing like a preggo in labor.

I heard Chicho's voice over the agony. "I'm going to do you a favor, Juno. We go back a ways, you and me, and I'd hate to see you get yourself hurt, understand? Get out of here now, and I won't tell Captain Mota about this. Piss me off any more, and you're on your own."

The woman bouncer stood over me aiming two lase-pistols—one of them mine—at my head. Looking up, I caught an up-skirt view that I couldn't enjoy in my busted-ball condition.

"Who is this geezer?" she wanted to know.

Chicho was about to answer when a voice at the door said, "Drop it." A uniformed cop came through the monitor-tooth curtain, his standard-issue drawn.

The woman let the lase-pistols slip out of her fingers.

Shit! I raised my hands to protect my face. One gun smacked the back of my left hand and tumbled harmlessly to the side. The other bounced off my jaw with a painful thunk.

"Nice." I glared at her.

She gave me a smart-ass grin.

Taking the weapons as my own, I slowly stood, my hand smarting, my package aching. *The things I do . . .* "What kept you?"

Officer Marek Deluski shrugged. "I didn't know you needed help."

Hunched over the way I was, I had to crane my neck to see the kid's eyes. They looked truthful, but I couldn't say for sure. I could picture the dumb shit staying outside and peeking through the curtain, secretly enjoying watching me get my huevos scrambled before coming to the rescue. This new squad of mine had a serious loyalty problem.

Now that I was back in control of the situation, this was the perfect time to exact a little retribution. I thought about shooting the pimp somewhere nonfatal, maybe in the knee, or maybe frying a hole through one of those fancy offworld shoes on his feet.

But I didn't do that shit anymore. Even after taking a groiner.

I forced my torso upright with a groan, my face frozen in a nasty leer. The woman tried to keep her tough-girl act going, but with the tables turned, I saw fear under those long, mascara-caked lashes.

I looked into Chicho's eyes. "You ready to quit this pissing match and talk business?"

Chicho crossed his arms, a sour expression of defeat on his face. He glanced at Deluski's weapon then sat on his desk, his ass dropping through the holo-ledgers.

"Truce?" I asked.

He gave me a nod.

I tucked my lase-pistol back in my waistband and passed the other weapon back to the female bodyguard. She thanked me, a sign that our little spat was already forgotten. That was the way things were in the muscle business. There were times to carry a grudge, and there were times to have a short memory.

I gave Deluski the eye, and he holstered his police-issue.

To Chicho, I said, "I'm back in business. I'm taking this alley again."

After a theatrical sigh he said, "C'mon, Juno, you can't be serious with this. Captain Mota's not going to let you steal his territory."

"It's not his. He's the one who stole it from me. I owned this alley for twenty years. The way I see it, Mota's just been look-ing after it for a while."

Chicho rubbed his jaw. "Listen, don't take this the wrong way, but you gotta know your time is past. You were one hard-nosed collections man, I'll give you that, but times have changed. I mean, look at you. What happened to you anyway? You look so thin."

"I'm on a diet."

"You need to eat, friend. You don't look good. You get that wife of yours to cook you up a nice meal."

My heart lurched at her mention. "Niki died." I could only mutter the words.

"What?" His face looked a little less rodent, a little more human. "How did she die?"

"She just did," I non-answered.

"Shit, that's a tough break."

I had no words. I just stood there.

"Where's she buried?"

My voice barely audible, I said, "Out in the jungle."

"You didn't put her in a cemetery?"

"What's it to you?"

He looked offended. "What if I want to send flowers?"

"Why? You didn't even know her."

"It's common respect. Somebody dies, you send flowers. Why'd you bury her in the jungle?"

"That's what she wanted," I said, hoping to end this line of conversation.

"She got a marker?"

I gave him an annoyed shake of my head.

"Why not?"

I felt the pressure building. "Who do you think you are, asking me this shit? It's none of your fucking business."

"Jesus, you don't need to get all worked up. I'm just trying to figure out where to send the flowers. I wasn't accusing you of anything."

I didn't know whether to be ticked or touched. "Just fucking forget the flowers."

He shrugged acceptance. After an uncomfortable silence, he asked, "So you want to take over protection duty?"

I nodded.

"Tell me how a washed-up cop is going to keep KOP off my ass?"

A cheer went up outside. The sun must've just dropped.

The Big Sleep had begun, the first seconds of three weeks of darkness now ticking by.

"My word is still good over there," I lied.

He gave me a skeptical stare.

"Paul Chang and I ran that joint for twenty years. Chang was the greatest chief this planet ever saw, you know that. They're still loyal to me. Me and Paul's memory. I tell them to leave you the hell alone, they'll leave you the hell alone."

"You still got that kind of pull?"

"Listen, I know how fucked up KOP has gotten since Paul was killed."

"Chief Chang wasn't killed. He ate his gun."

"Paul would never kill himself." I pointed my shaking finger at my heart. "I was there. I know what happened."

He shrugged his shoulders and offered an unconvinced, "Whatever you say."

I wanted to shove the truth down his throat and force him to swallow. But I hadn't come here to argue about Paul. I'd come to continue my slow climb back to the top of KOP.

"Listen," I said. "We're on our second chief since Paul. The mayor and the new brass are clueless. Nobody's running the show, which means KOP is splintering into a thousand little pieces. Everybody can see it, and that's exactly what's got people wishing things could go back to the way they used to be. Cops are turning to me to unify KOP again. I remind them of a better era. Tell him, Deluski."

"He's right," said the young uniform. "Juno's got standing. Everybody says so."

Chicho nodded his head, like he was believing the lies. "Okay, so tell me why I should make the switch. You gonna charge less than Mota?"

"Ten percent less."

I could see the pesos dancing in his eyes. Greedy bastard.

Time to hook him deep through the gills. "That's the rate I'm offering to everybody else," I said. "But maybe I can arrange a special rate for you."

"I'm listening."

I bet you are. "You get all the other pimps and madams in this alley on board, and I'll give you a year for free."

Chicho's beady eyes churned. "Make it two years, and I won't limit my influence to just this alley. I got connections with snatch houses all over this city. I can make you fucking rich."

"See, there's the reason I came to you first." I gave him a broad smile. What I'd said was the truth. Chicho was an operator of the highest order. Those dark eyes were always crankin' on one angle or another.

"I think we can do business," he said. "But I'll tell you, saving only ten percent might be a tough sell. These people are taking a risk making a switch like that. I know you think you can handle Mota, but that guy can be vindictive when he wants to be."

"You don't have to worry about Mota. When I talk to him, he'll back out."

"You have that kind of influence over him?"

"We have a history," I said without elaborating.

"Okay, I hear you, but I still think it'll be a tough sell. A lot of these people were glad to see you gone."

"You'll have to be persuasive."

"I can try, but you could make it a lot easier, couldn't you?"

I let that hang in the air for a moment. "Fine. I'll charge twelve percent less than Mota." I knew he was scamming me. He'd sell them at ten and pocket the difference.

"Now you're talkin'." The pesos in his eyes were spinning. He held up a finger. "But wait . . . how do I convince them that you're pulling the strings over at KOP? These people are a suspicious bunch. Don't get me wrong now, I trust you just fine, but these people aren't always easy to please."

"You tell them to watch out their windows tonight. I'll be out there with a crew of detectives and unis guarding this alley. That'll be proof enough."

"Why do we need you guarding the alley?" His face darkened with realization. "Don't fucking tell me."

I nodded. "Riots."

two

THE alley was silent except for the buzz of hungry flies and the rustle of geckos scavenging through the garbage. The crumbled asphalt, littered with brandy empties and crushed lizard masks, reeked of spilled shine and vomit. The party was over. The whores had closed their legs and then their doors. The band had exhausted its playlist and moved on. And the offworld youth, they'd taken their debauchery elsewhere.

Alone with only two of my crew members, I paced the alley crosswise, back and forth, my hands in my pockets, my jaw clenched, my shirt ruffling in the jungle breeze.

My new crew numbered five, which meant three of my boys were late. Deluski was here, of course, and Wu had just arrived, but the others were dragging their feet, a sure sign of insubordination. They'd be here soon, I told myself. They had no choice. I owned those assholes. Yet they took every opportunity they could to make me sweat. I checked the time. Only ten more minutes before the lights went out.

The Lagarto Power Authority was shutting the power down regularly now. They simply couldn't keep up with our increasing energy demands—so they claimed. Everybody knew the real reason. A hundred years of deteriorating equipment and outright mismanagement had finally taken its toll. Our energy capacity was on the decline, just like everything else on this planet, especially the standard of living. Electricity rationing was just the latest punch in the face for a planet that had already taken a full ten count.

For two weeks now, the city had suffered through rolling power outages. And when the lights went out, so did the riffraff: criminals and opium heads; unemployed and undereducated; anarchists and militants; disaffected youth and the hopelessly impoverished. Night after night, they'd mobbed the streets with unbridled anger. Their vicious, uncontrolled rage would spread like wildfire and they'd leave nothing but tornado-like paths of destruction in their wake.

Because of the riots, the power authority stopped broadcasting the times and locations of the blackouts to the public, and instead notified only the police. The theory was that the bad elements from all over the city wouldn't know where and when to gather. So far, the practice hadn't proven to be very effective. Apparently, every neighborhood had plenty of homegrown bad elements to get shit going without needing imports.

I checked the time again. Seven more minutes.

"The others will be here," said Paolo Wu, his downturned brows tugging at the scar under his hairline. "Froelich said he'd bring at least ten unis with him. We'll keep this alley secure."

I gave the hommy dick a nasty stare. "He should've been here an hour ago. If you humps can't be reliable then I have no use for you."

"Don't get your sack in a twist. They'll be here."

I paced like a caged tiger, my temper on a slow simmer, my energy positively toxic. On my next pass, I made sure to veer into Wu's space, forcing him to get out of my way. The little brush-back was a not-so-subtle reminder of who was the alpha.

If those assholes didn't show soon, the whole deal could fall through. I'd told Chicho there'd be a crew of cops out here. A *crew.* Two cops and a past-his-prime enforcer didn't qualify. I needed a show of fucking force to bluff the pimps and madams into believing I was pulling the strings at KOP.

Kripsen and Lumbela finally entered the alley. That made four out of five. The recent arrivals were in full riot gear—helmets, full-length body shields, shocksticks, and cans of fireline hanging on their belts.

"Where the fuck have you been?" I demanded.

Freddie Lumbela looked down at the ground. "We couldn't get away."

"Bullshit."

"They just deployed us," he said defensively. "Until ten minutes ago, we were trapped on a fuzzwagon with the rest of the unis who got called in on crowd control. We snuck away the first chance we got."

"Anybody see you leave?"

"I don't know."

"What kind of answer is that?"

"An honest one."

I shook my head and started pacing again. These stiffs were fucking worthless. And where was Froelich with my force of ten?

Kripsen chimed in. "What do you expect, Juno? We're on duty. We can't just walk away whenever we want. At some point, people are gonna notice."

"Will any riot police be coming this way?"

"I doubt it. Our orders were to guard the banks around the corner. This block's expendable."

"There been any changes in the schedule?"

"Nope. Blackout in five minutes."

I made eye contact with Wu. "Where the hell is Froelich?"

"I don't know, but he'll be here."

"What did he say when you talked to him?"

Wu rubbed the scar on his forehead, a broad groove that ran from one temple almost to the other. The way I heard it, he got the scar from standing too close to a competitive knife fight, one of those betting matches they run under Koba's many bridges. "I didn't talk to him," he said. "I left a message."

"You telling me your partner doesn't take your calls?"

"Jesus, Juno, I called him four times, okay? He didn't answer. What the fuck do you want from me?"

A serious loyalty problem. That was what I had. That was why I was so hot to secure a revenue stream. If I could fatten their wallets, they'd start thinking working for me wasn't so bad. As it was, they were doing it because they had no choice. This crew had gotten into some bad shit a couple months back, some really bad shit. They fucking stank of it. They'd conspired with offworlders. They'd betrayed their own people, selling them off to be killed by offworlders who wanted to play executioner.

These assholes were *traitors*. Rat bastards, every one of them.

They hadn't been the brains of the operation. Hell no. These humps didn't have that kind of smarts, and they'd proven it when they'd let me catch them on film. *The Killer KOPs*. That was what I called my little documentary. It wasn't a very long movie, barely three minutes, but still a pretty good flick.

Set in an abandoned warehouse, it starts when five cops enter through a cockeyed door and come face-to-face with one of their co-conspirators, a pudgy little local on the verge of squealing their devious deeds to investigators. The Killer KOPs are nervous and fidgety, you can see it on their faces. Wu keeps rubbing at that scar of his, and Deluski stands in back, shifting from one foot to the other. They're desperate, see. Their traitor bosses are already dead, and they're out to cover their tracks.

Wu pulls his piece. The porker knows too much, and they can't trust him to keep quiet. Wu fires, and the beam of his lase-pistol burns through hair and skull and brain. A piece of the porker's head comes free and falls to the floor.

It's done. Deluski is staring at the corpse, his jaw gaping, his face ashen. Lumbela and Kripsen grab the de-lidded corpse by the arms and legs, and Deluski holds the door as they haul it out into the rain. Wu gives a look to Deluski, his finger pointing to the scalp on the floor. Deluski, the low man in their little cop clique, steps over to the porker's lid and pinches a lock of hair between forefinger and thumb. He lifts it off the floor and rushes out with his arm extended, like he's carrying a rat by its tail. Wu and Froelich are the last to leave, the pair of hommy dicks disappearing into the pouring rain.

Roll credits . . .

Like I said, not a bad flick. I harbored no illusions about these bastards—bad men through and through. But I knew a thing or two about bad men. Bad men could be useful. I was on a mission to take back the police department, and a mission like that required the accumulation of power. And if I had to start with these five misfits, so be it.

Instead of turning my movie over to KOP, I kept it for myself. And when I'd screened it for the five of them, they became mine.

I checked the time again—any second now. Where the fuck was Froelich with my ten unis?

Wu kicked at a gecko. "How long is this thing going to take? I need to call my wife and tell her when I'll be home."

"You kidding me?"

"She worries when I don't come home on time."

"Fucking unbelievable," I muttered loud enough to be heard. I couldn't be bothered with this shit. "Tell her you won't be home. Tell her to use a vibrator."

His scowl made the scar on his forehead dip. "Some husband you must've been. No wonder she decided to off herself."

Without thinking, I snatched hold of his shirt and yanked his scarred face up to my own. "You watch your fuckin' mouth!"

Wu was grinning in my grasp, enjoying the fact that he'd gotten to me. What he'd said was true enough. I *had* been a bad husband. And had I been a better one, Niki might not have done herself in.

But that didn't mean I was accepting opinions on the matter, especially from Paolo-fucking-Wu.

A door opened and the woman bodyguard came out. Maria was her name.

She froze when she saw me. I must've looked ready to kill. Probably because I was. Snapped back to my senses, I remembered that we were likely being watched from the windows above. I released the bastard. It didn't look good to have anybody see us fighting among ourselves. With a self-satisfied smirk, Wu brushed at the stir of wrinkles my fist had left on his chest.

"I came to help," said a tentative Maria. "Where do you want me?"

Before I could answer, the lights went out.

Looking up, I tried to calm myself by taking a moment to look at the thousands of tiny pinpricks of light twinkling in the sky. That was the good thing about these power outages. You could see so many stars when the city lights went out. The only good thing.

"Um, can I ask a question, boss?" asked Lumbela.

It took me a few seconds to respond. "Talk."

"What's the plan?"

"We wait." A riot was about to start. Of that I had no doubt. The only question was whether the storm would drift our way.

I stepped out of the alley and into the street. Weeds bent under my shoes. This street was overdue for a good scorching. The Lagartan jungle was a persistent bastard. Inch by inch, street by street, the weeds and vines slithered across the pavement and up the walls, relentlessly seizing territory from a lazy population. You could slash it, and you could burn it, but you could never stop it. Once the roots dug in, you couldn't get rid of the shit.

I heard my crew complaining behind my back. No matter. They could bad-mouth me all they wanted. My roots had already dug into them.

I looked off into the darkness and listened. I could hear people above me. They were leaning out their windows and venting their frustration. This was a city that had had enough.

For ten minutes, maybe longer, I waited, my senses tuned to the nervous energy all around me. People milled about, curiosity seekers and troublemakers, their voices anxious and agitated. I heard the sound of crashing glass in the distance. I caught a whiff of smoke from an unseen fire. They were getting right after it tonight.

Running footsteps. I flicked on a flashlight and caught sight of a young punk sprinting my way. "They're coming!" he yelled. "They're coming."

Forgetting we had a gal in the mix, I called to my crew, "We're on, boys!" I aimed my flashlight at Kripsen and Lumbela. "You two set up a fireline right here at the alley mouth." Fireline was cheap but effective. You just squeeze out a thick bead of gel and light it. It would burn hot, and it would burn tall. With it, you could create a firewall of the literal variety.

Freddie Lumbela shook his black head, his skin a few shades darker than your typical Lagartan brown. "No can do, boss."

I shined the flashlight directly into his face. "What the fuck are you talking about?"

He used a hand to shade his eyes. "These cans of fireline are used up. This is the fourth riot we've worked this week."

"You couldn't swap those cans for new ones?"

"KOP ran out. They're getting more shipped in next week."

"Yet you two decided to keep carrying empties around?"

"It's in the regs for riot gear. We're required to carry fireline."

Holy hell, where did I find these humps? I played my flashlight across their tense faces. This would be so much easier if I had my ten uniforms.

"Okay. Here's how we're going to do this. I want a single line. Spread out wall to wall to cover the alley mouth. Nobody gets into this alley, got it? Use any force necessary. And you two put some flashlights on the ground and aim 'em up at us. We want people to see us when they come barreling around the corner."

"Hey, guys," said a voice holding a flashlight up to his face. Froelich. "I'm not too late, am I?" His shaved head was beaded with glistening sweat, like he'd really raced to get here. He wasn't breathing hard, though. It wouldn't surprise me if he was just trying to make it look good, stopping off on the way to dump a cup of water over his head.

"Where are my uniforms?"

"Just a minute behind me."

I told him to get in line. No time to ream out the late bastard.

I took my position, Maria to my right, Wu to the left. I leaned toward Maria and took a sneeze-worthy blast of perfume up the nose. "You know you don't have to stay. Chicho doesn't pay you enough for this."

"I'm staying." Her voice was firm enough to put any argument to rest.

Things were heating up on the street. I couldn't see much, but I could hear plenty—hustling feet, fierce shouting, more shattering glass. Lase-fire crackled upward, a red beam stretching seemingly up to the stars themselves. I pulled my lase-pistol from my waistband and clutched it tight in my left. I pressed the weapon against my heart, where everybody would see it. I tucked my shaky right into my pocket to keep it out of sight. Damn thing was a nuisance.

We held our ground as the voices thickened, more and more of them all the time. People tried to stay clear of us, but it was getting harder as the sheer size of the crowd forced their collective movement wide. Kripsen and Lumbela stayed active with their shocksticks, and Maria took to waving a lase-blade from side to side.

People flowed past like a river of angry white water. Our line held firm as the crowd inched closer and closer. Aiming at the ground, Deluski squeezed off a long burst of lase-fire, scoring the pavement with a searing stream of heat, forcing the tide to dance back to a safe distance.

Six of Froelich's uniforms finally arrived and filled the gaps in our line. Still not quite the show of force I was hoping for, but it was enough to convince the eyes watching from above I still held sway over KOP.

My plan was finally coming together.

A pair of teens charged. Wu drove the butt of his weapon into the face of the one on the left. The teen staggered backward, his hands to his face, blood oozing out from between his fingers, and then, just like that, he was sucked back into the angry tide, disappearing in the dark of night. I blocked the other teen with my body. He threw a punch at me, the eyes in his flash-lit face aflame.

I took the blow on my cheek and felt the sting of the shot, but I knew it was nothing serious. The kid had no meat on his bones. I swung my piece and caught him on the ear. At impact, the feral quality in the kid's eyes instantly disappeared. It was like the demon that had possessed him was suddenly exorcised. Just a scared child now, couldn't be more than thirteen or fourteen. I couldn't let him stand there. We needed to keep this area clear so we wouldn't get overrun. I shoved him backward. Had no choice. He lost his balance and fell under what seemed like hundreds of feet.

A fire broke out in the spice shop across the street, the madness of the mob scene now illuminated by a hellish, flickering glow. I looked for the kid, but couldn't find him. I hoped he'd managed to pick himself up.

Already, I knew the kid's face would stick with me. I had a helluva photo album going in my mind, the mementos of a lifetime of brutality. Over the years, the faces' features had faded, all of them meshing and mixing into little more than a brown-skinned blur, but their expressions . . . I remembered their expressions—shock, fear, disbelief, hatred, humiliation . . .

Begging faces. Bleeding faces. Broken faces.

Quite a gallery.

I'd never escape the violence. It was clear by now that I was damned to spend the rest of my days repeating the pattern over and over. Served me right. A bastard like me didn't deserve anything better.

I just had to trust that some good would come out of my mission to take back KOP. It might take years, but when I succeeded, Maggie Orzo would become chief. My on-again-off-again partner wasn't corrupted like the rest of us. A chief like her would make a difference. I couldn't let myself doubt that. Not ever.

And besides, I couldn't imagine my life without the mission. With no Niki and no mission, I'd be left with nothing but emptiness.

I looked up and down our line. Kripsen and Lumbela were holding their ground, acting like real pros. They'd had plenty of practice the last couple weeks. The rest of my crew were doing the same, finally proving their worth. Even Maria looked confident. Chicho had scored himself a winner.

I tried to process what my eyes were taking in: a gang of

punks with clubs, a woman with a baby cradled in one arm and a stolen chicken flapping in the other, an old man swinging a lase-blade at geriatric speed. Looters were everywhere, their arms overflowing with swag.

Shit started to rain down from the windows above the street, bottles and plates, chairs and lamps, all of it crashing down to the pavement from three, maybe four stories up. They were trying to protect their homes by heaving whatever they had handy down on the rioters' heads. The mob scattered. People ran for cover, tripping and trampling.

I'd never seen anything like this. The scene before me was so . . . so *raw*.

I felt an unusual spark down deep, down where the emptiness was centered. I puzzled at it for a while, wondering what it was. It grew stronger, this strange feeling gaining power inside me. I felt it emerge from the murky depths.

It spoke to me. It was calling me, drawing me into the madness.

Not since Niki died had I felt anything so pure. I let myself indulge the feeling. Magnificent relief washed over me. Gone was the guilt and the self-pity. Gone was the pain. Gone was the burden of the mission.

I couldn't believe I'd missed it all these years. The secret to life was so simple. All this time, all I'd had to do was surrender.

Dizzy with euphoria, I dropped my piece and stepped out into the glorious insanity.

Heading into the eye of the storm, I stole a look over my shoulder. My bewildered crew members watched me go. Nobody made a move to stop me. They didn't care if I got myself killed. I'd be doing them a favor.

I'd be doing myself a favor.

My senses were alive, my skin tingling. I felt the winter breeze pull at my hair. I felt the battered pavement under my soles. It was beautiful, really, the way the pits and ripples dipped and arched, like somebody had made a sculpture just for the feet to appreciate. Shattering ceramics sprayed my legs. I turned toward where they exploded. Even in the low light, they looked like starbursts. The last few stragglers stumbled about, some of them bloodied, all of them covering their heads. A brandy bottle exploded nearby, the spray jumping high enough to dot my cheek. I smelled cinnamon and cumin and anise, the flaming spice shop exuding odors like a magnificent stew.

I closed my eyes, savoring the aroma.

I reached for the sky, inviting the worst, and waited for the end.

three

A LAUNCHING spacecraft rattled the windows. My lids peeled open. I was on my sofa, and curiously, I was still alive.

How long had I been here? The emptiness had hold of me now. It wasn't so bad, really. I couldn't feel anything when it held me. I just wanted to sleep. In fact, I should be sleeping right now. I closed my eyes and shut out this godforsaken world.

My phone jingled. Had to be Maggie. I'd blocked all other calls.

I wondered if it was day or night. It didn't much matter, but I was curious. The Big Sleep could really screw with your sense of time.

I let the phone take a message. Maggie's holo lit up the room. I could see colors moving through my eyelids.

"Juno, it's me. It's Maggie. Hey, I'm running late for dinner." *Nighttime. Definitely nighttime.*

"Listen, can we push it back a half hour? Let me know."

Right. Dinner. Forgot about that. Lucky she called or I would've been a no-show. I fumbled for the phone, and in order to keep my half-asleep voice under wraps, I texted a response: *No problem.* And then I unblocked other calls.

I checked the time. *Fuck me.* Even with the extra half hour, I didn't have much time to get ready. I dropped my feet to the floor and stretched my arms up for the ceiling, my muscles aching, my head still swimming with the tail end of a fading buzz.

I lifted myself off the sofa and stumbled down the hall without looking at the bedroom door. I didn't go in there anymore. Too much Niki in there—clothes, shoes, jewelry, hairbrushes with long strands of black hair trapped in the bristles, *her* hair. And the smells, the perfumes and creams and lotions. No, I didn't go in there anymore. I couldn't.

Making it to the can, I watered the mold-lined bowl, then stepped into the shower and started rinsing away the stink of an all-night booze binge. A bandage washed off my bicep. I looked at the gouge on my arm. Not bad. It should heal up nicely if I could keep it clean. Amazing that was the only damage. Deluski and Lumbela were the ones who'd saved me. Lumbela paid the price, his melon taking a hit from what looked like a flying teacup. The resulting spray of shattering ceramic peppered my arm, one shard taking a good slice.

I remembered them pulling me back to the alley, both of them ducking, me walking upright, lost in a world of my own.

Upon reaching the alley, I remembered catching a whiff of Maria's perfume, and it was as if somebody had cracked smelling salts under my nose. Snapped out of my desperate trance, I slowly became aware of my wide-eyed, white-faced crew.

Stunned and confused, I had no idea how to feel. Happy I'd been saved? Angry they'd interfered? Even now, I still didn't know what to make of the episode. But standing there in that alley, with flashlights in my eyes, hearing a chorus of "What the hell's wrong with you," I'd had to cover quickly. So I made up some shit that made it sound like I'd just put them through some kind of sick-fuck loyalty test.

Figured it was better than letting them know I *was* a sick fuck.

I doubted they bought it, but I told myself it didn't matter. It wasn't like they could quit and join some other cop clique. They were property. My property.

I should've known they'd come to my rescue. Had I been thinking straight, I would've realized they had no choice. I'd told them more than once that if anything ever happened to me, their little hit flick would air for the public.

I turned off the water, grabbed a musty towel and walked naked back to the living room. I kept my clothes there now. I found a pair of white pants that almost looked fresh. As for shirts, I saw none that wasn't balled up, piled up, or left for dead.

I peeled back the flaps of a box I'd pulled from the bedroom closet before closing the bedroom door for the last time. Old shirts folded and stacked. I chose a pullover-style short-sleeve. Buttons were a bitch with my shaky right. I shook out the folds, and a pair of sunglasses fell free. Strange. I didn't remember owning any sunglasses.

They were probably a gift. Niki used to buy me tons of shit I didn't want. I'd probably never worn them. I'd just stuffed them in some drawer, where she eventually found them and jammed them in this box of forgotten crap. I was such an ass-hole. She'd gone through all that effort to buy me something nice, something she thought I'd like, and I'd dismissed the gesture. Would it have killed me to wear them a few times?

She must've been confused when she found them. Why hadn't I put them in the car? Or brought them to work? And then she must've realized that I didn't want them, that I'd rejected her gift. That I'd rejected her.

My gut was rolling over, my eyes stinging. *Fuck this bullshit.* I didn't have time for this sorry-ass crap. *Just get the fuck over it already.* The mission. *Think about the mission.*

I moved into the kitchen and grabbed the empty brandy bottle from the table. It had been three-quarters full last night. No wonder I still felt partly loaded. I put the empty back in its

crate with the other empties and set the crate out on the balcony with all the booze crates.

Exiting out the front, I went down the steps and headed into
the courtyard, jungle vines grasping at my ankles. I'd really let
the place go to hell. I was tempted to grab my sickle, if I only
knew where it was. I'd probably left it leaning against a wall
someplace and now even it had been overtaken by the sprawling growth.

I stomped and kicked my way out to the street. The road was
clogged with cars and bikes darting through the gaps. The air
tasted of exhaust. This was the only planet I knew of that used
fossil fuels. When you can't afford to import good tech, you
do what you can, and that included reviving centuries-old tech-
nologies like the internal combustion engine.

I decided to hoof it so I could walk off the last of my buzz. I
didn't like Maggie seeing me drunk.

I rounded the corner and spotted a group of kids under a
streetlight. Their clothes were filthy, same as their faces. I watched
one of the young teens squirt a bead of industrial glue into a
plastic bag before holding the bag over her nose and mouth. I
walked past as the bag ballooned in and out below her faraway
eyes.

My phone rang.

Captain Emil Mota.

I'd intended to pay him a little visit after the riot. He needed
to know he'd been replaced. But that riot had really fucked me
up. When it was over, I couldn't have crawled into a bottle any
faster.

Evidently, he'd gotten word another way. "Yeah," I said into
the phone.

Holo-Mota skimmed alongside me as I walked, and like all
the holos used by the phone system, he had this ridiculous,

pasted-on, ultra-happy attitude. Phone holos were incapable of matching the speaker's mood. Nothing but broad smiles and twinkly eyes. One of the crueler jokes played by offworlders on us poor and simple folk.

"What the hell do you think you're doing?" His sour tone clashed with the sugar-coated holo floating alongside me. Cheap-ass holograms.

"That alley's mine again," I said, matter-of-fact.

"But you're not a cop anymore. You can't do this." The fact that he was whining instead of demanding was a good sign, a sign that this would be as easy as I'd hoped. This hump was still afraid of me.

"Don't fucking tell me what I can't do."

He didn't respond for a few. Memories must've been running through his mind. Memories of him strapped to a chair, me standing over him, my fists pummeling that pretty face of his, his sharp, long-lashed eyes going puffy, that primly refined nose swelling up to double size.

My stomach twisted under the brutal truth of my enforcer's past, the guilt ripping me up like it always did. But I had no choice except to forge ahead. I put some extra steel in my voice. "You remember what happens to people who defy me, don't you?"

"But protection money is for cops."

As if there were a rule written somewhere.

As if rules mattered on Lagarto.

"Protection money is for protection," I said. "Where were you last night when that neighborhood burned? You weren't earning that money so they hired somebody else. You got what you deserved, so quit your bitching and stay the hell out of *my* territory."

I hung up, relieved that I'd managed to stay in don't-fuck-with-me character for the duration. I couldn't afford to let attacks of conscience throw me off my game. I had to stay focused. It was all about the mission.

I owned that alley outright now. Mota wouldn't fight me. The guy was a political animal, smart as hell, and a real up-and-comer at KOP, but he was also a pretty boy, the kind who shied away from street duty, a born bureaucrat best suited to public relations.

I'd been surprised from the outset that he'd entered the protection racket. Never would've thought a guy like that had the balls for it. Strong-arming wasn't his style. But as a captain, even a captain of the bullshit PR division, he could order around as many well-hung unis as he wanted.

I crossed the street, my eyes blinded by headlights, my feet chasing away dozens of geckos feasting on some kind of road-kill. I crossed a makeshift footbridge over lazy canal water flowing underneath.

No, he wouldn't call my bluff. I was sure of it. He wouldn't want to risk another beating. Those memories were still fresh in his mind, probably fresher in his than mine. A decade had passed, but shit like that never goes away.

Back then, he was a desk jockey working the KOP lockup. Paul Chang had put him in charge of collecting buyouts for petty crimes. You want to get your friend or loved one released before charges are filed with the Koba Office of Justice, you come make an offer. Cash only.

Smart as he was, Mota had a real knack for scoring maximum coin. So smart that he thought he could skim a little for himself. Who would know? He thought he could stay a step ahead of Paul.

He couldn't.

Enter me and my two fists.

Phone rang. Mota again. "What?"

"I won't let you do this," he said, like he'd found a spine.

"That alley's mine." He'd probably spent the last five minutes psyching himself up for this. "I'll haul your ass in if I have to."

I laughed. "You'll haul me in? What kind of threat is that? You wanna hear a threat? You keep this shit up, and I'll bash your fucking face in. Again."

Holo-Mota stayed silent.

I needed to keep pushing. His little bout of courage had to be quashed. "The chief used to like you, you know. When he sicced me on you, he told me to go easy. Nobody will be holding me back this time."

"You got some nerve mentioning the chief," he countered. "You ratted him out when he needed you most. You're nothing but a two-bit snitch."

My temples pulsed. My feet picked up their pace, my shoes clomping angrily on the pavement. Holo-Mota stayed on my wing, his apparition floating alongside.

Snitch. Squealer. Rat. I'd heard the accusations before. I'd been hearing them in my head since the day Paul was murdered.

Paul's enemies used me to bring him down. They threatened my wife. They forced me to turn on him. They used me to get him fired. And then they killed him and sold it as a suicide.

"I'm no rat," I said through grinding teeth. "I was set up. Everybody knows that."

"You caved. All that tough-guy bullshit is just an act." He was on a roll, his tone getting more confident with every word. "Down deep, you're just a pussy, and everybody knows it. Cops aren't afraid of you anymore. They laugh at you. You're pathetic, you hear me? You're just a washed-up boozehound. A shaky old man crying over his lost love."

I let him finish, my cheeks burning, my temper building. Then I uncaged the enforcer inside me. "You talk to me like that again, I'll kill you." I'd stopped walking, my eyes aimed at the sweet smile on Mota's holo-face.

As he let seconds tick by, the headlights of a passing car momentarily shined right through him. Then he said, "Fucking try it."

four

FUCKING Mota. I twisted the napkin in my lap, wringing it into
a cord, tighter and tighter.

I was sure he'd back down. No way would he call my bluff.
That pretty-boy pencil pusher had no business running a protection racket.

Fucking Mota.

The Punta de Rio was packed, every table occupied, wait
staff making the rounds, a crowd of offworld tourists milling
in the lobby. The menu was expensive, but so were Maggie's
tastes. This place was the go-to spot for anybody feeling nos-
talgic for Lagarto's brandy era, back when barges carrying
brandy fruit used to dock right outside to unload their cargo.
The decor was nautical, antique anchors and tow ropes, fishnets
and brandy barrels. Windows ran around the circumference,
all of them opened wide to let a pleasant breeze float through.
Outside, I could see a well-lit derelict riverboat that had been
refurbed into a museum.

I sipped my tea. Maggie was talking, had been for a while
now, saying something about her promotion to squad leader.
The words entered my ears but not my mind. I couldn't focus,
my buzz now fully dissipated to be replaced by a vicious head-
ache. I needed a hit in a bad way. Every drunk knew the best
cure for a hangover was more booze.

But not in Maggie's presence. She'd once admitted I was a
father figure to her, and a father ought to set a good example.

"This is already way tougher than I thought." She swept back the dark hair that had fallen over her emerald eyes. I still wasn't used to the eyes. They used to be blue, but she'd had them changed out. Rich as she was, she could afford to get them swapped with the seasons. These were her winter eyes, she'd told me.

"Those guys don't respect me." She shook her head.

Despite missing most of what she'd said these last few minutes, I got the gist with that final statement. "It's only been a few weeks. You have to give it time. They'll learn how capable you are. Just like I did."

She smiled, her teeth sparkling as bright as her eyes. With a mischievous grin, she said, "Yeah, you were pretty slow to catch on, weren't you?"

All I could do was nod. It hadn't taken me long, though. Not long at all. Her type was rare. Paul Chang was the only person I'd ever known who could match her intensity, drive, and purpose. She was on a mission of her own, a mission to bring order to this city, to make it a place where justice ruled, where people could count on the police for protection. She was determined to make it a place where she wouldn't have found her father alone on the street in front of their home, blood oozing from a charred wound in his chest.

She'd be chief one day. I'd see to it that nothing would stop her. Koba needed her.

Paul Chang and I had already taken our shot at changing this city, but KOP was corrupt, the levers of power smeared with shit. The only way for us to move up was to hold our breath and grab hold. Beat-downs and frame jobs. Cover-ups and payoffs. Forced confessions and back-alley executions. To seize control, we had to outcorrupt the corrupt.

By the time we reached the top, we'd become no better than those we'd replaced. Fucking classic how it worked out.

This time would be different. It wasn't too late for Maggie. She had the capacity to play dirty when she had to. I'd seen it more than once. But her dark side *had* to stay under wraps. The dirty work had a way of soiling you, rotting you from the inside out. I knew that better than anyone.

The dirty work was my job, and mine alone.

The waitress arrived to refill my tea. I was starving. Where was the food?

I noticed Maggie looking at me funny. "What?" I asked.

"When were you going to tell me about the sunglasses?"

"What about them?"

"You have a black eye under there?"

"No. They were a gift."

She rippled her brows. "You do know it's dark out, don't you? No sun for weeks?"

"I know." I didn't elaborate. "Tell me about Wu and Froelich."

"Don't try to change the subject. Are you going to tell me why you're wearing them or not?"

"No." Let Maggie think I had a coon eye. I didn't care. "Wu and Froelich," I repeated. "They been behaving?"

After a reluctant pause, "I guess so."

"I told you they would."

"They have no choice, Juno."

"True. But at least you have two obedient squad members. The rest of hommy will eventually follow their example."

She leaned forward, planting her elbows halfway to the table's centerpiece. "You should've turned them in, the whole lot of them. They belong in the Zoo."

"What good would that do? They wouldn't survive a week in prison. This way you have a loyal following."

"I don't want them on my squad."

"Yes, you do."

"I can't have bad eggs stinking up my staff."

The food arrived. Grilled fish over rice with two 'guana eggs blanketing the top. The eggs looked overcooked, two slate-colored eyes staring out from a lake of white. It was as if the cook heard Maggie say "bad eggs" and fried some up to order.

"What's with the eggs?" I asked the waitress.

"No sunny-side-ups during the Big Sleep. We do 'em all over-easy this time of year. The offworld tourists think it's a kick."

Offworlders. Fucking over this world wasn't enough for them. Now they'd gone after my eggs.

"Wu and Froelich killed a man," said Maggie as soon as the waitress stepped away.

Forgetting the eggs, I leaned toward her, keeping my voice soft, my tone strong. "Are you really going to make me go through this again? I have Wu and Froelich under my thumb, and they have their hooks into a whole bunch of uniforms. Add in Deluski, Kripsen, and Lumbela, and we have a whole squad. We can't piss that away. You want to be chief someday, we have to take every advantage we can get." I didn't mention my new protection racket or how I would expand the new revenue stream into a river of police power. She wouldn't approve.

Her phone rang, and she looked at the display. "I have to take this."

I shook my head at her back as she stepped away. She couldn't get to the top just by acing her goddamned performance ap-praisals. This was KOP we were talking about. She needed me. She needed what I could do.

I dug into my fish and eggs—tasty for the first few mouth-fuls, but turning blah shortly after. My taste buds were like that these days. Everything I ate went from grand to bland in three bites or less. I pushed the fish around my plate, taking an occasional bite as I waited for Maggie to return.

The crackle of a bug zapper drew my attention toward the kitchen. The hostess carried a handheld, shaped like a carpet beater but made of wire mesh instead of cane. I watched her meander among the tables, picking flies and mosquitoes out of the air, each one incinerating with a satisfying spark.

A group of young offworlders stood to leave, their appearances morphing as I watched, their flawless skin going furry, teeth sharpening into fangs, noses elongating into snouts. The newly minted pack of werewolves thought they were hot shit, prancing out like supernatural show dogs. *What a bunch of punks.* Like we locals were supposed to be impressed by their high-tech bullshit. I looked at their vacated table, where they'd left behind a huge spread of barely eaten food. Wasteful bastards. At least the kitchen staff would eat well tonight.

Maggie came back, her heels clopping on the mold-spotted floor, her face bunched in frustration.

"Sorry," I said. "I didn't think you'd mind if I started my dinner."

She dismissed my remark with a brush of her hand. "I don't care about that. It's good to see you eating."

"What's wrong?"

"I have to go out on a murder."

"Send Wu and Froelich."

"They're not answering their phones. That's some thumb you've got them under. Now I have to go with Josephs." She dropped pesos on the table. "We'll continue this later." She hurried across the dining room and out the door.

The waitress appeared. "What did you do to your date?"

I looked up. "I need a brandy."

"She's a feisty one, isn't she?" She cocked her hip to one

side and tugged at an earring. "What you need is a mature woman."

"Brandy," I repeated, practically snarling the word.

"Your loss." Her hip snapped back into place, and she headed for the bar.

My phone rang. Maria the bodyguard. I listened to what she had to say, my teeth biting down on my lip.

The brandy arrived by the time I hung up. I slugged the glass down, hoping the spurned waitress hadn't added a splash of saliva.

I waved for another glass of instant courage. I was going to need it.

Fucking Mota.

I leapt for the riverbank, one foot landing in the mud, the other splashing water halfway up my pant legs. I guess the skiff wasn't as close as I'd thought. Next time, I'd have to remember to push up my shades for a better look before I jumped.

I waved at the skiff's pilot and started scrabbling up the riverbank to the sound of the boat's motor puttering for deeper water.

"Here," said a voice.

Looking up, I saw a hand reaching over the embankment's edge. "That you, Deluski?"

"Yep."

Taking hold of his hand, I scrambled the rest of the way. "Kripsen and Lumbela here yet?"

"They're just up the way there."

"Good." I fell in step with the young officer, one shoe squishing with every step.

Kripsen and Lumbela approached, both of them wearing white, loose-fit linens. Kripsen's were too long in the legs, the short man's cuffs dragging on the ground. Lumbela's whites shone bright on his dark skin. They fell in alongside, the four of us now marching in a line.

"What's up, boss?" asked Lumbela. There was a small bandage under his temple.

"Maria called. She said a uni's been posted at the head of the alley, and he's scaring all the business away."

"Just one cop?"

"That's what she said." One cop. *One.* Mota was an amateur. After his little show of bravery on the phone, I'd expected him to make a move, but not one so feeble. He had no clue what he was up against. Like I said, he had no business running a protection racket.

"Anybody heard from Wu and Froelich?" I asked. "They won't answer their phones."

"They went upriver," said Lumbela. "They like to bet on the lizard fights up there."

"Why won't they pick up?"

"Did you tell them they'd be on call?"

Is he serious? I actually stopped to stare at him.

"If they didn't know they were on call, they might've turned their phones off."

I was speechless. Genuinely speechless.

He caught on. "You expect us to be on call all the time?"

"Twenty-two-fucking-seven."

"Okay." We started moving again. "Good to know."

We turned left. A bonfire raged in the middle of the street, making the air reek of smoke and ash, melted plastic and burned rubber. Several people worked the asphalt with fern-frond brooms, creating piles of debris left by the riot.

Silently, we marched from one ravaged block to the next. Out of the corner of my eye, I caught Lumbela checking me out. I tried to ignore him, but he kept watching me instead of looking where he was going, his shoes scuffing and bumbling.

"What the fuck?"

"I—I was just wondering if you could see okay with those glasses?"

"I see fine."

A pair of butchers wheeled a cart of monitor carcasses up to the closest fire. They each grabbed a pair of thick, stubby legs and swung the gutted lizard from side to side, counting one-two-three before heaving the carcass into the flames, where it landed like a heavy log, a cloud of sparks kicking up for the sky. We passed the cart as they grabbed hold of a second monitor. By the smell of it, the meat had been taken by the rot. The power was back on in this neighborhood, but not soon enough to save their unrefrigerated stock.

What a fucking mess this city was, the riots just the latest blight on an already spoiled fruit. It was hard to believe Koba once had thrived and bustled with energy. Those days were long gone, gone for generations.

Every step took us closer to where it happened. I remembered the way it felt when I'd let go, when I'd surrendered to the madness. Exhilarating. Pure. Totally insane. My stomach fluttered, and my feet felt light on the ground. I did my best to purge the strange emotions inside me. Now wasn't the time.

I looked where the spice shop used to be—nothing but a pile of charred rubble. An old woman sat on the pavement outside and used a piece of paper to scoop spilled spice into a plastic bag, picking out pieces of glass in the process.

We stepped up to the lone uniform at the head of the alley.

"Hey, fellas," he said. "That you, Juno?"

Son of a bitch. Not Jimmy.

"Shit, I knew it was you soon as I saw that hand of yours.

Shit, man, why don't you get that fixed? I bet them doctors can give you some pills or somethin'."

I knew this kid. Jimmy Bushong. Ex-army and a fellow Tent-towner. I'd met him during the Vlotsky case and helped him get a post at KOP after he gave Maggie and me the inside dope on his army unit. "What are you doing here, Jimmy?"

"Jus' followin' orders. My sarge told me to stand right here by this alley. I asked him why, and he told me the order came from up the chain. Pretty fuckin' weird if you ask me, but I ain't com-plainin'. This shit's way better than workin' riot duty. This neighborhood sure got worked over last night." He punctuated the statement with a whistle.

"You got that right."

"What you guys up to? You come down to get some action?"

"How did you guess?"

"I ain't goin' to stop another badge. You go on in if you wants to. With me scarin' the little action they's gettin' tonight, they ain't busy in there. I bet you can get some discounts tonight. I'm talkin' bargains galore."

"I bet so," I said with a lascivious leer. "We're going to give those whores a helluva workout, aren't we, boys?" I gave De-luski a guy-to-guy elbow.

Picking up on my lead, Deluski said, "Shit, they're gonna have to sit on ice when we finish with them."

The rest of my crew played their parts, horndog smiles all around.

I leaned toward Jimmy. "So how do you like the job so far? Been about a year, hasn't it?"

"You know how it is, ain't so much fun with all them riots and shit, but it's way better than the army. Livin' in the jungle, fightin' them warlords." He shook his head. "It ain't no picnic, you see what I'm sayin'. I gotta thank you for gettin' me this job, Juno. I sure do owe you one."

"You don't need to thank me. You earned your place. All I did was ask them to move your app to the top of the pile."

"Shit, that ain't nothin' small. You done helped me, and I ain't never goin' to forget it."

Lumbela asked, "You wanna come in with us, Jimmy?"

"No. I best stay out here."

"It's our treat."

Jimmy was tempted. I could see it in his eyes. But he shook his head no. I liked Jimmy. Good kid. And probably a good cop.

Lumbela put his arm over Jimmy's shoulder. "C'mon, man, nobody's gonna know."

"I hear you, but I gots a new girlfriend, see."

"So? We won't tell her." Lumbela shook Jimmy's shoulders in a big-brother way.

"I know, but she's been real good to me, so I best stay out here." Poor kid had no clue of the danger he was in.

With one arm already over Jimmy's shoulder, Lumbela swung his other arm across his chest, completing the bear hug. Jimmy still didn't get what was happening, not until Kripsen snatched his piece. "Hey, what the fuck are you doing?"

Lumbela and Deluski wrestled him into the alley. He was kicking and thrashing now. I looked up at the hookers peering down from open windows—lace and leather, poofed hair lit by flashing neon.

"Let go! Let the fuck go! Juno? Tell these fuckers to let me go."

I wanted to let him go. I really did. But I needed to put an end to this pissing match with Mota. He'd called my bluff, and now it was time for me to call his. I had to send him a signal he wouldn't forget. The mission didn't allow for half measures or nice tries. The mission wasn't for the timid. KOP needed to change. This broken world needed to change.

"Juno?" called Jimmy, his voice cracking, his eyes pleading. "Why you jus' standin' there? Fuckin' help me!"

It hurt me to hear the innocent fear in Jimmy's words. He was a fellow Tenttowner. He trusted me. My dinner threatened to come up.

I swallowed to keep my food down. "Break his legs."

five

MIDNIGHT had passed. I couldn't sleep.

I lay on the bed, my fingers laced under my head, listening to the sound of a bedframe scraping across the floor upstairs. Lumbela was really getting at it up there. Been going like this for ten minutes now.

I was in one of Chicho's screw suites, lying on a bed with fresh sheets. I'd insisted on fresh sheets. And even with the clean sheets, I made sure to lie on top. And fully clothed.

I was pretty damn sure Captain Mota would stand down, but until I could be absolutely certain, I'd stay here. No point making myself easy to find. For that reason, I'd dumped my phone too. Last thing I needed was to get arrested.

I was less concerned for my crew—cops didn't arrest other cops—but thought it best for them to lay low anyway. Deluski and Kripsen were bunking down the hall. And Lumbela was upstairs rearranging the furniture, making a goddamned racket. *Fucking idiot.*

Literally.

I turned on the lights. Geckos scurried and bedbugs scattered. An iguana stayed on the wall, a mane of spikes framing his face like military-inspired flower petals. His charcoal skin had turned fluorescent-pink along his spine like it always did during mating season. 'Guanas were especially brave this time of year. They'd leave themselves exposed for days in an effort to attract a mate, waiting in the starlight, their neon pink skin glowing with desire.

I wished my life could be so simple. Eat. Sleep. Fuck. If I could only be reduced to my biological urges. No love. No hate. No pride.

No guilt.

Using the room phone, I called a few fences I knew, waking them up until I found one who had a hoverchair in stock, one of those nice offworld models. I told the fence to send it to Jimmy's room at the hospital. *No, don't put my name on it. Make it anonymous.*

Jimmy. I could still hear the sound, the sickening crack of bone.

Fuck me. And fuck Mota for making me go this far.

Somebody knocked.

"Come."

The door swung open. "I saw your light was on." Maria held up a bottle of brandy. "Wanna drink?"

I nodded with enthusiasm. Sobriety was a bitch.

She stepped in, her hair and her mini both teased up to hooker heights. She pulled out a couple glasses from a rolltop liquor cabinet and poured. I took a deep swig, and sweet liquid fire burned down my throat. She sat on some kind of hammock apparatus that hung from the ceiling. Swinging, she snuggled herself into the folds, her ass hanging out through a hole in the bottom until she snapped a mesh flap in place.

I took another gulp, just about draining my glass. Damn, that was good. Looking at Maria nestled into that contraption, I mentally cycled through sex positions, trying to figure out how to use that thing.

I was stumped. And glad for it. Made me feel like I still had at least a drop of innocence somewhere inside me.

"Why are you doing this?" she asked.

Her left eye was decidedly puffy. I searched for other signs of bruising, but couldn't see through the layers of foundation on her cheeks.

"Sorry I hit you."

"Goes with the job, right? Why are you doing this?"

"Doing what?"

"Taking over this alley."

The 'guana stared at me like he was waiting for an answer. I pulled my shades from my shirt pocket and slipped them on, darkening the iguana's pink stripe to the color of blood.

I looked at Maria, her brown-sugar skin closer to chocolate now. She gave me a puzzled look, but didn't ask about the shades. "You're not in it for the money, are you?"

"Why do you say that?"

"Look at you. Those are decent shoes, durable, but nothing fancy. You don't wear a glitzy watch. You're dressed in whites like any other joe. If you were about the money, you'd be showing off what you got. That's what pimps do. Madams too."

I downed the rest of my glass, stood and walked over to her for a refill. Damn, her perfume was strong.

"You should get that hand fixed." She poured brandy into my wavering glass. "I know a doctor who works cheap. She does a lot of work on the girls around here."

"Tit jobs?"

"Yeah. And other stuff."

"What kind of other stuff?"

"Other stuff," she repeated with a shrug. "I bet she could fix that hand."

I took my place back on the bed. "Not interested."

"She's an offworlder. Or she used to be. She lives on-planet now."

"Why?"

"I don't know. I guess she likes it here."

"So how did you end up working for Chicho?"

"He took me in when I was eleven."

"You hooked for him?"

She nodded. "But I wasn't very good at it. I was young, so I did well with the pervs at the beginning, but when my tits started coming in, I knew my time was limited. The other girls were prettier, and they knew how to work the johns better than me. I tried to compensate in the looks department by learning how to do my makeup and my hair real good like this."

I wanted to laugh.

"But even then, I couldn't compete. So I had to find another way to make myself useful."

"And you chose security?"

"Why not? I still get to beat men off. I just do it a different way now." She gave me a mascara-caked wink, her lashes coming together like two rakes. "You never answered my question. You're not doing this for the money, are you?"

"No."

"Then why are you doing it?"

"It's complicated." I had nothing more to say on the subject. I sipped my drink, uncomfortable silence taking hold.

"That was some riot," she said after a while.

"Yeah."

"You just about got yourself killed, you know."

"I know."

"What were you thinking? The sky was fucking falling, and that's when you decided to stroll on out?"

"You ask too many questions."

"You remind me of some of the girls around here." She poured herself another. "I'm talking about the ones who drink and drug and fuck like they're on a mission."

"What kind of mission?"

"I wish I knew. It's like they're out to kill themselves, but they don't have the guts to just slash their wrists and be done with it. Is that who you are?"

"No. I'm on a different kind of mission."

"That's what they all say."

I tiptoed out, trying not to wake Maria, who was conked out on the sex swing. I hadn't slept all night. My haunted thoughts wouldn't allow it.

I found an empty room with a phone and tried to set up a conference call with Wu and Froelich. Wu answered. Froelich didn't. I'd have to wake up that asshole in person. I told Wu to meet me at Froelich's boat. It was time I took those two homicide bastards to task. Fuckers thought it was okay to go out gambling and not answer my calls? That shit was going to stop.

I strolled out the door and through the riot's wreckage, my shades dimming out some of the details. This duller form of reality suited me fine. The morning was hot. A southern breeze carried scorched air from the vast southern deserts that suffocated so much of this planet. Lagarto's only oasis was here in the jungles of the northern pole. If you could call this lizard-infested, riot-ravaged, poverty-stricken, mold-spotted city an oasis.

I chartered a skiff and rode the Koba River. A single light-bulb swayed on the end of a wire that hung from the rusted roof, golden light oozing out across black water. Pairs of monitor eyes reflected out of the darkness, accusing me with their cold, reptilian gazes.

Arriving at the dock, I handed the pilot some bills and climbed a ladder to the pier. I wandered the stalls, passing tables full of fresh fish on ice and racks of gutted 'guanas on hooks.

Spotting a small tub full of squirming salamanders, I stopped to order a taco. I stood by as the cook skewered two 'manders and dunked the squirming pair into a jar of peppery batter.

They came out completely coated, their battered legs and tails wriggling as they went into the fryer. Next, she held a flatbread in one hand and used the other to spatula on a thick swath of aromatic paste made from local spice. My stomach growled as she spooned on the riverfruit salsa. Then came the sprinkle of bitter cloverweed leaves. I waited as the fryer bubbled, the smell of grease and wood smoke making my mouth water. Finally, she pulled the skewer out of the fryer, crisped 'manders impaled on the end. Folding the flatbread into a taco, she used the bread to pinch the golden-brown critters off the slender rod. "Hot sauce?"

I nodded, paid up, and bit through the flatbread, crunching on the 'manders in the center. Tangy. Must be juveniles. The older ones tasted muddy.

Wu stepped up just before I took another bite, and I decided to take a bite of him first. "Hey, asshole, you left us hanging last night."

"Sorry, but me and Froelich, we were upriver—"

"I don't want to hear it." I chomped into my taco, hot sauce dripping out the other end. I walked as I chewed, forcing Wu to follow.

"Kripsen and Lumbela filled me in on last night," he said.

"Did you thank them?"

"For what?"

"For doing your job."

"What? Now I'm supposed to be the leg breaker?"

"You and Froelich should've been there. And you motherfuckers better quit dodging my calls." I chomped off another bite and kept at him, my words slurred. "I thought you were supposed to be the badass of this gang, but when the serious shit comes down you're nowhere to be found." I licked hot sauce off my lips, my tongue on fire. "You know what you are? You're a pussy."

He grabbed my arm and pulled me up close, our noses almost kissing. "You take that back." His temples were pulsing, the scar across his forehead darkening.

"Pussy." I grinned while I chewed, daring him to try something. His nostrils flared, and his lips pinched down so tight that they resembled the scar on his forehead. He didn't take a swing. He couldn't. I pressed my taco hand into his chest and pushed him out of my way, leaving a grease stain over his heart. If he didn't like being called a pussy, then he better grow a pair and do what he was told.

I was walking again. My appetite was gone, but I forced myself to take one more bite before tossing the scraps into the weeds with the candy wrappers and broken bottles. Wu trailed behind me, but not far—I could hear his shuffling footsteps. Sulking bastard.

"This it?" I pointed my bobbing finger at a listing barge. Froelich had once told me how some of the lower compartments flooded decades ago, making the old junker sit cockeyed in the water.

"Yeah," Wu mumbled as he stepped up alongside me. "His place is on the second deck."

"Let's wake him up."

We climbed the long gangway, and reaching the top, we started across the slanted decking, our shoes sinking into spongy moss. We ducked through a bulkhead and went up a set of rust-eaten metal stairs that—due to the barge's tilt—sat at an awkward angle.

"Heard from pretty-boy Mota?" asked Wu.

"No. But we don't have to worry about him anymore. Not after last night."

"Good. You know he's a fag?"

"Where'd you hear that?"

"Around."

I kept one hand on the sweating steel wall as we headed down a long corridor that leaned heavy to starboard. My shoe slipped and I went down, my knees crumpling, my left side smacking into the deck. *Christ.*

Wu laughed, the sound of his delight echoing up and down the corridor.

I slowly stood and evaluated the damage. One ankle felt a little gimpy, and my hip would surely bruise, but no more than that. "What the hell happened?"

"You fucking fell."

I pushed my shades up to the top of my head and studied the floor. *There's the culprit.* I reached down to touch a glob of yellow goop that had been smeared under my shoe. I held my fingers to my nose for a smell. "Fly gel."

"Somebody must've spilled."

The gel killed flies and eggs. Lagartans used it to clean cuts and abrasions. Without it, an open wound would be squirming with maggots inside five minutes. Lagartan flies acted fast. And they were damn good dive-bombers, expert at dropping their eggs from the air.

"There's more up there," said Wu.

We followed the sporadic trail of drops to a door painted sloppily with the name FROELICH.

"Did Froelich cut himself last night?" I asked, uncertainty creeping up my spine.

Wu shook his head no and opened Froelich's door. I followed him in, my hand on my piece. He flicked on the lights. The cabin was small—bed, kitchenette, toilet—and from the entry, it slanted downhill to the left.

The nightstand had been toppled, contents spilled on the floor. Oils and lubes. Condoms and cock rings. My eyes turned to a splatter of gel that marked the far wall, more gel on the floor underneath, and then a trail leading behind the bed, as if somebody had thrown something against the wall, where it fell, then rolled down the slanted decking.

Wu and I stepped slowly around the bed, following the trail to a severed head. Coated in fly gel, it rested where the wall met the floor, a vertebra poking out from a savagely chopped neck stump. I toed a gooey ear with my shoe, rolling the head faceup.

Hemorrhaged eyes stared from behind the gel mask. His mouth was agape, the black hole clotted with gel.

Froelich.

six

"No," said a shocked Wu. "No fucking way."

I pulled my shoe away, and Froelich's head rolled face-down, his vacant gaze aimed at the floor but angled to one side, his nose acting like a mini-kickstand. What was that on his cheek? A tattoo?

I squatted down for a closer look. A ring of interlocked snakes, two of them, each one swallowing the tail of the one in front. Where did that come from?

"No fucking way," repeated Wu, shaking his head slowly from side to side.

Froelich was dead, reducing my crew by 20 percent. My gut was heavy with dread. Events were reeling out ahead of me, and I had no way to rein them back in. I'd lost control.

Mota. Had I misjudged that pretty-boy son of a bitch? I couldn't believe he'd take it this far. Would he actually kill one of my crew? A fellow cop?

Wu's face was as pale as my own, his scar a faint pink line. "He was my partner," he said, his voice barely audible.

I sat on the bed's crumpled sheets and tried to see it another way. Maybe it wasn't Mota who did this. Froelich had enemies, lots of them. It might not be my fault. It might not have anything to do with me. That tattoo on his cheek was some weird shit, wasn't it?

And why kill Froelich? Cop killings brought too much attention. Killing me was the smart move.

Unless Mota couldn't find me.

Or he was crazy.

"What do you mean you don't know?" Maggie's hands were on her hips, her jaw jutted. We stood in a private corner of the barge's deck, behind one of the cranes, isolated from the hommy dicks and the med techs. I leaned on the rail, the deck's listing slope making it the only comfortable way to stand.

I hid behind my shades. "I don't know anything about this."

"Don't give me that. Talk."

I didn't know what to say. That I was back in the protection business? That I broke a good kid's legs last night? That I already got one of my crew killed?

Wishing it all away, I looked out at the river, at the black water flowing gently in the starlight. I tuned into the way the barge swayed with the silent current, my mind syncing with the lazy rocking. Maggie asked another question, but I wasn't listening. The river. It was calling me. The mad spark lit inside me. I recognized it this time. I felt reality leaking away, and I let it go. Gladly.

I stared straight down at the water. It stared back. Smiling, inviting. All I had to do was jump this rail. After a quick drop, the river would welcome me with a burst of spray, a celebration of liquid confetti. I'd drop below the surface and let her hold me in her cradling hands. Sinking, I'd let her carry me in her cool flow until she ushered me away from this world.

A finger poked my arm. "Talk, dammit. What do you know about this?"

I was transfixed by the water. Seduced. I didn't want to break the trance.

"I'm talking to you, Juno."

The trance crumbled. Dizzy, I gripped the rail and willed my melting knees to lock.

"Juno?"

I ripped my gaze off the water the way you rip off a bandage. Reality was back, the spark extinguished.

"What's wrong with you?"

I glared at her, my eyes burning straight through my shades.

"Seriously. What's wrong?" She reached for my hand, warm fingers making contact. "You're scaring me."

Hearing the fear in her voice, I felt a shift inside, chafing annoyance once again getting overwhelmed by the guilt and gloom. I couldn't handle this shit, emotions cycling like mad, moods swinging like hyper monkeys. What the fuck was wrong with me? "I'm okay." I tried to sound believable. "Really, I'm fine."

"No, you're not. Jesus, look at you. You look like you're about to pass out."

"I'm fine. I don't see a severed head every day, okay? It's got me a little screwed up."

"Oh, no, you don't." She smacked my hand. "Don't pull that shit with me. You and I both know you've seen worse."

I didn't want to bullshit her. I really didn't. But coming clean was out of the question. This whole fucking thing could be blowing up in my face, but I had to keep it contained as best I could. And to achieve containment I had to keep her out.

She waited for an answer. I had to say something. Something that would explain why my fingers were gripping the rail like a lifeline. Something believable.

I started into another line of bullshit, but it caught in my throat, nothing more than a mangled syllable coming out my mouth. I tried again, but couldn't spit it out, another false start dying before I could utter it.

Maggie's sharp eyes shone in the lamplight, her bullshit meter on full alert. I sighed, my posture deflating, my ego wilting.

"I miss Niki." I adjusted my shades, the shades Niki had

given me. Underneath, my eyes misted as painful seconds drifted by.

"I know you do. She was carrying too much weight to keep living."

Yes, she was. For the twenty-five years we'd been together, she tried to stay afloat. She really did. But the weight dragged on her ankles like an anchor until she couldn't swim any longer. There were things in life you just couldn't shake, and being raped by your father was one of them.

Footsteps approached from behind. "There you are. I've been lookin' all over for you two."

Just what I need. Josephs. Mark Josephs. Maggie's newest partner and a grade-A asshole. I rubbed my chin to cover my quivering lower lip.

"Juno, you old dog, what the fuck have you done this time?"

"He and Paolo Wu found Froelich," answered Maggie.

I cleared my throat and tried but failed to sniffle my nose clear. Using my index finger, I stabbed away a tear that leaked out from under my shades.

He leaned in to get a closer look at me. "What the fuck? You cryin'?"

"No."

"Cryin' over Froelich?" He threw up his hands. "You gotta be fuckin' shittin' me. Why you gettin' all weepy over that dickhead?"

"Fuck off."

"I'm just askin'."

"Leave him alone, Mark," said Maggie.

"What's today's date? I'm gonna mark my calendar. The day Juno Mozambe cried. This shit's historic."

A different type of spark ignited: anger. I was well acquainted with this kind. "Fuck off," I said, my shaky right strangling the rail.

Josephs held up his hands in mock surrender. "Whoa, don't get your titties twisted now. I'm just lightenin' the mood. Bringin' a little cheer like I always do. Why are you always so serious?"

I told myself to relax. *Let it go. Just let it go.* I peeled my fingers off the rail and shoved them in a pocket. I shifted my feet, muscles uncoiling, and even tried a smile.

"That's better," he said. "You gotta quit bein' so touchy. Don't be a bitch now."

My nerves jingled and my eye twitched. I was ready to pummel this stiff. That was what I needed, a good fucking fight.

Maggie put a hand on Josephs's shoulder. "Listen, Mark, why don't you let me talk to Juno alone?"

"No." He pulled his shoulder away. "We're gonna do it together. We're supposed to be partners, right?"

"I really think it would be better if you let me handle it."

"Fuck that. If you didn't wanna work with me, you shouldn't have asked me to be your partner."

"What the hell are you talking about?" Her face screwed in disgust. "Nobody else would have you."

"That ain't it at all. It's not that they don't like me. Those dickheads don't want to be outshined is all." He flashed his pearlies. "Nobody likes to be fiddle number two."

Hang in a little longer, I told myself. All I had to do was answer a few questions. No big deal. Then I could move on. I could find a bar and drink until the emotions stopped swinging. Drink until I couldn't feel. "Fucking ask your questions already."

Josephs hit Maggie with a self-satisfied smile, like he'd just won a prize. The bastard was like a jungle tick the way he loved to get under your skin.

"What are you waiting for?" she asked him.

He turned to me. "How did you find Froelich?"

"Wu and Froelich went upriver last night to do some betting on the monitor fights. Wu wasn't sure if he made it home
okay. We tried calling him this morning and he didn't answer,
so we came down here to check on him."

"That it?"

"That's it."

"What's the deal with that tattoo on his cheek? You ever
seen it before?"

"No. The killer must've stamped him."

Maggie asked Josephs, "What's the status on the search?"

"The unis tell me this boat's clean. We think whoever did
this did it somewhere else, then dunked Froelich's head in fly
gel to preserve it before bringin' it here." To me he said, "Now
why don't you tell me where you fit in with Wu and Froelich."

"We're buddies." Poker face.

"Fuckin' bullshit. You got some shit goin' with them two,
and you're gonna tell me what it is."

"We're just friends. Pals."

"We got a dead cop. We can't let that go unanswered. You
know that. If you three were into some shit, you gotta let me
know. You back to your old tricks?"

Maggie chimed in. "You know who did this, don't you, Juno?"

Possibly, I thought with locked lips.

"A cop is dead," said Josephs. "Fuckin' decapitated. You understand how much pressure's gonna come down on us? If you
know somethin', you can't keep us in the dark. You can't."

I felt the pressure, their combined heat bearing down on
me. But I held strong. "I told you everything I know."

Maggie seized my wrist. My heart started it was so sudden.
"Don't you dare shut me out." She raised an accusing finger,
aimed it at the spot between my eyes.

"Trust me," I said. "You don't want any part of this. Leave
it be."

"Part of what?"

"I can't even say for sure it's related."

"Talk."

I didn't like the way she was looking at me, her brows dipped in a deep V, her lips pursed, her pretty face gone sour. Her pointing finger felt like a drill aimed at my skull.

My resolve broke like I was a two-bit snitch. I wanted to keep her clear, but this was Maggie, my very last connection to the world.

"A badge," I said, the words bitter on my tongue. "Froelich might've been killed by another badge."

Maggie's drill of a finger went limp.

Josephs's face went blank, any vision of a clean case shattered. "Christ. The instant I saw you I should've known we were fucked."

Josephs was old-school KOP. A pimp kills a cop, and it's time to stomp some pimp ass. An O-head kills a cop, and it's open season on every junkie who has the bad sense to sleep in an alley. A cop kills another cop? That's a fucking minefield.

"Fuck me," he said. "Don't tell me he's brass. He better not be brass. Is he brass?" He hung on the answer.

I nodded.

"Fuck! I hate you, Juno. You know that? I've always hated you."

Their phones rang, both at the same time. A holo blinked into existence just beyond the rail. Captain Emil Mota's feet floated high over the water. "You two running this investigation?"

"Yes," they responded.

"I just got a tip. A credible tip. I want Juno Mozambe brought in for questioning."

seven

I FLEW through holo-Mota, diving for the river, my shades gripped in my left. My hands punctured the water, next came a slap to the top of my head, and then I was under. I plunged deep below the surface, my ears feeling the pressure. I kicked deeper, waiting for the mad spark to ignite inside me, hoping it would come so I could end this miserable existence.

No such luck.

It was cold down here. My ears hurt and so did my strained lungs. Not so rapturous after all.

I needed oxygen. Aiming straight up, I flutter-kicked for the surface. Breaking through, I sucked air into my lungs. I couldn't believe this shit. Damn river spat me out. Bitch didn't like the taste of me.

I looked up. Maggie was there, looking down at me, her expression unreadable from this distance. She gave me a wave. Josephs was there, too, flipping me a double bird.

Holo-Mota reappeared as Maggie must've called him back. She'd hung up with him as soon as he mentioned my name. From there, things had gone quick, her saying I better get out of here, Josephs saying they couldn't just let me walk away with all these cops wandering the pier, and me solving the problem by swanning overboard.

Soon they'd be telling Mota how they'd just tried but couldn't find me. I must've already left the scene. No, they didn't know where I'd gone. Now what was this tip all about?

I scanned the ship's rails. I couldn't see anybody but Maggie and Josephs. Nobody else had seen me. I quietly breaststroked away, aiming for a set of docks just downriver.

Water dripped from my clothes, forming a puddle on the tile floor. I shivered under the blasting aircon. From behind a long row of glass cases, a sharp-eyed woman stared at me with one brow cocked in puzzlement.

I held out my shades, drops of river water falling onto the glass counter. "Sorry." I tried to wipe off the water, but wound up smearing it around. Under the glass, rows and rows of earrings and necklaces glinted through the resulting blur.

I unfolded my sunglasses so she could see how one stem had bent when I hit the water. Through chattering teeth, I asked, "Can you fix this?"

I lay on the bed, wearing a brand-new set of cheap whites that I'd bought with some soggy pesos. My good-as-new shades covered my eyes.

Maria sat in the sex swing, her bare feet on the floor, her toenails painted pink to match her bra, which peeked out from under a tit-hugger top. My wet clothes hung from the cables that supported the sex swing. So did my drying pesos, two dozen bills clipped on like tiny flags, each held in place by a nipple clamp posing as a clothespin.

We didn't speak. She seemed to sense I wasn't in a conversational mood. My mind was grinding and churning, processing and plotting. Mota had overplayed his hand. The guy was a suit, and suits had no business poking around in a murder investigation. Not when they worked in PR. Shoving his weight around with Maggie and Josephs was an overreach. They didn't report to him.

I never doubted Maggie and Josephs would let me go. Tense

as things were between Maggie and me, we had a history. And Josephs, he was an everyday cop, and everyday cops had a long tradition of anti-suit sentiment. He'd let me go on principle. The SOB didn't like being told what to do.

But Mota would keep pushing. He was already trumping up a bullshit tip to turn KOP against me and my boys. KOP was too fractured for his plan to work in full, but he didn't need complete success. Shit, all he needed was a single kiss-ass. Just one trigger-happy uniform with designs on currying suit favor and I was fucked.

Whether Mota killed Froelich or not, he had to be corralled. And fast.

But he hadn't responded to my threats. Or a pair of broken legs.

I knew what I had to do. It was the only way to get the mission back on track. There was no other way to be sure my new protection business would succeed.

The competition had to be eliminated.

I had to kill him.

I tried to tell myself I shouldn't feel guilty. I ran tired, old rationalizations through my head. Things like, *It's his own fault for not backing down.* Or, *Anybody stupid enough to buck me isn't worth the air he breathes. Eye for an eye, tooth for a tooth. You fuck with a monitor, you get an assful of teeth.*

I had a million of them, but none helped, the familiar pit of guilt-tinged self-loathing making my stomach ache.

I had to kill him.

There it was.

"You met my sister yet?" asked Maria, her lashes gunked up with so much mascara that her lids and upper cheeks were dotted with semicircles of mascara tracks. I couldn't see the bruise I'd given her. Whether it had faded or had just been covered by a few coats of foundation, I couldn't tell.

"No."

"She works here. She's got a pretty face. She's gonna do good at this."

"How old is she?"

"Fifteen, but she looks older. Most people think she's seventeen or eighteen. I've been saving up to get that doctor I was telling you about to do some work on her."

"I thought you said she was pretty."

"She is. She'll get regular business, but we have to think long-term. Most of these girls don't think like that. They spend their money as fast as they earn it. They never think about what's going to happen when their tits start sagging. What are they going to do then?"

Somebody less jaded would've told her to get her sister the hell out of here. The girl was only fifteen. It wasn't too late to get her back in school.

Instead, I told Maria her sister was lucky to have her looking out for her.

"She's a smart kid. Someday we're going to start our own house. If we're really good about saving our money, we can do it in ten years or so."

"You think a new set of tits will earn her that much?"

"It's not just the tits. She's gonna get some work down below, too."

"What kind of work?"

"This doctor can insert motors and stuff down there so she can give her johns a ride they won't forget."

"Motors?" I asked, disbelieving.

"Not that you can see. They're all internal, small little things. But they're powerful as hell. I mean they'll vibrate your wang off. And there's other settings, too." She counted fingers. "There's roll, and jerk, and squeeze, and twist. Oh, and they lubricate."

My jaw was on my chest. Robo-fucking-snatches? "Guys dig that shit?"

She nodded emphatically, her teased hair bowing up and down like a tree in a windstorm. "I know a girl over at the Red Room who got the procedure. She has to turn 'em away. Now I admit there's some who aren't into it. She says she gets johns who come in for a curiosity fuck and never come back, but she also says there's tons more who won't do regular girls anymore. She has a waiting list."

"How long have these things been around?"

"Not long. Offworlders have had 'em for years. I don't even know how long. But they're new on Lagarto. As far as I know, that offworld doctor was the first to offer the procedure down here."

"Does Chicho have any girls who have one?"

"Why? You wanna try it out?"

Surprised at the question, I stuttered a no.

She cocked her head to one side like she was confused by my reaction. "I think I'm starting to get you."

"You are?"

"You're one of those sentimental types, aren't you? You can't separate sex from love. Big and bad on the outside, but soft and squishy on the inside."

Soft and squishy? Try twisted and tortured.

"Don't look at me like that," she said. "I wasn't trying to insult you. I think it's sweet, really."

Christ. Don't tell me she's coming on to me, this ex-hooker with the big hooters, and the big hair, and the big perfume.

The room's phone rang.

I answered quickly, jumping at the chance to escape this conversation. Deluski appeared, the badge on his holo shining extra bright. "It's Wu, boss, he just went into the Beat."

Any relief I felt was instantly erased. I was up, shoving my feet into my shoes. "I told you guys to lay low. Why didn't you stop him?"

"We tried, but he wouldn't listen. He's in there looking for Mota."

eight

I HUSTLED from the back of the cab. Deluski waited on the curb outside the longtime cop bar. A flickering lamp blinked across his youthful face. Together, we barged through the double doors. The place was quiet. Unusually quiet.

Heads turned our way, uniforms and brass, badge bunnies and bartenders.

Wu stood by the bar, crocked off his ass, swaying to and fro, a bottle in one hand, a half-full glass in the other. "Where are you?" he shouted, the words sloshing out his mouth. "Where is that fucking faggot?"

The crowd gave him plenty of room. Other than some hushed muttering, nobody spoke. They appeared to be waiting for his tirade to run its course. Any normal night, a guy disrupts everybody's good time and somebody would've dragged him out back for a thumping. But Wu had just lost his partner. They were in a generous mood.

Wu brought the bottle to his lips, forgetting the glass in his other hand. He tipped his scarred head back for a swig, and his body followed, back arching, feet backpedaling—but still drinking—until he smacked into the bar. Glasses jumped, and bar stools tumbled.

I wished I could laugh like some in the crowd, but my heart was racing, my pulse double-timing. I scanned the clientele, searching for threats, searching for agents of Captain Mota. Did he have a crew like I did? Was his influence bigger than I thought? He wanted me brought in for questioning. How far had the word spread? How many of these jokers were ready to smooch some suit ass?

I spotted both Kripsen and Lumbela. They looked relieved to see me. I gave them each the eye. *Let's do this thing.*

I approached the bar, Deluski riding shotgun, Kripsen and Lumbela joining from the sides, a four-man show of force.

"Where is he?" yelled Wu. "Where is that bastard? I just wanna ask him some questions. I wanna ask him if he killed my partner."

We passed cop tables, brandy in glasses, tin cups full of shine. Badge bunnies watched us pass, their faces painted with rouge and lipstick. The hairs on my neck prickled, and sweat broke on my brow.

I stepped straight up to Wu and took a fistful of his collar. "Let's go."

I turned and made for the door, my boys fanning to the sides, me dragging Wu along. My boys walked with purpose, their hands on their pieces, putting out a pure don't-fuck-with-us vibe.

Wu's garbled protests sounded behind me. *Dumb fucking undisciplined piece of shit.* He'd put us all at risk tonight. His drunken posturing was a colossal show of stupidity, though I had to admit he couldn't have stumbled into a more effective means of putting out word that Mota might've killed Froelich. True or not, the accusation would pass from cop to cop on whispered breath until the whole of KOP was infected.

I eyed the last couple tables. I felt a tug on my improvised leash, fabric slipping through my fingers. Wu tried his escape, but I recovered in a hurry, my hand seizing a tighter hold on his collar. Buttons popped off his shirt as he tried to pull free. Stumbling, he went down, his body falling on top of the brandy glass in his left hand. The muffled crunch of glass made me wince.

I yanked him upright. His hand was bloodied, his pants torn. He held the bottle tight to his chest with his other hand like it was a baby. I told him to heel by giving his collar a rough yank. The door. I had to get him out that door.

Wu threw the bottle. Heads ducked to a chorus of startled screams. The bottle exploded against a wall by the door. A shower of brandy and glass rained down on a table of cops and their dates. They jumped up in unison, the women looking at their stained dresses in disgust, the men aiming steamed stares at us.

Christ. The men were approaching.

I glanced at Wu, at the fear creeping into his eyes—he knew how bad he'd fucked up. A group of four brandy-splashed beat cops met us, their chests out, their nostrils flared, testosterone flowing strong. Three more cops joined from another table, one of them a woman.

"That boy's gonna apologize," said the one in front.

My crew stood their ground, their hands gripping their undrawn weapons. I let go of Wu and stepped up to meet the uniform in a cop face-off. Nobody in my crew was going to fucking apologize. I'd never allow us to look so weak. I didn't care how in the wrong Wu was. He was one of *mine.*

"Tell him to apologize," said the uni.

Four on seven. Make that eight now that another cop had joined their ranks. I took my sunglasses off, folded them, and shoved them in a pocket. I pulled my piece out of my waistband real slow and deliberate. With the handle pinched between thumb and forefinger, I held it up in my swaying hand.

This was what I needed. A good fucking fight, consequences be damned. If Mota had one of his agents in the crowd, so be it. My enforcer juices couldn't be tamed.

Somebody came and collected my weapon. And everybody else's too. The air hung heavy with anticipation. Badge bunnies hopped away. Suits hung in the corner, spectating from afar. A pair of uniforms joined our side, and I recognized them as a couple of late arrivals from the riot. Two of Wu and Froelich's boys.

A bartender yelled from behind the bar, "Take it outside. You want to be welcome in here afterwards, you take it outside."

The stiff opposite me turned his head to talk to his newly formed gang. "Yeah, let's move it outside."

That was when I hit him, dropped the fucker with a right to the jaw. I ran over him, my shoe stomping his balls on my way to bull into the next hump. I drove my shoulder into his chest and ran him backward until we tumbled over a table, and the gates of hell broke loose behind me.

The gates of glorious hell.

I was on my back taking shots to the face, my hands covering and taking the worst of it. I tried to buck the bastard off me, but my strength was sapped. Nothing to do but take it. He snuck one through my guard, my head going dizzy.

"You can't hurt me," I spat. Another fist came down. "That all you got?"

Somebody pulled him off, telling him it was over. "Easy. Take it easy," said a voice.

I couldn't see straight. Too much blood in my eyes. I wiped my face with my shirt. Hands picked me up and ushered me toward the door. I bumbled over collapsed tables and broken chairs before being ejected out to the street. Finding a lamp-post to lean on, I rubbed my eyes clear and took a long look at my scraped and already swelling knuckles. I grinned. I could still throw a punch.

Looking down, I found Deluski and Kripsen sitting in a patch of weeds, their lungs heaving, their faces bloodied like mine. Behind them Wu lay passed out with geckos crawling all over him. I swept at the flies buzzing around my head. The smell of blood must've been driving them mad.

Lumbela was across the way, his arm draped over the shoulder of the uniform I'd dropped, the two of them laughing. The uniform's girl stood nearby, arms crossed, her impatient foot going *tap, tap, tap*. That stiff had another fight coming later tonight. I laughed, deep and hard. I'd forgotten the joy of genuine laughter.

Somebody handed me a can of fly gel. "You're gonna need this."

"Yeah. Was that you pounding my face?"

"That was me." He flexed his fist. "You got one hard face."

I scooped out a gob of gel and slathered my brow to kill any eggs that were already there. "See any other cuts?"

He tilted my head back in the lamplight and gave me a good once-over. "I don't think so, but I can't tell for sure."

I rubbed gel over my knuckles. "Good fucking fight."

"Shit, yeah." He patted my shoulder and brought the gel to Deluski and Kripsen.

I walked over to them. "Can you guys get Wu home?"

"You bet, boss," said Kripsen.

"Let me borrow your phone."

Kripsen handed it over. It took me only a few seconds to get the address before I tossed the phone back to him. Fun as it would be to buy everybody a round, it was time I shoved off.

I found my piece in a pile of weapons on the walk and tucked it into my waistband.

"Where you going, boss?" asked Kripsen.

"I got something I gotta do. You guys get Wu home."

Suddenly remembering, I reached for my shirt pocket. Good. My shades were still there. I pulled them free and gave them a look. They'd made it through just fine. Smiling, I slipped them on.

I started hoofing, purpose in my gait. I didn't care that my head ached, didn't care about my ribs and knuckles either. I wore the wounds like badges, something to be proud of. I'd kicked some ass and tagged myself a fucking force.

I didn't want to think about where I was going. I wanted to enjoy the moment. *Good fucking fight.*

I was back.

Nobody would care that I'd taken a beating at the end. What they'd remember was me not backing down. They'd remember how I threw that nasty sucker punch, how I'd stomped that hump's nuts.

Confidence surged through me. The tattered mission was restored, achievable. I'd take back KOP. My will was too strong. My desire was too great.

I was putt-putting the river on a rented skiff, a breeze drying the blood on my face.

I was very aware of the fact that nobody had made a move against me at the Beat. Even when I was down, catching face-fuls of knuckles, nobody tried to arrest or kill me. That told me Mota's influence over KOP was minimal. Captain or no, he couldn't turn the police against me. He was a middle manager, a bureaucrat, nothing more. He didn't send a crew to guard the alley last night. The best he could do was to get a single uniform posted. A clueless uniform. Jimmy.

I wasn't going to feel bad about Jimmy. Not tonight. I was serving a higher purpose. Together, Maggie and I were going to change this city.

Mota was just a bump in the road. A temporary hurdle. And I was going to end this thing tonight. I was going to kill the bastard.

I angled the boat into one of the many canals built when Lagarto's brandy trade was the agricultural envy of the Unified Worlds. I passed houses on stilts, drawn curtains and dark windows. An offworld flyer rose into the Big Sleep's perpetually black sky. Unusual for this neighborhood. Not many offworlders ventured into the residential districts. The dumbass had probably got lost and decided to get his bearings by taking an aerial view. The flyer banked left and headed for the river, buzzing rooftops with its ear-rattling shriek.

I ducked my head as I passed under a low bridge, viny growths scraping through my hair. I turned left and entered a broad canal. Both banks were lined with stilted homes jutting over the water. I couldn't stop myself from remembering: Niki grew up not far from here. She'd still lived with her parents when Paul and I staked out their home. Back then, Paul and I were young guns hot to make a name for ourselves by nailing a big-time drug dealer, Niki's father.

Hour after hour, day after day, we'd spied through the windows, watching her brush her hair and read her books and change her clothes. I fell for her. It was as simple as that. I fell, and fell hard.

The earliest days were the best. We each had our demons, but we were still young and stupid enough to believe that our love for each other would conquer all. I didn't need to stop my enforcer's ways, and she didn't need to face the ugly truth that her son-of-a-bitch father had raped her.

But the happy days didn't last long. The shit we were carrying kept getting in the way, so we broke up and reunited, broke up and reunited, over and over until we each found a way to contain our demons. For me, the secret was booze. For her, pills.

But even then, the demons never stopped nipping at our souls. They took tiny, little bites, nibbles so small we didn't even notice them until our hearts and souls had been completely devoured.

She'd had the good sense to escape her torment by leaving this world. And me, I was still here. Why, I didn't know.

Mota's house shouldn't be much further. Afraid of making too much noise, I turned off the motor and let the boat coast to a stop before grabbing a pole. I stood in the stern and stabbed the water, driving the pole deep down into the mud, and propelled the boat with a shove. Quietly, almost silently, I moved toward my destination.

Stroke by stroke, I made my approach. Monitors lurked in the water, their reflective eyes watching me pass.

I stopped.

This was it. Mota's place. Light from a neighbor's outdoor lamp penetrated enough of the shadows to let me see his back wall. Weighted by the relentless strangle of jungle roots, the porch had partially separated from the rest of the house and hung down in the water.

I'd expected something nicer. Looked like Mota's intensely manicured image didn't extend to his house.

The bedroom light was on, shadows shifting on the ceiling. He was home. I poled the skiff to the opposite side of the canal and drove it as far as I could into a thicket of mangrove. I sat down and waited for the light to go out. I'd do him in his sleep.

I'd be the prime suspect. Thanks to Wu, my feud with Mota had been well advertised. And it wouldn't take much asking around to learn of my new protection racket. They'd come for me. A cop killer.

Did it matter that Mota might've killed a cop himself?

I doubted it.

Were this the old days, I wouldn't sweat it. Back then, I had protection at the highest level. Between Paul and the Bandur cartel, I had free rein. I was untouchable. Bulletproof.

Shit, Mota never would've challenged me in the first place.

Damn that SOB. Why couldn't he have stood down like he was supposed to?

The guy had grown tougher than he used to be, a bona fide badass. But had he gone so bad he could've chopped off Froelich's head? That shit was savage.

The timing of it was hard to contradict. Froelich must've died just hours after I ordered the breaking of Jimmy's legs. Who else could it have been?

I told myself it didn't matter. Either way, Mota had to die. The mission required it.

My face hurt. I probed my features with my fingers. They felt strange, like I was wearing a puffy mask. My side ached, like somebody had shoved a shiv between my ribs. Despite the pain, I had to smile. *Good fucking fight.*

The bedroom light went out. My heartbeat moved up a tick. I checked the time. I'd give it a half hour, let him get into a deep sleep first. Let him dream his last dream.

I spent the next thirty concentrating on how I was going to beat the rap. The obvious move would be to frame Wu. After that stink he raised tonight, he'd be an easy mark.

But he was one of mine. That dumb, scar-headed asshole was one of mine.

I twisted my brain, trying to figure a way. All raps were beatable. There was always a way. And I was a fucking master, a frame-job maestro. Evidence was my paint, crime scenes my canvas. The perfect scam was out there. I could find it if I just concentrated. *Think, dammit. Just think . . .*

Fuck this brainy shit. I'd kill that dickhead and take his body with me. I'd take it out to the jungle and find a nice private place to dump it. The jungle made quick work of corpses. Geckos and 'guanas. Beetles and maggots. Give it a couple days, and he'd be mulched into shit.

I poled the skiff out from the mangrove and crossed the narrow canal, pulling up to his dilapidated back porch. Broken posts sat atop bent pilings, the collapsed floor half submerged. I tied the boat to a loose beam.

I pushed my shades up onto my forehead. I needed to see. Carefully, gingerly, I stepped onto the porch. Floorboards creaked. The rooftop swayed. *Shit.* I froze, my heart pounding, my throat dry, my teeth clenched tight. I reached for my piece, my ears waiting for the sound of approaching footsteps, my eyes zeroed in on the bedroom window.

Nothing.

Breathing easier, I moved toward a window, not the bedroom window, but the one on the opposite side of the door. This section of the porch was underwater. I stepped slowly into the drink, taking care to keep from slipping on river muck. Cool water seeped into my shoes as I popped the screen and crawled silently through.

I was inside. A rush came over me. I was unstoppable. A fucking force.

My inner enforcer was in charge now.

I slunk down a hall, water squishing in my shoes, the bedroom door my target. I carried my piece two-handed to keep the shaking under control. Mota didn't know what was coming. *Wakey, wakey, pretty boy.*

The bedroom door was open. I filled the door frame, my piece trained on the bed, bathed in the blue glow of a holoclock. Mota's fine features were an unearthly mix of radiant light and shadow. He snored loud, deep sawing echoing off the walls.

I looked to his right. From under the crumpled sheet, thick black locks spilled across the pillow. Mota wasn't alone. And he wasn't gay. She slept with her mouth wide open, a model's face caught in an ugly pose. My piece shook in my hands. I had to fry them both. No witnesses. Whoever she was, she had to die.

I tried to level my weapon.

Tough luck, lady.

Wrong place, wrong time.

Shit fucking happens.

I was on a mission, dammit. KOP needed to be conquered. This world had to change.

I couldn't steady my hands, my aim wobbling out of control. Sweat stung my eyes.

I had to kill them. The mission required it. I couldn't blink. Paul and I never blinked when we took KOP so many years ago. *Fucking do it.*

But she was an innocent. *You don't hurt women, Juno.*

Conflicting urges yanked at me like a pair of monitors tug-of-warring over a fresh kill. My knees shook, and my heart pounded explosive beats. I couldn't make myself pull the trigger. But Mota had to die. He wouldn't stop until he turned KOP against me.

Pull the trigger, Juno.

But my trembling finger wouldn't move. She was innocent.

And with every second of hesitation, I felt the mission crumbling away. I wasn't up to the job. I could see that now. I didn't have what it took. Not anymore.

I spun away, out of the door frame, and pressed my back against the wall. My lungs heaved for air. Must've been holding my breath.

I moved down the hall, away from the snoring, into the living room and slumped onto the couch. This whole thing was a joke. I couldn't take over KOP. I wasn't even a cop. What was I thinking?

Why did I even care? This world was beyond saving. People were mostly assholes anyway. I shouldn't even give a shit.

With total certainty, I knew the mission was dead. Dead, dead, dead.

So was Niki. My Niki.

And Paul.

I realized I was dead too. My body just didn't know it yet.

I wanted the mad spark to come. The crazy sensation that could sweep me away from this world. I tried to summon it— *come out, come out, wherever you are*. It didn't come. Even it had abandoned me.

I held up my lase-pistol and studied it in the dark. This gun was all I had left.

I brought the barrel into my mouth and sucked on the metal composite, my finger fondling the trigger.

Still, the mad spark wouldn't come. Fickle bastard.

Do it anyway. Just fucking do it. I came here tonight to end this, and I still could. *Pull the trigger.*

A tear trickled down my cheek. I couldn't breathe, not with my nose running and my mouth stuffed with metal. *Just do it already.* My lungs felt ready to burst. I was getting light-headed. Dizzy. *Do it!*

I pulled the weapon out of my mouth. *Fucking coward. That was twice you couldn't pull the trigger.*

I sank deeper into the cushions and dropped my shades down over my eyes. I listened to snoring from down the hall. I didn't know how long I sat there. One minute? Ten? An hour? I couldn't tell. But I stayed put until long after the tears dried and my nose cleared.

I still tasted metal. I licked my shirt to scrape the taste off my tongue.

A phone rested on the coffee table. Mota's phone. He must have left it there when he went to bed.

I called Maggie, holo-free. I got voice mail, hung up, and tried again.

I was numb. From head to toe, nothing but numb. I called her again. And again.

She picked up, her voice a middle-of-the-night croak. "Yes, Captain?"

I kept my voice down. "It's me, Maggie. It's Juno. I'm using Mota's phone."

"Why are you using Mota's phone?"

"I trashed mine, didn't want to be tracked."

"Where are you?" Her voice turned urgent. "Why are you whispering?"

"I'm at Mota's place. In his living room."

A pause. "What?"

"I came to kill him."

"Jesus Christ. What's wrong with you?"

"I really fucked up, Maggie."

"You killed him?"

"No, he's in bed, sleeping. He's with somebody. I couldn't do it."

"Can he hear you?"

"I don't know. He's snoring pretty loud."

"Get out of there. Now, Juno."

"I started something I can't finish."

"Are you moving?"

I stood up. "I am now."

"Good. Now keep moving."

"Did you hear me before? I started something I can't finish. I really screwed up."

"No fucking kidding."

nine

I couldn't sleep. I lay in the dark. Blinking neon splashed the far wall. A loud groan came through the wall behind me. Somebody was getting their money's worth. At this hour, he must've paid for an all-nighter.

I'd managed to sneak in without waking Maria, who was crashed in the sex swing, her big hair catching every strobe of neon in its net and briefly lighting up firefly style before fading to black.

Despite Maggie's insistence, I'd refused to go to her place after leaving Mota and his girlfriend sleeping in their bed. It was the middle of the goddamn night. I couldn't intrude like that. I'd intruded enough when I woke her.

I'd meet her in the morning. I'd survive the night without doing something drastic. Starting early, she and I would talk it out. That was what she said. That was enough to keep me going.

I watched the window light up with the crimson glow of neon, then blacken with the dark of night, on and off, back and forth, no telling which would eventually win my soul.

I laughed at myself, at what a fuckup I was.

Maria woke. "When did you get in?" She rubbed her eyes.

"An hour ago."

She yawned and stretched her arms. "I've been waiting for you. I wanted to warn you that a couple guys came looking for you earlier."

"Who?"

"They didn't say. I think they were from upriver."

"How do you know?"

"One was wearing a panama hat, one of those cheap ones they make out of straw."

"What did you tell them?"

She adjusted her position in the swing. I didn't know how she could sleep on that thing. "I told them I hadn't seen you."

"They say why they were looking for me?"

"No."

Nice. Now a pair of strangers were after me. They'd have to take a fucking number. "Does Chicho know?"

"I didn't tell him."

We stayed quiet for a while. She dropped a foot to the floor and used it to rock herself, red light slashing across her face with every flash from the sign outside. "You know Chicho's already bringing in protection money from the other snatch houses."

"I figured."

"If I were you, I'd ask to see his books. He'll short you if you don't keep on top of him."

"You think his books are accurate?"

"Yeah. That man keeps track of things. He's smart that way. I've been asking him lots of questions. I gotta know how to do numbers to run my own house. It's actually . . ."

I stopped listening and pulled Mota's phone from my pocket. It still worked. He must not have noticed it was missing yet or he would've ordered it wiped. The bastard was probably still snoring away.

I opened the pics folder, and the first shot materialized over the bed. I squinted at the bright light until I slipped on my shades. Mota stared at me with a pearly-toothed grin, hat square on his head, badge shined bright. It was his graduation photo. I moved to the next pic, and the next. Mota waving from the deck of a boat. Mota posing by a new car. I jumped from pic to pic: Mota, Mota, Mota.

He liked to take pictures of himself, hundreds of them, the holo-slide show floating above the bed: Mota rubbing his chin, pensive-like; hands on hips with a faraway look; leaning on a door frame, looking oh so casual. He had all the poses down.

Maria was still talking, going on about her plans for the future. I motored through Mota's photos, tossing her an occasional "uh-huh" as if I were listening.

What's that? I stopped and moved back a pic.

"Find something?" she asked.

I stretched the holo-pic's edges in order to enlarge the image. It was a street market, rugs and wood carvings under jury-rigged tents. Mota stood in the foreground, his arm over the shoulder of another man, a man with a shaved head and a round tattoo on one cheek. Fucking Froelich.

Froelich and Mota? I checked the file's time stamp. Six months old.

But that couldn't be. Froelich never had a tattoo. I thought the killer must've stamped him when he chopped off his head. I zoomed in to get a closer look at the two interlocked snakes, each one eating the other's tail.

"What is it?" Maria asked.

I spun the 2D image her way.

"Isn't that one of your crew? The one who showed up late?"

"Yeah. But he didn't have that tattoo."

"You know they make 'em so you can turn 'em on and off, don't you?"

"They do?"

"Offworlders been doing it forever. You've seen how they can shift their looks. But now locals can do it too. They can't afford to get the works like offworlders do, but a little tattoo isn't that expensive. They even make some that are animated."

I started back into the slide show, the next bunch of pics all candids of Froelich, some with the face tat, some not. And then came a string of shots of Froelich and Mota posing together. How weird was that? If I didn't know better, I'd think they'd been dating.

"Lovers," she said.

"You think so?"

"Definitely."

"Wu told me Mota was gay, but I didn't buy it. He sleeps with women."

"How do you know?"

Remembering the woman in his bed, I said, "Trust me."

"Maybe his snake don't like just one kind of hole."

I navigated pics, dubious of the gay lover theory until a shot of the two of them kissing clinched it.

I was stunned. Floored.

One of my crew had been dicking my enemy.

The streets were waking up, vendors hosing sidewalks, farmers wheeling pushcarts loaded high with spiralfruit and cilantro. Stooped porters labored by with sacks of grain strapped to their backs. The Phra Kaew market would open soon.

The Mota and Froelich slide show cycled through my head, pic after pic, my brain snagging on one picture in particular, this one of Mota, Froelich, *and Wu*, brandy glasses raised to the camera, standing behind a table stacked high with cash. As if discovering Froelich and Mota were sword fighting each other wasn't shock enough, there was Wu, consorting with the enemy. The pic was dated the twenty-first. The night Wu and Froelich ignored my calls. When they claimed to be upriver watching monitor fights.

The night Froelich got his head cut off.

My gut stung with the realization that long before I'd come

onto the scene, Mota had penetrated my crew, and maybe in more ways than one.

I had to know how deep.

Wu lived in this neighborhood with his wife and kids. I was going to brace that hungover shitbird. I'd throw the wife a few bills and tell her to treat the kids to a nice breakfast. Then I'd get after that son of a bitch.

I thought this would be easy. I'd picked on Mota for that very reason. I thought he'd go down without a fight. I didn't know he'd toughened up. I didn't know he was screwing one of my boys.

I didn't know shit.

Mota's phone chirped in my pocket.

I pulled it out and checked the display. The call was holo-free, and whoever it was, they'd blocked the name. I picked up but didn't say hello.

"Who is this?" Mota's voice.

"Who the fuck do you think?"

He stayed quiet for a few. "You broke into my house."

I didn't respond. No way I was going to admit it over the phone.

"You can't intimidate me, you hear me?" His voice rose in pitch. "You're going to pay for Froelich, you bastard. You're going to pay."

The phone went dead. Wiped.

I'll pay for Froelich? How was he going to blame me for that? He couldn't possibly think I killed him, could he?

The answer came in a sickening flash. If Mota and Froelich were lovers, he just might think I offed his boyfriend to intimidate him.

Jesus.

Mota and I were on a collision course. I could see that now. I'd started something that couldn't be stopped. No way to undo it. No such thing as do-overs. It didn't matter that I'd lost the will to fight, that I wanted out. It wouldn't end before one of us was dead.

I needed Maggie. I couldn't trust myself. I needed somebody with a level head, somebody who could see straight. Somebody who could call me on my shit. Somebody who had a moral compass that wasn't spinning in circles. Maggie.

But first, Wu.

I turned right. A narrow alley closed all around me. Light slanted out from workshops on either side, illuminating the alley with a weave of dim beams. I passed basins filled with clothes soaking in dyed water. Up ahead, a pair of women dumped a tub. A rush of crimson water came running down the stained pavement. I moved to the side and let the tide roll past. They dumped another tub, and this time it was yellow water—smelling of saffron—that ran past and found its way into a storm drain.

I walked through a battered gate and up a set of mossy wood steps that led into a short tunnel. As I walked, I ducked beneath hanging moss that tickled my face as chittering lizards gave me an earful. I skipped up another short set of steps at the tunnel's end and entered a courtyard surrounded by apartments, the patio freshly torched and dusted with ash. A tree stood in the center, its branches hanging low, weighed down with ripening brandy fruit. I walked up four flights to the top floor and around to the opposite side. I looked down at the treetop, leaves rustling in the breeze.

I rapped on Wu's door, then waited a few before giving the door another pounding. His wife must've gone out early with the kids, probably walking them to school. Good. I kicked the door this time, giving it some extra boot. *Wake the fuck up.*

A thought tickled. This was the Big Sleep. No school on a holiday.

I tried the knob. Not locked.

I stepped inside, my hand on my piece, my heart already bumping my ribs. Putrid air assaulted my nostrils. Two tipped lamps rested on the floor with dented lampshades, angles of light slicing the walls. Dirt from a toppled houseplant ground under my shoes. I held my lase-pistol out front and followed its quivering lead into the kitchen; dishes in the sink, a drippy faucet, a sweaty fridge spotted with mildew. I backed out and peeked into a bathroom with chipped linoleum and musty towels.

A droning buzz drew me into a dark bedroom. The air was rank. I fumbled for a light switch and flicked it on. Toys sat on the floor. Bunk beds stood against the wall. *Don't fucking tell me.*

Flies swarmed over the beds. *No.* I stepped forward, repeating the word no in my head with every footfall. Flies bounced off my face and plinked off my shades. Small forms rested under the sheets of each bed. I peeled back one of the sheets, and the image before me seared into my brain as if a hot branding iron had entered through my eyes. Pink PJs squirmed with geckos. Her hair was speckled with maggots, a plastic barrette on one side.

As bile rose in my throat, I lifted the other sheet. Another girl, another abomination.

I exited the room, my shaking piece still taking the lead. I moved down the hall, thick patches of black flies marking the floor and walls. They took off when I stepped near, briefly revealing spills of blood before resettling.

The master bedroom was bustling with activity. Flies swarmed. Geckos scavenged. 'Guanas fed on a naked body that lay on the floor. Wu's wife. I moved in close. The stench was so bad I had to breathe through my mouth.

I tucked my piece under my arm and clapped my hands loud. Lizards scattered. Flies went airborne. I pushed up my shades and took in the unfiltered horror.

She'd been stabbed several times with a lase-blade. The wounds were charred and partially cauterized. I clapped again, then picked up a stubborn 'guana by the tail. Its body twisted, and its legs reached, and its bloodied mouth snapped at the air. Her breasts were gone. Not eaten. Gone. Cut off. Her chest butchered by jagged wounds. Same with the vagina, a roughly etched triangular wound marking the place it should be.

Unlike the stab wounds, the mutilations weren't charred. Killed by lase-blade, then butchered with a knife.

I dropped the iguana on the floor, and it scrambled in for a bite of bicep. Light-headed, I forced myself to survey the rest of the room. Then a second bathroom. No sign of Wu.

I took another look at the body. Big mistake. My hand went to my mouth, and I hurried down the hall, my steps unsteady, my balance shot. I lurched into the living room, my world spinning, and dropped into a chair. I swallowed hard. *Breathe.* The air stank in here, but not as bad. I swallowed again.

I set my piece on my lap and told myself to get a grip.

Fuck.

I needed a phone. I had to call Maggie.

The front door opened. My heart leapt out of my chest. My hands jerked in surprise, my lase-pistol falling between my legs. A man stepped in, a stranger, not Mota. *Not Mota.* Dark eyes peeking through an unruly mop.

Spotting me, he did a double take. He had something in his hand, something round, something with hair. He held it by the lower jaw like it was a handle, his fingers hooked over the bottom teeth.

I grasped for my piece, my fingers curling around the grip.

He heaved the head at me, fly gel spraying loose, a spinning blur of hair and ears and neck stump coming my way. Being seated, I couldn't dodge it, but I slowed it with a forearm before it caught me in the chest, gobs of fly gel splattering my face.

Wu's scarred head landed in my lap, empty eyes staring, stretched mouth hanging open unnaturally wide. I was up, the head tumbling free, bouncing off the coffee table and rolling across the carpet.

Jesus.

I squeezed off a burst, the air catching fire. The beam crackled into the door frame, melting the paint and scorching the wood underneath. I corrected my aim, sweeping to the right, but too late. He'd already gone.

I hurdled one of the fallen lamps and rushed out the door fast, too fast to make the turn. I hit the railing, my shades flying off my head and down into the courtyard. *Shit.* The railing gave, just enough to make me think I was going over, metal scraping and rattling, but holding. He was almost to the stairs. I took another shot, a jittery beam missing high and wide— couldn't shoot for shit.

I tore after him, my veins coursing with adrenaline-fueled fire. He killed those girls. I hit the stairs. My feet barely made contact as I hurtled down the four flights. Just as I hit the courtyard, I saw him disappear into the tunnel. I kicked up clouds of ash as I ran, my heart pounding in my ears, my chest heaving for oxygen. I sped into the tunnel, his footsteps sounding ahead of me, my face whipped by mossy growths. Out the other side, I dropped down another set of stairs and turned into the alley. Skidding on wet pavement, I went down, my left elbow taking the worst of the impact. I slid through dyed water, my whites staining red and yellow. I scrambled back to my feet. *Where is he?*

One of the women I'd passed earlier pointed at an open door. I sprinted past pedestrians who hugged the walls, colored water splashing and spraying. I barreled through the door and up a long staircase, then into a narrow room filled with two long rows of sewing equipment. Wheezing, I scanned the room.

Machines hummed. Scissors clipped. Lazy fan blades spun overhead.

Where was that prick? That monster who murdered children in their sleep.

I stalked down the aisle. People slowly noticed me, their machines stopping midstitch, the room getting quiet. Wide eyes stared at me and my quivering lase-pistol. Dyed water ran down my leg. Flies clouded around me. Must've cut myself when I wiped out.

I scoped faces, left and right, seeking and searching. He had to be in here somewhere. The only other door was closed, latched from the inside with a hook and eye. No open windows. I studied expressions. Somebody must've seen him. All eyes were trained on me, all but one pair. A man who sat close to the door, eyes aimed down at a wheeled bin next to his worktable.

I got you now. I moved toward the bin, getting in close where I couldn't miss, shaky hand or not. I could see him now, his head and chest poking out from a pile of cloth scraps. I crept up, steadily closing. He hadn't seen me. He was looking at the worker, his finger making the shush sign over his lips. I stepped closer, my piece extended in front of me, ready to fry the fucker.

He saw me. He was young. Not a kid, but young. Eighteen? Twenty? His blocky chin was peppered with razor stubble, his nose long and blunt. Brown eyes sat in the sinkholes of his face, and his hair ran wild as the Lagartan jungle.

He watched my piece shake out of control. He measured his chances, gears cranking behind his eyes. *Don't even think about it.* I marched the last few steps, leaned over and slowly edged the wavering weapon toward his face, planting the barrel on his left eye.

He made himself small, trying to shrink deeper into the bin.

I added some pressure, driving the barrel deep into his eye socket. "Who the fuck are you?"

He slunk further down into the bin, his face cringing with fear.

I smelled glue. I thought there might be an open tube on one of the workspaces nearby, but then I saw the tube poking from his shirt pocket. The tube's cap sat crooked atop a sticky mess of spillover. Bastard was a huffer.

I gave his eye a jab. "Start talking."

Somebody appeared at the door. I glanced up: Maria. What was she doing here?

My forearm exploded in pain. My piece fell harmlessly from my fingers. From under the loose scraps, his hand had grabbed hold of me, but it wasn't a hand. Metal teeth dug deep, down to the bone. Blood flowed. Flesh ripped. Nerves screamed.

I howled in pain, tried to pull free.

His face shifted. Skin turned charcoal gray. Ears recessed. Hair disappeared. A forked tongue tickled my nose.

I was in a full panic. I jerked and yanked but couldn't break free. Blood sprayed, and muscle stripped off the bone. My free hand dug at his face, fingernails sliding over beaded skin.

The sizzle of a lase-blade passed by my ear and tore through the side of the bin. Maria took another swipe at him but the bin tipped before she could land the blade. I fell and hit the floor, my mangled arm popping loose.

Half buried by scraps of bloodstained fabric, I rolled onto my back, my ruined arm quivering with waves of unbelievable pain.

He ran for the far door, Maria in pursuit.

A puddle of blood spread from my arm, warm liquid soaking into my shirt. I felt sleepy. So sleepy.

ten

"You awake?"

I grunted.

"The doctor will be back soon."

My eyes were open but I couldn't see, my vision blurred and clouded. I blinked, and blinked again, but couldn't clear the haze.

"She's going to fix you up," said the voice.

I tried to speak but failed, my throat seizing.

"It's okay, Juno. Really."

Who was that? Where was I? I tried to sit up but couldn't. Something was holding me down. I puzzled over what it was, but my cobwebbed concentration couldn't figure it. I tried to sit up again and felt a band pressing into my chest.

Fear took hold. I pushed harder, my lungs constricting, my face flushing with effort. My arms, my legs . . . I couldn't lift them. Straps dug into my skin.

"What's wrong? Are you okay?"

I lost it, my blurred vision turning blood red. I jerked against the restraints. "Let me go," I shouted, my voice suddenly working again. I thrashed about, straining to bust loose.

I felt hands on my shoulders, a soothing voice. "Relax, Juno. Stop. You're going to hurt yourself."

I kicked and twisted, pushed and pulled. The strap across my chest made it hard to breathe. It didn't take long for me to run out of air, and then out of steam.

I smelled something. Perfume. Lots of perfume. So much that it almost drowned out the smell of antiseptic.

My vision began to clear. I could see Maria's face, her eyes. "Get me out of here," I said between heavy breaths. "Get these straps off."

"Listen, Juno, I brought you to a doctor. Your hand got fucked up, and she's going to fix it."

I looked around. Whitewashed walls and industrial lighting. Maria leaned over me, her cleavage in my face, hair brushing my cheek. "It'll be okay. She's a good doctor. I was telling you about her before. Remember? She's going to do some work on my sister as soon as I have the money."

My hand got fucked up? What was she talking about?

Memories came to me. Bad memories. The little girls. Wu's butchered wife. Wu's flying head.

Like an overflowing toilet, the foul memories kept bubbling up. The lizard-man. My arm. Muscle hanging off exposed bone.

Was that shit real?

I didn't want to look, but I lifted my head off the pillow and let my eyes wander slowly down my right arm. Shoulder to bicep. Bicep to elbow. Elbow to forearm. Forearm to *nothing*.

I sucked in a breath. Oh hell. My hand was gone. *Gone.*

I implored Maria with my eyes. "Get me out of here."

"It'll be okay, Juno."

"Untie me."

"Don't be scared. You're safe here."

"Let me go, dammit."

"Does it hurt?"

"Fucking untie me!"

"Stop it. Just stop it for a minute, okay? Now tell me, does it hurt?"

I had to think about it. "No."

"See? The doctor knows what she's doing. She blocked your pain receptors."

"Why am I tied down?"

"You're a fitful sleeper. You needed a transfusion, and you kept pulling out the needle. As long as you stay hooked to that IV, she thought it best to keep you secured."

"I'm awake now. Take off the straps."

"Let's call the doctor." She jabbed at a button on the wall, pumping it several times. "Let's see what she says."

I looked at my arm. Bandages ran from the elbow down to where my forearm ended, about halfway to where my wrist should be. I bent my arm at the elbow. Bandages bunched and wrinkled. I bent it as far as the straps would let me and straightened it back out.

"I got you a good deal," she said. "I know price probably doesn't matter much to you since you'll be hauling in plenty of protection money, but I still haggled her down good."

Footsteps echoed from the hall, quick, efficient steps. The doctor walked in. "You only need to push the button once."

"Yes, Doctor. Sorry."

"What are you? A damn monkey?"

Maria's eyes twitched at the verbal blow, but she stayed silent and lowered her gaze.

The doctor turned to me. She forced an offworlder's smile, two rows of perfectly positioned ivory. Her black hair was shot with gray, and she sported glasses that gave her a bookish air.

She sat next to the bed, indifferent eyes giving me the once-over, her smile more like a sneer. "I'd shake your hand, but . . ."

Not funny. I didn't try to hide the contempt on my face.

"No sense of humor? Don't tell me you lost your funny bone in that hand." The joke came laced with enough condescension to make it a put-down instead of a pick-me-up.

I wasn't buying the bitch's getup. Offworlders didn't need glasses. They didn't gray. And their skin didn't wrinkle into crow's-feet. This whole pseudo-schoolmarm look of hers was nothing but a bullshit attempt to make herself look doctorly.

She was a fake. Offworlders were all fakes, changing their looks on a whim, shifting and morphing. Chameleons.

"You cut my hand off without asking me. You're a butcher."

She brushed my complaint away with a swipe of her hand. "I'm going to attach an artificial hand for you. I picked out something special."

"I want to see it."

"And ruin the surprise? No. I don't do work to order. I'm an artist. Don't worry, when I'm finished with you, I guarantee you'll be thankful."

"She's right," said Maria. "She does amazing work."

I was not a canvas. I had to get out of here now. "Untie me."

She acquiesced with a nod and started unbuckling. "Do you know how lucky you are that Maria brought you to me instead of one of those filthy hospitals?"

Somebody appeared in the doorway, a teenaged boy with milky eyes on chocolate skin. "Would you like some tea, Doctor?"

The doctor's head snapped around to look at him. "Can't you see I'm busy?"

He bowed his head and blinked his cataract eyes. "My apologies." He walked away.

She turned back to me, her eyes rolling behind her glasses. "That boy has a lot to learn if he thinks he's going to make it as my houseboy."

Maria asked, "Can you fix his eyes?"

"Not if he doesn't learn how to follow directions."

She undid the straps. I breathed easier and easier with each uncoupling, and I sat up as soon as the last strap slithered off.

"Hold out your arm so I can change your dressing."

I had my arm pulled in tight, hugged to my body. I didn't trust her. I had to get out of here.

Maria gave me the eye. The doctor made a don't-keep-me-waiting face. "You need fresh bandages. The wound has to stay clean or the rot will set in."

The rot had taken my mother.

Reluctantly, I lifted my half-arm and let her start unraveling. I watched the layers peel off, steeling myself for my new reality. The last bandage fell free. My hand was gone, an empty space where it should be.

I raised my arm. It had a cap on the end, some kind of thick, plastic-like substance that sealed the wound, a dozen or more vinelike tendrils holding it on.

She was going to give me a new hand? A hand of her choice.

Fuck that.

I had to get out of here.

I held my arm out straight. It held steady. Didn't shake anymore.

I could deal. I was plenty used to having only one good hand.

I could fucking deal.

With my mind made up, I sat still and let the doctor dress my arm with a fresh set of bandages. When she finished, I made my intentions clear. "Pull the IV. I'm leaving."

"Not until I take measurements for your new hand."

"Pull it."

Maria tried to intercede. "You're not thinking straight. She's a great doctor. The best."

I looked the doctor in the eye. I wanted to enjoy this. "She's a hack. Tit jobs and robo-snatches. Artist, my ass. Real doctors cure the sick."

The hack glared at me, cheeks burning, eyes smoldering, her carefully constructed doctor's face not so doctorly anymore.

I held my left arm up and nodded at the IV. "Pull it."

"Fine. Be a cripple." She reached over my torso to my left arm and yanked the IV tube like she was starting a cheap outboard. I didn't feel it. I could get used to this no-pain thing.

Maria watched the doctor go out the door before she got in my face. "What's wrong with you?"

I nudged her back with my left and stood. A bead of blood formed on my arm where the needle had been.

"I'm going to kill you if you screwed this up for me."

The drop broke loose and I swiped it away with my . . . my stump.

I was in my underwear. "Where are my clothes?"

"They were stained. I threw them away. Sit down and think it through."

"Shoes?"

"Under the bed."

I used my toes to pull them out one at a time and slipped them on. "My money and my gun?"

"In the drawer. Listen, why don't you wait here while I go buy you a set of whites. It'll give you a chance to think."

I didn't want to think. I wanted to leave before that bitch doctor cut off another part of me.

I walked out the door. Maria's voice sounded behind me. "You can't go out in your underwear."

Looking left, I spotted the houseboy. "Where's the exit?"

He pointed to a set of steps.

I took them down and threw open the door at the bottom. Greeted by a blast of party noise, I moved into the street, a jungle breeze kissing my skin, clouds of O smoke wafting on the black air. Music blared from a dozen open doorways, the combined sound mixing and mashing into a pulsing cacophony. The street was filled with a large herd of offworld kids bucking and braying.

Bangkok Street.

I refused to be bothered by the strange looks coming my way. I spotted a clothes counter down the way and made straight for it. As I cut through the herd like a wounded lion, everybody gave me plenty of room.

I glanced to my right. Maria's big hair had fallen in lockstep with me.

Wearing more bandages than clothes, I stepped up to the counter. "Whites," I said to the kid who had watched me approach with saucer eyes. He grabbed hold of a pincer device and used it to reach for some pants that sat on a high shelf behind a crowd of cheap BIG SLEEP '89 T-shirts.

A full-length mirror stood between the counter and the dressing curtain. I forced myself to take a look. Bronze skin overrun by an unhealthy gray, like I'd been rolled in ash. I'd lost a lot of weight, my underwear hanging loose around my pelvis. When was the last time I could see my ribs?

A dead tree with a bough sawed off. That was what I was.

The kid tossed aside the pair of pants he'd pulled down after checking the size. "Too big."

I looked at Maria, a frown on her face.

"What?" I asked, innocent-like.

"You better not have screwed things up for me."

"I wouldn't let that woman touch my sister."

"Don't you get it? She's an offworlder. The local doctors can't do the shit she does."

"She's a hack, and I won't be her lab rat."

"Dammit, Juno, she was going to help you. I got you a deal."

"Who asked you?"

Anger flared in those mascara-lined eyes. "Who asked me? I saved your damn life."

She was right. Without her, I would've bled out on the sweatshop floor. As unsure as I was that being saved was a good thing, I had to admit she'd tried to be a friend. For that I should show some respect. "You're right. Sorry." I cranked up the sincerity in my gaze until she acknowledged the apology with a smirk of acceptance.

The kid passed me a pair of white linen pants. I set my piece on the table, took hold of the waistband with my left, and shook out the folds. I slipped in a leg. "Were you following me?"

"Remember those two guys who came looking for you? I was worried they might be waiting for you outside, so I followed you until I saw you go into that apartment. At that point, I figured you were safe so I went and got some breakfast. I was eating eggs up at one of those rooftop places when I saw you go running underneath."

I tried to slip my other foot in but couldn't hold my pants correctly with the one hand. I let myself lean against the counter while I forced my foot into the pant leg. I tugged the pants up and started fumbling with the button.

"Jesus Christ, let me do that."

I stood there like a four-year-old letting her button and zip me up.

"What's wrong with you? You gonna go through the rest of your life with one hand?"

I chose not to respond.

"You know that cap is just a temporary, don't you?"

I shook my head no.

"You can't just leave it like that. And when those pain blockers wear off it's going to hurt like a son of a bitch." She caught the surprise on my face. "You really are a dumb shit, aren't you? You wanna go back inside?"

I looked across the street at the door I'd exited a few minutes earlier. The door was unmarked, anonymous. I looked up at the second-floor windows, dark glass staring down. "No."

The temporary cap would have to do for now. I had more

pressing matters, like the fact that Mota hadn't killed Froelich or Wu. There was a serial out there, a fucking lizard-man.

And one by one, he was killing my crew.

I clenched my fists but was half robbed of the sensation. *Christ.*

Time to move. "Where the hell is my shirt?" I snapped at the kid. "What you waiting for?"

He nervously cleared his throat. "Um, short sleeve or long?"

eleven

A PIECE of me was missing. I was unbalanced. Incomplete. Not whole.

I had to get it back.

But it was too dark behind this tree. Couldn't see shit. Was it asking too much to get a little daylight?

I looked up, my gaze climbing through boughs and leaves, and settling four stories up on police tape wound around a railing. Right where I'd almost gone over this morning. Would've been quite a fall.

The courtyard patio was quiet, no sign of KOP. They'd probably wrapped the crime scene hours ago.

Gotta be around here somewhere. I roamed, my squinting eyes straining to see the ground. I kicked something, felt it through the toe of my shoe. I reached down with my right but came up short. Forgot. I switched to my left and pawed through ash and crisped leaves.

There. I blew out a sigh of relief and unfolded the glasses with a snap of my wrist. Lucky I hadn't stepped on them. I held them up in what little light there was. They'd survived the fall intact, thanks no doubt to landing in a soft bed of ash.

I blew off the dust and slipped them on with a relieved smile.

I was whole again.

"Juno, you stupid hump, where the fuck are you?"

I picked my way back through the tree's weeping canopy, the rustling ruckus serving as my answer.

Detective Mark Josephs approached from the patio entrance, Maggie following a few paces behind. "We got your message. Who was that who called us?"

"Maria. A friend." I didn't know what to do with my right arm. Hide it? Give an empty wave? I let it hang by my side. "Thanks for coming."

The courtyard tree had me cast in night shadow. Maggie hadn't noticed yet. "We spent a few hours working the crime scene upstairs. Wu's wife and kids are all dead, butchered, but there may be a witness. Somebody took a couple shots at the killer and chased him down to a sweatshop before getting himself wounded and disappearing. We were ready to start canvassing hospitals when Lieutenant Rusedski pulled us off the case."

"He say why?"

"He said a second dead cop makes this case too high-profile to run a regular investigation. He's going to create a task force and run it himself."

"You ask if Mota was behind the move?"

"No. I figured Rusedski just didn't want me working such a big case."

"Why not?"

"He doesn't want to share the spotlight. He thinks I'm after his job."

"Are you?"

"I just got a promotion."

In other words, not yet.

I dropped the first bombshell. "Mota didn't kill Wu."

Josephs dropped his jaw. "The fuck you say? You said it was brass who did Froelich."

"I didn't say I was sure."

"You shittin' me? Dammit, Juno, that's a helluva thing to be wrong about. How do you know he didn't do it?"

"Because I'm your witness."

"You were here?"

"I was inside when the killer came back with Wu's head."

"That was you in the firefight?"

"Yeah." I raised my right. "Caught the short end of it." Bombshell number two.

Maggie snatched me by my new short sleeve and pulled me out into the light of a patio lamp. She stared at the void where my hand should be. "Why aren't you in a hospital?"

"It's all fixed up," I lied. "No big deal."

"No big deal?"

"The thing didn't work right anyway."

Her voice gained volume. "Shit, are you crazy? We're not talking about a broken phone. You lost your hand. Your *hand!*"

I shrugged. I was getting used to the idea.

"Dammit, Juno, you should be in a hospital."

"I can deal."

"Are you kidding me? You can deal? Is that all you have to say?"

"Um, yeah."

She popped me in the chest, a quick shot with her fist.

"What was that for?" I said with max indignation. "What do you want me to say?"

She turned away and started pacing, her angry heels muffled by a carpet of ash.

I looked at Josephs. "What am I supposed to say?"

Josephs shook his big, round head. "This is some fucked-up shit. Even for you."

Maggie paced, left and right, back and forth. I stayed silent, letting her work it off. I didn't know why she was so upset. I really didn't.

"Does it hurt?" asked Josephs.

"I'm on pain blockers."

With a sigh, Maggie stopped pacing and ran her fingers into

her hair. She squeezed down on her long locks like she was wringing the agitation out of her face, forcing it all the way down into her tapping foot. "Tell us about the killer."

I gave them a description. Tall. Skinny. Dark hair and darker eyes. Skin the color of dead vines.

"A local?"

"Right down to the ratty clothes. But this punk could shift. He became a lizard just before he clamped my arm."

"A lizard?"

"Beaded skin. Forked tongue."

"I don't know many locals who can shift. Could've been an offworlder in disguise, couldn't it? Maybe the killer goes native to blend in with us."

"No, I saw a tube of glue in his pocket. He's a huffer. Offworlders can afford better drugs than that."

"If he's too poor to buy good drugs, how did he afford the tech he needs to shift?"

"I don't know. But trust me, the guy's a local. He was too ugly to be an offworlder."

"Did he bite you?"

"No. He grabbed me with his hand, but his hand had teeth. It was like being bit by a monitor, except the teeth were made of steel."

Maggie's phone rang before I could explain. Abdul Salaam's holo appeared, bald head and thick glasses. I grinned at the sight of him. The old coroner was a longtime friend. "Have you seen Juno?" he asked Maggie without saying hello, the urgency in his voice at odds with the holo's saccharine smile.

"He's right here."

"That blood from the sweatshop, the DNA says—"

"It's his. We know."

"He okay?"

I stepped up close to Maggie to get in range of her phone's

receiver. "Just a scratch, Abdul. Have you passed my ID up the chain?"

"Of course not. Not until I talked to you. Want it hushed?"

"Yeah. I'm getting enough heat as it is." I tossed a deliberate glance in Maggie's direction.

"No problem," said Abdul.

That was what I loved about him—as dependable as he was loyal. A true friend. When Paul and I ran KOP, Abdul was our chief evidence manipulator, the king of faux forensics—ginned-up genetics, phony fingerprints, bullshit blood spatter . . .

When we needed a frame, he'd be ready with wood and nails.

"What else do you have, Abdul?" asked Maggie.

"I heard you and Josephs got pulled from the case."

"True, but we're going to keep at it awhile."

"Because of Juno?"

"Yeah, because of Juno," she said with subzero enthusiasm.

"I know how that goes. Have you heard the rumors floating around?"

"That Juno had something to do with Froelich's death?"

"Yeah, and there's another one going around that says Captain Mota in PR was responsible. I've heard it both ways."

"They're both false."

"I figured as much. This killer's a vicious bastard. At first I thought that after being stabbed, Maribela Wu was attacked by a monitor. The wounds where her breasts and vagina used to be look like bite marks, but what kind of monitor would target just those three locations on her body? So I measured the wounds, and they didn't measure right to be bites."

I knew what that was about. I broke in to describe the killer's steel-trap hand—the way it came out of nowhere, the opposing rows of fanged metal. He was a biter instead of a chewer.

"You get nipped? Is that where the blood came from?"

"Yeah. The thing clamped down strong as a motherfucker."

"You sure you're okay?"

"I'm fine," I said with more emphasis than necessary. I didn't need Maggie chiming in.

"That steel hand sounds high-tech enough that it has to be an offworlder, don't you think?"

"He was a local."

"You sure?"

"Yes."

"It okay if I pass what you've told me along to Rusedski?"

"Yeah. The sooner we squash the rumors about me and Mota, the better."

Maggie asked Abdul, "Ever seen a hand like that?"

"Maybe. I searched the database for bodies with similar bites. We get a lot of corpses that have been fed upon, but I filtered for people who were fed upon by bigger game."

"Find any that were beheaded?"

"No. So either Froelich and Wu were his first victims, or he's killed before but the decapitation is new."

"Any with missing sex organs?"

Good question.

"Plenty, but I ruled out the ones that had been eaten all over. That left me with one male found naked with missing sex organs and minimal damage elsewhere."

Josephs spoke up, a devilish smile on his face. "So unless those monitors suddenly developed a taste for sausage . . ."

I rolled my eyes. *Asshole.*

Maggie spoke into the phone. "How easy would it be to mistake our killer's bites for monitor bites?"

"Pretty damn easy. Unless you had a reason to check for monitor saliva or the presence of one of the bacteria strains that live in their mouths, you wouldn't know. Even though the bites I found on Maribela Wu were smaller than a typical

monitor bite, you could mistake them for bites from an imma-
ture monitor, or maybe a really big iguana. Postmortem bites
are common enough that you wouldn't look that close unless
you had a reason."

"But this is all theoretical, isn't it?" I asked. "You can't pin
that body in the database on our killer with any certainty."

"True. But I thought you might find it interesting that he
had a tattoo on his cheek."

My doubt evaporated. "Two snakes?"

"Two snakes," he confirmed. "Just like Froelich's."

Abdul was on to something. Theory solidified into fact.
"We need an ID on that stiff."

"The name is Franz Samusaka."

"Where was he found?"

"I'll send you the info. The first responders found his death
suspicious enough to call in Homicide, but the hommy dicks
ruled it an accidental overdose."

"You think they were covering it up?"

"It's likely. This is KOP, right?"

"Who were the detectives?"

"Froelich and Wu."

Fucking figures. Those two beheaded assholes were pissing
me off with this convoluted bullshit.

"You want me to keep Samusaka out of my report?"

I told him yes. Keep Rusedski in the dark. The lieutenant
was too close to Mota to be trusted.

"I'll see you day after tomorrow, Juno?"

"For what?" I made no effort to hide my confusion.

"Robert's graduation party."

Right. Paul's son was about to graduate from the Academy.
Paul's widow was going to throw him a party after. "Let me get
back to you."

"You don't sound very sure."

I wasn't. "Later, Abdul."

After a quick thank-you, Maggie let him off the hook. Then her emerald eyes turned on me, their radioactive glow making it clear she wouldn't be doing the same for me.

"You said Captain Mota did Froelich." Her eyes burned hot in the dim light.

"I said he might have done it."

"You don't accuse a cop unless you're sure," said Josephs. "You let that scar-headed Wu shoot his mouth off about Mota at the Beat. Now that Wu's dead, what are people gonna—"

Maggie stopped him. "That's not the issue here. If Mota didn't kill Froelich and Wu, then he's got no stake in this. So what's his beef with you, Juno?"

"Beats me."

"Yeah," said Josephs. "What the fuck?"

I tried to shrug it off like I didn't know.

Maggie kept at me. "Why is Mota poking his nose in this case? Why is he spreading rumors about you?"

"How should I know?" I tried to say it straight, nonchalant, but my voice betrayed me, a defensively high pitch giving me away.

Josephs stepped toward me. "Don't play innocent. Talk."

"Talk," echoed Maggie with her uranium stare.

I tried to conjure my enforcer's face, a shield of pure steel to keep out the radiation. It wouldn't come, my inner enforcer running for cover. "Fine! Fucking fine. You want to know? I took over his protection business."

Maggie closed her eyes and shook her head.

"What protection business?" asked Josephs.

"Mota was taking money from the snatch houses in the alley near Floodbank."

"When you say you took it over, you mean you bought him out?"

I shook my head no. "I did it old-school."

"You and what army?"

"Me and my crew."

"Don't fucking tell me. Froelich and Wu?"

"Them and a few others."

"You that hard up for cash?"

"It's not about the money."

"Then what is it?"

I looked at Maggie. She was pacing again.

"Well?" asked Josephs.

"KOP has to change," I said.

"What does that have to do with it?" He turned to Maggie. "What's he talking about?"

Maggie stopped pacing to look at me, her expression unreadable.

I repeated my defense. "KOP has to change."

She turned on her heel and walked away.

twelve

"You think he uses a saw? Or maybe he chops the head off with an ax or something?"

"Can you shut up with that shit?" said Deluski.

"Don't you want to know how he's going to do us?" asked Lumbela. "We're next."

I rubbed my arm, a dull ache creeping through the pain blockers. "This isn't helping."

It was long past midnight. Other than the occasional drunken giggle or groan, the whorehouse was quiet. The four of us were in my room, Lumbela and I sitting on the bed, Deluski on the floor, Kripsen leaning against the wall, the slow-burning cig in his hand matching the expression on his face.

"We can't assume he's after all of us," said Deluski. "Wu and Froelich were partners. It could be just the two of them he targeted. It's probably somebody they put away who just got sprung. Plus Juno said the killer might've done another one before Wu and Froelich. Far as we know, that body didn't have anything to do with us."

I leaned forward. "Listen to me, boys, I can't say if we're targets or not, but we're not going to sit back and wait to find out. As long as Mota keeps butting into Wu and Froelich's investigation, we can't trust KOP to catch this guy."

I sharpened the edge in my voice. "This fucker killed two of ours, you hear me? He slaughtered Wu's wife, his little girls."

"And he took your hand," said Kripsen.

"And the son of a bitch took my hand." I made a chop with my abbreviated arm. "Whether we're targets or not, we're going after this freak. You with me?" I met them eye to eye, one at a time, soliciting nods of agreement.

I had them. I could see it in their faces. Gone was the resentment they'd harbored against me. I wasn't their blackmailer anymore. I was their leader, the guy who'd made it through scrapes way worse than this. I was the one who could keep them alive.

"Besides, it's about time you shits learned to do some police work. Did any of you know Froelich was gay?"

"Froelich wasn't gay," said Lumbela.

"He was." I nodded with certainty.

"Really?" Lumbela's eyes were wide open, the whites showing bright against his dark skin.

"No fucking way," said Kripsen.

"He and Mota were seeing each other," I said. "They were lovers."

"Get the fuck out of here."

"I saw the pictures."

Deluski spoke up. "I knew he was gay."

Kripsen flicked his ashes on the floor. "Bullshit."

"No, really. You remember that friend of his who would come drinking with us sometimes, the thin guy with the gold tooth. I saw them holding hands."

"Why didn't you tell us?"

"It was none of my business."

The group stayed quiet for a few, lost in their own thoughts. Kripsen puffed on his cig. "This shit's hard to believe. I mean, us and Froelich, we'd go chasin' tail together all the time."

"Ever seen him catch any?" I wanted to know.

Kripsen thought about it. "I figured he was shy."

Lumbela threw up his hands. "Aw, shit, think of all the times we'd go piss on a wall, all of us whipping out our wangs. Fucking Froelich must've been checking us out."

Kripsen laughed at him. "You are such a dumbass."

"What?"

"You think he wants to peep when we're pissing? There ain't nothing sexy about a dick that's pissing."

A smirking Lumbela came back with, "How would you know when a dick is sexy?"

Are these humps for real? "Shut up already! Save this crap for another time. What's important right now is to understand that Mota thinks we did Froelich. He thinks we killed his lover to send him a message."

"He does?"

"Wouldn't you? We broke his uniform's legs."

"But Froelich was one of ours. We wouldn't do one of ours."

"What if Froelich and Wu were really on Mota's side?"

Confused stares all around.

I elaborated. "Mota had something going with Froelich and Wu. They were in business together. Anybody know anything about that?"

They threw one another questioning stares. Nobody had answers, and their bewildered gazes eventually came back to me. It wasn't surprising Wu and Froelich had frozen out these three. Why cut their share three extra ways?

What pissed me off was Wu and Froelich let me pick a fight with Mota without clueing me in.

"Here's the deal, boys. While we were suspecting Mota killed Froelich, he was thinking it was us trying to intimidate him into backing down. Mota even threatened me, told me I was going to pay for Froelich."

"Ironic," said Deluski.

Lumbela gave him a sour face as if to say, *Why the fuck are you bringing big words into this?*

"Listen to me," I said. "We're exposed on this. If Mota finds out I was at Wu's crime scene, he will become more certain than ever that I was the killer. The evidence will lead away from us, sure as shit, but the task force might be coaxed out of following the real trail. It all depends on how much sway Mota has over the investigation. The sooner we bring the real killer down, the sooner we clear our names, and if we are the serial's next targets, the sooner we make ourselves safe."

Kripsen blew a cloud of smoke. "What's the plan?"

Ghost pain made me wish I could rub my right hand, my right wrist. The best I could do was keep massaging my shoulder. "I need one of you to write down names of all the people you guys have fucked over. You bastards have done some ugly shit. I need to know who might be looking for retribution. I want that list before I wake up in the morning."

Lumbela pointed a thumb at himself. "I can do that."

I turned to Kripsen. "I need you to get down to the Office of Records and pull Froelich and Wu's case files. You know as well as I do that some things don't make it into the public record, but it's a good place to start. Comb through those files and write down anything that could be related."

I turned to Deluski. His eyes looked older than they had a few days ago. "I need you to go down to the morgue to see Abdul Salaam. You know him?"

"Yeah."

"Tell him I sent you. Get paper copies of everything he's got."

"Paper?"

"I don't want anything electronic. Until we get the Mota situation under control, I'm too hot to get on the grid. I need you to work up a history on that body with the tattoo. I want to know everything there is to know about him."

"Got it," said Deluski before erupting in a broad smile.

"Something funny?"

"No." His grin turned sheepish. "It's just—"

"It's just what?"

"I was just thinking. It's almost like we're real police again."

There was hope for this one. "Like real police," I acknowledged. "Now get out of here so I can sleep."

They headed for the door. I lifted my aching arm and swung it back and forth, hoping a little movement might bring some relief.

"You gonna be okay there?" asked Deluski from the doorway.

Damned if I know. "I'm fine."

"What kind of lizard did he turn into?"

"What does that matter?"

"Monitor? Iguana?"

"He didn't turn into an actual lizard, you know."

"More like a man in a lizard mask, I know. But were there any markings? Stripes or ridges?"

"Stripes. Rust red stripes."

"How many?"

"I don't know. Two, maybe three. Who cares?"

"Ridges?"

"Fucking quit bothering me with this shit."

"You sure you don't need something for that arm?"

"Yes, dammit. Now get the fuck out."

"Good night, boss."

The door swung shut. I lay back and let my head rest on the pillow. I stretched my arm out alongside my body. *Shit, that hurts.* It was going to be a long night.

A knock came on the door. "Yeah?"

Maria poked her head in, more hair than head. "Those drugs wear off yet?"

"Yeah."

"I got a bottle."

"Now you're talking."

I didn't want to open my eyes. My hungover head hurt. Same for my arm.

And that smell wasn't helping. Like somebody was trying to smother me with flowers. Fake flowers. The kind of perfumey shit that comes from a can. I felt something on my chest. It wasn't one of those straps from the doctor's. This was warm. An arm.

My eyes opened. I was clothed. Maria was clothed too, her usual—skimpy and slutty. When was she going to learn she wasn't a hooker anymore?

I remembered waking up when she'd told me she was tired of sleeping in the sex swing. I remembered wanting to object when she squeezed in next to me, but I didn't object. Not when I felt her warmth against me. Not when I felt her nuzzle into my shoulder.

I was letting this relationship get too cozy. We'd have to have a little talk. She had to know I was a one-woman guy. I put on my shades. Niki's shades.

I slipped out from under her arm and climbed out of bed. One-handed, I undid my top two buttons and wrestled my shirt over my head. I nabbed a clean one from the pile on the floor and put my arms through the long sleeves. Leaving it un-buttoned, I tucked my piece into my belt and stepped out of the room.

Closing the door behind me, I found a sheet of paper taped to the door frame. I pulled it off and scanned the list of names Lum-bela had compiled. Not as long as I thought it would be. I shoved it into my ass pocket and moved down the hall, my left hand working the shirt's snaps on the way. Lucky for me, it was one of the shirts Niki had modified by substituting snaps for buttons.

Hookers were lined up outside the showers. They looked domestic in their robes, their hair pillow-pressed into all kinds of hair spray horrors. I checked the time. Just past noon. Early morning for a whorehouse.

I snapped the last snap and wondered what to do with my right sleeve. Roll it up? Pin it up? Fuck it. I let it dangle like a limp dick.

I hit the stairs and strode toward the front door. I had to find Maggie, set things straight.

"Juno."

I stopped. Marek Deluski approached, his uniform starched and pressed, a green folder pinned under his arm, a steaming round of fried dough in his hand. "Hey, I got those papers you wanted." He held up the bread. "You want some? They're making these in the kitchen."

My rumbling stomach said yes. I followed him into the kitchen, the smell of warm bread wafting about magnificently. A pair of hookers worked the fryer. Rounds of golden bread were bubbling inside. The hookers wore aprons over their work clothes—fishnets down low, hairnets up top. Next to the fryer sat a pile of fry breads atop a wire rack. I took one, doused it in honey, set another on top, then folded them up like a taco.

I bit into them. They were crunchy and chewy at the same time. Sweet honey oozed across my tongue. *So good!* I really should eat more. I should schedule it. Three times a day like a regular person.

"Let's walk," I said between bites. "I gotta go see somebody."

"Who?"

I blew off the question. "Did you go through the files?"

"Yeah." He took the folder he'd been carrying and tucked it under my half-arm. "I took a cab over here so I could skim through them on my way over."

"What did you find?"

"The dead guy who had the same tat as Froelich, he was rich."

"Did you know him? Ever seen him with Froelich?"

"No. But Froelich didn't make a habit of parading his boy toys around."

Approaching the front door, I took a peek at the entrance to Chicho's office. Fractured beams of light shone through the monitor-tooth curtain. He was in, and it was probably about time I collected my first payday.

But not now. Now I had more important things on my mind. "Did you know Froelich and Mota were lovers?"

"No. I didn't even know they knew each other. How did you find out?"

"I saw pictures of Mota and Froelich together." I followed Deluski out the door and down the stairs.

"Where did you get the pictures?"

"Mota's phone. He had a picture on there of himself with Froelich and Wu, the three of them clinking glasses over a stack of cash."

"That's how you knew they were in business together?"

I nodded yes before taking another bite of bread. Half of it was gone already.

"How did you get Mota's phone?"

"Stole it."

"Damn. How did you pull that off?"

"Broke into his house."

We left the alley. The street was pretty well cleaned up by now and open to traffic. Wouldn't be long before all signs of the riot were erased. We headed for the river.

Deluski said, "What I don't get is how the killer got Wu to go with him."

"What do you mean?"

"Well, he went to Wu's place to kill Maribela and the kids

there in the apartment, but he took Wu somewhere else, killed him, and brought his head back."

"Yeah?" I took another bite of bread.

"So how did he get Wu to go with him?"

After a bewildered pause, I said I'd been wondering the same thing, even though I hadn't. Hadn't even occurred to me. But Deluski was right. Wu must've been home when the killer arrived the first time. Otherwise, there was no reason to go there twice. Had the killer met up with Wu somewhere else and murdered him there, he could've done the wife and kids when he brought the head over.

But he'd been there twice.

Deluski continued. "I can't figure it, boss. I don't see Wu going with him. Can't even imagine it. Not after what he'd done to his family."

I popped the last piece of bread in my mouth and chewed on it awhile. I couldn't figure it either.

Why hadn't I started thinking on this earlier? This was some obvious shit, and I'd totally missed it.

We came to the river. Fishing boats were moored to moss-draped docks, and I could see a few pedestrians carrying ice-filled bags of whole fish, water leaking out the holes. I stepped up to the river's edge and, keeping the folder pinned tight under my half-arm, I punctured a film of algae to put my left hand in the foul-smelling water. As I shook my hand to wash off the honey, a small patch of clear, agitated water formed around my fingers.

I pulled my hand out of the water, flicked off the big drops, and rubbed the rest into my pant leg.

Deluski asked, "So if this same guy killed that Samusaka stiff Abdul found in the database, then why didn't he decapitate him too?"

This one I had thought through. "I figure he's tired of being

anonymous. After his first killing got passed off as an overdose, he wants to make sure everyone knows he killed Wu and
Froelich. He wants credit."

"Do you think that was why he killed them? Because they
didn't give him the credit he deserved for killing Samusaka?"

"I don't know. That's why we need all the info we can get
on Samusaka. What did you find out?"

"That file I gave you is pretty sparse. You'll have to look it
over yourself in case I missed something, but it doesn't say
much except Franz Samusaka's death was ruled an overdose.
This was eight months ago. I did see his father is wealthy,
though. Hudson Samusaka is an oil man."

"You have time to dig some more this afternoon?"

"No. I'm already late for a function at the mayor's mansion."

"Guard duty?"

"Yeah."

"You better get going then."

"Later, boss."

I watched him walk away. The kid was proving himself
smarter than I thought. I wondered how he got hooked into
this gang of misfits in the first place.

Gotta find Maggie. We had to talk. Recalling the way she
looked at me last night made me feel like hands were kneading
the fried dough in my stomach.

I needed a phone. And a ride. I aimed for the docks. I'd ask
around, see if I could bum a phone off somebody. I stepped out
onto the planking. Wood bent and whined underfoot. I heard
something slip into the water, something big. Monitor.

Lights on strings swung in the gentle breeze as I passed
empty boats, fishnets piled like dirty sheets, barnacled hulls
scraping against pilings. I found a young fisherwoman sitting
on an upturned bucket, her fishnet spread across her boat. She

labored at the net's edge with a needle and twine, attaching coins as weights. She had a burlap bag full of half-pesos, the ones with square holes cut in the center.

"A phone?" I asked.

Without looking up, she shook her head no.

I moved farther down the dock, setting my sights on a boat up the way.

From behind, creaky footsteps approached. Quick footsteps. More than one set. My heart kicked into a new gear, and I moved my hand to my waist, making ready to drop the folder and grab for my weapon.

A voice said, "Stop." A lase-blade sizzled to life.

thirteen

"WHAT'S your name?" The voice was close, the crackle of the lase-blade even closer, too close for me to pull my piece without getting carved.

"Mark." A dry-mouthed lie. "Mark Josephs." I slowly turned around, my raging heart already running at a full sprint.

Two men. One held the blade up to my face, bright red light blaring through my shades. The other held a gun, the lase-pistol hanging lazily by his hip. He snatched the glasses off my face and tossed them over his shoulder before giving my mug a critical once-over. "It ain't him," he said. "He don't look right to me. Mota said the guy would be a big bruiser. This shit's skin and bones."

Mota. These two worked for Mota.

"Look at the eyes, though," said the one with the blade. "Don't that look like him?"

With them both mesmerized by my big browns, I wanted to go for my piece, real slow so they wouldn't notice, fry the bastards' balls off before they knew what happened. But I couldn't drop this folder in my hand without telegraphing my intention.

And I had only the one damn hand.

I was fucked.

Fear rippled up and down my spine. I leaned way back, away from the blade, my feet creeping backward of their own volition, my wincing backpedal taking me to the dock's edge. I didn't want to go down like this. Scared. Helpless. Weak.

Not like this.

"Who are you?" asked the one with the blade, a panama hat with a monitor-hide band on his head. The frayed straw brim cast his eyes in latticed shadow. He pressed a finger against the bar-fight bruise over my brow.

I let the fear show in my voice. Didn't have to try very hard. "I told you. M-Mark Josephs. Who are you looking for? You want money?"

Their faces were hard, their sneers well practiced. They wore crisp whites that shone pink in the blade's glow. These were the guys Maria warned me about, the ones from upriver who had come looking for me. Must've gotten tired of trying to find me and posted themselves somewhere outside Chicho's.

"Who was that cop you were with?"

My face broke into a sweat, the heat of the blade burning my cheek without making contact. I wanted to move back, but my heels were nearly hanging off the dock's edge. A river fly popped off the blade in a flash of light. *Fuck.* "I don't know. We just met at a snatch house. I paid for an all-nighter, and he came in for a nooner, I think."

The one on the right grabbed my dangling sleeve and felt around. "He don't got a hand."

"Mota said his hand would shake. Shaking hand ain't the same as no hand. I told you it wasn't him."

Unconvinced, he asked, "What happened to your hand?"

"Got bit off when I was a kid. Monitor attack."

"It ain't him. We should get back," said the one.

"What's in that folder?" asked the other.

I tried to think fast, my mouth opening as if I had a lie ready. But nothing came out, my synapses firing blanks. "Um, see for yourself." I lifted the folder but fumbled it away before he could take hold. Papers slipped free and fell to the water.

"C'mon, we gotta get back," said the one.

"Yeah." His partner took one step away then lunged at me and feinted a swing, the lase-blade's fiery arc swiping in my direction but stopping short of making contact.

I flinched like a scared little gecko. Tipping backward, I tried to regain my balance, my arms flapping like a one-winged bird until I went over. I plunged into the water, briefly sinking before popping back up, my face covered in a film of river muck, one of Abdul's case files stuck to my shoulder.

They laughed, the cocksure bastards. A grade-school bully kind of laugh. I stayed where I was, treading water, taking it like a bitch until they moved off.

I swam to a ladder, grabbed hold with the left, hooked the right over a rung and climbed. I felt my lase-pistol squeeze out from my waistband but couldn't make a move to catch it without losing my grip on the ladder. Fucking thing plunked into the water a second later.

I hauled my ass up to the dock and immediately scanned the riverbank, my eyes searching for a panama hat. I caught sight of Mota's thugs just as they disappeared down a street that led in the direction of Chicho's alley.

I found my shades where they'd fallen and slipped them on. The smart move was to call myself lucky and move on. I was unarmed. And in more than one way. I should quit while I was ahead. Live to fight another day.

Just let them go.

I had the shakes. I told myself they wouldn't last. The butterflies in my gut would soon settle. Everything was okay.

Just let them go.

But their laughter still echoed in my head, their damned mocking laughter.

The 'fraidy-cat shakes shifted into roaring rumbles of rage. The butterflies in my gut became angry jungle wasps.

Mota thought he could take me out with a pair of upriver thugs?

With my nerves ringing and my inner enforcer humming, I stormed up the dock, right up to the boat with the young fisher-woman. I jumped in, my feet thudding against the hull. Wide-eyed, she sucked in a terrified breath. The coin she was about to attach to her net slipped from her fingers and disappeared in the folds. I snatched the sack of coins. She didn't protest. She knew better.

I marched to shore. The anticipation of violence coursed through my body. Reaching the riverbank, I kicked off my shoes. Couldn't make a quiet approach with them squishing.

I pursued. I felt no pain in my arm. Couldn't feel the pebbles under the soles of my bare feet. My face burned hot like it was still baking in the glow of the lase-blade, my soul crazed with a fire that my soaking clothes couldn't cool.

I could see them now, the SOBs, walking shoulder to shoulder just a short ways ahead, but on the opposite side of the busy street. I started across, dodging cars and bikes, pushcarts and pedestrians. I tightened my grip on the sack. The coins felt plenty weighty.

Pedestrians dodged out of my way as I ran the last couple steps toward the one who had held the gun on me. My left arm took a wide, hooking swing, the sack of coins bearing down on his head. He turned around just in time for the sack to pound him on his right ear. He crumpled to the pavement like a rag doll.

The one with the panama hat reached for his weapon. I sank the sack into his gut. His blade and hat tumbled free as he collapsed to his knees. He was still sucking air when my next blow took him in the shoulder. The sack exploded on impact, a shower of coins crashing to the pavement. He tried to stand, coins shedding off his back, but hardly made it halfway up before I clubbed him back down with my stump.

Harsh, stinging pain shot up my arm. I brushed it off, just like I brushed off the shouting from behind me, the onlookers' protests hardly penetrating my senses. I kicked him in the gut, stomped his ribs, worked him up and down. I dropped to one knee and leaned over him, water from my hair dripping on his face.

The questions spilled out of my mouth. "Who are you? How do you know Mota? What kind of shit is he into? Do you know Wu and Froelich?"

He couldn't respond, his eyes bleary and bewildered. I tried to bring him back with a slap to the cheek, but he was too far gone, eyes rolling up in his head. I stood and evil-eyed the crowd encircling the scene. "Don't fuck with me!"

Some took off. Others stepped back. Nobody looked me in the eye.

I bent over and raided the bastard's pockets. Cigs. Cash. Rubbers.

And a badge.

Wet pants chafed my thighs. The soles of my feet stung like they were crisscrossed with cuts. Insistent throbbing nagged my arm. I'd busted something open in there. My empty shirt-sleeve was stained crimson and dotted with clinging flies.

I made it back to the docks.

Shit.

Somebody had made off with my shoes.

I glanced at the clock while the barber counted my soggy bills. I'd been in the barbershop for over an hour now. A cut. A shave. Fresh bandages for my arm. I'd sent the barber's daughter on a gofer run. New shoes. New pants. Yet another new shirt.

The barber finished counting the pesos. "That'll do. Glad we could help you today, but you really should get that arm checked by a doctor."

I walked out. Wasn't in the mood for advice. I crossed the street and went down a set of damp, mossy steps into a basement bar. The room was long and narrow, coffin-like. The bar ran down the right side, nothing more than a rigged-up series of old doors laid end to end and suspended from the ceiling by a collection of ropes. No room for tables.

I took the stool on the end and ordered a brandy. The bartender reached for a bottle sitting on a shelf hung from a wall that glistened with sweat.

"How about a phone?" I asked.

"Gimme a minute." She stepped away to attend to two empty-glassed customers who sat at the far end.

I sipped my drink. Just a little sip. I didn't come to get drunk. Just needed to take the edge off, make it so I could think straight.

I pulled the shield out of my pocket and held it up to the light. YOP. Yepala Office of Police. Yepala was farther upriver than Loja. Five hours by boat. A town deep inside warlord territory.

I rubbed the badge with my thumb. Yepala cops. Christ.

I'd left them on the pavement. Fucked them up pretty good. To get out of there, I'd had to plow my way through a circle of concerned civvies. A do-gooder tried to stop me, a little man who said something about how I wouldn't get away with what I'd done. I shoved the sap to the ground, where he had the smarts to stay.

Then I saw his kids. Two young boys, one already crying, the other about to. I hoped they'd learn the right lesson, that their father was courageous. Principled. But they were just as likely to grow up thinking their dad was a pussy. Knocked to the ground by a one-armed man and afraid to fight back.

That was the way of things on Lagarto.

I set the badge on the bar and stared at its shiny surface. Instead of sending a couple common thugs, Mota had sent cops to do me in. Yepala cops. I couldn't make sense of it. If there was one thing this city had in abundance, it was thugs and dirty cops. Why outsource the job to YOP?

Unless they already had a relationship. Unless whatever Mota, Froelich, and Wu were into also involved those two cops. I remembered the night we'd broken Jimmy's legs, how Wu and Froelich didn't show because they were upriver at a monitor fight.

Or maybe they were doing business in Yepala. What kind of business, I could only guess.

The bartender returned with a phone. I called Maggie. No answer. I talked to her voice mail. "Hey, Maggie, it's me. It's Juno. We need to talk, okay?"

I set the phone on the bar, next to a doorknob that poked up like a mushroom.

What the fuck was I doing? That was what she was going to ask me. I was going to have to tell her all about the mission. It made so much sense a few days ago. Start with a small crew and work my way up. Soon I'd have all of KOP under my control. I'd done it once. I could do it again.

But that was before two of my crew got decapitated. Before I ordered Jimmy's legs broken. Before I realized Mota was going to fight me to the end. Before I lost my hand.

Before I chased Maggie away.

Shit, and now I'd even injected myself into the nightmares of two teary-eyed kids.

A teen entered carrying a heavy washtub. He waddled forward, and with a clunk, set the washtub on the floor. He pulled off the tied-on plastic bag that served as a lid so the bartender could have a look. Clumped white mash soaked in a pool of clear liquid. I could smell it already, the familiar burn of shine climbing up my nostrils.

The bartender took a tin cup down from a shelf and used it to scoop up a sample, which she set in front of me. "Try this and tell me what you think. I don't drink anymore."

I tilted the cup up to my pinched lips and carefully sucked alcohol out from the mash. Shine blazed a path along my tongue and down my throat, the heat running all the way down to my stomach.

"Good," I said, remembering a time when shine was all I could afford.

She had the teen drag the tub behind the bar while she got some money together.

I took another pull. Pure fire with metallic overtones. Tasted just like my gun.

The memory of it made me want to spit. Gun barrel on my tongue. Finger on the trigger. I'd almost done it. Almost. So what was keeping me from eating my piece right now? It seemed like a fine time. Before I paid for my drink.

But those cops had scared me on that dock. I was afraid of dying. That had to mean I wasn't done, didn't it?

I snatched the phone back up and tried Maggie again. Still no answer. Tried Josephs instead.

"Who is it?" came his gruff voice.

"It's Juno. Maggie there?"

"Yeah, but she doesn't want to talk to you."

"Put her on."

"You deaf? She doesn't want to talk to you."

I wasn't taking no for an answer. I spoke superslow, carefully enunciating each word. "Put . . . her . . . on."

A beleaguered response came back. "Hold on."

What was I going to say when she came on? I scrambled for something as the seconds ticked nervously by.

The connection went dead.

Shit. She hung up on me. Maggie had hung up on me. *Shit. Shit. Shit.* I slapped the phone down on the bar, sent the hanging wood door swinging on its ropes.

"Woman trouble?"

I sucked down the rest of my brandy. "Gonna need another one of these."

I watched the amber liquid fill my glass. It'll be okay, I told myself. Maggie will come around. Just needed a little more time.

And if she didn't . . .

I couldn't worry about that. Not now. I had to focus on the immediate. I imagined Mota with Wu, Froelich, and two Yepala cops, all of them standing around a stack of scratch.

I clutched my glass tight and took a hearty swig. *Mota, you pretty-boy son of a bitch. What are you up to?*

fourteen

I'D lost the files—drowned in the river—but I remembered the name of Lizard-man's first vic. Franz Samusaka. Died dickless with a tat on his cheek.

The taxi dropped me curbside. Actual curbs in this neighborhood. Sidewalks too. No foot-tramped paths of dirt running through walls of weedy growth. Here, the walls were man-made, brick and mortar with spirals of barbwire on top.

I rang the bell next to the gate. A voice came through the speaker. "Yes?"

"I'm here to talk to Samusaka."

"Mister or Missus?"

"Whoever's in." I waved my stolen YOP badge for the cam.

The gate buzzed, and I pushed my way through. Floodlights lined the pristine walkway, colored tile with unbelievably bright white lines of grout running in between. Must be somebody's job to scrub away the mold every day.

The grounds were large, walkways snaking off in various directions, leading to guesthouses or garden houses or bathhouses or whatever other kind of houses rich people invent for themselves. Straight ahead was the main house, a brandy-era mansion of austere stone and iron. Deluski said Samusaka was an oil man. The resurgence of the internal combustion engine had done wonders for the family bank account.

A housekeeper in a blue dress with a white apron met me at

the door. "You'll have to wait in the study. Mrs. Samusaka is entertaining guests. I'll let her know you're here."

I followed the housekeeper down a long, broad hall with a gold chandelier overhead and marble slabs underfoot. Below the staircase, a door opened of its own accord, and she ushered me through.

Left alone, I wandered the small room, my shoes sinking into luxurious carpet. One wall was taken up with bookshelves stacked with leather-bound volumes, another with photos of oil pumps working the scorched dunes to our south.

A globe turned slowly on a desk. Lagarto's bottom three-quarters were dominated by the color of toasted bread, mountains and valleys all the same dead-leaf brown. Oceans broke it up with sprawling, rippling splotches of aquamarine. The globe's top was textured with a lush green that swayed as if in a breeze.

I reached a finger for the jungle, expecting to poke right through the hologram's surface, but the globe was real, the ruffling jungles soft like felt. I traced the Koba River's snaking path and my finger came away wet. Fucking magic, what off-world tech could do.

A woman appeared in the doorway. Black hair hung straight down to her shoulders. Stern eyes sat in deep sockets. A necklace draped from her neck, a diamond pendant hanging from a gold chain, her dress cut just low enough to give it proper room to sparkle.

"Mrs. Samusaka?"

"Yes. I'm Crystal Samusaka."

"I'm Detective Mozambe with KOP. I was hoping we could talk."

"I'm very busy right now."

I smiled and gestured at the chair. "Which makes me appreciate the time all the more."

She sat and crossed her legs, her knees poking out from under the hem of her dress.

I sat on a small sofa. "I'd like to talk about Franz."

"He died in August."

"Tell me what happened." Starting vague is best when you
don't know what you're looking for.

She squinted at me, the resulting crow's-feet the first sign she
was old enough to have an adult son. She took in my shades,
the empty right sleeve, the bar-fight bruise on my forehead.
"Who are you? You're not a cop, are you?"

"I used to be."

"What do you have to do with my son?"

"I'm looking into his death."

"Why?"

"I think he was murdered."

Her squint narrowed to the point where I couldn't see her
eyes. "This isn't funny. It's time I get back to my guests." Despite
her words, she didn't move.

"Do you believe the official story that he ODed?"

She stared at me, lips pursed, arms crossed.

"Did he have an opium problem?"

Nothing. Her left foot tapped at the air.

"Listen," I said. "You could really help me out by being open
with—"

"You want money, don't you? This is some kind of scam."

"I don't want any money. What I want is the truth."

"You want truth? Then tell me who you really are. How did
you know my son? What was he to you?"

I took a deep breath. "My name is Juno Mozambe. Like I
said, I used to be a cop."

"And now?"

"Now I'm a businessman."

"What kind of business?"

"The kind you can't talk about," I said with finality. She wouldn't get any more.

She fingered her necklace, pinched the pendant between her fingers. "I should throw you out."

"But you want to know what happened to your son. You don't believe he overdosed."

"How would you know?"

"Because you're still here."

She dropped the pendant. "Tell me how you knew my son."

"I didn't. But somebody's killing people, and I think he started with your son."

"This killer, he killed somebody close to you?"

"Somebody I was responsible for." I leaned forward in my seat. "Did your son have a drug problem?"

"He liked to party. He was only twenty-two. Nothing wrong with that at his age. But he wasn't an addict. When the police found him and told me how he died, I refused to believe it. For a long time I refused to believe it."

"But you eventually accepted it?"

"Until now. If this is some kind of scam, I swear I'll—"

"It's not. Where did he like to party?"

"He mentioned a place called the Maze a few times."

"Did you know about the tattoo on his cheek?"

"He didn't have a tattoo."

"He did. It was the kind you can turn on and off. Two interlocked snakes in a circle, each one eating the tail of the other. Do you know what that's about?"

"No."

"Was your son gay?"

She rubbed the pendant, her face a blank mask. She uncrossed her legs and crossed them the other way.

"Mrs. Samusaka? Was your son gay?"

"He might've been."

"What does that mean?"

"It means just what I said. I didn't pry into his private affairs."

"Can you think of anybody who would've wished your son harm?"

"No."

"What about your husband? He have any enemies?"

She shook her head no.

"This could be important," I said.

She dropped the diamond pendant and picked it back up.

"I'm not trying to poke into your husband's business, but I'd like to check out his enemies, see if any of them could've killed your son."

"My husband doesn't have enemies."

"C'mon, Mrs. Samusaka, he's a very successful businessman. You and I both know there are no angels in business."

She looked down and smoothed the hem of her skirt. She was shutting down. My instincts said push. My instincts always said push. I leaned in as far as I could, my ass on the edge of the sofa. I upped the urgency in my voice. "Tell me who his enemies are. Who did he screw over? Tell me."

She stood. "I will not be bullied by a stranger in my own home. You need to go."

Not before I exhausted my arsenal. "If you loved your son, you'd tell me." *That's right, lady. No fucking shame.*

The low blow had the desired effect. Her cheeks turned red. Same with the skin under her necklace.

I stayed in my seat with the hope of coaxing her back into hers. I softened my tone. "I'm sorry I said that. I'm really sorry, but I get carried away sometimes. Listen, in business, people get screwed, right? I'm not a cop anymore. I don't care who your husband screwed over or why. I only care about how it relates to your son's death. Please sit and talk to me."

I'd done it just like my fuckhead father used to do my mother. Hit her hard, then go sweet. Abuse then apologize.

I waited for her to spill. She was hiding something.

She gestured at the door. "Good-bye, sir."

I stubbornly crossed my arms. I wasn't going anywhere.

"It's time for you to go."

I stayed, my ass cemented to the sofa.

With a huff she walked to the door and went out.

I stood to follow, ready to chase her through this house if I had to. I reached the hall and did a double take when I found the housekeeper waiting right outside the door. Had she been out there the whole time? "This way," she said curtly.

A man rushed toward me from down the hall, tailored pants swishing over his legs. Mr. Hudson Samusaka. "Who are you?"

The housekeeper responded eagerly. "He was asking about Franz." Damn snoop. "I called you right away." Damn brown-nosed snoop.

"Yes, Paulina, you did the right thing." He dished the compliment like a pat on the head. Crystal Samusaka stepped over to stand next to her husband.

"Answer my question," he demanded. "Who are you?"

"He says he's—"

"I'd like to hear it from him, *dear.*" He grabbed his wife's wrist and gave it a tug. She lowered her head and meekly took her place a half step behind him. The housekeeper was already positioned slightly behind. She knew her place.

"I came to talk about your son. I think he was murdered."

"Who do you think you are coming to my home, *my* home, and bothering me with this garbage?"

"I was just—"

"I don't want to hear it. Get the hell out."

I opened my mouth to protest some more but could see the futility of it. Hudson Samusaka held his head high, nose aimed upward, chin jutting like he was completing a chin-up. Like he'd spent his whole life keeping his head above us riffraff.

He tapped his ear, activating some kind of communication device. "Who let this joker in here? I want him out, you hear me?"

Defeated, I headed for the door.

"Where are Kripsen and Lumbela?"

Deluski scratched his nose. "They got called in on riot duty."

"Again?"

"Half of Villa Nueva went dark an hour ago."

"Fucking blackouts." I shook my head and looked up at the sign above the door. MAZE. The name of this club was all I'd managed to weasel out of Samusaka's mother. That was one touchy family. The rich were naturally suspicious. All that money to protect. Giant nest eggs resting in a forest full of starving vultures.

Maggie should've been there with me. Wealthy as she was, she would've known how to put Samusaka's mother at ease. How to deal with Samusaka's prick of a father. Maggie's family was old money. Brandy-era plantation owners. She knew the ways of the rich.

We should be working together.

Deluski lifted his shirttails, a pair of lase-pistols tucked in his belt. "I brought an extra like you asked." He handed a weapon over, and I tucked it into my waistband. You never knew when those Yepala cops might show again.

Deluski pulled open the door, and we stepped inside. Heads turned. Men's heads. A dozen or more gave us the eye. I could practically hear the pings of gaydar. This was Franz Samusaka's favorite hangout. I was tempted to call his mother and cinch it for her. *Your boy liked outies, not innies.*

I scoped the room. Crammed tight with tables and booths,

the place was near full, and uniformly male with a few fag hags thrown in. A small dance floor jammed to club music, sweat-streaked faces bouncing and swerving in a melee of arms and legs and pheromones.

I led us forward, not really knowing what I was looking for. We meandered through tables, drawing a multitude of stares. Appraising stares. Who-the-fuck-are-you stares. Stares that said, *fresh meat.*

I stopped at a table of five, flashed my YOP badge, and raised my voice over the music. "Did you guys know Franz Samu-saka?"

Quintuple no.

"Marvin Froelich? Emil Mota?" More negatives. I moved to another table. Same questions, same responses. Deluski went off to question the bar. Old-fashioned police work.

I canvassed from table to table. "Ever seen a tat with two snakes in a circle? How 'bout an offworlder with a steel trap for a hand?"

I wandered up a short set of stairs into a second room—sofas and settees, mood lights, and opium smoke. This room had its own bar, little more than a window cut into the wall. I stepped up and ordered a brandy from the shirtless bartender, dropped a generous but soggy tip on the bar. "Did you know Franz Sa-musaka?"

"We don't kiss and tell around here." He nabbed the bills and abruptly turned his back to wash glasses in the sink.

Brandy in hand, I turned around and leaned against the bar, my eyes soaking up the scene. Gay porn on vid screens. Sofas loaded with entwined twinks, frenching and fondling. Flames milled around, libidos in overdrive. Flirtatious winks and waves ricocheted off the walls. Shit, there were more pup tents in here than in Tenttown.

I spied an offworlder in the near corner, inside a circle of admirers. His shirt was unbuttoned, hairless pecs and tight abs on display. He had a brandy in one hand, and he held the other out front. Some caterpillar-like creature snaked through his fingers, coiling and uncoiling, slithering and sliding. Always in motion. Some kind of genetically engineered pet.

One of his admirers held up a thumb and the offworlder transferred the creature. Fluffy fur wrapped the thumb, then wound back and forth between outstretched fingers. Delighted shrieks sounded over the bar's hubbub.

The offworlder finished his brandy, and his gaze turned toward the bar, his eyes snagging on my stare. He stepped out from his group and came my way, his legs scissoring inside nut-hugger pants. Despite the still air, the back of his shirt flapped like he was walking into a breeze. His hair blew too, long raven-colored hair that whipped in fictional wind. Vain bastards with their high-tech bullshit.

"I saw you watching me. Do we know each other?"

"No."

"In that case, I'm Angel. And you are?"

"Straight."

He lifted a brow. "Forgive me if I doubt that, the way you came in here acting so butch. It's quite the look you've got going there. Badass shades. A bump on your forehead like you're a tough boy." He took hold of my empty sleeve. "Oh, and this is a nice touch. Where's your hand? Is it detachable?"

I leaned back to pull the sleeve from his hand. "You been coming here awhile?"

"You could say that."

"Ever know a guy named Franz Samusaka?"

"Maybe. Why do you want to know?"

"I'm looking into his death."

"You police?"

I lost patience. Not sure I had any in the first place. "Did you know the fucker or not?"

He acted taken aback, his lips forming a playfully exaggerated O. "You've really got that rough-boy act down, don't you?"

"Not an act. Did you know him?"

"No."

"Then fuck off."

I watched the chill overcome the charm, twinkly eyes going dark, disarming smile going flat. "As you wish," he said. "I'll leave you be after I get my drink."

I went back to scanning the room. A couple sat scrunched together on an ottoman. One was holding a jar up to the light. I could see something small and black inside. He unscrewed the lid and tapped the glass facedown against his palm in an attempt to dump out the object. Whatever it was, it held tight to the side of the jar. He and his partner giggled like teenagers until it finally popped loose.

The offworlder I'd told off brushed past me, his brandy glass now filled. He stopped to look back at me. "You know what you need? A good fuck."

I pretended like I didn't hear until he moved off. Asshole offworlder was used to people bowing at his feet. I studied the couple on the ottoman. One of them was picking at the black object with his fingers, trying to get hold of something. Finally succeeding, he pulled it free and made a show of holding it up high. It dangled from his fingertips—black and oily. And wiggling.

A snail, I realized. He'd pulled it from its shell, and now he closed the snail in his fist and squeezed, black juice oozing out from between his fingers and down his hand. Holding his hand over his open mouth, he let the thick black drops fall to his outstretched tongue.

He popped what was left of the snail into his mouth and

chewed, an oily drop running down his chin. His lover swiped away the drop with his index finger, and they smiled at each other, the snail eater grinning inky teeth.

Deluski appeared at my side. "Get anything?"

"Did you see that?"

"Yeah. I watched somebody eat one in the other room. A guy told me it's an aphrodisiac."

The couple stood and walked to the back, then through a curtain, briefly exposing a set of stairs that led up to what I figured to be some private rooms.

"You think it works?" I asked.

"Hell no." He laughed. "You know how people make up stories to sell worthless crap."

"Learn anything?"

"I got a couple guys to admit they knew Samusaka, but that's as far as it went. You?"

"Dead fucking end."

"What's our next move?" Deluski seemed eager, totally digging his first crack at playing detective. The kid impressed me. Made me think he might be worthy of being my number two. Might be.

I asked, "You ever tell me how you got sucked into this?"

"Sucked into what?"

"Into this gang. What's left of it anyway."

He rubbed his chin. "It started with a girl."

"A girl?"

"Yeah. I wanted to impress her, show her I could take care of her. She had this ex who kept bothering her. You know the type, the clingy kind that can't let go. I went to see him, wanted to talk some sense into him."

"You give him a beat-down?"

He nodded, his eyes looking distant. "I didn't want to. I really tried to talk to him, but all the guy understood was fists."

"Some people are like that," I said, thinking I might be one of those people.

"Yeah, well, this guy turned out to be Wu's cousin, and he went to Wu for help. That's when Wu came to me and told me that he could get me fired. All he had to do was file a report."

"Unless?" With Wu there was always an "unless."

"Unless I did a job for him. He had this whole plan of how he was going to steal a shipment of O. He had a tip that a container had just come in, and it was sitting in one of the abandoned shipyards. What he wanted me to do was knock it into the water. There'd be no guards, he said. That was the way these guys liked to operate."

Already, his story sounded familiar. "Guards would just attract attention."

"Right. They thought it was better to just leave their shit out in the open. There were so many shipping containers on that pier nobody would stumble upon the opium unless they knew where to look for it."

I listened closely even though I already knew how this one was going to end. I'd run the same con.

Deluski carried on, his voice getting deeper and harder to hear, as if he were telling the story of how somebody close had died. "He gave me the container number and told me where to find it. It was right where he said it would be, locked up tight and sitting close to the water. I hooked it to a tugboat I'd rented, and I pulled it off the pier and let it sink just like he said. You see what he was thinking?"

"He wanted to make the drug dealers think somebody hauled their container away."

"Right. They'd go searching the river, looking for a big boat, and while they were off doing that, he'd go back with a small fishing boat and dive for the O. I thought he was a genius."

"But?"

Deluski's voice continued to lose volume. I had to lean in to hear him. "But when he dove down to the container, he found bodies inside. A whole family. He showed me pictures of them. A man and woman. Three kids. All drowned. They were trying to get off-planet. A barge was going to come by and sneak them into the spaceport as cargo. I'd sunk the wrong container."

Deluski was practically shaking. He had to know the truth. I looked him in the eye, my face as sober as my words. "The whole thing was a con. That container was empty. It's still down there. Still locked up tight."

"I know." His voice was solemn as an undertaker's. "I eventually figured out it was all bullshit. But at the beginning . . ." He let out a sigh. "At the beginning, I thought it was real. Wu helped me cover it up. I owed him, and I started doing regular jobs for him. By the time I realized I'd been had, I was in too deep. I still remember those pics. Those kids *still* feel real to me. Fucked me up good."

I swallowed what was left of my drink and slapped my glass on the bar. A story like that required a good belt. Hard to believe I used to pull that con myself. Some cruel-ass shit.

Right in front of us, a couple sat pressed together on a sofa, lips mashing, hands exploring. Helluva place for a conversation like this. To the rest of the Maze's clientele, Deluski and I probably looked like a good match. Like we'd just had a moment.

Over in the corner, I caught the offworlder watching me. I shot him a nasty stare. Asshole. Offworlders were all assholes.

Deluski's story was common enough. Decent kid catching some bad breaks. Ground up like so many others in the mill of corruption that was KOP.

"Wu screwed you," I said. I wanted to see what he'd do if I gave him an easy out. "Everything that's happened since wasn't your fault. You had no choice."

"Wu was a grade-A prick, no doubt about it. I'm not sorry he's gone. But . . ." He shook his head. "But I had choices every step of the way. Some of the things I've done . . ." His voice trailed into dust.

The kid was the real deal. Man enough to put the blame right where it belonged.

We stood in silence for a while, lost in thought. My arm itched. I poked at the bandages through my sleeve, dug my fingernails into the fabric to get a little relief.

He broke the silence, barely, his voice hardly a whisper over the bar's din. "I'm going to burn in hell."

"Tell you what. When you get there, you ask for me and I'll show you around."

He chuckled and patted my shoulder. "Thanks, boss. Now tell me, what are you after in all this?"

I gave him the only answer I had. "I don't know."

He threw a nonchalant wave of his hand. "I'm sure you'll figure it out."

I seized on the statement. "What makes you so certain?"

He thought before answering. "Listen, I was Wu's man for a time, and later Ian's until you killed him and took us as your own. That's three bosses I've had, and all three of you were power-hungry bastards, but you were the only one who understood that power comes with responsibility."

I arched a doubtful eyebrow.

"You ran KOP. You and Chief Chang. You two were dirty as hell, everybody knows that, but you never stopped running a police department."

"You give us too much credit."

He shrugged off my comment. "All I know is the city ran a lot better when you were in charge."

"Quit blowing smoke up my ass. You can be honest with

me." A fly buzzed by my face. I took a swipe at it but came up short. Damn missing hand.

"I was being honest."

Time we quit pussyfooting. Time to put it out there. "You telling me you wouldn't stab me in the back if you had the chance?"

His jaw held firm, his eyes tightening in the corners. "You referring to the vid?"

Of course I was. *Killer KOPs.* "Wouldn't you cut my throat for a chance to destroy it?"

The corners of his mouth lifted, a sly smile forming. "Absolutely."

I reflected a wily grin back at him. Kid had some balls. Definite number-two material.

"Screw this place," I said. "Let's get out of here."

We beelined our way out the back exit, down some stairs and up a short alley to the street. The Maze's front entrance stood just a couple meters away. Misting rain drifted down from the starless sky, and caught in the glow of passing head-lights, formed temporary galaxies of twinkling light.

I sucked deep on O-free air. "Let's hit some more gay bars. We need to find a connection between Froelich and Samusaka besides their taste in tattoos. Call Kripsen and Lumbela. See if they can ditch riot duty. We could use two more bodies."

"Can't call them. You know the regs. Police radio only."

"Call them anyway. They'll answer for us."

"KOP disables their personal phones during riot duty."

"Since when?"

"Since a few riot cops got calls from their families and aban-doned their posts to protect their homes. Duty first. Want me to call Dispatch, see if I can get a message to them?"

"Yeah. Have them call us first chance they get."

He placed the call, and a hazy KOP holo-logo appeared in the mist. For an investigation like this, the person I really needed was Maggie. Kripsen and Lumbela were piss-poor substitutes.

A woman came out of the Maze, an offworld woman, full lips, man-eater eyes, her hair a fountain of brown ringlets that splashed over her shoulders in a rippling cascade. She stood under the sign, cobalt-blue neon bathing her fair skin. She looked up into the mist, a blue halo forming around her face. I hadn't seen her inside. Must've been on the dance floor.

I paid no attention to what Deluski was saying to Dispatch. My eyes were riveted. There was something familiar about this woman.

She came my way, tight pants, loose shirt, her eyes meeting mine. She winked like she knew me.

And I knew her. But from where?

She stepped past me, her dewy hair sparkling in the beam of a streetlight.

It hit me. The hair. That same abundant flood of curls streaming across Mota's pillow. I hadn't realized she was an offworlder at the time. Too dark. How she knew me I didn't know. She was totally asleep, her mouth hanging wide open when I had her and Mota in my sights.

Deluski hung up, the KOP logo blinking out of existence. "That didn't sound right."

"What?" I asked absently, my mind weighing what was the better move. Confront her or follow her?

"According to Eddie at Dispatch, Kripsen and Lumbela just got pulled off the riot. They were sent to the Cellars."

She crossed the street. I started walking.

Deluski followed. "Did you hear me? They were sent to the Cellars."

She turned left at the end of the block. I hastened my pace.

"Boss?"

I crossed the street and ran up to the corner. I peeked around just in time to see her get into a cab. *Shit.*

"Who is she?" asked Deluski.

I waved my one and a half arms in an effort to hail a ride. No fucking cabs. I looked to my left and already her taxi was lost in a swarm of taillights. I dropped my arms. *Fuck.*

"Who is she?" repeated Deluski.

"Mota's girlfriend."

"Seriously? I thought he was gay. You think she turned him straight?"

I rubbed my jaw. I couldn't pin Mota down. The bastard kept finding new ways to surprise me. Screwing one of my boys. Siccing a pair of Yepala cops on me. And now an offworld squeeze.

"Did you hear what I said about Kripsen and Lumbela?"

A fly plunked me in the forehead. Damn things were pissing me off.

"Boss?"

"Yes, dammit. I heard you. They got routed to the Cellars."

"Does that sound right to you? Who gives a shit about the Cellars? Nobody lives in there. No businesses either."

"Did Dispatch give a reason?"

"Eddie said vandals were spotted in the area."

"Nothing strange about that. They get a call from a citizen, they have to send somebody."

"Not when there's a riot going."

Again, a fly kamikazeed me. *Dammit!* I swatted at the little shit, once, twice. A cab pulled over. "Fucking move on!" I shouted at the driver.

The driver leaned her head out the window. "Why did you wave me down?"

"I was swatting at a fly."

She called me an asshole and pulled away. Unbelievable.

"Maybe the riot is over," I said.

"That's just it. Eddie said Villa Nueva's still dark. The riot's in full swing. It's a bad one too."

Deluski had a point. Why peel a pair of officers off a riot when you could send somebody else?

"Think it's a setup?"

Dread sprouted in my gut. I could feel Mota's hand behind this. I could *feel* it, his fingers itching at my spine.

fifteen

OUR taxi dropped us at the edge of the darkness. The driver refused to go any farther. Said she couldn't take chances like that.

I took off my shades, stuffed them in a pocket. "You ready?"

Deluski pulled his piece. "Let's do it."

I drew my weapon, and we ran into the blackout, Deluski in the lead. He had the flashlight we'd bought off the driver. I'd go without. My hand was already full.

I couldn't lose Kripsen and Lumbela. I'd already lost two men. No more.

No fucking more.

The Cellars were ten, maybe twelve blocks away. The street was empty. Deserted. I stayed close on Deluski's tail for the first block, but my lungs were far from equal to his. "Slow down," I wheezed at his back. He complied, dropping his speed from young buck to old fuck.

I kept my eyes aimed at the ground and followed the bobbing beam of his flashlight, getting in the rhythm when he stopped short. I smacked into him, my face bouncing off his shoulder, the taste of blood in my mouth.

"Sorry." He swept the flashlight beam left and right. "Don't we have to turn here?"

We stood in the center of an intersection. He three-sixtied the beam, hitting all four corners: shoe store, fruit stand, rubble from a collapsed building, another fruit stand. I knew where I was. I'd been here a few nights ago, on my way to the Punta de Rio, the restaurant where I'd met Maggie. "Ahead another block, then left to the river."

"Got it." He was off.

I hustled to catch up, then settled back into the pace. Misting rain didn't keep me cool, and sweat broke on my forehead, in my pits. We made the turn, our footfalls echoing in the silence like ticks of an old clock on a sleepless night.

Block after block, we approached the river, the nicer parts of Villa Nueva falling away behind us, brick and asphalt giving way to clumps of weeds and brush, the air heavy with the smell of wet mulch. This patch of urban jungle was once a bustling port, a buzzing, booming link of the supply chain from the long-gone brandy era.

Deluski's flashlight flitted over the signs of neglect: glue jars huffed clean; used rubbers tossed from car windows; bottles and cans; cig butts and O pipes. We hurdled vines, dodged shrubs, stomped through knee-high grass, coming ever nearer to the Cellars.

Deluski slowed. He swept the flashlight beam across an angled plane of greenery. Starting from ground level, the plane sloped upward, rusted metal showing through in places. This was the roof, one side of a massive A-frame that sheltered a man-made inlet big enough to hold a barge.

We ran alongside, seeking a usable entrance. Deluski stopped to aim the flashlight at a pair of doors lying flush with the ground, his beam settling on a locked chain running through the door handles, the links knotted with roots and vines. This place was condemned a decade ago. A deathtrap. Supposed to be sealed up.

We moved on, passing two more properly chained entrances before reaching a pair of doors flapped upward, a bolt cutter lying on the ground. I could see the first steps of a long staircase that I knew tunneled into the earth, down, down, down to the Cellars, a series of cavernous rooms buried beneath the inlet.

We started our descent, my piece clutched tight, too tight, like I was trying to hold on to a slimy fish. A fly buzzed my ear. My stump had to be bleeding again, must've bumped it without noticing. No other way to explain why the damn pests had been dogging me since the gay bar.

Already, the air felt cooler. The Cellars were designed to provide a constant temperature year-round, each meter of depth providing further protection against the scorching Lagartan summer. Perfect for brandy's long-term aging process.

We descended one step at a time, our movements deliberate, careful, nervous, weapons aimed at the black shadows hiding ahead of the flashlight beam. My lungs protested the stale air; legs quivered from overuse; eyes stung with salty sweat.

The bottom was near, a tall, arched doorway emerging from the dark like a tombstone, the last two stairs submerged in floodwater. I stepped down, ankle-deep water filling my shoes, the spaces between my toes. We took the last stair, cold liquid soaking our calves. Deluski swept the beam from side to side. Brandy casks sat on rusted shelves, rows and rows of them bathing in still water. We entered a tunnel of tipped shelves. I had my eyes peeled, my ears dialed in. Shattered casks poked out of the water like shipwrecks.

We sloshed to the row's end. The water was now above our knees, my already exhausted legs resisting the extra work. Up ahead, Deluski's beam found a lift, one of many that were once used to lift casks to the surface, where they could be loaded onto a barge docked in the inlet overhead.

We about-faced and started up another row. Casks towered overhead, water dripping from cracks in the ceiling, plinks and plunks echoing all around. I tried to shut out the fear of the ceiling giving way, river water crashing down on our heads in a violent torrent.

Water crept up my thighs, every centimeter a shock to my never-cold Lagartan skin. We stopped at the foot of a metal monster, long arms reaching out, the robotic stock picker frozen with rust and crusty mold.

"This is going to take forever," I said. "They could be anywhere down here."

"They might not be down here at all. They could've gotten scared off. If we smelled a setup, they could've too."

Deluski's phone rang. My heart jumped at the sudden ringing. *Shit!* To free up a hand, he tucked the flashlight under his arm, making everything but a small, rippling circle of light on the water go dark.

"Fucking silence that shit."

"Sorry. Forgot. Call's coming from a blocked ID."

I felt a twinge in my gut. Something was up. "Answer it."

"It's a vid."

"Live feed?"

"Yeah."

"Turn off the outgoing vid before you answer."

"Got it. No holo-projection down here. We'll have to watch it on my screen."

I dragged my rubbery legs through the water until I stood shoulder to shoulder with him. "Go."

Dim yellow light jittered across several racked casks of brandy. The camera was as dizzying as the lighting, bouncing, weaving, until finally it steadied on two men, *my* men. They were both on their knees, water up to their waists, faces sagging with resignation. A third man stood behind them, panama hat tilted down to keep his face in shadow. A lase-blade fired up, its red glow casting the scene in hellish fire.

No!

Panama took hold of Kripsen's hair and sliced his throat. Flash-fried blood misted upward among puffs of curling smoke. Kripsen's eyes rolled up in their sockets, blood streaming, life draining.

Blood pulsed in my temples, my face on fire. FUCK! FUCK! FUCK!

Panama shoved Kripsen forward. A splash of water kicked up at the camera, and the camera jumped. "Fucking watch it," came a voice with a pissy attitude.

I knew that pretty-boy voice. Mota. With no conscious thought, my arms came to my face and started to knead, the butt of my weapon digging into one cheekbone, the butt of my right arm into the other.

The screen shook in Deluski's quivering grasp.

Kripsen wasn't moving. He was doing the dead man's float.

Bile stewed in my gut. We were too late. Too damned late. Lumbela was about to die, and we were powerless to stop it. The Cellars were too big. They could be anywhere within this network of interconnected underground warehouses. We'd run out of time.

Lumbela's hair was in Panama's grip, head tilted back, Adam's apple bulging, eyes pleading, begging. The blade scorched and charred its way through skin and muscle and windpipe. Panama let go of his hair, and Lumbela briefly splashed under the surface before slowly rising to the top.

Deluski didn't speak. But I could hear him breathing fast through his nose, the sound raking in and out.

Panama wasn't done. He turned the floaters over, their blank eyes staring, throat wounds gaping, mouths hanging open and filled with water. Panama pulled Kripsen close and reached a hand toward the wound. Kripsen's still face went underwater as Panama worked his fingers inside his throat. He pulled his hand out, bringing Kripsen's tongue with it. He left it like that, red flesh poking from a mouth that wasn't a mouth. A Lagartan necktie.

I wanted to scream, but they were down here somewhere. Possibly *near*. Mota and Panama. They were going to pay.

Panama moved in to dress up Lumbela.

"Turn it off," I said. "We'll fry the fuckers on their way out."

Deluski understood. He was already moving, heading back toward the staircase, his legs high-stepping through the water. I was right behind him, doing a sloppy imitation, bumbling and stumbling, my stride a splashy sort of scramble.

The water shallowed nearer to the stairs, my gait taking on a semblance of normalcy. Deluski used the flashlight to help me pick a spot behind a cask that had a good line of sight.

"You set?" he asked.

"Yeah. Don't shoot until I do."

"Got it." He splashed away, light jouncing for a minute then extinguishing when he found his spot.

My feet and ankles were still in the grip of cold water, an aching numbness taking hold. Wet pants chilled my legs. A water-splashed shirt clung to goose-bumped flesh. Focus. I held my piece tight in my left, my eyes searching for a break, any break in the pitch black dark. They'd come this way. They had to.

Mota and Panama. I'd passed on my chances to kill each of them. Kripsen and Lumbela had paid the price for my stupidity, the ultimate price. My once-fearsome crew was now reduced to one.

I clenched my jaw to keep my teeth from chattering, wiggled my unfeeling toes. Mota had been asleep when I had him in my sights. *Asleep*. All I'd had to do was squeeze the trigger. But I was weak. Soft. Felt sorry for the piece of offworld ass spooning alongside him.

And Panama? I'd left him beaten and bruised but all too alive. *Fuck.*

I tried to take satisfaction from the fact that Panama's YOP partner didn't show on the vid. I'd clocked that bastard over the head good. That SOB probably still wasn't seeing straight.

I let my piece hang by my side. Didn't want a tired arm. I'd have plenty of time to take aim as they approached. The sound of dripping water pinged hollowly off the walls. I ignored the fly buzzing around my head. *Focus.*

Neckties. Panama gave my boys fucking neckties, the calling card of the jungle warlords. I couldn't wait to fry the fuck out of him. Mota too. Despite the chilled bones in my shoes, this time there'd be no cold feet.

Yepala was General Z's territory. The general was famous for employing an army of children. Decades of war had taken its toll on the adult population so now he drafted children.

But what was the connection between Mota and General Z? I remembered the picture: Mota, Froelich, and Wu standing around a pile of cash. Opium money? It was possible.

But would General Z order the murder of two Koba police? That was a risky move for the warlord. A move as ballsy as that could provoke a nasty backlash from the Lagartan army.

So perhaps Mota and Panama weren't conspiring with the warlord at all. Yepala was on the edge of the general's territory, a place where nonopium trade and commerce were freely permitted. Those two SOBs could be operating an independent business inside the general's territory.

I saw a light ahead, and I put thoughts of drugs and warlords out of my mind. The light blinked in and out as they passed behind one obstruction or another. Then it split into two lights.

Mota and Panama.

Panama and Mota.

I raised my piece, my heart quickening its pace. They were

mine. Darkness was my shield. I was invisible, a ghost with a gun.

Mota and Panama. Panama and Mota. They made slow, sloshing progress. My finger was on the trigger, waiting, anticipating.

Ready.

A phone rang. One of theirs. "Who the hell is that?" asked Panama, his voice distant but audible.

"It's him again," said Mota. "It must be important. Hello?"

Not yet, I told myself. Be patient. Let them get nice and close. Close enough that I couldn't miss, even with the left. No need to rush it. They couldn't see me. Couldn't see Deluski.

Not yet.

Their lights went out. Their silhouettes disappeared. The sound of splashing water.

What the fuck?

I resisted the urge to open fire. Couldn't give away my position. I had to stay between them and the door. As long as I did, the upper hand was mine. Only one way out of here.

Water dripped. The fly buzzed. My breath pumped in and out. Otherwise, quiet. Total, absolute quiet.

The phone call. Whoever the bastard was he had tipped them off. Ambush up ahead. But who? How?

The air came alive with red fire. My eyes went blind, bright light overwhelming me. An oven blast struck my cheek, eyelashes curling, skin burning. I dropped down, taking cover behind the cask, my body in a crouch, my ass dipped in the water, face pressed into the wood.

I could feel the cask shake as lase-fire ripped into it. Smoldering wood chips rained on my head, and smoke filled my nostrils. I looked left, my vision fuzzy and blurred. Through the haze, I could see return fire coming from Deluski's position, the beam terminating in a confusing red-black smear.

How did they know where I was? Fucking heat sensors. Had to be.

A chunk of wood bounced off my shoulder. My cover wouldn't last much longer.

Fall back to the stairs. Cement and rock would hold better than rotten wood. I sank into the cold water, stretched my legs out so my torso went all the way in. Good luck finding my heat signature now. I took a second to locate the staircase in the deep-red glow of lase-fire, then I sucked in a breath and dropped in my head. Underwater, I scrambled for the stairs, doing a swim-crawl. Water exploded around me. Microcurrents struck me like punches, wild surf tinted bloodred with lase-fire.

Hot water scalded my face, my ankles, my gun hand. I turned back, paddling, crawling, lunging. My head struck something hard. I came up and sucked air as I tapped around with my weapon, the sound of hollow wood answering back. Another cask. I pulled myself upright, my back leaning against my new cover.

Bastards saw me. Even when I went underwater. *Shit.*

Lase-fire erupted from the staircase, momentarily silhouetting Deluski's crouched form. He'd managed to fall back unhurt. All their fire was focused on me.

It was me they could see. Not Deluski. How?

From behind, I heard splashing. They were closing. Deluski searched with his flashlight and took some potshots, but the splashes came closer.

I couldn't stay here. But I was farther away from the stairs than I'd been on my first try—no chance in hell I'd make it. Deluski's position was more and more vulnerable with our enemies' every wet step forward.

I had to move.

"Run!" I yelled at Deluski. I didn't stick around for a response. I took off in the opposite direction. I held the trigger down, squeezing off a long burn and chased the light. Stinging with exertion, my legs fought the water, my knees kicking up spray that flash-fried in the lase-beam.

The lift. Its shaft ran up to the surface. There had to be a service ladder or staircase nearby. Had to be.

The water deepened, now up to my thighs. I dropped in and swam. A beam sizzled by. I dove deep, my stomach scraping the floor as I stroked forward through the black water, my lungs on fire, my eyes seeking the lift. Flashes of red light penetrated the dark, but couldn't penetrate deep water.

I came up for a puff of air, the back of my head catching a steamy spray, scalp on fire. I went back down, cold water extinguishing, soothing. I hit something with my stump, pain ricocheting up and down my arm. I came up for another puff, afraid to surface for more than a sip.

Air. I needed more air.

I steered left, edging closer to toppled shelving. I picked my way into a gap alongside a cask, splinters digging, my weight centering underneath me. I stood upright and sucked air, my piece taking aim.

Fire came at me, two beams tearing at the cask. Couldn't fool those fuckers for a second. I aimed at the beams' source and returned fire. Their beams went dark. I jerked the beam around, attacking the black with a fiery scribble.

I heard splashes. Couldn't see shit. I fired off another burst. "Stay back, motherfuckers!"

The splashes stopped. I kept up the fire, stalling for time. I needed oxygen before the next big push.

The sound of sloshing, swooshing strides started back up. They were on the move again, and they were close. Too close. I needed more time. More air. But I had to go. I burned off a burst in the direction of the lift, red light illuminating a door to the right of the lift entrance. A stairwell. Had to be.

Better fucking be.

Not far. I could do it in one breath. I could. I filled my lungs full and dove under. I made frantic frog strokes, my stomach skimming over the floor, bubbles blowing out my mouth, red light blinking in and out. The door. It was all about the door.

I hit the wall and peered up, the door handle briefly blinking into existence as a burst of lase-fire tore into the door. I stayed crouched below the surface and dropped my piece to free up my only hand.

Desperate for air, I made a quick snatch, my hand darting out of the water to grab the door handle. I yanked down and pulled at the door, but it wouldn't budge. *Fuck.* My fingers stung with searing heat—another flash of lase-fire setting water to a boil.

Ignoring the pain, I tried a push instead of a pull, and the door swung open. I slipped inside, remembering to reach back for my piece before pushing the door closed. I stood and sucked air, foul, fetid air that tasted sweet as hell.

I opened fire, a cloud of steam bursting out of my weapon. Red fire lit the small space. Stairs. I started up, then stopped and turned back to fry the door handle. I hit it with a sustained burn, the rusted metal quickly taking on a red glow.

I waited for the door handle to turn, waited for the fried-flesh scream that would accompany it, a vicious smile on my face. It didn't turn. But they must've arrived by now. Yet the door handle didn't turn. I took my finger off the trigger, and I heard the sound of water splashing against the door. Fuckers were throwing water at it, trying to cool it off.

How did they know?

A fly buzzed my ear. *You're still with me, are you?*

Oh shit. The fly.

I swiped at the little fuck, then sizzled off a burn, but couldn't hit the bob-and-weave bastard. I'd been bugged.

I hustled up the stairs, my lase-pistol lighting the way. I made it up three flights before hearing the door open below. I kept going upward, water squeezing over the lips of my shoes. I was spent. Aching-chest, toasted-muscle, ready-to-vomit spent.

But I kept going. Up and up and up.

I heard them clomping and grunting. Mota and Panama. Panama and Mota.

I kept firing my pistol at the ground, the red glow illuminating the stairs. I hit the next landing, turned around and started up another flight. Flight after flight, I kept moving, refusing to quit. Fuck Mota. Step, step, step. *Fuck, fuck, fuck.*

I burst out a door into open space. I was inside the A-frame, the large, barge-sized inlet lying before me. I ran for the water, the inlet's mouth sitting to my right, the river just a few meters away, lights twinkling on the far shore. The fence was my last obstacle, a chain-link job that stretched across the inlet's mouth to keep out boats.

I heard the door crash open behind me, but I was already airborne, the lase-pistol flying from my fingers, my body aiming for the water. I splashed in and kicked downward. The fence wouldn't go down to the bottom, I was sure of it. This was Lagarto. We did everything on the cheap.

I kicked down, pressure in my ears. I grabbed the fence with my good hand and pulled myself deeper. I ducked under, metal scraping my back, the current grabbing hold.

I stroked upward, and popped up to the surface for just a second before going back under, a beam missing high and wide.

Free. Fucking free.

sixteen

I SWALLOWED river water, mud-flavored muck sliding down my throat. I fought to stay afloat while a stitch shanked me between the ribs. My arms and legs begged me to give in. I vomited again. Small fish came for the free food and surrounded me in a flip-flop frenzy.

The riverbank was visible, a dark shadow that underlined the burned-out, blacked-out port of Villa Nueva. The grim sky of the Big Sleep hovered overhead like a giant hand primed to push me under.

The current was slow but persistent. Unrelenting. My adrenaline tank was empty. My swim stroke was dangerously labored. The river told me to quit. She whispered in my ear, told me she could take away my pain.

You can't have me. You spit me out, remember?

She got mean. Told me I was a curse, a blight on this world. She told me my touch was the kiss of death. Kripsen and Lumbela. Froelich and Wu. Wu's wife and daughters. All dead.

Even Niki, she said. Your wife killed herself to get away from you. Give in. Do everybody a favor.

Bitch had a point. But I couldn't afford the luxury of death. I had responsibilities. I had to set things right with Maggie. I had to avenge my crew, Wu's little girls.

I choked down another unintentional gulp of river water and swung my stubborn left arm over again to slap the water with an open palm. I took yet another knife at the water with my half-arm. One after the other, stroke after stroke, my eyes always on the shore.

My feet made contact with the bottom, my shoes finding traction in the silt. The cramp in my side kept me hunched as I waded through floating garbage. I trudged forward, my body rising out of the water. I picked my way into jungle brush, solid ground now underfoot. The stitch in my side started to unthread and the defeated river could only shout insults at my back.

I emerged from a thicket onto an empty street at least a dozen blocks downriver from the Cellars. I spat bile. My spent body felt ready to collapse.

A buzzing sound grazed my ear. Damn fly was a persistent bugger. It must've operated off a combination of motion sensors, heat sensors, DNA sensors, and whatever other kind of sensors would keep it on my ass.

Mota and Panama could still see me. They would come for me. They would.

I swung a tired arm at the fly, but it was far too fast and agile to be swatted away.

An idea lit inside my mind. I ran. The fly followed.

Streetlights flickered into life, the hum of restored electricity sounding all around me. Windows lit and neon glowed. Now that the blackout had ended, heads poked out of doors, faces searching for signs of trouble. They watched me run, their strange stares a perplexed mix of curiosity and fear.

I checked over my shoulder. Nobody followed. Nobody but this damn fly.

A toenail scraped uncomfortably in my soggy shoe. My thighs stung as they chafed in wet pants, and my lungs heaved in and out, in and out.

I'd been bugged. How? When? I forced my weary mind to go back in time. Fucking concentrate.

Mota's girlfriend. The fly had been with me since she tossed me that wink outside the gay bar. *Offworld skank bitch whore.*

I checked over my shoulder again. Still clear.

People came out of their homes. Neighbors milled about and shopkeepers checked for damage. I spied the Punta de Rio up ahead, the same restaurant where Maggie and I had eaten. Despite the late hour, their clientele was just now filing out the door. They must've stayed inside for the duration of the blackout. Safer to ride it out inside.

I raced to the entrance. Legs exhausted, my ungainly steps clapped against the pavement. People moved out of my way, alarm in their eyes.

I rushed inside and dodged a waiter who tried to tell me they were closed. I weaved past empty tables with burning candles and tips waiting for pickup. Busboys yelled at me, told me to stop, but I charged through their demands, my eyes tunneled on the back office. I burst through the door, startling the manager, and scanned the shelves: canned goods and holo-time sheets. There it was.

I paid no heed to the agitated protests and grasped the handheld bug zapper I'd seen the waitress use a few nights earlier. *Where are you, you little bastard?*

Spectators went silent in their confusion, the manager, the busboys, all of them wondering what the fuck was wrong with me. My eyes caught on a black dot buzzing in zigs and zags. I powered up the zapper and swept the racquet-like end toward the dancing dot. Electricity popped in a blue flash. The racquet jumped from my grasp and a starburst of smoking, spiraling cinders drifted down.

I was back on the street, hoofing as fast as stiff legs would allow. The bridge wasn't far. A car came around the corner. I ducked behind a stoop and peeked through a cluster of vine leaves. The car crept by: a panama hat rode in the passenger seat.

The car rolled toward the restaurant. Mota and Panama were going to check on my last-known location.

I gave it a few before coming out. I'd picked up a hitchhiker from the vines, felt it crawling and brushed the bug from my hair. My scalp screamed in protest, like I had a wicked sunburn under my hair, sun in the form of lase-fire and steamed water. A second burn stung my cheek, and my half-arm screamed too, ghost pain gripping me like a too real, invisible fist.

Fucking hell of a night.

Deluski and I were too slow. The image of Kripsen and Lumbela showed bright in my mind, the necktied bastards sticking their tongues out at me. I could see Wu's little girls, innocent young things who would never again know joy or love.

Mota, Panama, and that psycho lizard-man. They'd all left their mark on me.

I'd brandish the scars like banners, lift them high as I carried them into battle. I was on a mission.

Numb legs carried me onto the bridge. I looked down at the river, streetlights illuminating an eddy, silent water spinning, meandering, wandering. Me, I was walking in a straight line.

"I didn't quit!" I called to her.

She didn't answer.

I wouldn't be intimidated. This was still *my* turf. It was important to be seen. I strode right up the middle of the alley. My sore feet clomped with purpose, half expecting to be fried apart.

I trod past a group of hookers on a smoke break, all girl talk and garter belts. I looked over their heads, saw that Chicho's office light was on. Good. I wouldn't have to wake up that stiff. I was short on cash. And short on time. Mota and Panama would eventually come here looking for me.

I tried to take Chicho's stairs quickly and almost fell, my tired legs having to be coaxed along. I stepped through the door, a shiver of relief rippling up my spine. I'd made it in alive.

I took a quick peek into the tiny barroom to see if Deluski was inside. The kid would know to meet me here after we'd been split up. But the barroom was empty. I told myself not to worry. He was probably upstairs somewhere.

A pair of young offworld johns with just-got-laid grins came from the back, a hooker on each elbow. They eyed me with concern, the missing hand, the damp clothes, their faces saying it all—don't tell me you shop here too? Arrogant bastards were worried that they'd just dunked their toothbrushes into the same glasses I made a habit of rinsing in.

I gave them a wink before walking past and pushing my way through the curtain of monitor teeth. Chicho sat at his desk, tallying holo-receipts. Didn't he know how late it was? In a big house brimming with big tits, big numbers were his only aphrodisiac.

"Tax time," I said.

His eyes went straight to the part of me that was missing. "Where's your hand?"

"Got it fixed so it doesn't shake anymore."

He studied my face, looking for a sign, any sign, I was joking. My gaze was pure steel. Stainless.

He shook his head, beady eyes incredulous. "You are one crazy-ass son of a bitch, you know that?"

I stood on the spot where Maria had given me a nutter. Seemed like a long time ago. Still felt bad about punching her. "Time to pay up," I repeated.

"It's a little late for that, isn't it?"

"I saw your light was on. I have a busy day tomorrow. Figured I'd get a jump on things."

He didn't look ready to drop the missing-hand thing. His eyes had returned to the empty space hanging by my hip. He opened his mouth like he was going to ask a question, but a glance at my biz-only face talked him out of it. "How do you want it?"

"Cash."

He whistled as if to say, *tall order.* "I don't have that kind of scratch lying around. I can probably scrounge some up from tonight's till. The rest will have to wait until I can hit the bank tomorrow."

"Fine." I didn't want to bring up Mota, but I had to know if he and Panama had come around. My heart ticked up a notch as I tossed the question his way. "Heard from Mota?" I held on to my stone face while hanging on the answer.

"Nope."

I acted like I'd expected that response, my voice cocksure. "See, I told you not to worry about him."

Nodding, he said, "That you did, Juno. That you did."

This was going better than expected. Mota hadn't made his reappearance yet. He'd eventually try to reclaim his racket, no doubt about that, but the bastard probably had the good sense not to come to Chicho until after he'd snuffed me. Cleaner that way.

For the time being, Mota's silence worked to my advantage. This little partnership between Chicho and me was still new. Fragile. If Mota started making waves, fears would have to be calmed, hurt feelings would have to be salved, and knowing Chicho, new rates would have to be negotiated.

But this was shaping up nicely. A sweet little collect-and-go.

Except Chicho was still sitting there, as in not hustling to get my dough. He kept nodding his head, eyes crinkled like he was thinking on something important. "Hey, did you know the cops who got axed?"

Shit. I kept my response minimal. "I knew them."

"Two of them. Their heads cut off." He scratched his chin. "I saw their pics on the news, thought I recognized one."

So much for a quick collect-and-go.

"The one with the scar. Wasn't he here for the blackout the other night? One of your boys, wasn't he?"

I couldn't deny it. He knew.

He moved up in his seat. "The other one. Was he one of your boys too?"

I nodded.

He slapped his desk. "Fucking hell. What kind of operation are you running?"

Never let your mark see weakness. I shrugged it off like it was no biggie. "So I lost a couple. What you getting all worked up about?" Two dead crew. Ho-fucking-hum.

"Mota do that shit?"

"Hell no. It had nothing to do with him." And that was the truth. I kept the fact that he'd offed my other two dead crew to myself. If I was lucky, those bodies would stay underground for a good long while.

Chicho didn't look convinced.

"Those were serial killings. They say that on the news?"

"They hinted that way but didn't say for sure."

"It wasn't Mota." My voice was chock-full of conviction. "I told you I took care of that pretty boy. You'll never hear from him again."

Chicho angled his head slightly so he could look at me sidewise with mistrustful eyes. "You on the level?"

I shouldn't have to justify myself to this pimp. I let some anger seep into my voice, a little righteous indignation. "You've known me for how long?"

"Too long."

"Try twenty years. Twenty long years. All that time, I've always been straight with you. So get the hell over whatever bullshit has you doubting me, and get me my damn money."

"I put my neck out for you, Juno. I've got this whole alley singing your praises. Better protection at a cheaper price and all that. How's it going to look if this shit gets out? You know what happens if people lose confidence in their protection? They'll stop paying."

"So don't tell them Wu and Froelich were mine. Keep your trap shut, and you won't have to worry about it."

"They were here." His voice rose as he stood. He took a step toward the window. "They were right outside that goddamned window. Any of the pimps or madams in this alley could've seen them, and I don't have to tell you how recognizable that scar-headed motherfucker was."

"Those pimps or madams mention him to you?"

"No."

"Then nobody recognized him. Quit your bellyaching."

He stepped back behind his desk and leaned in. "I'm trying to sell your services to a half dozen houses outside this alley. What am I supposed to say when they ask why your boys are dying left and right?"

I could see it now, what he was doing. He was trying to put me on the defensive. Trying to seize the upper hand in our partnership.

Not going to happen. I took a big step toward his desk, big enough to bump it with my thigh. We stood face-to-face, the desk holding us apart. "You tell them my rep speaks for itself."

"Not fucking good enough." He punched at the air. The desk standing between us seemed to shrink. "I'm putting my name on the line for this."

"You quit that shit right now!" I chopped at his desk with

my good hand. "I came to you with a gift, dammit. I could've brought the same deal to anybody, you hear me? But I came to you, you stupid prick. I thought you'd have the smarts to take proper advantage."

"Fuck that. Don't act like you did me a favor, like you took a chance on me. I took a chance on *you*, you dumb fuck." He was working himself into a fit, his hands jerking around, his words coming out in a blustery blast. "You were nothing when you came in here a few days ago. Just a burned-out ex-cop. A sad-sack widower. You were nothing. *Nothing!*"

I felt spittle land on my face. His red-faced mug was ready to burst. His voice got real low. "You want to get paid, you show some appreciation."

There it was. Prick just made his play, talking to me like I was *his* employee, like I was *his* muscle. He'd figured it out. He'd seen the ragtag group I'd put together, figured out that my influence over KOP was mostly a mirage. He'd seen hints of weakness, and he was going to wring it for all it was worth.

He thought I'd fold, thought I needed this gig in a bad way, thought I needed it to feel important. He figured me for desperate, desperate enough to give him control of this racket in order to stay on his good side.

But I knew this SOB, knew what made him tick. Thanks to me, he was going to collect a piece of every trick turned in this alley. Every dick sucked. Every pussy fucked. A piece of every last buck.

He'd been sitting here in this office for days now. I could picture it, him working through the projections, charting it out, the zeroes added to his bottom line giving him a hard-on. Hour after hour, he'd been salivating over those zeroes, fawning over them like he could screw them.

He was hooked. I *knew* it. Through-the-gills, jonesing-for-a-fix hooked. Look at him, his eyes greedy as they were beady.

Time to set him straight.

I pulled off my shades so he could get a good look at my eyes. Ice. "Apologize."

"What?"

"For talking back to me. Apologize and make it sweet before I replace your ass."

I stepped through the curtain, big-ass wad of cash in my damp pocket. Deluski and Maria waited in the lobby. "We heard you were here," said Maria, her V-neck top cut low enough to show the top edges of a lacy bra, breasts squeezed up and in. Her eyes were dominated by eye shadow, deep blue swaths coming down like gaudy drapes with each eye blink. "We were worried."

I smiled and—not wanting to send the wrong signal— patted her shoulder buddy-to-buddy style.

Deluski gave a relieved grin. "Glad to see you made it, boss."

"Same here." I held him with a suspicious eye, knowing that in his case, the concern might not be so selfless. *Killer KOPs* would've gone public had I died.

"Sorry it went down like that." He dipped his head. "I didn't want to leave you to fend for yourself."

I gave him an appraising look. His brown eyes hung heavy in their sockets. He raised his brows, but they weren't strong enough to lift the weight of a long night. The guilt seemed genuine.

"Don't sweat it. I ordered you to run. You did right."

A skeptical smile. "What happened down there?"

"I ran like hell." I stepped in close, leaned forward so nobody but Deluski and Maria would overhear. "We can't stay here any longer." I asked Maria, "Know anybody with tight lips who can put Deluski up tonight?"

"What about you?"

"I have to go see somebody, but I'll have to crash eventually. Can you get a place with room for two?"

She bit her lipsticked lip. "I'll come up with something."

"When you find a place, take Deluski over there. Then call the Iguana King Hotel and leave the address for Joe Chin."

"Who?"

"Just tell them a Joe Chin will be checking in tomorrow."

She nodded her head, understanding.

I put my hand on Deluski's shoulder. "Wherever she brings you, stay there until I come for you in the morning."

Things settled for now, I went out the door.

Maggie. I had to see Maggie.

seventeen

MORNING. The traffic—both foot and wheel—told me so. I'd been sitting on these steps for hours, waiting for her to come out. Didn't want to wake her up. She was plenty pissed at me as it was.

Rain came down in a constant patter. Water streamed out from a pipe under my feet and ran down a cement gutter before disappearing into an underground pipe. The courtyard was secluded, trees and vines trimmed and shaped, the jungle tamed into a garden. Damp moss filled the air with mustiness.

The door opened behind me. She came halfway down the steps and turned to face me. "What are you doing here?" A porch light lit her face, but her voice was anything but bright.

"We need to talk."

She looked down at me, at my rumpled clothes, my up-all-night eyes. "No, we don't. I can't talk to you when you're like this."

"Like what?"

"Don't play stupid. You know exactly what I'm talking about. And take off those damn sunglasses."

I semi-complied by pushing the glasses up to the top of my head. My scalp hurt like hell.

"What were you thinking?" Her voice was amped with impatience.

"I fucked up."

"You think?"

"I didn't know Mota would fight me. I thought he'd crumble."

"You are unbelievable." She shook her head. "You really don't get it, do you?"

"Get what?"

She kept her voice low. "You still think this is a problem of execution. You think you picked the wrong protection racket to take over. Christ. It ever occur to you that taking dirty money is illegal?"

"What do you want me to say? I'm sorry?"

"An apology isn't going to do it. Good-bye." She rushed down the stairs, took the first step into the rain.

I couldn't let her go. "I did it for you," I called before she got far.

She spun on me, her face flushed, brows stabbing downward.

I stayed seated but forged ahead, undaunted. "I was trying to build a power base. You can't be chief without—"

"Stop!" She jumped on my words and stomped them into the ground. "Don't you dare put this on me. *You* fucked up. *You.*"

"I was trying to—"

"Shut up! Just shut the hell up."

I shut up. My insides hung heavy. I couldn't stand to see her angry, couldn't stand that I'd brought that ugliness to her face. The creases marring her forehead, the squint-wrinkles spoiling her eyes, the thorny little lines surrounding crimped lips, they were all my work, all of them strokes from my black paintbrush.

She was so angry I saw myself in her face, my ugly side reflecting back at me. I wanted to crawl into a hole.

Fix it, Juno. You have to fix it. I told myself I could, that it wasn't too late. She hadn't left. She hadn't given up on me. Not yet. "One question."

She stayed silent, glaring.

"What did you see in me?"

Her brows quirked as if to ask, *What the hell are you talking about?*

"When we first met, when we first partnered up, what did you see in me?"

She stepped out of the rain, up onto the bottom stair, droplets in her hair, water dotting her face.

I needed an answer. "What did you see?"

"I saw a broken man trying to fix himself."

I rubbed my stump. "So what's changed?"

"Everything. You're going the wrong way. Can't you see that?"

"My head's been a little screwed up."

"A little?"

"My intent was right, Maggie. My intent was right."

She started to protest, but I stopped her by holding up my left hand. I wouldn't let her talk me out of it. *My intent was right.* It was true. It *had* to be true. How else could I live with what I'd started, the shitstorm I'd unleashed?

I needed her to see. To understand. "You saw more in me than that."

She folded her arms, her green eyes wary.

I pressed. "When you learned who I was, my history, why didn't you drop me as fast as you could?"

"Because I could see you didn't want to be that person anymore. I thought you wanted to redeem yourself."

"I did. I *do*. You know damn well that's why I wanted to take KOP back. You know I wanted you to change it, to make it better than the clusterfuck Paul and I left behind. But that's only half of it, isn't it? Enough with the redemption story. Tell me the other reason."

She came up two steps so she could look down at me again.

"Stop twisting things. What you're doing is wrong. You took over a *protection* business. You're pocketing *prostitution* money."

I didn't like that tone, that holier-than-thou, white-horse-riding tone. I leaned way forward, my ass coming up off the step, my floored soul coming off the mat. "Of course it's fucking wrong." I spat each word. "But doing right isn't enough. Not for this screwed-up world. It's never been enough."

My voice got loud, words stampeding from my mouth. "You think I enjoy being me? You think this shit is easy?"

She backed away, the heat in my voice knocking her down a step.

"I pay the price," I said. "Fucking every day, I pay the price. But I do what it takes. If I have to, I'll paint the fucking streets with blood. You know why?" I clenched my fist, pounded it on my leg. "Because doing right doesn't change anything. Because doing right isn't worth shit!"

My wad shot, I dropped back down to my seat, my face on fire, my body shaking, my soul standing tall.

Maggie stared back at me, her stern face giving away nothing.

"It's a taker's world," I said. "A taker's world."

We watched each other, pieces said, guts spilled. I didn't need to say the other reason she kept me around. She knew damn well what wasn't said, that she saw in me something she lacked. Something she needed to get where she wanted to go. The capacity to go all the way, to sink the knife to its hilt, to slice the throat all the way through to the bone.

She needed a vicious bastard like me.

But she showed no forgiveness in her green eyes, no give at all. She was right, and I was wrong, and with this quiet stare, she was making sure I knew exactly what she thought.

I'd said what I had to say. I stayed silent, wondering if this was it. If this was where our paths forked.

I refused to believe it. We'd been through too much together in the short time we'd known each other. Our bond was too strong, our codependence too great.

"I can't have you running a criminal enterprise." Her voice was rock certain. "Quit the protection racket."

"I can't let Mota take it back."

"Why not?"

I took a long time answering, the last ounce of pride I had left making me reluctant to reveal the depth of my mistakes. "He killed Kripsen and Lumbela." There. I'd said it.

She closed her eyes and shook her head. Her jaw dropped like she was about to speak but nothing came out. She tried again but managed only a stutter. I'd knocked the words right out of her.

"He cut their throats. He's working with a pair of Yepala cops. I put one in the hospital, I think, but the other one gave my boys neckties. Mota, Wu, and Froelich were running some kind of business in Yepala, something far bigger than a protection racket. We have to find out what it is."

Her dropped jaw stayed where it was.

"Mota's got an offworld girlfriend who helped him try to knock me off. I have to find out who she is and where she fits in."

She closed her mouth and rubbed her face with her hands.

I kept dishing it out, puzzle piece after puzzle piece. Mota and Froelich were lovers. Froelich and Samusaka had matching tats. Froelich, Wu, and Mota were all in business together. Samusaka was the gay son of an oil baron whose family was less than cooperative.

Somehow, it all fit together. The lizard-man serial killer too. It all fit together.

I told her I'd put the puzzle together, and when I finished, I was going to destroy it. I'd blow the whole thing up, and I'd watch the fragments burn. Wu's little girls deserved no less.

She listened to every word, sharp green eyes taking it all in.

"I need your help."

"Quit the protection racket."

Frustration spilled into my voice. "You need a power base to be chief."

She shook her head no.

"This is how it's done."

"We're doing this different."

"Dammit, Maggie, you think you can get to the top by doing a good job? You think they look at attendance records? 'Boy, she's punctual, let's make her chief'? To be chief you have to *take* it. It's a taker's world."

"I won't do it like you and Paul did. I won't climb over the backs of pimps and hookers and drug kingpins. I won't be corrupted." She leaned forward like she was about to throw a dart. "I won't let myself turn into you."

The dart drove deep. Pierced me in a place so deep that a shallow man like me ought not to feel it.

She crossed her arms. Emerald eyes bored in. "Drop the protection racket or we're done."

Her will was so much stronger than mine, her moral center more fixed. Judging by the look on her face, she knew she'd won, and now she was just waiting for me to figure it out. I'd come here to remind her of why she needed me, but she'd upended the thing. She'd done it so skillfully, so completely that my arguments floated adrift, meaningless.

Nothing to do but marvel at what *I* saw in *her* at the beginning.

I surrendered with a defeated nod of agreement.

Her green eyes softened, emeralds becoming less cold, less chiseled. She shook her head at me with a disapproving smirk, then sat down next to me, letting out a what-am-I-going-to-do-with-you sigh on the way down. "A taker's world? Have a damn heart, will you? It wouldn't hurt to give a little."

She was right. Always right.

I ran my fingers into my hair and instantly regretted it, the root of every hair feeling like a sharp needle against my burned scalp. After a prolonged wince, I said, "You may never get there doing it your way."

"I know." She sounded sure. Like she'd made peace with it.

"I can't let Mota take his racket back. Not after what he did to Kripsen and Lumbela. They were my responsibility."

"Drop the racket after we bring him down."

We kept quiet for a long time, content to be in each other's presence, listening to jungle rain drum on the roof and the patio tiles, reunited in our mission for change.

Change. Whatever that was.

eighteen

THE skiff rode low in the water. A tourist vessel. We had cushioned seats under our asses, elbow rests for our arms. Overhead, a red-and-white-striped tarp stretched over a metal frame, ropes of light twining around the poles.

Deluski and I sat near the back, Maggie and Josephs a row ahead of us. Maggie kept one of the boat's floodlights trained on the riverbank, her face focused, concentrated. Light skittered across trees and tangled foliage. Jungle overflowed the riverbank like bread raised over a pan's lip.

The pilot's gray hair was tucked under a tied scarf, her cheeks wrinkled and wind chapped. She held the throttle open, the skiff plowing a deep furrow in the black water. Josephs had told her we'd lost a boat last night. "Came unanchored or some shit," as he'd put it. He told her we wanted to search the riverbanks to see if it ran ashore. He didn't mention the real goal of our search: bodies.

A list of monitor fun facts hung from a crossbar, the requisite campy chomp taken out of the corner. Did you know Lagartan monitors have four rows of teeth? Did you know they can stay underwater for forty minutes? Did you know monitors have redundant hearts?

Two hearts. Maggie's early-morning words replayed in my head, how she told me to have a damn heart. As if I didn't have one. As if the lizards were up a deuce on me.

I looked over at Deluski, at his world-weary eyes. They

didn't suit a kid his age. A young cop like him should be enjoying himself, chasing tail and partying his nights away. Not searching the river for the beheaded corpses of his comrades.

I pulled the big hunk of Chicho's cash out of my pocket. I roughly split it in two and handed half over. He looked at the dough, his eyelids broadening. "What's this for?"

I leaned over so he could hear me over the motor. "You're the only one left. You get their cuts now."

He nodded, his mouth screwed to one side. "Mind if I give some to Lumbela's sister? Lumbela's been supporting her. She has young ones."

I didn't want the details. The shit I'd started was rippling outward, sewage spilling from one life to the next. I didn't need to know where it all went. I had enough wrecked lives to my name. "It's yours," I told him. "Do what you want with it. Got a pen?"

He fished in a pocket and pulled one out.

"Write this down."

He nabbed an advert for the tour company from a plastic holder attached to the side rail.

I recited the Net address first, then a set of credentials that would give him access to *Killer KOPs*.

He looked at the paper. "What's this for?"

"Your movie. Destroy it."

His head snapped up, his eyes locking on to mine. "This the only copy?"

I nodded.

He shook his head like he couldn't believe it. "You fucking with me?"

"No."

He stared at the paper, lips moving as he read it to himself. "You're free."

I waited for him to show some appreciation. A nice big

You're a lifesaver would've been nice. Or maybe a little *I'm so lucky you came into my life.* I would've taken anything, even a simple thank-you. But it didn't come. He just folded the paper and pushed it into his shirt pocket, his face frozen in thought. Maggie said I should give a little. She didn't say anybody would thank me for it.

Deluski leaned forward in his seat, fingers laced tight together. Must've been killing him not to be able to destroy the vid file right this second, but he'd wisely dumped his phone after last night's escape.

I sat back, told myself it didn't matter if I got any thanks, told myself to enjoy the comfy ride. I looked toward the shore: a dock jutted into the water, lights bobbing on either side, grills flaming up, the smell of lunchtime fish drifting on the air.

"You laying me off?" asked Deluski.

I spoke without looking his way. "Stay on or not. Your choice."

"I'll stay on until this shit gets resolved. Then I don't know."

I nodded. Fine.

Maggie pointed at a buoy. The pilot took her cue and aimed the boat in the direction of her extended finger. According to the report, Franz Samusaka, the oil man's kid, was found in an old house built over the marshy runoff between the city and the spaceport. I thought it possible the killer would reuse the dump site.

Wu and Froelich's heads had been recovered, but that left a lot of corpse unaccounted for.

The skiff sliced into a narrow channel. I looked at the pilot. The nerves on her face were as plain as the wrinkles, her thoughts easy to read. Why would your lost boat go drifting in here? I calmed her fears with cash, a few bills hitting the mark.

We putt-putted through the dark, trees scratching the tarp overhead, hanging moss snagging on the vertical supports. A branch caught on the foremost pole and bent back like a whip, leaves scraping off before it slipped loose and slapped the next pole down. A dislodged gecko landed on the floor. Josephs pinned it under his shoe, picked it up and tossed the wriggler over the rail.

The channel widened. Maggie swept the floodlight left and right: tree trunks standing in still water, vines hanging down, fanned roots reaching into the water like green brooms. The motor churned through a patch of reeds, deep gurgles belching from the water. I leaned forward to peer over Maggie's shoulder. Her digital pad showed a map of the exact location of where Samusaka's body was found. We were close.

The marsh stayed connected to the river this time of year, shortly after the rainy season, when the water level was still high. But most of the year, it was a self-contained swamp, the narrow channel we'd just passed through becoming a bridge of land during the drier seasons.

Maggie guided the way with her gesturing hands as the pilot eased the skiff forward. The floodlight caught a post sticking out of the water, a bouquet of ferns sprouting from the top. Then another post emerged from the black, a second remnant of a long since collapsed dock. The pilot glided us alongside the sparse collection of pilings to a large, stilted house that stood at least two meters above the water.

"There." Josephs pointed at a rope ladder dangling over the edge of a grand wraparound porch. The pilot idled the motor and let us coast the last bit to where Josephs grabbed the ladder. Holding us in close, he let Maggie start up first. Then went Deluski. I followed with my one-handed best. Going up wasn't bad. Getting over the top was a challenge. Deluski had to drag my ass over by snatching hold of my belt.

Last, Josephs handed up a couple flashlights before starting the climb himself.

Maggie and Deluski ran the flashlight beams up and down
the outer walls, illuminating peeled paint and furry moss. The
place must've been something in its day, a vacation home built
on a broad platform that had fared better than the dock since
being abandoned who knew how many decades ago, probably
when the spaceport was built so close.

We headed for the front door, the decking littered with brandy
empties. I spotted a huffed-up tube of glue. Lizard-man was a
huffer. I bent down and touched a finger to the spillover near
the tube's cap. It felt tacky. He'd been here recently.

I let Josephs bag the tube. If we were lucky, we might score
a fingerprint.

Deluski stopped next to a hole in the floor and kept his light
trained on it until we'd all safely passed. Josephs scraped open
the single-hinged door. Inside, an old sofa sat in the middle of
a large room, where there was more seating in the form of
overturned crates and shine tubs. Curlicues of stripped wall-
paper clung to the walls. So did the stink of stale booze.

This was a party den—tin cups and shot glasses, cig butts
and O pipes, ashtrays made of cans sliced in half. A pile of shattered bottles sat under a broken-out window, the sill badly
chipped and pocked. The local sport must've been throwing
empties through the window from the couch.

Flashlights scanned the floor, where condom wrappers had
gathered like fallen leaves. Deluski threw a light on a flickering poster strung from a dead chandelier, the strobing image
some kind of music vid. "Teenagers."

"Yep," said Josephs. "Horny little bastards must come at
night."

Maggie aimed her light at a staircase. "Samusaka's body was
found upstairs."

We stepped forward, floorboards creaking, and filed up the
stairs. I felt the rumble before I heard it, a launching spacecraft

shaking the steps under my feet. We topped the staircase, Maggie in front, Deluski right behind, Josephs and me in the back. The spacecraft's roar intensified, walls shaking, our eardrums rattling with thought-piercing racket.

I plugged an ear against the deafening roar. I trailed in back, my nose wrinkling at the twinge of death on the air.

I followed the rest into a bedroom. The smell was getting riper, the screeching roar digging, drilling into my skull.

I scoped the scene, seized by the image before me. My jaws clenched and my innards twisted. The image overwhelmed me, my eyes protesting as much as my bombarded ears. Decibels drowned out all thought.

Two beheaded bodies were propped on a mattress. One on all fours, the other kneeling. Mounting. The bodies posed for an assfuck. They looked like mannequins, their skin shiny like polished plastic. But the smell. The smell left no doubt this was real flesh and bone.

The ship's roar faded, replaced by a ringing in my ears. Drawing closer, I could see they were dickless, with meaty red gashes where their genitals should be. A meter-long spike ran through the two of them, pinning them together like a toothpick through a stuffed flatbread. It ran through the lower back of the kneeler, into the anus of the one on all fours, then protruded out the crotch wound, the single spike making a reasonable facsimile of both their missing hard-ons.

They wore their badges, the pins running through their right nipples. Froelich and Wu.

"What the hell are we dealing with?"

I didn't realize I'd asked the question aloud until Josephs responded. "A fairy. One fucked-up fairy." His voice sounded distant over the hollow ringing in my ears. "He actually cut their dicks off," he said to himself as much as anybody. "Heads and dicks both. Beheaded 'em two times."

My arm twitched with the firsthand memory of the killer, teeth sunk into my flesh, reptilian eyes reflecting back inhumanly.

Maggie moved up for a closer inspection. "How are they staying upright?" She was over the shock, her mind already reasoning, analyzing. She tapped one on the arm with her flashlight, a solid clink sounding back. "They've been dipped in something like varnish."

Deluski rushed out. Nobody tried to stop him.

Josephs snickered. "Punk's got weak knees."

I didn't let Josephs's words penetrate as my mind struggled to inch forward, wheels slowly turning with the need to make sense of the senseless.

Froelich and Wu had been here before, in this very room. They'd investigated Franz Samusaka's death and ruled it an accidental OD. They said his missing member was munched away by lizards postmortem. And they got a powerful family like Samusaka's to accept it.

I couldn't fathom why Froelich and Wu would cover for this cock-chop bastard. Why sweep away Samusaka's murder with lies?

Froelich knew Samusaka. They had matching tats. Friends? Lovers?

Nothing made sense. Nothing.

"The killer craves attention," Maggie said.

"Cocksucker's got flair," responded Josephs. "I'll give him that."

I nodded my head in silent agreement. The killer reveled in his work. He must've been pissed when his killing of Samusaka was passed off as a bullshit OD, his art tossed in the trash as idle scribble.

He wanted attention, wanted everybody to know who he was, what he was capable of. He'd been ignored before, and

Froelich and Wu had to pay for showing such disrespect. He'd brought what was left of their corpses back to the site of their crime. And in doing so, he'd retroactively claimed credit for Samusaka. He was erasing all doubt, doing his best to get the attention he deserved. His head-tossing, child-killing, assfuck-posing best.

We'd returned to the living room, Maggie, Josephs, and I. We'd come to escape the smell, but the stink of my mutilated crew members stayed with me, in my clothes and nostrils.

Josephs shined a light through the window. "You out there?"

Deluski stepped into the beam, hand over his eyes. "Yeah." His voice didn't sound right, like he was out of breath. He wiped his cheek on his shoulder.

"You cryin'?" asked Josephs.

Deluski turned his back. The kid had finally cracked, like his newfound freedom had set him free to feel. I wished I could console him. But that shit wasn't me.

Josephs swung his light on me. "Why are you and your boy cryin' all the time? What kind of pussy-ass show you runnin'?"

I let his words pass through me. Not in the mood.

Maggie moved her light around the room. O pipes. Chewed leather shoes. An empty box of rubbers. "The killer must've spent significant time here. He's dropped bodies here twice now. This place is important to him."

"Maybe he was slumming here."

"Or he's a student. There's a prep school ten minutes down-river."

"Is that where you went?"

She put her phone to her ear and asked for San Juan Diego Academy. To me, she said, "No. It's for the troubled kids. Uniforms and curfews."

"Hey, boss," called Deluski from the window. "Come check this out."

I stepped over and leaned through the broken-out frame. I tried to get a good look at the kid, see if he was still crying, but couldn't see more than a shadow. His light was aimed at a tree. "You see it? Right there on that branch."

I saw it. An iguana, eyes reflecting like little pools of molten brass. Over the eyes stood row after row of don't-fuck-with-me spines. The spines ran halfway down his back like a cape of thorns. "What about it?"

"Is that the kind of lizard the killer turned into? See the rust-red stripes on his cheeks."

"No. Our guy didn't have spines."

"Do you remember how many stripes?"

I couldn't remember. Didn't want to. Steel teeth clamped down. Flesh ripping, tearing off the bone.

"Well?"

"Quit bugging me with this shit."

"Don't you want to know why he shifts into a lizard?"

I shook my head and swung around. Maggie was off the phone, waiting for me. "Franz Samusaka was a student at San Juan Diego Academy. Graduated two years ago."

I bit my lip, gnawed on the new fact. This place was a hooky haven. A place for troubled kids to get in more trouble. The killer could've been Samusaka's classmate.

Deluski rapped on the wall. "Somebody's coming."

I stopped breathing and listened, the distant buzz of an approaching outboard motor sailing through the broken window. Instinctively, I reached for my piece. But I had no piece. Or a hand.

Maggie and Josephs fared better, lase-pistols drawn and already moving for the door.

We stepped outside. Deluski kept his back to us. "I think there's two boats."

Josephs pounded his way to the porch's edge. "Who are these bastards?"

Maggie pressed her flashlight into my chest. "Go inside. You too, Deluski. We'll tell whoever it is that this is a crime scene."

I squinted at the dark, my eyes straining to see the approaching boats.

"Go inside," Maggie insisted. "We can handle this."

Deluski headed inside; I still couldn't see his face. He tugged my shoulder, and I let him guide me, allowed myself to be backpedaled inside the door. He pulled the door most of the way shut, and I stood with him, shoulder to shoulder, watching the boat lights through the cracked door until the lights disappeared under the plane of the porch. We moved to a window and stood on opposite sides. I watched and waited, broken glass under my shoes, shards pressing into my soles, jagged breaths puffing out my mouth. I kept my eyes zeroed on the rope ladder, half-hitches wrapped around rusted cleats.

Maggie and Josephs stood outside, their backs silhouetted by dim haloes. Maggie tucked her weapon into a pocket. Josephs dropped his to his hip and gave us a wave. I breathed easier. Whoever had arrived wasn't a threat.

I could see Maggie and Josephs talking, their hands gesturing, but I couldn't hear their voices, the sound swallowed by motors.

Engines silenced. The rope ladder tensed, rope scraping against the decking. Hands came over the porch's edge, then a head, blocky features under wavy black hair. Lieutenant Rusedski, Homicide.

"It's the good guys," said Deluski, his voice solid, his emotional episode apparently forgotten. "Wanna go out?"

I weighed my options. I didn't know where I stood with

KOP. Mota had been telling lies about me, spreading rumors. The bastard had tried to implicate me in his boyfriend's decapitation.

I half listened as Rusedski gave Maggie the biz: *What are you doing here . . . I took you off the case . . . I should bounce you out of Homicide . . . you call yourself a squad leader. . . .*

Maggie took the punches with stoic poise. Josephs let her take the heat. Prick stood off to the side, doing the innocent bystander routine. Finally he spoke up, asked how Rusedski knew to come here.

The killer tipped them off. Called the tip line himself.

By this time, several med techs had climbed the ladder, piling up cameras and lights. Hommy dicks milled. They'd soon be ready to come inside. Lights flicked on, the porch bathed in eye-piercing bright white.

I had to make a decision: run away or face Rusedski.

KOP couldn't be serious about me. Rusedski would have questions but nothing more. I couldn't see it any other way. Mota's rumor mill must've collapsed by now, blades falling off as Rusedski's task force looked at the evidence. Witnesses had seen the killer eat my arm in that sweatshop. KOP would have sketches of him. They had his voiceprint too, now that he'd called in. They knew he wasn't me.

Nothing to fear.

What else was I going to do anyway? No fucking way was I going to jump in the river again. She'd been a bitch to me.

I ducked and stepped through the window. Sore muscles creaked and moaned, made me regret my choice of exit.

My appearance silenced all conversation. Unis and med techs and hommy dicks looked at me, then the void where my hand should be, then at Rusedski, who hadn't noticed me yet, back to me, then the rope ladder, people still coming up, eyes back on me.

I didn't like the way they looked at me. Like I was a storm cloud about to ruin their picnic.

Deluski appeared alongside me. I gave him a questioning look. He seemed as confused as I felt.

Rusedski noticed me now, his eyes bouncing between me and the ladder. Hands came over the porch's edge. Grabbing a cleat, a man pulled himself up the rest of the way. He stood straight, with a fine nose, expressive eyes, and a tailored uniform with a glistening badge under captain's stripes.

My upper lip curled into a snarl, my hand into a fist.

Nobody spoke. Nobody moved.

The jungle closed in on me, its humming monotone scratching at my pulsing eardrums.

His lips curled into a smug smile.

I wanted to pound that nose. Drive a fist into his slick smile. I'd done it before, pulped that pretty face of his. Him tied to a chair, me teaching him not to cheat the chief. Teaching him four knuckles at a time.

But this wasn't the time.

Mota came toward me. "Juno." He extended his hand. "Truce?"

The bastard was putting on a show, acting like he was the bigger man. My jaw was squeezed too tight to speak. He and Panama killed Kripsen and Lumbela, pulled their tongues out their throats.

I felt eyes on me. Cops and med techs. Maggie and Josephs and Deluski.

And Mota—long lashes planted around bright whites. He stood there with his hand stretched out, taunting me.

I rushed him, planted my shoulder in his gut, drove my legs through the impact, and brought him down in a crunch of cracking wood. Shades hanging on one ear, I used my weight to hold down his squirming form. I wedged my stump under his chin and brought down my fist.

Fire exploded in my eyes, a thousand needles dipped in chili paste. I sucked wasps into my lungs. I couldn't see, couldn't breathe. I rolled off him and swiped at my eyes with my shirt-sleeves.

Mota grabbed me by the hair. My burned scalp went electric with pain. On a gust of hot air, a whisper blew in my ear: "I'll cut your throat next." I felt it in my ear canal, the searing burn of chemicals. It was still on his breath, whatever he'd spat in my face.

He let me go and voices gathered. Hands grabbed hold and pulled me to my feet. I tried to cough out the wasps, wracking, stabbing, excruciating pain. I let myself be led, Maggie's voice nearby. A shove sent me over.

The river took me. She kissed my eyes with cool water. I filled my mouth, let her rinse out the chemicals, cleanse the pain. River wasn't such a bad bitch after all.

nineteen

I STRODE down Bangkok, 'mander-on-a-stick in my left. I bit
off a leg and crunched it down, hot sauce sizzling on my tongue.

Rusedski had been a pain in the ass. After I'd refused to go
down to the KOP station, he kept me at the scene for three
hours, asking his questions, grilling me on how I knew Froelich. And Wu. *What's with you and Mota?*

*Why are you wearing those sunglasses? You have an eye condi-
tion?*

Three hours I'd had to put up with his shit, my face still
burning with whatever Mota had spat in my eyes. I did a lot of
coughing. A lot of tear dabbing. Even more stonewalling.

Three hours. I was there when he chased away Maggie,
Josephs, and Deluski. I was there when Mota took off with a
self-satisfied wink, and when they knocked the railing off the
staircase so they could carry Froelich and Wu's shellacked
bodies down, somebody's bright idea to carry them by their
skewer, three dumb-as-hell med techs on each end of the pole,
hauling Froelich and Wu down the stairs like they'd bagged
big game on a safari.

Un-fucking-real.

I put the stick up to my mouth and bit off the shoulders
along with half of the torso. I really did need to eat more
often.

Bangkok Street was prepping for a long night of partying.
Street vendors arrived on bikes, umbrella-topped grills in

tow. Strippers headed to work, high heels dangling from their hands, skimpy numbers on hangers. Offworld kids sat in restaurants, shopped for souvenirs, and generally acted like the pampered brats they were. Debauchery would be coming soon.

I gnawed off what was left on the stick and dropped the splinter of Lagartan bamboo on the ground. I stopped for a bag of soda and sucked it dry as I watched the place across the street. The upstairs lights were on.

I borrowed a phone from a street vendor and called Josephs. The results on Lizard-man's tube of glue were finally in. As I'd expected, Lizard-man hadn't been careless enough to leave us the gift of fingerprints.

I had to find another way to ID him.

I looked at the door, the door I'd come out one hand less than when I went in. Lizard-man could shift. The fork-tongued fuck could turn his hand into a steel trap. And Lizard-man wasn't the only one who had been enhanced. Mota had his mouth modified so he could spit liquid fire without burning himself in the process. Did that mean false lips and eyes? Artificial skin?

Locals didn't usually go for that kind of shit. Even the rich ones. Tummy tucks and tit jobs were more their style. Face-lifts and erection extensions. To shift like Lizard-man, that was something different. His skin changed texture. His ears recessed. His tongue split. That was some high-end work. Not the kind of thing you could do with a little silicone or a scalpel and a fat vac. To shift like an offworlder, you needed motors and mind jacks. Digital tissue. Fleets of minibots in the bloodstream.

They must have gotten offworld tech installed somewhere. Somewhere cheap, somewhere with low standards.

They needed the kind of doctor who wouldn't think twice about installing a robo-snatch in Maria's fifteen-year-old sister.

I crossed the street, dodging offworld pedestrians, and gave the door a loud rap. The door swung open. A teen stood in the frame, the boy assistant I'd seen here before, the one with the milky eyes. Like poached eggs with dishwater yolks.

"The doctor in?" I asked with a grin.

"No."

"I can wait." I stepped over the doorjamb and forced him aside.

He put his hand on my elbow. "You'll have to come back later."

I started up the stairs. "Doc! You in, Doc?"

"You c-can't d-do this."

I ignored his stutters. "Doc? Where are you, Doc?" I hit the top of the stairs and started down the hall, pushing open doors on the way. "Doc?" I threw open another door. Tanks on tables, tanks on the floor, stacked all around. Body parts were growing inside, flesh clinging to circuitry, growing around it, enveloping it. Fingers. Hands. Legs. Suspended organs swam in fish tanks.

"Who the hell are you?" A woman's voice.

I spun around to face her. "Hey, Doc, it's me. Remember?" I waved at her with my half-arm.

"I tried to stop him," said the teen, his milky eyes gone sour.

She motioned her servant away with a toss of her hand, kept her eyes on me. "What are you doing here?"

This woman cut off my hand. Cut it off without asking me. But I needed information. Needed to know if she'd done the work on Lizard-man. I needed that name. I capped the well of anger inside me with a casual smile. "I had time to rethink this missing hand. Sorry I was so rude before, but it was quite a shock, losing a part of me."

She squinted suspiciously, her crow's-feet sinking deep into the sands of her face.

I opened my mouth, words stalling in my throat. It wasn't too late to play it straight. To drop the charade and ask my questions like I was a regular cop. Except I wasn't a cop, meaning she had no reason to talk to me.

"You still got that replacement hand?"

She nodded like she'd expected that question. "Have you had your dressings changed?"

"No."

"Come." She stepped down the hall.

I took a last look at the lab, a shiver tickling the hair on my neck. I followed her into an exam room. It could have been the same one I was in before, but muddled memories made it difficult to pin down. I sat on the padded table and unbuttoned my shirt.

She was dressed most undoctorly—silk shirt, tight pants, like she was ready for a night on the town. But the stressed buttons and taut fabric of her shirt didn't fit right over her rack.

Her shirt was wrong. My brain scratched at it. I was missing something.

I took off my own shirt, and she pulled up a stool. Seeing the bloodstained bundle of bandages, she spoke with a scolding tone, "What happened here?"

"Got in a bad scrape."

She let it pass with a head shake and an unfriendly smirk, her chilly bedside manner on full display. Made me want to ask what she thought she was accomplishing with her glasses and salt-and-pepper hair. Why play the middle-aged doctor when you weren't going to back it up with a warm personality? Or any personality at all.

She yanked tape and started unraveling. "I know you said you don't do work to order but—"

"I don't," she interrupted.

I continued on as if I hadn't heard her. "In my line of work I could use something with a little punch, if you know what I mean."

"Be more specific." Her face stayed flat when she talked, her voice unreadable.

"I'm talking weapons."

She took her eyes off the bandages and looked square at me.

"Maria told me about some of the work you do for her hooker friends, so I figured maybe you do stuff for bodyguards like me?"

"You're a bodyguard?"

"Bodyguard. Bouncer. Whatever pays."

She pulled off the last of the bandages, exposing the blood-caked cap affixed to the end of my arm, and the viny tendrils holding it in place. She dug scissors from a drawer and clip-clipped the air.

"Those sterile?"

"I'm a pro. I won't cut you."

I tensed as she leaned in and snipped the first tendril. She pinched the severed piece in her fingers, and I felt a tug as it pulled free. Barely felt it at all.

"So you want a self-defense system?"

"Yes."

"I've done weapons before." I waited for her to elaborate, for her to say she once did a hand that could morph into a steel trap. She snipped another tendril. "You never told me how you hurt your arm."

"Didn't Maria tell you?"

"No."

I had a lie ready. "I took a day job at a bottling plant and got my hand caught in the machinery."

"Bad luck." She dropped another tendril in the trash.

"So what can you do for me?"

She snipped at the tendrils. "I don't take directions from my patients." Her tone was as sharp as her scissors. "I go where inspiration leads me."

"But Maria told me you've installed very specific equipment for some of her hooker friends."

"I let them tell me what area of the body they want me to work on, but that's all. My practice is not a lunch buffet. Only an artist can be trusted to shape the human body."

She pulled the cap off the end of my arm. I didn't look. Didn't want to know what was down there after so much neglect. I kept my gaze focused on her, pictured her with a saw in her hand, going at my arm. *My* arm. I breathed deep, gritted my teeth. *Get a grip.*

She opened up a small pack of gauze, bunched it up in her hand, and poured some alcohol into the center.

I kept my arm still, fighting the urge to jerk free. This butcher cut off my hand.

"Doesn't look too bad." She took a deep whiff of my wound. "You're a lucky one. I don't smell the rot, but I'd like to get some antibiotics into you just in case."

"Sounds good." I tried to sound cool. Calm.

"Be right back." She went out the door.

I wanted to get out of here, jitters tingling in my feet and legs. I didn't want her touching me again. But I hadn't scored any info yet. I told myself I was being paranoid. Just some antibiotics. *You need the antibiotics.* I knew damn well how regular antibiotic injections kept my mother alive a year longer than most.

I could do this. A quick injection, and it would be over. I'd never have to let her touch me again. We could get back to talking about a new hand. Back to steel traps. I could con her into giving me Lizard-man's name as a referral.

A figure appeared in the door. The teen with the clouded eyes. He had a syringe in his hand. "I have your antibiotics." He stepped forward, the syringe filled with clear liquid.

Clear. A sick twinge rolled in my gut. It should be brown. I'd injected my mother plenty of times. Always brown.

"I'll need an arm," he said.

I pointed at his hands. "Wash those things first."

"I already did."

"Wash 'em again so I can see you."

He nodded glumly, turned around, and moved to the sink, setting the syringe on the counter before running the water.

I slipped up behind him, slow, silent. He shut off the water, reached for a towel. I nabbed the syringe, bit off the cap with my teeth. He spun, tried to back away, but I'd already sunk the needle into his thigh. He let out a squeak as I dropped the plunger. Antibiotics my ass.

Milk-filled eyes curdled. His balance shifted. Legs noodled. I left the needle in his thigh and eased him down into a crumpled mass of angled limbs. Couldn't afford to make noise.

I moved to the door, listened first, peeked out second. I crept into the hall and headed for the stairs, the sound of a hushed voice ahead. I pressed my back into the wall, moved toward an open doorway, shoulder blades sliding over bumpy plaster.

"Just get down here." The doctor's voice.

A pause. She was on the phone.

She spoke again. "I'm putting him under until you get here."

I stopped at the edge of the door frame. The stairs were so, so close, but I stayed where I was, afraid to cross the open doorway. I couldn't let her see me. Couldn't give her the chance to unleash whatever offworld tech she had inside her. Recessed lase-pistols? Plague pins? Who the fuck knew?

"Bye."

Shit. I should've gone for it already. I heard footsteps. *Fuck.* I backed down the hall, away from the stairs, and ducked through a door. A bathroom. Stalls and urinals. A shower. Three sinks.

I went for the window, turned the handle and pushed open both sides. I looked out, sized up the drop. Two stories down to a dimly lit alleyway. An ankle-breaker if I ever saw one. Damn. Damn. Damn.

"Juno?" I heard her call from the hallway. She'd found her assistant. "Where are you?" A door slammed down the hall. Then another that sounded closer. "Emil Mota told me who you are. Where are you?"

If I was going to jump it had to be *now*.

But it was too high. Too damn high. I took off a shoe, dropped it out the window, and ran into the shower.

"I wish I'd known who you were the first time you came in. I wouldn't have stopped with your hand." She was in the bathroom, her voice so near, so cold, so cruel.

Heartbeats pounded in my chest, my ears. I peeked through the gap between the mildewed shower curtain and the mossy wall, dewy water soaking into my shirtsleeve.

I could see her now. She was at the window, leaning through to get a good look down. *See the shoe and believe it. Please believe it.* Lungs ached to keep up with my double-timing heart, but I kept my breathing slow and constrained, breaths squeezing in and out of my mouth.

She pulled her head back inside the window. *Believe, bitch.*

Seconds passed. Long, super-stretched seconds.

"It's me again," she said. "He's gone. Bastard jumped out the window."

A pause. She was on the phone again, the device wired somewhere inside her skull.

"He got spooked and ran. You still coming, Emil?"

Pause.

"We're going to Yepala. Book a flyer."

Pause.

"Yes, tonight."

She slammed the window shut, sealed it with a turn of the handle, and moved out of view. I turned my head, pointed an ear in her direction. I listened for footsteps, had to know when she'd left the room.

I heard the hollow sound of wooden soles on tile. *Step, step, step.* Then nothing. Shit. She was having second thoughts. For good measure, she was going to do a quick search. She was going to kill me, take me apart piece by piece and kill me.

I heard a zipper, a rustle of cloth, then the sound of liquid streaming against porcelain. I told myself to breathe again. She was taking a piss.

But I hadn't heard her go into one of the stalls, hadn't heard any of the doors.

I leaned to the right. Carefully. Tentatively. Painstakingly. I edged my eye past the other side of half-drawn curtain. She stood with her back to me, facing the wall.

Understanding bloomed in my head. Her shirt made sense now, why it didn't fit right.

A man's shirt.

She was at the urinal, hands in hose-holding position.

The good doctor had a dick.

twenty

I TOLD the kid to cut the shirt into strips. He was the same clothes vendor I'd come to in my underwear after escaping the doctor's office the first time. He knifed through the shirt, making nice long strips of fabric while I hid behind a row of hanging tees, my eyes zeroed on the doc's door, phone conversations replaying in my head.

Mota was coming to meet her. *Him*. She was a him.

The kid finished, the shirt now reduced to a pile of makeshift bandages. For disinfectant, I dunked my stump into a jar of fly gel, a yellow glob sticking to the end. I put my eyes back on the door and stuck out my arm, told the kid to mummy it up good.

Dumbass doctor should've fried me the moment he saw me. But he tried to get cute with it, playing the good doctor, sending in his pasty-eyed patsy with a needle. Apparently, violent confrontation wasn't the doctor's way. Before this was done, I'd make sure he knew it was mine.

The kid layered on the last strip. He pulled a safety pin from a rusted tin box. "I don't have any tape."

"No problem."

I let him pin it and went back to spying, my bare foot tapping the asphalt.

I spotted a hat poking above the crowd of offworld kids. *Panama*. I watched it come down the street, bobbing on top of the crowd like a leaf on a river.

My pulse punched my temples, and hate stoked the fire inside me. I wanted my weapon. Wanted to feel its cool grip in my palm, feel its heft, finger the trigger. Just a little squeeze was all it would take to loose the fire burning within. Just a little squeeze.

But I had no weapon. I pinched my lip between my molars and squeezed. Panama approached the doctor's door. Mota was with him. I could see him now, the crowd thinning enough to expose his smooth strut.

They went inside. I paid the kid and waited.

It wasn't long before the door opened again. Three of them came out. Mota, Panama, and . . . *I'll be damned* . . .

Raven hair and silk shirt, offworld tech somehow making both blow in a wind that didn't exist.

I knew that guy. The gay bar. He'd hit on me.

He wore the same poured-into pants the doctor had worn inside. The same silk shirt that had barely held together over her buxom chest now draped and shimmered over his muscular frame. This had to be the doctor's regular appearance, his true gender on display.

It must've been quite a shock when he spotted me in one of his favorite haunts, sniffing around, asking questions. He knew me. He'd already cut off my arm. He would've called Mota, told him somebody was asking about Franz Samusaka. Using the phone in his head, he would've transmitted a vid stream of me, and Mota would've told him who I was.

Mota would've come for me, but he couldn't. Not then. Not when he was hiding in the Cellars, lying in wait to ambush my boys.

So he told the doc to sic that damn fly on me. That way he could come for me later.

They moved away from the door, and I noticed spinning snake tats on Mota's and the doctor's cheeks. The same tats as

on Froelich and the dead Samusaka kid. A gay-boy's club was
coming into focus. A matching-tat dick clique.

The crowd quickly engulfed them, everything but the panama hat. I pushed my way through hanging shirts to the
pavement and followed with a tilted, one-shoed gait.

I wracked my brain to remember what she'd been wearing.
Mota's girlfriend. When she came out of the club. Silk shirt.
Tight pants. I was sure of it. Just like the doctor had been wear-
ing inside. Just like he was wearing right this second.

Understanding brought a knowing sneer. They were all the
same person. The gay playboy. The doctor. Mota's girlfriend.
The *same* person.

Mota was *gay*. Not bi. One hundred percent flame just like
Wu thought. His girlfriend was a man, a drag queen who could
raise tits and sink an Adam's apple; a cross-dresser who could, at
will, broaden hips and sprout a big, gaudy mop of hair. A tranny
who swapped out everything but the plumbing.

I was sure that with offworld tech even that was possible,
but evidently, shedding his thing wasn't his thing. Even as a
woman, he pissed standing up.

The panama hat turned right. I sped up to the corner, then
stopped to let the hat reel out far ahead. The crowd was less
dense on the side streets. I'd be easy to spot if I didn't keep my
distance.

Mota and Dr. Tranny. Lovers. Mota and Froelich. Lovers. All
three together. Franz Samusaka too.

They turned again, and the trio ducked through a gate with
armed guards standing on both sides. I strolled straight past,
head down, no eye contact with the guards. I hustled to the
end of the block and stood outside a schlock shop: porn vids,
monitor-tooth necklaces, neckties made to look like brandy
bottles.

I fake-studied a rack of palm-frond fans, my true gaze aimed up the block to the guards holding their posts, the red tips of their cigs glowing with every puff. From this angle, I couldn't read the painted sign over the door, but I knew the place. Bresner's Sky Cab. The biggest flyer rental company on the planet.

I waited for ten minutes, maybe longer—the shopowner giving me the stink eye—until I heard the roar of liftoff. Ear-splitting thunder rumbled down the street. Windowpanes rattled in cheap-ass frames while monitor-tooth necklaces gnashed on their hooks.

The flyer appeared above its rooftop landing pad and passed overhead, lights bearing down, wind lashing my hair. The flyer moved off, the roar growing steadily softer before fading to nothing but the echo in my ears.

They were going to Yepala. On the phone, the doc had said so. They were all in business together, and that business was centered in Yepala. What did that war-torn wasteland have to offer? I knew I'd have to go up there myself to figure out this shit. But not tonight. Tonight I had a social call to attend to. If I wasn't already too late.

I headed up the block and strode between the guards to the office inside. I asked my question and pulled bills from my pocket until I got an answer.

Dr. Tranny had a name. Angel Franklin.

The skiff slid under a dark bridge into a narrow canal. Almost there.

Dr. Angel Franklin. The name washed through my head over and over like foul water through a sewer pipe. I tried to eject it from my thoughts. Time enough to look him up later.

I paid my fare and hopped out of the skiff onto a private dock, walked to shore, then started along a well-lit, fresh-burned trail through jungle scrub. Recent rains made a paste of ashy mud stick to my shoes, my newest pair. I'd needed to replace only the one I'd tossed out the doc's window, but you couldn't buy just one.

I rapped on the back door. Paul Chang's door. I wiped mud off my shoes, scraping them back and forth over a coarse-bristled mat. The door swung open, a stranger waving me into the kitchen with a drunk grin. Didn't know the guy. Likely one of Pei's relatives. Paul's wife came from a family so big that Paul used to joke about needing name tags.

Catering staff stood at large sinks with steamy water running over clacking dishes. I was late. Paul's son's graduation party was about wrapped.

I walked through the kitchen, which was cavernous enough to be gaudy. Paul liked to show off, and the deceased chief had the money to do it. Selling KOP's services to the Bandur cartel yielded a sweet income.

Acting as his enforcer, I'd made a nice haul myself. Not that I had much to show for it. Spent most of it as it came in, and dropped most of the rest on Niki's medical bills, all that money wasted trying to save a woman who wanted to die. I would've given anything to save her. Anything. But she didn't want to be saved.

I centered my shades on my nose and looked at what was left of the cake. Less than half remained, but it had clearly been shaped like a badge. *Congrats Robert* was written in icing. Paul's son a cop. What would Paul have thought? My first instinct said proud, but considering how Paul's reign ended, with him disgraced and a hole blasted through his head, I couldn't be sure.

I exited the kitchen and entered the dining room. The caterers had set up quite a spread, platter after platter of picked-over cured meats and spiced fruit. A basket of bread sat at the table's end. I reached for a piece, but stopped when I saw the mold spots. Couldn't leave bread out for more than a couple hours.

I'd spent a lot of nights in this room. Niki and I. Paul and Pei. Knocking back a few, eating dinner, knocking back a few more.

I palmed an empty spot on the table where Niki used to sit, felt the cool wood against my skin. I shouldn't have drunk so much those nights. The memories would be clearer now, easier to reach, easier to touch.

It was right here at this table that I'd told Pei about Paul, told her he was dead. Told her he had been murdered. Told her KOP was going to sell it as a suicide. No, she couldn't fight it. The mayor and the new chief were in control now. She *had* to swallow it. She had to accept that her husband would forever be remembered as a criminal and a coward. If her kids were going to have any future at all, she had to swallow it.

One of the caterers came in, started bussing platters. I moved into the living room. Only a dozen or so hangers-on were still milling about, mostly cops, longtime vets and pensioners. Eyes avoided my face, checking out my arm with sideways glances.

These were Paul's loyalists. His inner circle. There was a time they all reported to me, but that was a long time ago. Now, they didn't know how to deal with me. They knew I had no choice but to turn on Paul. I had to agree to testify against him. It was the only way to keep Niki out of jail. But justified or not, I was still a traitor. You don't clap a traitor on the shoulder and ask him what he's been up to. You don't give him a mock punch in the gut and tousle his hair. You don't shoot the shit or tell the old stories. You don't talk to a traitor at all.

Pei marched up to me in white pearls, gold earrings, long red-lacquered nails, strappy high heels jabbing the floor. "Nice of you to show up." She noticed my dangling sleeve, grabbed hold of the empty part to verify the vacancy. "What happened?"

Every eye in the room was now fixed on me. "Robert here? I came to congratulate him."

Using my sleeve as a leash, she led me away from the stares, back into the privacy of the dining room. "He moved on to another party over an hour ago. You let him down, like always. Now what happened?"

"Will you tell him I came by? Tell him I'm sorry I missed him."

She was much shorter than me, her neck craned back to look me in the eye. She pulled my shirtsleeve down like the branch of a Lagartan melon tree, then pulled my face down like it was some out-of-reach fruit, pulled it down so she could machete it off.

"You didn't have a service for Niki, you bastard. How could you do that to her?"

I poked my chest with my thumb. "My wife. My decision."

"She was *my* friend, damn you. You robbed me of the chance to say good-bye." She tossed the sleeve from her long-nailed hand. "You always wanted to keep her to yourself, didn't you? Well, she wasn't yours. You didn't own her."

I felt my cheeks heating, my heartbeat knocking at my ribs. I didn't need this shit. Words bubbled up inside me. Bad words. Hateful words. But this was Paul's wife. *Show some respect.*

"Where did you get those glasses?" She snatched them off my face and inspected the frames.

Chandelier light made me squint. I held out my hand, curled my fingers a couple times as if to say, *Gimme.*

She held my shades up to the light in order to read the fine print on the frame. "Where did you get these?"

"I found them in a box. Niki must've given them to me."

"They were Paul's."

I didn't understand.

"I bought them as a birthday gift when we were still dating. He said he lost them."

What was she talking about? I felt dizzy, reached for a chair.

"See." She pointed at the frame. "I had them personalized. It says *Paul Chang* right here."

I forced out the question I didn't want to ask. "How did the glasses get in my closet?"

The makings of a spiteful grin formed at the corners of her mouth. "You didn't know?"

I pulled the chair close, leaned against it. Needed it to keep upright. A giant hole was burning in my chest.

"Remember when Paul and I split up for a few months after he was promoted to captain? You and Niki were going through a rough patch around the same time. The first year after you two got married, you were always going through a rough patch." She spoke like she was dishing to her gossipy friends, her fingers wrapped around my heart, lacquered nails digging in. "Paul told me about it when we got back together. He told me *all* about it."

I had to get out of here. *Now.* Forcing shaky feet into action, I went toward the door and banged my way through. A caterer steered clear as I rushed across the kitchen—heads snapping my way—and busted out the back door like a drunk in sudden need of a toilet.

I swallowed bile and hurried down the narrow path toward the river, away from this house and the people inside it. I kicked at one of the lights stuck in the ground, uprooted the thing and would've sent it flying if not for the cord that ran through it to the other lights. I went for the lightbulb with a heel, busted it in a pop of shattered glass.

I went off the path, shoes slip-sliding over scorched, muddy earth until thick, black jungle stood tall all around me. I took a swing at it, my fist busting through leaves and fronds, rage filling the hole in my chest.

Niki and Paul.

Paul and Niki.

Screaming, I lunged deeper into the jungle, arms swinging like sickles, breaking stems under my feet. I grabbed with my left hand, ripped and pulled at the foliage, clumps of torn greenery coming free. I struck a thin tree with my right arm, took hold of the skinny bastard and tried to uproot the fucker, but a thousand vines refused to let it go. I punched at the vines, chopped at them with the blunt blade of my right arm, and yanked at the tree again. I kicked and pushed and yanked and shoved. The bastard was coming down!

I pulled with all my might, sweat dribbling in my eyes, lungs sucking air. The damn tree wouldn't budge. The jungle never budged.

I let it go and raised a leg to give the stubborn bastard a last karate kick. Ended up on my ass.

I stayed there, waiting for my lungs to quit heaving. Waiting for the sweat to quit dripping. Waiting for my heart to quit ripping into a million little pieces.

twenty-one

ANOTHER day of darkness would begin soon. I'd tossed and turned the night away with sparse dozing, turbulent thoughts, and disturbed images.

Niki and Paul. I told myself that it was a long time ago. Paul had spied on her just like I had. He'd watched her sleep and talk on the phone, watched her put on her makeup and eat her breakfast. It was natural for him to develop feelings, wasn't it? He'd split up with Pei, and Niki and I were fighting like we always did right after we were married. They were both lonely.

I told myself again that was a long time ago. I shouldn't care. I told myself they were dead. I should let them rest.

I told myself a lot of things, but none could yank the thorn of betrayal embedded in my heart.

My wife. My best friend.

I could feel the pressure building in my blood and behind my eyes.

Breathe. Just breathe. This was a perfectly nice bed. It would be a damn shame to smash it up; a shame to rip into the mattress and tear out the stuffing; to snap the frame under stomping feet and demolish the walls with a bedpost sledgehammer. All of it a damn shame.

I *had* to stop thinking about them.

I rolled onto my side. A lopsided curtain hung over the door, lopsided because the withered fabric had lost its grip on a third of the rings. A triangle of light came through where the curtain hung folded over. I followed the glowing beam's path past three figures on the wall—two geckos and one Jesus—followed the beam down to where it died on the floor.

A church guesthouse. That was what this place was, where Maria had set us up for the night. It was one of several attached buildings surrounding a courtyard with a fountain and a blinking sign that read, HE DIED FOR YOUR SINS.

Deluski slept a couple doors down. I'd peeked in on him when I arrived. He'd been snoring with a twisted, strangled sheet snaking between and around his limbs. I wasn't the only one with restless dreams.

I'd also spotted the phone on the dresser by his bed. A cheap, anonymous phone. No doubt, Deluski had used it to erase his movie. First chance he got, he'd connected up and deleted that era of his life.

I stretched out my legs. I could barely see the dimly lit Jesus staring at me from his perch on the crucifix nailed to the wall. He died for my sins. So did Kripsen and Lumbela.

Four dead crew. They weren't all my fault. Lizard-man got credit for Froelich and Wu. But Kripsen and Lumbela, they were on me, victims of my arrogance. *Seize a protection racket. From there, seize KOP.* I was fucking insane to think I could pull off that shit. I wasn't even a cop.

I rolled onto my back . . . fussed with the pillow . . . readjusted the sheet . . . flipped the pillow . . . pulled the sheet back up.

No more of this bullshit. I sat up. No matter how desperate I was to sleep, it wasn't going to happen. I had too many derailed trains of thought, too many poisoned memories.

Niki and Paul.

What the fuck was I supposed to do with that?

I grabbed my pants and struggled to pull them on one-handed. Damn nuisance. I carefully zippered over my skivvyless package

and coaxed my still-sore muscles out to the hall. That run-in
with Mota and Panama in the Cellars had taken a toll on these
tired bones. I ambled down to Deluski's room and shook the
curtain on his door, brass rings jingling on the steel rod.

"Yeah?"

I poked my head through the curtain. "I need your phone."

He picked it off the dresser and tossed it my way. I snatched
it out of the air left-handed and headed back to my room,
pleased that I hadn't tried to make the grab with my missing
right. I was finally catching on.

I kept the light off, stripped off my pants, and dropped back
into bed. I punched in a name: Dr. Angel Franklin.

Born ninety-three years ago. Smooth-skinned bastard kept
himself young. Offworlders were damn good at defying time,
their bodies riddled with antiaging drugs and a steady supply
of replacement organs. Their life expectancy was more than
double ours.

He was originally from Earth, someplace called Slovakia,
wherever the hell that was. Started the fourteen-year journey
to Lagarto in 'sixty-nine.

Fourteen years. Nobody made that trip anymore. Not since
the brandy market tanked. The Earth–Lagarto trade route was
called the sucker's rainbow now, named for the fourteen-year
stream of immigrants who arrived after the economy collapsed.
All of them setting off for the promise of work and a new
world. All of them following a rainbow cut through the heavens
to the pot of gold called Lagarto. A decade and a half's worth
arrived after the collapse, my great-grandparents among them,
all of them caught in transit after the pot of gold had already
been looted and picked clean.

Yet Dr. Angel Franklin made the same voyage. Why coop
himself up inside a metal tube for more than a tenth of his life
to come to this green hell?

I checked out his professional history, and the question answered itself. He lost his medical license in 'sixty-eight, revoked for ethical violations. That was all it said. *Ethical violations.* He'd set off for Lagarto just a few months later.

He'd come here to practice medicine, or his twisted version of it, away from the rules and the regulators, to a place where rules were for sale.

I heard the clacks of high heels on tile coming this way. The curtain swung aside. Backlit explosion of hair. Miniskirt silhouette. Maria. "You like the place?"

I set the phone on my chest and turned on the light, carefully propped the pillow under my head to keep from aggravating my burned scalp. "I owe you one."

"You owe me more than one. Don't you ever sleep?"

"Not often."

She walked over and slumped into a chair by the bed. Her breasts were squeezed into a faux-leather halter top.

"Long night?" I asked.

"Long but quiet."

"Business slow?"

"Not bad. By quiet, I meant no problems."

"Chicho know you're gone?"

She shrugged her shoulders and turned up her palms. "I don't know. I doubt he'd care this time of night. The johns are all gone except for the all-nighters, and they never cause trouble. Any luck with whatever you're working on?"

I mimicked her don't-know gesture.

"You know, you never told me what you were after in all this."

"That's because it keeps changing."

"What's the latest?"

"I'd settle for catching the bastard who did this to me." I waved my right arm. "That, and stopping Mota."

"What about expanding your protection business?"

"That can wait." Despite my promise to Maggie, I couldn't bring myself to say I was giving it up. Truth be told, I wasn't sure that was a promise I could keep. "What do you know about the doctor?"

"No more than you already know."

"Keep away from him."

"Her."

I shook my head. "She's a he."

"Really?"

"Stay away from him."

"Why?"

"He works with Mota."

"On what?"

"No idea, but don't trust him with your sister."

"Where else am I supposed to get the work she needs?"

"I'm sure the johns love her just the way she is."

"I'll think about it," she said, absent sincerity. She unstrapped her shoes and kicked them off. "Can I use your shower?"

"Help yourself."

She stood and disappeared into the bathroom. A knob squeaked and pipes clanked somewhere under the floor before I heard the sound of sputtering, drizzling water.

I didn't want her getting any ideas when she came out. I picked up my pants, and after thinking on it a bit, decided to try the lying-down method of pulling them on. A minute's labor proved the method promising.

I brought the phone back to Deluski, woke him up to tell him we were leaving in an hour.

Back in my room, I reached for my shirt when Maria came from the bathroom, towel wrapped around her, wet hair slicked back, her cheeks stripped of rouge, her lips bare. She crinkled up her brows in disapproval, like she was upset I'd dressed. "You have a comb?"

I shook my head no as I pulled on my shirt. I sat on the bed and started on the buttons. Why so many?

She took a seat at the end of the bed and combed her hair with forked fingers. Free of her high hair and her makeup mask, she looked like a different person, loud features turned plain, muted. I put my eyes on my buttons.

"You were married for a long time, weren't you?"

I gave a slight nod, a bare-minimum response for a subject I didn't want to discuss.

"Did you love her?"

I looked at Maria. She'd stopped combing. With no makeup to cover it, a faint mark from one of my knuckles still showed on her cheek.

"It was complicated."

"Complicated how?"

"It just was."

"Knowing how it ended, if you could, would you trade away your time together?"

I didn't know. I suspected I never would.

"Would you?"

A larger truth came to mind. "If I could, I'd trade my whole life away."

She combed her hair again, her fingers catching on a knot. She worked at it with two hands until she pulled it free. "You're a strange man." She held her hand over the floor and shook a couple strands off her fingers. "Never heard of anybody taking over a group of brothels, but not going for freebies."

I went back to the buttons. Stupid things were tricky as hell.

"Christ, will you let me do that?"

"I got it."

She tugged on my sleeve. "Get over here."

I stood and stepped in front of her, smelled shampoo and hints of perfume trapped in her hair.

"You didn't line 'em up right. It's all out of whack." She undid the misaligned button. And another one. She reached inside my shirt, her hand warm against my chest.

"You don't want me," I whispered. "I'm damaged."

She slid her hand down my stomach, tingles drifting south. "I'm damaged," I repeated. "Broken."

She touched my arm. "It's okay. I'm damaged too." She freed the towel, terry cloth falling down to her waist. Her hands were back on my chest, wandering downward, as were my eyes.

Now I understood why she'd quit hooking. Why she *had* to quit hooking. I wanted my sunglasses. I needed a shield, needed something to dim this painful reality.

She took my good hand, put it on her right breast. "You can't tell when you can't see." She waited for me to say something, her fear-filled eyes tottering at the edge of a cliff.

I answered with my hand, fingers touching, squeezing, caressing, as if her breasts weren't scarred. As if she hadn't let some cheap, back-alley plastic surgeon hack her up. I touched them with my lips.

As if they were normal.

I touched with my half-arm.

As if I had a hand.

A clique of girls came into the library, voices at volumes only teens could achieve. Plaid skirts, *SJD Academy* embroidered on matching white blouses. Upon spotting the librarian's stern stare, they silenced themselves, faces contorted with suppressed laughter. They dropped books on the counter and busted back out the door, laughter like shattering glass. Maggie watched them go, a quirky smile on her face.

"Remind you of your school days?" I asked.

"The early days."

"Before your father died?"

She nodded, eyes sobering, the smile unquirking. "Find anything?"

"Not yet." I went back to the holo-pics, jumping one-by-one, holo after holo, Franz Samusaka's former schoolmates flashing by. Zits and chin fuzz. Slicked-back hairdos and caterpillar mustaches. Two more years of senior photos to go and so far, no sign of Lizard-man.

"Thanks for coming," I said.

She responded with silence, its barren emptiness ballooning in my chest. I couldn't do anything right. I said what needed to be said anyway. "Your help means a lot to me."

She didn't meet my eyes. Instead, she pretended to be interested in checking her earrings, like she thought they could've fallen out since we'd been sitting here.

I groped for something to say, desperate to find something that could penetrate the wall standing between us. "Where's Josephs?"

She drummed the table with her fingers. "Sleeping in. He said he'd meet up with us later."

"Does he know we're going to Yepala later?"

"I thought we could surprise him."

"He's going to throw a goddamned fit."

A sly grin formed. "Looking forward to it."

Deluski came through the double doors, back from the bathroom, and dropped into a wooden chair scarred with carved graffiti. Tall shelves stood behind him, rows and rows of mildew-stained books, the aging paper making the room smell old.

I stole another glance at Maggie's smile, soaking in as much of it as I could before I voice-ordered the yearbook forward, one holo shifting into the next, kid after kid, the same damn repetitive poses: the smile-into-the-camera look, the thoughtful chin-resting-on-fist look, the looking-off-into-the-future look. I stopped on a name. The kid I didn't recognize, but I did the name: Ang Samusaka.

"A brother?" asked Deluski.

"Looks like it. Why don't you go ask the librarian?"

He stood and went to her desk. Maggie leaned my way. "How long you going to keep him under your thumb?"

I rubbed my smarting arm. "I set him free already."

"Really?"

"He destroyed the video himself."

"But he's still working for you?"

"He wanted to see this case through. Kripsen, Lumbela, and the others were his friends. After this is over, I don't know. If he's smart, he'll go back to being a regular cop."

"Think he's smart?"

I shrugged my shoulders. *We'll see.*

"You know, it's nice to see your eyes again."

It took me a second to realize I wasn't wearing my shades. Paul's shades. I'd worn them long enough that I could still feel the plastic resting on the bridge of my nose, stems hooked over my ears. Ghost shades to go with the ghost pain in my hand.

"You done hiding?" she asked.

I tuned into my own breathing, air moving in and out, lungs inflating and deflating. I tuned into the other signs of life. My heartbeat. The ache in my missing hand. The pleasant memory of recent sex.

She waited for my answer. I put my good hand on her knee, felt the warmth through her pants. "I'm done hiding."

"That's good." She patted my hand. "That's real good."

I took my hand back and reluctantly, remorsefully forced my brain out of the moment, back into the past, focused it on my first sight of the lizard-man, standing in the doorway, Wu's lower jaw in his hand. I conjured up the killer's face as I navigated from pic to pic. Searching for that wild mop of hair. Those disturbed eyes. That cold gaze.

Seven years of class photos. Samusaka's class and the three years before and after. Close to the end now, the last year of San Juan Diego Academy's privileged but troubled youth cycling by.

"That's it." I rubbed tired eyes. Lizard-man wasn't a student here. He knew Samusaka some other way. Knew about the party pad where he killed Samusaka and later posed Froelich and Wu's bodies some other way.

Deluski came back. "Ang was Franz's brother. Graduated last year. Last the librarian heard, he was living in a hotel off the Square. She hears the kids talking about it. Sounds like he hosts a lot of parties there."

"Anything else?"

"I made a quick call to a cop friend I used to work with—"

"Did you use your new phone?"

"Yeah."

I felt an uptick in my pulse. "Why the hell did you do that? You should've borrowed the school's."

"I wanted to see if—"

"Ditch the phone."

He rolled his eyes. "The phone's anonymous."

"Not anymore. Dump it."

"This was a friend I called. He's not going to tell anybody."

I pointed my short arm at the trash can.

He rolled his eyes and tossed in the phone. The loud, metallic clunk drew a scolding stare from the librarian. Librarians must practice that shit.

"You know Maggie still has her phone. Mota could track us through her."

She shook her head no. "Mine's anonymous. I hid my police issue under the seat of a taxi."

I smiled at the thought of Mota following a taxi all around town. "What did your friend tell you?"

"I had him look up Ang to see if he has a record. He wasn't in the system except for a call he put in to report a B-and-E at his parents' house. I checked the date. It was only a month before his brother was killed. Think we oughta check it out?"

Hotel Koba. Ten minutes of asking around the school had scored us the name of the place. We followed the arrow down a set of stairs to a basement door and pushed our way through. Stone floors and sculpted light fixtures. Thick rugs under monitor-hide chairs. A front desk made of polished wood with a backdrop of gold-tinted mirrors.

"Ang Samusaka," I said to the desk clerk, a teenage girl in a purple hand-me-down uniform with overly long sleeves folded up at the wrists and a worn-through collar.

"Let me see if he's in." She touched a number on an airborne holo-grid to her right. "May I ask who's calling?"

"No."

Lines in her forehead arched at my curt response. "Um." She gestured at her earpiece. "It's ringing right now."

We waited.

"He's not answering." Not *He's not in*, but *He's not answering.*

"No problem. What's his room number?"

She hesitated until Deluski waved his badge. "Three-o-three."

Maggie pushed the elevator's up button, and steel doors slowly cranked open with a metal-on-metal scrape. Inside, a chamber-maid struggled with a tippy towel hamper that was missing a wheel from one of the front corners.

I reached with my half-arm but came up short. *Dammit.*

Deluski beat me to it, used his big hands to lift the cart's front end over the gap between the elevator and the floor.

We stepped into the now vacated elevator. The humid stench of soggy towels clung to the walls. The elevator banged and groaned up to the third before the doors took their time scraping open. We walked down the hall, shoes sinking deep into plush carpet.

Deluski rapped on the door. A punk kid answered, dark skin and fried eyes. No shirt, no shoes, wrinkled pants. Not him.

"We want to talk to Ang Samusaka."

"Ang!" he called over his shoulder before wobbling back inside.

We strode into the young Samusaka's suite and closed the door behind us. The room stank of burned herbs. Damn early for that shit. Another kid slept on the sofa, and to his left, a rolled herbstick burned on a saucer, and next to it a plate with a half-eaten frybread. The punk who let us in sat and called for Ang again before snatching up the bread.

A bedroom door opened. Ang came through fastening his pants and nabbed a shirt off the floor. He gave it a shake before pulling it over his shoulders. "Who are you?"

Maggie moved toward him, her shoe avoiding a food scrap on the floor. "We want to talk to you about your brother."

He pulled his shirt over visible ribs and started buttoning. "He's dead."

"We know."

"Who are you?"

Deluski pulled his badge, gave Ang a quick wave.

Ang rolled his eyes while his friend dropped his jaw and swiveled burned eyes between Deluski and the smoldering herbstick. The punk tossed the frybread back onto the plate. "Um, I'm still hungry. I'm gonna get some more food." He nudged the kid sleeping on the sofa. "C'mon, Jose."

Jose's lids slowly cranked open like the hotel's elevator doors.

"Cops are here." The punk shook Jose's shoulders. "C'mon, we gotta go."

Jose's lids couldn't hold, lashes dropping back down like they were weighted.

The punk ditched him and slunk out.

Ang took a seat. "You gonna tell me what you're doing here?"

Maggie pointed at the herbstick. "Put that out."

Ang leaned over and mashed the ashy end into the plate.

"Your brother was murdered."

"Cops said he ODed."

"Did he have a drug problem?"

"He ODed, didn't he?"

"How long have you been living here?"

"About a year."

"Why don't you live at home?"

"I'm an adult. I do whatever the hell I want."

Maggie moved in a step, getting close enough to brace him.

I passed his chair, posted myself directly behind it. People get nervous when they can't see you. He looked over his shoulder to find me, and I nudged myself out of his view.

Maggie leaned down to him. "You reported a robbery at your house."

"No. I reported that somebody broke in."

Smartass.

"He didn't take anything?"

"He didn't take any of my stuff, but he tore up my brother's room. My dad's study too."

"What did he take?"

"I don't know. My father and brother didn't say."

Maggie's eyes narrowed. "What does that mean?"

He twisted in his seat. "You'd have to know my father to understand. Man likes his secrets. My brother was just like him."

Maggie gave him a long, appraising stare before deciding to let it pass. "Was anybody home when he broke in?"

"Miss Paulina was."

"Who's she?"

"Our housekeeper. She was in her living space downstairs. She never heard anything until I came home from school and found the mess."

"How did the burglar break in?"

He shook his head. "Why are you asking me all this crap? Can't you just read the police report?"

I booted his chair. That startled the shit out of him, hands and knees jumping. Over on the sofa, Jose's eyelids flickered and went still. Ang torqued his body all the way around to look at me, his face part surprise, part fear. "What's your problem?"

"She asked you a question."

He faced forward again. "I don't know how he got in." His words were coming out quick now. "The police couldn't figure it out. They said somebody must've left a door open."

Deluski leaned against the arm of the sofa. "Ask him about the tattoo."

"What tattoo?" asked Ang.

"Your brother had a tattoo on his face."

"What about it?"

"What does it mean? Why two snakes?"

"It's a gay thing."

"Explain."

"The snakes are eating each other's *tails*. Get it?"

Maggie stared at him, her eyes processing.

"It's like they're sixty-nining," said Ang, as if he thought he needed to explain things to us old people. "The snakes, they're sucking each oth—"

Maggie put up a hand. "I get it."

"My brother and his friends got their tats at the same time."

"Like they were in a club?"

"I guess."

I pressed myself into the back of his chair, my eyes looking straight down at the top of his head. "Who was in this club?"

He looked up at me, counted on his fingers. "My brother, the doctor, a couple cops."

My thoughts braked on the word "doctor." "What doctor?"

"I don't know his name, but he's an offworlder."

"And the cops?" asked Maggie.

"I only met them a couple times, but they were tight, always holding hands and stuff."

"Names."

"One was called Froelich. Can't say whether that's a first or last name. The other name I don't know. Everybody just called him Captain."

"Good-looking?"

"I don't swing that way."

"Humor me."

"I guess so. My brother sure had eyes for him."

Froelich and Captain Mota. Together with Franz Samusaka and Doctor Tranny. Matching tats all around. All of them into the same shit. Froelich's nongay partner must've gotten dragged in along the way. "Is that it? Just the four of them?"

"Far as I know. I saw each one of them come out of my brother's bedroom at one point or another."

"They do more than screw each other?"

"What do you mean?"

"They had a business going."

"What kind of business?"

"You tell me."

He shrugged. "My brother helped find patients for the doctor, if that's what you mean. The doctor is a plastic surgeon. My brother would get a killer referral fee for all the rich friends he sent over."

"Anything else?"

"Not that I know of."

"Has your brother ever been to Yepala?"

"Sure. He went a few times to visit the doctor. The doc has a clinic up there, one here in the city and one up north."

"What does the doctor do at this clinic?"

"I don't know. I guess he does the same thing he does here."

Maggie jumped in. "You have a job, Ang?"

"No."

"You go to school?"

"Nope."

"Who pays for this place, a nice suite like this?"

"My father."

"You telling me he pays for you to bum around this place with no strings attached?"

Good question. I remembered the way Ang's father talked to his wife, the way she dropped her head like a dog before its master. The man was a control freak.

Before Ang could answer, the bedroom door opened behind me, a teenage girl coming through, her hands fastening the last button of her purple hotel-uniform blouse, a pinned-on name badge over her right breast: Mira Grabowski. "Um, good morning," she said, hands smoothing her hair, then her skirt, gold bracelets jingling on her wrists.

I turned back to Maggie just in time to see the disapproving look on her face. She had a low tolerance for girls like Mira, girls who got ahead by lying on their backs. Maggie dismissed the girl with her eyes and squared them back on Ang. "I asked you a question, Ang. Your father okay with you doping your life away?"

"I do whatever the fuck I want. He doesn't own me." The bravado was back; he was putting on a show for his girlfriend.

The girl walked past me to the center of the room. I told her, "We're having a private conversation here."

She rubbed the big-ass stone hanging off the gold chain around her neck, her gaze moving from person to person until she lingered on her boyfriend's face. "I'm not going anywhere. Who are you people?" Mira to the rescue.

"Yeah," said Ang, his voice gathering strength. "I'm done talking."

I looked at Maggie, Deluski too. I wanted more answers, wanted to use my particular expertise to extract them. But not this kid. This kid was a Samusaka. Big-time money and big-time power. The kind of power that could crush a has-been cop like me.

Best to keep biting around the edges; take what's offered and move on. Besides, when it came to unearthing the Samusakas' family secrets, something told me we'd just begun to break ground.

Deluski pointed to his watch. If we were going to make it to Yepala today, we best get going. We headed for the door, Mira Grabowski following us to make sure we left. I heard her call to Ang just before the door closed us out. "Who the hell were they?"

I followed Maggie and Deluski to the elevator, and we silently rode down to the lobby. We went toward the exit, the girl behind the desk watching us pass. She looked an awful lot like the girl upstairs. I scanned the name badge. *Dora Grabowski.* Sisters.

On a whim, I let Maggie and Deluski go ahead and stopped to talk to her. "What can you tell me about Ang?"

"We don't talk about our guests."

I put on my earnest face, made my voice sound concerned.

"You really want to protect him, knowing how he treats your sister?"

Her brows angled downward. "What are you talking about?"

"Hey, I don't want to cause any trouble, but you know he shares her with his buddies, don't you? She was doing Jose and that other one on the sofa when we walked in on them." I really was a wicked son of a bitch.

She dropped her hands to the desk and shook her head. "I told her from the beginning he was no good."

"Listen, I'd love nothing more than to get him out of her life. Is there anything a cop like me should know about him?"

She leaped at the chance. "He takes drugs."

I sucked a loud breath through my teeth. "Not good enough. You gotta know a family like his can buy him out of small-time trouble like that. Got anything else?"

She fussed with her hair, pulling at the strands hanging by her ear. I glanced back at Maggie and Deluski, who waited by the door, wearing matching quit-fucking-around expressions.

I took another look at the girl, still pulling at her hair, her eyes staring off to nowhere.

Maggie and Deluski were right. This was a waste of time. I turned for the door.

She spoke before I could take a step. "How about blackmail?"

I froze. *Fucking A.* I winked in my partners' direction before facing her. "I'm all ears."

twenty-two

I FELT Josephs's shoe bump my shin again. "Dammit, quit kicking me."

"Don't blame meee," he slurred. "You shoulda got a bigger boat."

"Put that bottle away already."

"Fffuck you, Juno, you stooopid drunk. Like you're one to talk."

I wished I could roll the bastard overboard. The guy had a way of pissing me off like no other. I searched for relief in the black sky, in the few stars that had found a break in the clouds. It had been an hour since we'd seen any onshore lights, the captain's calm piloting and occasional buoys the only signs we were going the right way.

"I still think he staged the break-in," said Deluski.

Five hours on this boat and Ang Samusaka's blackmail scheme still dominated the conversation. According to the hotel clerk, Ang had his father by the curlies, lording an incriminating vid over his head. The clerk had no idea what was on the vid, didn't think her sister knew either, but whatever it was, it was enough for Ang to turn his father's wallet into a help-yourself buffet.

Deluski's theory went like this: Kid and his dad were on the outs for one reason or another, kid decides to rifle his father's things, finds an incriminating vid of some sort, gets walked in on by the housekeeper, makes up a bogus burglary story to cover up the mess he's made of his father's study. Six days later, Ang moves into the hotel.

Maggie's voice came out of the dark. "Still doesn't explain why he raided his brother's room."

"He was trying to throw his father off, to make it look like somebody really broke in."

"But if he wanted to make it look like somebody really broke in, wouldn't he have busted a window or something?"

"I didn't say he was smart."

The hollow ping of a glass bottle sounded off the boat's hull. The bottle clanged around a bit before rolling down to the boat's center. By the sound of it, Josephs had finished the thing off. I leaned forward. "You still with us, Josephs?"

No response. Finally passed out, thank the stars. I should've left his ass on the pier as soon as I saw him buy that bottle. Dumbass wanted to pass it around, like we were going to party our way to Yepala.

Deluski pushed Josephs's knee with his shoe. "Remind me why we brought him along, Maggie?"

"He told me he wanted to stay involved." I could hear the shrug in her voice.

I felt a tap on my shoulder. The boat captain pointed to a cluster of lights up ahead. Yepala.

After jumping ashore to join Maggie and Deluski, I stretched a sore back. Long fucking trip. I checked the time: late afternoon, almost true night.

The charter boat captain aimed a pole at Josephs's slumped form. "What am I supposed to do with your friend?" Josephs's conked head hung straight back, mouth open like he wanted to catch raindrops. One hand was draped overboard, a couple fingers dipped in the water.

"Let him sleep it off. If he wakes up, tell him to stay on

board. You make it real clear, he goes to a bar we'll ditch his ass."

The captain used the pole to push off and revved the motor, the boat powering toward a collection of pilings jutting from the water where he'd tie up and wait for our return.

I took the lead up a narrow trail through a tangle of jungle, keeping to the boards embedded in the mud. Dim lights were strung overhead, and the air was ripe with damp peat. Fronds brushed my arms. Leaves dragged over my hair. I lifted a shoe, pinned a thorny shoot to the ground, and waited for Maggie and Deluski to pass before forging forward.

The jungle opened onto the street. Yepala unfolded on either side, squat buildings facing a rutted road. A motorbike putted by, mom, dad, three kids and a baby heaped on top.

We looked at one another, the same questioning faces all around. Now what?

We turned right—why the fuck not?—and passed in front of a market, blue tarps stretched over tables of piled fruit and spice. Chickens and 'guanas squawked inside cages hanging above butcher blocks. I recognized the market from some of Mota's pictures. He'd spent a lot of time here.

"You need a guide?" I looked down at the voice. A young girl, ten, maybe twelve, pinned-back hair, grunge-stained pants, jellies on her feet with dirt-blackened toes poking through the cracked plastic.

"You know an offworlder with long hair? Says he's a doctor."

She put a finger on her cheek, drew a circle. "Snakes?"

I nodded.

"He has a clinic in the jungle. He comes into town sometimes. I can take you."

Just at that moment, an older boy came out from the market and stepped in front of her. "I know the way. Half hour on foot."

The girl slipped around him, wedged herself between us. "I saw them first!"

He grabbed her by the shoulders and tossed her to the side. "Come, I'll take you."

She threw a punch, fist bouncing off his arm, her follow-up swing catching him in the ribs.

I liked her already.

"Cut it out." He geared up to give her another shove.

I put my hand on his shoulder. "She asked us first."

"But—"

I squeezed down, fingers digging in, words slowing. "We have our guide."

He backed up and ducked out of my grasp. "Don't fucking touch me!"

I took an aggressive step his way, and he darted off.

The girl stood tall, posture proudly erect. "Are you cops?"

Were we that obvious? "Why do you think that?"

"Some cops from Koba come to visit the doctor a lot."

"Do you know their names?"

"No, but one of them has a big scar." She drew a line across her forehead.

Wu.

"How many cops?"

"There's the one with the scar, and then there's the bald one with the same snake tattoo. And sometimes they come with a captain."

Wu. Froelich. Mota.

"What do they do here?"

"They go out to the doctor's to get a cask they take home to Koba."

"What kind of cask? The kind they put brandy in?"

She nodded.

"Do you know what's inside these casks?"

"No."

"So how do we get to the doctor's clinic?"

"If you want to pay for a car, we can drive halfway, but the hills get too steep after that. Too muddy after it rains. Or we can walk the whole thing."

I exchanged glances with my traveling partners.

Maggie bent down to the girl's eye level. "What's your name?"

"Evangeline, but everybody calls me Evie."

"Okay, Evie, I think we'd rather walk. It'll do us good after that boat ride." She didn't mention that we wanted to make a silent approach. Our goal was simple: figure out what the hell was going on up here and go home. No confrontation. Not here.

Evie started down the street, and we fell in line—me in back—keeping to the narrow channels between puddles and clumpy mud. I took a look over my shoulder and scanned the sparsely lit street for a panama hat. This was his turf.

Warlord territory.

We strode past food counters and refurbed tech shops, a clothing store with broken mannequins in the window, amputees sporting sundresses. Somebody called to us. I spotted him up ahead, sitting on a tire, trying to wave us down: a beggar in rags.

I looked away. If you don't want to give, you don't make eye contact.

I heard him call again and chanced another glance his way. He was off the tire now, crab-walking. Something wasn't right about him, the way he moved, crawling backward, his head twisted uncomfortably around so he could see where he was going. Curiosity got the better of me. I stopped and pulled a bill from my pocket and waited for him, his out-of-whack crab-walk striking a freaky chord inside me.

He came closer, his bare feet too short, toes too long. What the fuck? Hands. I realized they were hands.

I bent over and held out the money, waiting for one of his four hands to come off the ground and take it. Something snaked around the bill, wrapped it up tight and pulled it from my fingers. I jumped back, heart kicking. What the hell was that?

He smiled and laughed softly as he crabbed away, the money held up high with his tail.

"Juno," Deluski called. "You better get up here."

My legs obeyed and started moving to catch up, my gaze slow to unlock from the beggar. *What are you?*

I stumbled over a clod of mud and forced my attention forward. Evie was standing next to another young boy with a lase-rifle hanging across his chest. Maggie and Deluski faced them, Maggie digging into her wallet. "He wants money."

"Who is he?"

Evie said, "You have to pay to leave town to the north."

The kid waited with crossed arms, one elbow resting on the weapon's butt, the other on the barrel. His shirtsleeves were cut off, a scar tattoo of the letter Z raised on his arm, the scar tissue too perfectly lined to be made by anything other than a branding iron. I looked left, through the open window of a dance hall. Music played loudly, and a dozen armed boys sat at long tables with longer stares.

A pair of boys not much older than Evie came out squaring berets on their heads. General Z's soldiers. They joined ranks with the first boy.

Maggie handed the kid a bill. He looked at the denomination and shook his head. Maggie added a second. And a third. He still shook his head.

Maggie pulled out yet another bill but Evie stopped her. "That's enough."

The soldier boy stayed where he was. Hand out. Waiting for more. Evie took his hand, closed his fingers around the money, and told him to quit. She put her hands on his hip and pushed. He resisted with a straight face and rigid body. She drove with her legs until he finally tipped. He caught his balance and swung the gun around. "I want more money!"

We froze. Maggie, Deluski, and I were caught in the sights of a pubescent punk playing soldier.

Evie took Maggie's hand and told her to come. "You paid enough. He's just playin'."

Didn't look like he was playing.

Evie pulled Maggie's arm, "C'mon." Maggie took a tentative step, and another, me and Deluski following in her cautious footsteps. I felt an uneasy sickness in my chest. We were foreigners here. Didn't know the players, didn't know the rules. Foreigners.

Another beggar approached, this one a child, a protruding bump under his shirt, head shaved bald with some kind of input jack embedded in the center. *Christ.* Where the fuck were we?

My head swam, anxiety creeping up from my chest and settling around my throat. I pulled the lase-blade handle tucked into my belt, held it tight in my fingers, thumb perched on the button. Deluski paused for a moment to give the kid some money, put it in the kid's pincer-claw hand.

With my nerves now on razors, I kept moving, eyes bouncing left and right, watching, waiting for the next mind fuck. An occasional truck passed, workers standing upright in the truck bed, their clothes stained from a grueling day in the poppy fields. We passed homes with barred windows, guards sitting out front, resting on tipped-back chairs, weapons slung from their shoulders, glum frowns slung from their chins.

We reached the edge of town, the last streetlight falling

behind us, the pitch black darkness a relief to my overloaded senses. Maggie passed her flashlight to our guide. To me she asked, "Can you see all right back there?"

I kept my eyes aimed up ahead, where Evie and Deluski lit the way. "I'm good."

We crunched our way up the trail, weeds and dead branches snapping underfoot. We'd ditched the road as soon as we'd left town. Told Evie we didn't want to be seen, asked her if there was a back way.

The jungle trail was rough going. According to Evie, it wasn't used much, not since the road was built. We tripped through vines and scrub, my lase-blade slicing through the worst. We tramped through streams, pushed through brambles. My thorn-scratched, bug-bitten skin itched in a thousand places. Bug spray didn't do shit in deep jungle.

The unmistakable roar of a flyer sounded up ahead. We were close. I covered my ears as the grumbling bellow passed overhead, foliage whipping in the wind. I dumbly looked up, caught a shower of sappy detritus in my hair, my eyes, down my shirt. I coughed and spat, shook shit out of my shirt.

Flashlights and laughter, both aimed at me.

I wiped my face with my empty sleeve. A too rare smile broke on my face as I had a good laugh at myself, first time since forever ago. Evie and Maggie brushed flakes of I-didn't-know-what out of my hair while I winced against the pain of my burned scalp.

On the move again, Evie led the way until the bush finally thinned and opened onto an open field, where a pair of lamp poles dropped cones of light on a broad swath of poppies. We stayed low, flashlights off, watching for activity.

A building sat in the middle of the field, surrounded by several shacks. A two-wheeled track led to the road we'd avoided.

A sizable group of people worked the far side of the field, canisters on their backs, sprayers in hand, rags tied over their mouths.

I scanned for guards, scoped five in total, two monitoring the workers, three more patrolling near the main building, a two-story structure constructed of slats and poles under an open-air thatch roof.

I asked Evie, "Is that General Z's headquarters?"

"This ain't no headquarters." She laughed. "It's just the doc's clinic. Z runs whole villages up north. I portered a trip up there once."

"You're a porter?"

"My cousin is. He took me along as more of a runner. I don't eat much so it don't cost much to bring me."

"Ever seen General Z?"

She nodded. "He comes to Yepala sometimes to meet with his lieutenants and the sheriff."

"Who is the sheriff?"

"Carlos Aceves. He's a mean man. You watch out for him. He always wears a panama hat. He and the doctor are friends, which is why he lets the doctor have his clinic here."

"What kind of clinic is it?" asked Deluski.

She didn't have an answer for that.

Maggie took a seat in the weeds. "That flyer we heard heading south—think the doctor was on it?"

"Probably. He's always going back and forth to Koba."

I dropped down next to Maggie. Might take awhile for that last group of workers to call it quits. According to Evie, they'd walk the road until they passed the mud, to meet a truck that could take them the rest of the way back to town.

Deluski and Evie sat down, Evie right next to Maggie. "Can I see your earrings?" Her tough-girl voice had been replaced by something softer and sweeter.

Maggie pulled them out of her ears and passed them to Evie, who held them low to the ground before turning on a flashlight. "They're real pretty. Is that gold?"

"Yes."

"What about the stones?"

"Emeralds."

"They match your eyes. How'd they get so green?"

"They're not my original eyes. I was born with brown eyes, just like you."

Evie hung the earrings on a branching weed and studied how they dangled.

I turned my attention to the poppy field. Slowly, the workers peeled off, dropping their spray cans at one of the sheds and heading for the two-track road where a small gathering formed.

Evie took the earrings off the weed hanger and made to give them back but Maggie put up a hand. "You can keep them."

"No. They're too nice."

"The way you've helped us, you deserve something nice."

Evie forced them into Maggie's hand. "Somebody would try to steal them by cutting off my ears." Tough girl was back.

Workers continued to quit, my heart rate climbing as they did. Sneaking in there was going to be tough. Too much open space, and too many guards.

The last few workers headed in, the field lights flicking off right afterward. The compound, however, was still bathed in yellow as workers started to file down the road.

As a group, we moved into the poppy field and slowly started across. The deep dark made it difficult to pick our way through ragged rows of poppy plants, black leaves and stems and pods reaching up from blacker earth. We detoured around the lamp poles, afraid somebody would turn them back on.

Maggie whispered, "This is as far as you go, Evie."

I counted off some bills for her. "First sign of trouble, you go back the way you came."

"Got it."

We crept forward. Only three guards left. The other two were escorting the workers down the road.

We made our crouched approach, slithering through and around the poppies, our goal a wide stack of black tar bricks. Three guards, none looking this way. They were boys, young teens. General Z's army was a children's brigade. I doubted many survived long enough to be men.

We slipped behind the stack of bricks and peeked over them and around the side. I grabbed Maggie's wrist, put my half-arm on Deluski's shoulder. "You sure you want to do this?"

They both nodded. We had to know what was going on in there, had to know what game Mota, Panama, and the doctor were playing.

We had no choice but to break in and see with our own eyes. The local authorities wouldn't help. Panama ran YOP.

The planetary authorities wouldn't help either. This was General Z's territory, a lawless expanse of jungle villages and O fields. The Lagartan army would never tame this region. Truth was, the pols didn't want them to. Crush the narco-state and they'd have to stop milking the Unified Worlds for drug enforcement money, which they siphoned into their own pockets.

The three guards stood in a group, close enough that we could hear them chatting. We snuck from one stack of tar bricks to the next, approaching closer and closer, the first shed a few meters away. I looked at the main building. The windows, most of which were dark, were now in plain view. I checked the lighted ones, searching for moving shadows and prying eyes. All I found was eerie stillness.

Deluski led us toward the next cover, a low-to-the-ground

enclosure of tarps and hand-hewn wood poles. We crawled over hoses to the enclosure's edge. The clinic was a short distance ahead.

I moved around the enclosure, my shoulder getting wet as it brushed against the dewy tarp. What the hell was in there? "Wait," I whispered to Deluski. I pulled my lase-blade, held it close to the ground, and flicked it on. I stayed hunched above the blade to block the light, fiery heat baking my chest and chin. I sliced into the tarp, a good-sized gash, and I spread the opening wide, using the light of my blade to peer through.

Dirt. Rocks. Sprawling squash vines. A garden?

I saw something move. Barely. I strained to see in the red light, spotted it again. A burrowing shell. I could see more of them now, lots of them, coin-sized shells dragging sluggishly across the dirt, along the squash vines and leaves.

Deluski tapped my shoulder. "See anything?"

I turned off the blade. "Snails."

"Like the ones we saw at the gay bar?"

"I think so."

Maggie elbowed me. "What were you guys doing at a gay bar?"

Deluski peeked around the side. "Let's go. The guards are heading for one of the sheds." We dashed behind the clinic, pressed ourselves into the wall. We hustled down its length, stopping at the first doorway, a shutter on hinges.

Maggie pushed open the shutter and we were inside, stealing down an empty hall, weapons-first. Humming lights fluctuated to the sound of an unseen generator. As we went forward, our legs were tickled by ivy and ferns that grew through cracks in the wood plank floors. An unoccupied desk came into view, and we stepped up to it. Maggie put her free hand on the seat. "Warm."

We waited, listening. My heartbeat sounded in my ears. A

toilet flushed. We followed the sound to a curtained doorway and stopped to surround it. A hand swept the curtain aside and a guard came through. Maggie and Deluski plugged his ears with lase-pistols.

"Drop to the floor," I ordered. "Kiss the wood."

The kid spread his hands and slow-moed down.

I pushed my heel between his shoulder blades, my toes pressing his head into the floorboards like it was a gas pedal. "Kiss it."

I could feel the punk's lungs rising under my heel, quick puffs up and down. His head went all the way down, lips on wood. I lifted my shoe so Deluski could relieve him of his weapon and frisk the little shit.

I put my foot back where it was. "How many guards?"

"Four," he said, his voice cracking midword. I couldn't tell if it was distress or puberty that frogged it. "Three outside and me."

"Who else?"

"A nurse."

"What about the doc?"

"He left, took a flyer to Koba."

"Just one nurse?"

He nodded, his face mashing into the floorboards.

"Where?"

"I don't know."

I put some extra weight on my foot.

"Upstairs somewhere," he wheezed. "He makes rounds."

"Does he come this way?"

"Sometimes."

"Armed?"

"No."

I let up. "Call him."

"Manny."

"Louder."

"Manny! Get down here."

Maggie and Deluski waited by the stairs. The ceiling creaked overhead. I looked up and followed the trail of whining planks to the staircase, shoes clomping down. He reached the bottom, stunned eyes sizing up me and my piece. He was built like a gym rat, his head shaved bald as a bent knee. Dark-skinned biceps squeezed out of a tight-fitting tee tucked into belted designer pants. He wore rubber gloves on his hands.

Maggie and Deluski closed in on either side of him. He froze except for a quivering lip.

Maggie waved her weapon at him. "What's going on here?"

He hesitated, eyes clicking through his options. Deluski accelerated the decision making with a quick crack to the skull.

"A clinic," he blurted. "It's a clinic." He rubbed his head with his gloved hand, checked his palm for blood. "What did you do that for?"

"What kind of clinic?"

"Listen, I'll tell you whatever you want to know. This shit's not exactly a secret around here, but you best go see for yourselves." He hiked a thumb at the stairs and rubbed his head again.

Maggie, Deluski, and I traded glances. Nods all around. Maggie told him to give us the tour.

We filed upstairs, all five of us. I kept my piece buried in the kid's kidney. Deluski stayed with Nurse Manny, a fistful of the nurse's tee bunched in one hand, weapon in the other, gun barrel stabbed into Manny's spine.

We stepped down a short hallway, passing a room with a single bed on the left. "That's the doc's room," said Manny. "My room is way over on the other side."

Iguanas scuffled overhead, the rafters dotted with nests made from stolen fronds in the thatch roofing. We entered a long room, beds lined up barracks-style. We walked down the wide center aisle, my brain struggling to comprehend.

Maggie wandered, slack-jawed, her weapon hanging by her hip. She made to talk but her mouth just opened and closed like that of a dazed fish dying on a boat's floor. Pigment had drained from Deluski's face, his sand-colored skin turning a sickly olive.

My head spun, drunk on this fucked-up horror show. I felt ready to tip over. I drilled my piece deeper into my charge's side, made him wince and bite his lip. I kicked his legs from behind. "Get down."

Deluski ordered Nurse Manny down and looked for a place to sit, wobbly legs carrying him to the foot of an unoccupied bed.

I closed my eyes, just long enough to wish it all away. I opened them back up knowing it wouldn't be gone. They were still here. The man lying naked on his back, a quadruple amputee, six black insect legs coming from his torso and scrabbling at the air like an upended beetle's. The woman with air tanks for legs, hoses running from her metal thighs directly into her chest. The man encased in a bug shell, his face mostly hidden behind a chitinous mandible. The I-didn't-know-what lying in a bath, skin looking like gray rubber, a triangle of thick gray flesh hanging over the rim.

A fucking fin.

One of them moved. Three weapons took aim. She slipped out of bed with a thump. Her legs had been shortened, no knees or feet, the skin of her thighs covered with dense, thick fur. She started into an ungainly, stump-legged crawl.

"Don't mind her," said the facedown nurse, his bald head raised off the floor. "She's just going to the bathroom."

She humped and bumped to the aisle's end and turned for a toilet against the wall, used a step to get herself up. She looked young. Evie's age or thereabouts. Her face was flat. Dominated by big eyes. Down's.

What the fuck was this place?

Maggie put her shaky voice to the question.

"The doc does experiments here," said the nurse.

"What kind of experiments?"

"He's a genius, you know. Crazy, but a genius."

The toilet flushed and the girl slowly began the return trip.

Maggie stepped over to the nurse, looked down at him like a lizard had taken a shit on the floor. She stared at the back of his smooth head, her weapon hanging tensely by her side. Hair fell in front of her face, sweaty straggles dangling over dark eyes. "Explain."

"He's trying to make more effective workers."

"More effective?" She leaned down at him. "She can't walk!" I kept a close eye on her lase-pistol. Didn't want her doing something stupid.

"She can walk in space," he said.

"What do you mean?"

"I'm talking about zero g. Hands are all that matter when there's no gravity. You float from handhold to handhold. Legs just get in the way."

"The fur?"

"Say you need to turn a wrench or something. Doesn't work too good when your feet come off the floor. You have to anchor yourself, but do that with one of your hands and you've only got one left to work with."

"The fur?" Maggie repeated, her tone maxed out on impatience.

"Works like Velcro."

Velcro? Fuck me. I felt numb, my whole body ready to melt into the floorboards. Somehow, against all odds, I held shape as I watched the girl drag herself up a short ramp back to her bed.

Maggie was stunned into silence.

Velcro. Fucking fuck.

Nurse Manny pointed at the man with the bug legs. "That's another model the doc developed."

Model? The poor sap's eyes were lost in another world, legs clicking in a feeble attempt to turn himself over.

"The legs are way too weak to carry his torso down here, but get him in zero g and he'll be scooting up walls, across the ceiling. He'll be perfect for going EVA, won't need to fuck around with a jetpack or a tether."

"He has no hands."

"True. The doc still has to add those. That, or he might go with a prehensile tail. He's gotten good at those."

Deluski spoke up for the first time. "Why all this talk about zero g? The Orbital has artificial gravity."

"They're mining asteroids up there. Most are too small to worry about setting up any kind of permanent base. The space stations and space liners have gravity, but most of the mining facilities operate in zero g or whatever little gravity they get from the asteroids themselves."

"Have you shipped out any of these workers?"

"Not yet. He hasn't even tried any of his designs on real people yet."

Maggie raised her brows. "These aren't real people?"

"Shit no," he said. "This here is a vegetable garden. Nothing but cripples and retards. That one there was in General Z's army, but he got lobotomized by a shot in the head, burned a hole straight through. There's a couple more woundeds over there, the rest were dumped by their families. People around here are crazy superstitious. They think their kids are possessed when they don't come out right, so they sell their defectives to the doc. He doesn't buy them all. He's picky about his specimens."

Specimens. Cold-ass bastard. Maggie lifted her piece just a smidge, enough to make me call her name as a caution. Nurse Manny wrenched his neck around to see what was going on. Maggie's piece dropped back to her hip. "Continue."

"Before he starts doing real people, he wants to test his designs by chartering a shuttle to take the whole bunch out of the atmosphere. He doesn't quite have the funds yet, though. Soon as he does, he wants to close his plastic surgery biz in Koba. He funds this work here with the money he makes down there."

"Where does he plan on getting the *real* people?"

"People will volunteer."

"You must be joking."

"Listen, lady, where the fuck do you think you are? This is Yepala. We've got an army of kids terrorizing people. Girls around here get gang-raped every day. People will do anything to land an offworld job. And the offworlders will pay for labor. You know how successful the mining operations are. Those people can't wait to get a bunch of immigrants in to do all the shit work."

I didn't know what to say. None of us did. The horror of it all was beyond us.

Silence reigned for the next minute. Until a nervous Nurse Manny asked, "What are you going to do with me?"

The young guard glared at him. Manny said *me*. Not *us*.

Nobody responded.

He decided to keep talking, like he figured he was safe as long as he had something to offer. "The one in the tub can breathe underwater. Pivon has a moon that's all ocean. The waters aren't as developed as ours when it comes to sea life, but they do have these little shrimplike creatures that are evidently mighty tasty. Doc figures a swimmer would be useful untangling nets and shit.

"And Quentin, the guy fused into the bug shell, is designed

for EVA work. You attach a faceplate, and he's airtight. You know how much time workers waste suiting up to go into vacuum? The doc figures that making people EVA-ready could boost productivity by ten percent. Maybe more. Plus it'll be safer."

I stopped listening. I didn't want to know about the woman with air-tank legs or the young boy with sockets on the end of his wrists, myriads of attachments surely available for the right price. "Does General Z run this place?"

"Not the clinic. But he does run the opium operations. The guards are all his. This one's job," he pointed at the young guard, "is protecting the big storeroom downstairs. If the general knows there's a clinic out here, he's never shown any interest in it."

"So you work for the doctor and the doctor alone?"

"Him and the sheriff. This is the sheriff's land. He bought it real cheap a couple years back and had it cleared of jungle so he could lease it to General Z."

"Lease it?" asked Deluski. "Can't the general take whatever land he wants?"

"The money buys more than the land," I said. "It buys YOP too. Let's go. We got what we came for."

Deluski stood. "What do we do with these two? We can't let them send up the alarm until we're away."

Maggie raised her piece, the barrel leveled at Nurse Manny.

"Maggie? What do you think? Should we tie them up?"

Her contorted face was flushed.

"Maggie?"

She lowered the lase-pistol. "Get some rope."

Deluski rummaged for rubber tubing, made quick work of tying hands and feet and using bandages for gags. I inspected his knots. Looked solid. Didn't have to last long.

Maggie was already at the door, Deluski on his way. I made

like I was following but turned back. I put my lase-blade in the kid guard's palm. Pressed his fingers around the handle. "If your bosses find out we got past you, you're as good as dead. Nobody needs to know we were ever here."

The kid's eyes scrunched up. He was reasoning it through.

I didn't want Maggie doing anything stupid. Me, stupid was what I did best. "Best I can tell there's only one witness in here who can talk."

I saw understanding in his eyes. I gave Nurse Manny a wink as he struggled against his restraints and screamed into his gag. I turned and hustled to catch up.

Just before I exited the door, the unmistakable sizzle of a waking blade brought a smile to my face.

twenty-three

WE were outside, jogging past snail pens. Forgot to ask about the snails, dammit. Goddamn information overload in there.

We passed behind the last shed and sprinted into the darkness of the poppy field.

Evie met us and wordlessly led us back into the jungle. Flashlights on, we pushed along the trail, chirps and squawks sounding over the jungle's drone.

Maggie stopped in front of me, almost bumped into her. "We have to go back."

I took her wrist, dragged her along. "We can't do anything for them."

"We can take them with us."

"How? We can't parade them through town."

"We can't just leave them."

"We won't." I felt more centered than I had in a long time. Nothing like a dose of true evil to remind me I wasn't so bad. "We'll stop them. Just not tonight."

"But—"

"Not tonight." I pulled her along until she started walking on her own.

Evie stopped us, told us to turn off our lights. She snuck ahead to check the road, came back a minute later. "There's a patrol down the way."

Deluski whispered, "They must be looking for us."

"Agreed." By now, the arrival of a one-armed man in Yepala

had probably spread to the wrong ears. "How many soldiers, Evie?"

"Plenty," she said. "I hope you have a lot more money."

I doubted we had enough. If Panama knew we were in Yepala, he could've offered a bounty to the general's soldiers. "Is there another way back to town?"

"There's another trail we could take to get around that patrol, but when we get to town, you'll have to pay one way or another."

We'd take another. "Can you get home on your own, Evie?"

"What do you think?" Her words came loaded with attitude.

I loved this kid. I pulled a wad from my pocket, pressed it into her palm. "Take us to the trail, then get home without being seen. If you get stopped, you tell them you took us to the clinic and left us there. You got me?"

"I got you."

We slunk across the dark road, entered the jungle on the far side, picked our way through some brambles to a well-worn trail.

"That's it, Evie. On your way."

Maggie told her to wait. She pulled her earrings out of her lobes. "Take these."

"I told you somebody will just steal them."

"Hide them someplace."

Evie took them and ran.

We followed the trail for a kilometer or two, my heart leaping at every snapped twig. Finally, the jungle opened into a tamed expanse dotted with tin-roofed mud-brick homes. The area was illuminated by gas lamps that emitted piercing white light. "Where do you think the pier is from here?"

Deluski pointed at a church on the far side. "Should be near that church."

I agreed. "How you want to do this?"

"We walk straight through," said Maggie. "Act like we know where we're going. There's no guarantee that the patrol was looking for us. If we run, we're asking for trouble."

"Objections?"

Deluski shook his head no. We tucked our weapons away and walked into the village. As we passed homes, off-duty farmhands stared our way, and the sour smell of shine rode on the breeze. Wood fires pumped smoke through the gaps between walls and rooftops. People ate from bowls with their fingers, geckos dancing in the dirt, scurrying across tables.

We passed an open-faced two-story home on the right, the bottom level reserved for dry wood and a roped cow, the top floor a small deck for sleeping under the overhang. A young girl shoved branches into a clay wood stove. Flames licked at a steaming pot, and her soot-coated face gave us a once-over.

We strode forward, each step taking us closer to the pier and the river. A shirtless old man shooed us along, crazy eyes under wispy hair, ribs standing out like roots from a toppled tree. He hissed and nabbed a machete, brandishing it wildly before a family member scolded him and took the tool out of his hand.

I spotted a woman standing behind a post, a phone to her ear, her eyes tracking us step for step. Her lips moved, speaking unheard words into the receiver. I looked all around, found two others, phones to their ears.

Racing to rat us out to Panama.

I accelerated into a jog, my hand moving to my piece. Maggie and Deluski matched pace, the church still in the distance, its cross fashioned from scrapped street signs. Maggie had her phone out, holding it to her mouth, yelling into the speaker, "Josephs!"

A soldier appeared in front of the church. Then a second. I tried to stop, skidded, and slipped to the ground, my body sliding through the mud. Now there were three, four, a whole squad pouring into the church courtyard.

I scrambled to my feet and ran after Maggie and Deluski, who had already turned for the jungle to our right. I was in full sprint now, darting between houses, hurtling through family dinners, startling children and scattering chickens.

My right shoe slipped out from under me. I went down a second time, an uncontrolled slide taking me into a set of chairs. I was back up, untangling my legs, tossing chairs, as the rumble of clomping feet approached from behind.

I was running again, speeding for the jungle, knowing the river had to lie somewhere behind it. Deluski was the first to disappear into the green, Maggie a couple seconds later. I pushed my lungs to their limit and leapt into the darkness, branches and leaves, vines and brambles. A hand grabbed my shirt, Maggie's voice, "C'mon."

I followed as close as I could, my eyes straining to keep up with the jouncing beam of Maggie's flashlight. She yelled into her phone, "Track my signal! We're heading for the river!"

The crackle of lase-fire ripped overhead, burned leaves raining from exploding clouds of foliage. The undisciplined shits were taking potshots. If they were going to catch us, they'd have to follow us in. Whether they did would depend on how bad they wanted us.

The shooting stopped. I listened for following voices but heard only our own heavy footfalls and the rustle of leaves as we crashed through. These were the general's soldiers, not Panama's cops. I gave myself permission to hope they'd dropped their pursuit. Maybe the bounty Panama offered wasn't so big.

Another burst of lase-fire quashed that hope. We raced

through the snagging, slapping, scraping jungle. Lase-fire tore through the trees to our right. The soldiers were veering off course. Maggie and I responded by angling left, widening the gap. I could hear the sputter of an outboard motor ahead. The river was close. *Please be Josephs.*

We scrambled up a steep embankment, kicking and clawing through muddy earth and deep piles of damp leaves. The air turned fetid with overturned compost. I coughed and choked on mold spores, my feet churning at the slick slope.

Maggie crested first, me a step behind. We raced down the embankment. Josephs's voice called to us, the boat a short distance out, floodlight aimed our way. We dove into the water and paddled toward the floodlight. Josephs and the boat captain pulled Deluski on board.

The boat putted up. Maggie grabbed hold of the rail. "Turn off the light and the motor!"

The motor went silent. The light went dark. I held on to the rail and waited for Maggie to get pulled up. "Sssh. Nobody talks."

I heard voices upriver, the voices of boys. I could see them scanning the water with their flashlights, thirty meters upriver, maybe less. A real army would've spread out, cast a wide net as they moved through the jungle instead of going in follow-the-leader formation. Those kids weren't real soldiers. They had no training. No fucking clue.

I held up my arms, letting hands grab hold. They lifted me slowly, my torso rising out of the river. I winced at the water running off me, knowing every drop could be the one that they heard. Lucky for us, the punks didn't have the good sense to shut up and listen. Instead they argued and took random shots at the river.

My feet slipped from the water. They set me down on the deck. I didn't dare move. I just breathed, told my heart to quit

pounding. Minutes passed, and the river took us away in its
silent flow.

We putted under one of Koba's many bridges, city lights all
around. The journey was almost over. Maggie and I sat next
to each other, scratching at skin savaged by bug bites.

Deluski kept fiddling with the boat captain's phone, said he
was looking up some things. Josephs stared at the stars, his
gaze quiet and peaceful, not shellshocked like the rest of ours.
He hadn't seen what we'd seen. A goddamned freak show. The
kind of shit nightmares were made of.

The captain turned the boat into a canal. A nightclub floated
to the right, the crowd overflowing onto a pontoon dock, suits
and dresses, cocktails and party voices.

"He has to be stopped." She was repeating herself. Saying it
over and over and over.

"I know." The same empty response.

"KOP has no jurisdiction."

"I know."

"I can go to the governor. See if I can convince him to send
the army in to raid that compound."

"You can try." *But you know you'll fail.*

"If he refuses, I'll go to the press and amp up the pressure."

Which you know will simply spook the doctor into relocat-
ing. I waited for her to come to the same conclusion.

She shook her head. "There has to be a way to stop him." Back
to square one.

She knew the riddle had no legal solution. The doctor operated in General Z's territory, meaning the clinic might as well
be a million miles away, for all the authorities could do about
it. Shit, the General regularly slaughtered entire villages and
took the children as his soldiers. Gang rapes were a way of life
up there. If the pols hadn't found the will to do anything by

now, they sure as hell weren't going to start a full-scale invasion just because of a rogue doctor.

Yet she kept at the riddle, around and around, trying to solve the unsolvable. I had to admire her for it.

Deluski jumped up. "I got it!" He held out the phone for me.

"Got what?"

His grin was huge. Didn't know the guy had that many teeth. "The lizard the killer turned into. I found it."

I wasn't in the mood. "Not this again."

He put the phone in my face. "Fucking look at it already!"

I took the phone, studied the lizard's pic. Charcoal skin. Red stripes. Wide mouth. "Could be." I made to hand the phone back.

"Read the description, the part I marked."

Christ. I held it so Maggie could see and navigated into the text, skipped over the species name—some kind of Latin shit—my eyes pausing on the common name: stripe-faced man-eater. I read the portion he'd highlighted, the text focusing on the lizard's sexual habits. I took the information in, my smirk fading, my back straightening.

I soaked it up, let it mingle with the case facts, images gaining clarity. I read it a second time, read how the female attracts the male with those red stripes, stripes that get thicker and brighter during mating season. How the male stands on its hind legs, making himself look big, making himself look like good genetic stock. How they mate, the male inserting his genitalia, the female's vagina closing around it, a vagina made of a bonelike material that pinches down until it severs the male genitalia. Severs it in its entirety. Only then, after the genitals are severed do the muscles relax to release his seed.

Holy shit.

Maggie pulled the phone from my fingers to read it again. "Oh my God."

Deluski sat back down. "I told you I'd find it."

Maggie had her face practically pressed into the display. "That steel trap thing he snapped onto your hand. You think the doctor installed another one inside him?"

Josephs perked up. "Inside where? What are you humps talking about?"

Franz Samusaka, Wu, and Froelich all had their dicks chopped.

"Somebody gonna answer me?"

Chopped during mating. Holy fuck.

I rolled over. Again. I scratched my ankles, my neck, my ears. Damn bugs chewed the hell out of me.

I couldn't sleep. Again. Bad thoughts always came at night. Gave me a good reminder why I usually drank myself to sleep. Niki. How could she do that to me? I loved her. I trusted her.

The love was real. But I knew now the trust was an illusion. Our curse was too many secrets. Secrets that separated us like walls of glass that were so crystal clear that we could fool ourselves into believing we were in the same room all along.

I heard the now familiar sound of high heels clopping down the hall, heard the curtain slide open. Heard it close again. The sheet moved, somebody slipping under, a wave of perfume leaving no doubt who. She curled up next to me, warm skin pressed into my back, an arm worming its way under what was left of my right arm, sliding up my stomach, hand settling on my chest.

I looked at the window. Dark as ever. "What time is it?"

"Morning."

I scratched my ear, the back of my neck.

"You okay?"

"Got eaten up last night."

"Yepala?"

"Yeah."

"Did you find what you were looking for?"

"More." I rolled over to face her. "Found too much. Listen to me, do not bring your sister to the offworld doctor."

Her hand pulled away. "You can't tell me what to do."

"He's a monster."

"I'm not going to work for Chicho the rest of my life. And neither will my sister. We're going to start our own house, and the doctor is our ticket to better days."

I couldn't let her do it. I made the decision right then. Had to blurt it out quickly before I went back on it. "Take my business."

"What?"

"The protection racket. Take it."

She sat up. "Is this a joke?"

"Tell your sister to quit, and the two of you run the business."

She flicked on the light. I squinted at the brightness, her image a blur of hair and rouge and lipstick. "I can't run a protection racket."

"Why not?"

"Women don't run protection rackets."

"They're not bouncers either."

"You think I can face down Captain Mota?"

"I'll take care of him."

"What about the next Captain Mota? If KOP or a street gang wants to move in, how am I going to stop them? Sic my fifteen-year-old sister on them?"

"Throw my name at them. You need me to show up, I'll show up, flex my muscles, but the business is yours. You run it. You keep the money."

The corners of her heavily painted lips lifted, the beginnings of a smile. "You serious?"

I went to the gate and rang the bell.

"Yes?" came a voice from a speaker.

"I'm here to talk to Hudson Samusaka."

"That won't be possible, sir. Your face is on file, and it's on our no-entry list."

I sneered into the lens. "He'll see me. You tell him I had a nice talk with his son Ang. Couldn't shut the kid up."

No response. Good. Meant he was checking with his boss. I leaned against the gate and waited.

Worked better than a fucking key. The gate buzzed, the voice telling me Miss Paulina would meet me at the door. Samusaka had to find out what I knew.

I pushed through. My eyes took in the well-lit grounds. The walkways branched and merged into a meandering network of stone paths. Manicured hedges and fountains; stone walls and wrought iron railings; the air scented by flowers. I headed for the main house, my shoes clacking on stone.

The door was open, Miss Paulina standing guard, arms crossed over a blue dress, eyes staring down the length of her nose. "You again?"

I came up the steps. "Where is he?"

"In the study." She held out a hand like an usher.

"I know the way." I breezed past her into the foyer, got a few steps down the hall before turning back to face her. "I'll take a brandy. Make it a twenty-year." I was off before she could respond. Might as well act the part from the get-go.

I moved down the hall, then through the study's entrance. He sat at the desk, white dress shirt unbuttoned at the collar, sleeves rolled up, eyes sharp like monitor claws. I strode to the desk and took the seat across from him. Opened with a bluff. "You've been a naughty boy."

He bared teeth. "What did my son tell you?"

"Everything." My face was straight like a piece of rebar. Time to beat him with it. "Kid found your dirty little secret right here in this study. He ransacked this room until he found it, then made it look like somebody broke in. Kid's been naming his own allowance ever since."

Color leaked from his cheeks and pooled into a flushing triangle between his collar points and under his Adam's apple. "What do you want?"

Gotcha, asshole. "Truth."

"Or else?"

"Or your dirty secret doesn't stay secret."

His shoulders rode high, like every muscle in his body was tensed. "You want money?"

I shook my head. "I want answers."

He threw up his hands. "Ask your damn questions." Bluffed into folding. Game over.

I kept signs of victory off my rebar face. "You know your eldest son was murdered, don't you?"

He stayed silent, giving me a big spoonful of that hostile glare. I knew his type. Controlling. Domineering. I knew how he'd treated his wife the last time I was here, making her stand a step behind him. Prick was used to treating people like property.

A knock came on the door. Miss Paulina entered, brandy snifter in hand. She carried the glass to me and silently hurried out.

I sucked in a sip, swished it around in my mouth, tongue wrapped in flavor and the tingle of alcohol. I swallowed it down and set the glass on his desk. One sip was enough. Gave me a perverse satisfaction to know the busybody housekeeper would have to pour the rest down the drain.

"Murder. Killer cut your son's dick off."

He didn't flinch. "I know what happened to my son."

"Why did the police report it as an OD?"

"They wanted to save our family from the embarrassment."

"Telling the public your son doped himself to death isn't embarrassing?"

His granite face didn't budge.

"Detectives Wu and Froelich handled your son's case, correct?"

He nodded that rock on top of his neck.

"How much did you pay them?"

"Enough."

"You know they're both dead. They suffered the same fate as your son."

"Sorry to hear that."

"Did you know them before your son's murder?"

"No."

"But they knew your son."

"They did."

"How?"

"They were business partners."

"What kind of business?"

"I stayed out of my son's affairs."

These bare-minimum answers were pissing me off. Didn't he realize he'd lost? I'd bluffed him into folding, and now it was time he paid up. I wanted to crank up the pressure, use my leverage, but I still had no idea what his youngest son had found in this room, what he was dangling over his father's head, what had turned this take-charge alpha dad into a whipped cash register. I didn't know.

He moved up in his chair. "Are we done?"

I screwed up my face. "No, we're not fucking done. Your son was murdered, and I'm trying to catch his killer. Now why won't you help me?"

"I've told you everything I know." He pushed a button on his desk. "Paulina will see you out."

I stayed where I was, my brain struggling to comprehend why this blackmail angle wasn't scoring shit. If it worked for his son, why didn't it work for me?

Her voice came from the door. "Right this way, sir." She'd shown up fast. Too fast. Damn woman must've been eavesdropping again.

I couldn't make sense of why he was shutting me out. I looked into his eyes, closed windows staring back. I gave it one more incredulous shot. "What the hell is your problem? You telling me you'd rather I go public with what I know than help me catch your son's killer?"

The lights went out behind his closed-window eyes. "Goodbye, sir."

twenty-four

DELUSKI came strutting up, a small grin on his face. Kid was feeling pretty good about himself, finally pinning down that lizard. He could be a detective one day. A good one.

"Any luck with Samusaka?"

I fell into step alongside him. "No. He didn't say anything useful."

"Did you threaten to expose his kid's blackmail scheme?"

"He still didn't talk."

We turned left, into the university campus: boxy concrete structures, moss-covered walls, and rusted window frames.

Deluski pointed straight ahead. "Biology department should be up there. He's hiding something, isn't he?"

"Yeah, and whatever it is, it must be bigger than what his kid has on him. He tried to buy me off, but when I wouldn't bite, he just shut down."

We crossed a footbridge—foul-smelling canal water running underneath—and veered right, BIOLOGY painted over a door. Inside, we took the stairs up two flights, then down a short hall and in through a glass door to a lab with cages and terrariums, and white-coated techs with goggles.

A young man stepped forward. "Can I help you?"

Deluski flashed his shield. "We want to talk to whoever's in charge."

"That would be Dr. Stark. Wait here. I'll see if I can locate her."

We stayed put, eyes scanning across the glass enclosures, where iguanas—and tuataras and geckos, skinks and chameleons—perched on dead branches, and salamanders parked on leaves. It was feeding time, a lab tech moving down the line, pouring beetles from a coffee can.

"I'm Dr. Stark," said a tall, ponytailed woman with a horsey smile. "How can I help you?"

"We're interested in your stripe-faced man-eaters."

"Ah, the *lagartus lacerta zebrata*. You know how they mate?"

"We've read about it."

"Those poor chaps get a raw deal." She chuckled. "Why are you interested?"

"Part of a murder investigation. We can't say more."

"A murder?" She practically brayed she was so excited. "Nothing like that ever happens around here."

She waved for us to follow and led us down the long room with a clumsily unbalanced stride. Probably spent too much of her childhood in libraries instead of playgrounds.

She stopped at a cage sitting on the floor. "We keep a pair of specimens in here."

Deluski and I dropped to our knees. I put my nose up to the wire mesh and studied a lizard resting on a rock, sitting so perfectly still that it looked fake, like a kid's toy. Its body was as long as my hand with a cigar-sized tail that tapered down to a cigarette as it snaked through some leaves. "Is that the female?"

"No, that's a male. He's a nubby hubby now." She laughed at her own joke. "He mated two days ago. It's too early to tell if it took. He only gets one shot at it, you know. That's the female with her tail in the water."

I looked at her glassy eyes, stripes like three sets of crimson eyebrows. Broad, red-speckled lips. Skin the color of polished granite.

"Ever seen one before?"

I absently rubbed my right arm. "I think so."

"She lives up to her name, that one. She's mated four times, makes sure her husbands never cheat on her. She eats some of her young too, but only the girls. The practice assures that there are always more male man-eaters than female. Otherwise the procreative math wouldn't work."

A crawling beetle held the man-eater's attention; her head was swiveling like a turret.

Deluski stood. "Has anybody else come to talk to you about these lizards?"

"Not that I can think of. But we give tours from time to time, and we always point them out."

The man-eater attacked, her movement so quick that my eyes couldn't track, like she'd disappeared and reappeared in a new location, the beetle suddenly clamped between her red-speckled lips. She held it like a trophy for a few seconds, then started to chew it down, lips drawing in the beetle's shell little by little, until nothing but the legs poked out before they too disappeared.

I got to my feet. "Have you ever heard of anybody being obsessed with these things?"

"Obsessed?"

"Ever seen anybody who wanted to turn into one?"

She stroked her ponytail. "I don't understand."

I couldn't say it. Seemed too outlandish to put voice to it. *Ever heard of anybody replacing their back-door plumbing with a cock-chopping steel trap?* The thought sent a shiver down my back. Nerves jingling on heebie-jeebie overload.

I still couldn't figure how he got his vics to have sex with him. Froelich and Franz Samusaka were gay; maybe they got seduced into a helluva surprise. But Wu? That scar-headed stiff was straight as they came.

It was unfathomable. Wu's family was slaughtered, his little

girls killed in their beds, and that was when the killer decided
to hit on Wu. *I just axed your whole family, so how about you come
over to my place for a little man love?*

Deluski broke the silence. "These tours you give, ever had
anybody ask strange questions about the man-eaters?"

"Define 'strange.'"

"Strange. Weird. Out of the norm."

"Somebody tried to steal them once. Does that count?"

"Who?"

"I don't think I ever asked his name. This was a while ago.
Could've been a year, maybe more. He stuffed them inside his
shirt. He must've been quick, because nobody saw him do it,
but I later saw a tail poking out between the buttons."

"Did you call the police?"

"No." She shook her head. "Didn't want the hassle. I didn't
think anybody else saw, so I just held him back when the tour
ended and asked him to return them."

"What did he look like?"

"Young. I figured him for a student, although I never saw
him around here again. He had a thick mess of hair."

Deluski gave me a questioning look. I grinned on a surge of
hope. *Yeah, that could be him.* "We need a name."

"I really have no idea. But we do sign-in sheets for our tours."

My ass was planted on a bench in the Old Town Square. Street
vendors with woks and grills filled the air with an oily reek.
Pedestrians wandered about, children with balloons tied to
their wrists, young couples holding hands.

Deluski sat next to me busily scanning the names on the
sign-in sheets into his newest anonymous phone. I watched the
fountain, a circular pool surrounding a statue of four intertwined
iguanas climbing for the sky. Even the natives wanted to escape
this world.

Mota hung heavy in my thoughts. I knew I was going to have to kill him. Panama too. I reasoned it every which way, but there was no getting around the fact that it was them or me. The moment I first stepped into Chicho's office, I put us on a collision course. Them or me.

I had to do them right. Not like when I went out to his house. Couldn't let my nerves get the best of me. I had to be a pro.

The tricky part was getting away with it. But there was always a way.

Deluski elbowed me. "Got a hit."

"What?"

"One of the names showed up in Wu and Froelich's case files."

"Who?"

"His name is Bronson Carew, age nineteen. He went to the police with a rape complaint."

Rape. Interesting.

"His complaint was taken by Inspector Jeljili, but the case got passed to Wu and Froelich."

"How could that be? Wu and Froelich worked Homicide, not Sex Crimes."

"It doesn't say."

"When did this happen?"

"The day after the break-in at the Samusakas'."

The timing nailed it. Too big a coincidence for him not to be Lizard-man. *Your day of reckoning is coming, Bronson Carew.* "Call Jeljili."

He gave me a dark stare. "I just bought this phone."

"It was compromised as soon as you logged into KOP. Mota could be tracking us already. We call Jeljili then dump it and go."

"You're buying the next one. Do you know Jeljili?"

"Yeah. I'll talk."

I waited while Deluski rang him up, my thoughts centered on the man who stole my hand. A rape victim. I didn't feel sorry for him. I didn't care how hurt he'd been. He could've been raped a thousand times, and I wouldn't care. He didn't have to kill Wu's girls. He had to be punished.

Mota. Panama. Dr. Tranny. They all had to be punished.

Inspector Blake Jeljili's holo appeared before the fountain, tailored suit hanging on a trim frame, young eyes and a thick shrub of hair. I almost laughed at how comically ancient this holo was. Must've been scanned twenty years ago, long before that shrub of hair lost most of its leaves. Before Jeljili's waist tripled and his chin had twins.

Deluski passed me the phone.

"Jelly, this is Juno."

"Juno? It's been a while. Hey, I heard about your wife. Tough break."

"Yeah."

"What the hell did you do to piss off Mota? From what I hear, that queen's got a tiara up his ass over you."

"Anybody buying his BS?"

"Nobody I've talked to. The hommy boys are fed up with him meddling in their case. Rumor has it Froelich and he were lovers. You know anything about that?"

"Yeah, that one's true."

"Damn. Didn't know Froelich swung that way."

"I need some info."

"Can't help you."

"Just some simple questions about an old case."

"Listen, Juno, you know I always respected you and the chief. I really did, but these are different times."

"I just—"

"I can't help you. Shit, if anybody found out I was talking to you . . ."

"Just some sim—"

"I can't take any chances until you get cleared."

I raised my voice. "I have been cleared. I was questioned and cleared by Rusedski himself."

"People are dying all around you, my boy. You heard Kripsen and Lumbela got killed?"

"No." Seeing wasn't the same as hearing.

"They got necktied. Word is you and that Deluski kid were chummy with them."

I looked over at Deluski. He had his head in his hands, probably wondering if he'd ever be able to shake these questions. Wondering if he'd ever be able to erase the stain of sins.

The kid needed to chill. This was just a negotiation. He was mistaking Jeljili's questions for accusations. Everything in this city was negotiable. Everything. I spoke into the receiver. "I don't make the kind of scratch I used to."

"Don't gimme that. I know you, Juno, you always got something going. Am I right?"

Deluski gave me a bewildered stare while we haggled over price.

The money settled, I asked my question: Bronson Carew. Rape complaint. I want the whole story.

"Yeah, I remember that kid. He was one scary freak. He came in with this vid, said it proved he was raped."

"You watched it."

"I watched the whole thing. Hours and hours of it. Must've been shot over several days. It looked like they were living in an abandoned house, just a crappy old mattress on the floor."

The party house where he'd staged Franz's body. And later Froelich's and Wu's.

Jeljili rolled on. "I couldn't help the kid. He wasn't raped. He never objected, never said no. He didn't cry or call for help."

I already knew the answer but asked anyway. "Who was the alleged assailant?"

"Franz Samusaka. A rich kid. Father's an oil tycoon."

I clicked the new facts into place. "I know who he is. Did you question him?"

"Absolutely. Found out his house was broken into the day before Carew came into KOP. Didn't take a genius to know Carew was the burglar."

I processed the new info, incorporated it into the building narrative.

Jeljili continued, "Franz Samusaka denied the rape. Said it was consensual, which it was. This freak was digging for gold. Scored some high-class ass and now he wanted to get something for it."

"Did Carew say he wanted money?"

"No. But it's obvious, isn't it? The Samusaka kid wanted me to return his stolen property, but I couldn't do that."

"Of course not."

"This was evidence in a potential rape." I could practically hear him smile, he was so pleased with himself. Translation: he wanted to get paid. "That was when Franz called in Froelich and Wu. He knew them somehow."

"And?"

"And they brokered an arrangement."

"The vid?"

"I heard it got lost."

Of course it did. "That it?"

"That's it."

I tossed the phone into the fountain. "Let's move."

I took a chair next to the wall so I could look down on the Square.

Deluski went to the bar to pick up drinks, and came back say-ing, "I don't get it. I thought Ang Samusaka staged the break-in in order to cover for the fact that he trashed his father's study."

I sipped my ice water, eyes tracking a panama hat that had just entered the Square. Its owner walked with a second man. It was too dark and too far to see faces, but I knew who they were. They walked toward the fountain.

Deluski was still waiting for an answer. "Well?"

I'd already reasoned it through. "Ang found the mess in his brother's room after Carew broke in to steal the alleged rape vid. Then Ang took the opportunity to ransack his father's study before reporting the break-in to the police. Whatever Ang found, he's been using it to blackmail his father ever since."

"But that doesn't explain how Carew could've broken in without leaving any jimmied doors or broken windows."

"True."

Panama circled the fountain. Mota climbed onto a park bench so he could get a better view of the crowd. I aimed my left index finger in their direction, cocked my thumb like it was an antique-style gun. *Bang.*

"So how did Carew get inside?"

"Somebody must've let him in."

Panama stepped into the fountain, water up to his knees, reached down and fished out Deluski's phone. He held it up for Mota to see.

I aimed my finger. *Bang.*

He got out of the fountain and spiked the phone on the ground, drawing startled glares from passersby.

A smile came to my lips. I reveled in their frustration. They had scored some early points on me, but that was before my head was straight. Before I'd purged the booze out of my blood. They couldn't match me now. I was a fucking master.

They moved out, heading in the opposite direction. I pumped finger shots into their backs. *Bang, bang, motherfuckers.*

I stared at the ceiling. Snails. It had to be the snails.

I heard Maria call my name from down the hall and sat up on the bed a second before she stepped through the curtain. "Hey, I can't stay for long or Chicho will miss me. The evening rush will be starting soon."

"What's up?"

"Just wanted to make sure you're still breathing."

I gave her a wry grin and sucked in a couple life-proving deep breaths.

"Where's Deluski?"

"He's trying to track down the bastard who did this to me." I lifted my arm. "The guy went off-grid a year ago."

"But you know who he is?"

"We do."

"So what are you doing lying around here?"

"Thinking. Ever seen anybody drink snail juice?"

She raised her overplucked eyebrows. "Snail juice?"

"Supposed to be an aphrodisiac."

Her eyes lit with recognition. "Oh, you're talking about the genie. It's supposed to do more than that."

"Tell me."

"Supposed to make a person open to suggestion. Like when people get hypnotized. 'Your wish is my command.' I don't know if it works, but I was there when Mota tried to sell some to Chicho. He claimed that it only took a drop to put somebody in a sex trance."

"Sex trance?"

"It's like you tell them what to do and they do it. Can't help themselves. Mota said this particular species of snails produces some chemical they use as a defense mechanism. Makes hun-

gry iguanas get disoriented or something, and discourages
them from eating more snails. Mota said the snails he was selling had been enhanced with a concentrated version of the
chemical."

"Did Chicho buy any?"

"No. What would be the point? You don't need a snail to
make a hooker fuck your brains out. That's what money is for."

It finally made sense. The new fact meshed with other facts.
I turned and twisted them into proper place.

A little drop was all it took for Franz Samusaka to turn
Bronson Carew into his sex slave. He ordered Carew to enjoy
it so the vid wouldn't look like rape. Carew might not even be
gay. No wonder he went psycho.

Fueled by humiliation and victimization, he fixated on the
stripe-faced man-eater. That was one badass bitch. Couldn't
fuck her for free. He fantasized himself as the victim turning
all powerful. *You want to rape me? I dare you. C'mon, do it. There
you go. That's it . . .*

Snap.

A shiver rippled down my back.

The fantasy was so powerful he made it real, got a steel trap
installed inside himself. He re-created the rape by using the
snails on Samusaka and brought him back to the original scene
of the crime. Then he forced his rapist to rape him a second
time, but this time he turned the tables. Took his pound of
flesh in revenge.

God, a fantasy like that must've dominated his every waking thought. The urge to do it again grew over the months
since, the drive like a tidal force, pressure building day after
day until the bursting point, when he chose two more victims,
the men who covered up Samusaka's crime. They deserved it.
They were accessories, rapists by proxy. He made them attack
him, made them mount him.

It was the doctor who did this. Genetically engineered a new breed of snails and kept them in a pen outside his clinic. Wu, Froelich, and Mota were his distributors with connections to the gay community as well as the brothels. The trio headed upriver every so often to pick up a new cask of snails. The pile of cash in that picture of them was their latest ill-begotten haul.

And Panama was their partner. A Yepala sheriff who took his cut of the profits in exchange for providing muscle as well as allowing the doctor to run his clinic on his land.

Maria sat next to me. "What's wrong? You look lost."

Not anymore, I'm not. The doctor had to be stopped. He'd brought us the genie. The ultimate date rape drug. The bastard was a menace. A scourge.

Her phone rang. "It's Chicho."

"Take it."

I stood and walked into the bathroom, lifted the seat with my shoe.

The genie.

A sickening thought came to mind. Lizard-man might've made Wu kill his own family, his own girls. Jesus. I didn't know if the drug was strong enough to make somebody do a thing so horrendous, but if it could make him shove his junk into a steel trap, then what couldn't it do?

The sudden urge to vomit overwhelmed me. I dropped to my knees and gagged into the toilet. Jesus.

I flushed and stood on my quivery legs. Maria was still on the phone. "Where? Tell me where!"

I hadn't paid any attention to her conversation until now. A rush of alarm struck, and I was out the door.

She was pacing, Chicho's holo moving to and fro to stay in front of her. I stepped through him, into her path, grabbed her by the elbow. "What is it?"

Words came out in a frantic, hyper stream. "My sister. A john attacked my s-sister. She's g-going to the hospital."

"That you, Juno?" asked holo-Chicho.

I took the phone from Maria. "It's me."

"A john cut one of my girls. What are you going to do about it?"

"Who is he?"

"He goes by the name J.T. I'm paying you for protection, you better take care of this."

"You know his address?"

The address popped in over his holo-head. I read it twice before hanging up.

I passed the phone back and looked into her terrified eyes. "Go to the hospital. Take care of her."

"He said she lost a lot of blood."

I guided her toward the door. "Just go. I'll take care of everything else."

I watched her hurry down the hall. A john cut her sister, and Chicho wanted me to rough him up.

I wasn't buying it. A john my ass. Chicho cut her himself. That rat bastard had gone back to Mota and helped him and Panama set their trap.

The showdown was near.

twenty-five

THE Rojo Caballo.

I sized up the hotel from a neighboring rooftop, eyes scanning up and down six stories of stone staircases and long outdoor walkways. Lights shined inside windows of the lower levels. The upper levels were dark and empty. Vacant. Abandoned.

This was the address Chicho gave me. The address of the supposed knife-happy john.

I scoped the two-tiered roof, its ragged tarps and gnarled rebar. Scrap metal rested in piles. Scaffolding had been there so long it could be mistaken for part of the structure.

The address came complete with a unit number: P2. *P* for penthouse, *2* for the two men who were about to die.

A light glowed inside one of the rooftop unit's windows. Probably just a flashlight positioned to make me think the john who had cut up Maria's sister actually lived there. I kept my eyes on the shadows, primed to spot movement of any kind. But they were keeping cool. Disciplined.

The smart move was to stay clear. The smarter move was to take advantage. They were planning to kill me on that rooftop. That meant they'd taken great pains to make sure they hadn't been seen getting up there. And that meant they hadn't told anybody of their whereabouts.

Which meant they'd made my job of getting away with murder that much easier.

Mota's setup was a yawner. Did he really think he could lure me to my death with that flimsy-ass story? That shit was grade-school.

I crossed the rooftop, feet tromping through leafy vines and ripped tar paper. I climbed a wall and jumped down to a lower rooftop, the long bag slung over my shoulder bouncing on my back. All I had to do now was hurdle that rail, cross that balcony down there, climb out onto that ledge, jump across this alley.

I checked the time. Maggie should be along any minute. Careful to stay in shadow, I leaned out and peered down at the street, where a jam of cars was gridlocked like bathroom tiles, pedestrians walking the grout lines. Horns and shouts echoed up the alley walls, the noisy sounds of a dysfunctional city.

There she was, crossing the street. Even from way up here, I recognized her, that confident stride, black locks waving in a light breeze. Maggie passed the Rojo Caballo's front door and entered the alley, reaching a staircase and starting up.

I moved again, butterflies lifting off in my gut, pulse beating faster. Harder. I walked to the edge and stepped off, dropped a meter to a balcony, the landing muffled by a soft bed of moss. I ducked under a pipe, detoured around a ventilation fan, and sidestepped my way out onto the ledge.

I looked down at the hotel. Maggie was on the fifth floor now. She tried a gate that led to the roof but found it locked. Mota and Panama had seen to it that there was only one point of entry, meaning Maggie would have to walk to the opposite end to the other gate. She stepped along the outdoor walkway, heels crunching crumbled concrete, hotel rooms on her left. Door, window, door, window, door, window . . .

I caught a glimpse of her face as she walked under a light, the beam catching a rock jaw and eyes like jade.

She passed below my position. I kept still. She had no idea I was here, no clue what I had planned.

I hadn't liked lying to her, but I did it. I'd told her I was ready to surrender my protection racket to Mota. I just needed her to negotiate the truce.

I'd told her all about Maria's sister getting cut, and how I thought Mota and Panama would be on the hotel's roof ready to ambush me. She could go in my place and work out a deal.

But it was all a ruse.

What I really needed was for someone to draw out Mota and Panama from their hiding places so I could kill them.

I couldn't feel bad about using her. Not now. Not until it was over. Time enough to repent later.

She was on the other end of the hotel now, going through the unlocked gate and disappearing up the stairs. I could hear her call Mota's name. "Don't shoot! It's Maggie Orzo."

I used my left to put the earpiece dangling on my shoulder into my ear. I recoiled at the volume when she shouted his name again. The bug I'd dropped in her hair had a sensitive pickup. She'd never find it. Small like a flea.

I sloughed the bag off my shoulder and reached in, pulled out a lase-rifle, unfolded the stock and snapped it into place.

"Captain Mota?" I heard in my ear. "Come on out. I came alone." *So she thinks.*

"What the fuck are you doing here?" Mota's voice.

"I'm unarmed," she said. "Juno's not coming. He didn't fall for that story Chicho told him. He knew it would be a trap. He sent me to negotiate a truce."

So she thinks.

I dropped the now empty bag, watched it sweep and sway its way down to the alley far below. I checked the rifle to see if the telemetry from Maggie's bug had been received. Green light.

"Who is this?" Maggie's voice.

"I'm a business partner from upriver." *Maggie, meet Panama.*

I gauged the distance across the alley. Two meters. A drop of, say, four. I could clear it easy. No problem.

I looked straight down. The alley was long and narrow with evenly spaced lights, the last one infected by a jittery flicker. I figured it best to jump now in case the jitters were contagious.

I held the rifle out front and pushed off with both feet. Air blew through my hair and billowed my shirt, my stomach climbing into my throat. I dropped as I crossed the narrow alley, sailing over the blacktop far underneath. I cleared the hotel wall, feet reaching for the roof of one of the penthouse units.

Contact.

Knees buckled.

Impact.

The rifle wrenched out of my hand. My body folded up, my chin driving into my knee with a clap of teeth. I fell backward, my back and head striking the wall.

Too stunned to move, I stayed where I was, my heart pumping mad beats. My lungs sucked wild breaths. I swallowed blood. My chin, teeth, and jaw suffered from a wicked uppercut. I thought the forward momentum would've been enough to take me into a roll, but my downward trajectory must've been too steep.

I fumbled for my earpiece, stuck it back in my ear. Maggie's voice came through the dazed fog. "He doesn't care about the protection business. You can have it back."

"And in exchange?"

"All we want is the doctor. We've been to that hellhole he calls a clinic. He's using people as lab rats."

"That's a little outside your jurisdiction, don't you think?" Panama's voice.

"He has an office here."

"He doesn't do anything illegal here. And what he does in Yepala is my jurisdiction."

They hadn't heard my fuckup of a landing. I tested my legs, couldn't feel them, but they moved when I told them to. I forced myself onto my hands and knees, started feeling around for my gun, thorny weeds poking and scraping.

I crawled on numb knees. It felt like I had two more stumps. My hand made contact, fingers wrapped around the rifle. I pulled the weapon up, pressed the cool steel of the barrel against my cheek. I struggled upright, using the rifle as a third leg.

Maggie spoke in my ear. "Juno offered to sweeten the deal."

Mota laughed. "Now you're saying he wants to buy his way out? What happened to the empty threats?"

I took slow, lurching steps, wobbled and weaved, toddler-like, toward the open arms of scaffolding pipes. I hooked my arms around them and leaned out, took a look, couldn't make visual. My weapon required line-of-sight.

I went to the corner, looked in another direction, couldn't see them. Shit.

I looked into the gunsight, studied the rifle's display. I saw numbers. Coordinates. Maggie's bug was reporting her exact position, its camera eye picking out Mota and Panama, calculating their positions, feeding the data into the targeting system. Somebody smarter than me would know how to read this thing. They'd do some quick math and know right where to go. All I saw was random numbers. Shit.

"It's too late for him, Maggie. He can't undo this. It's time he paid for all the shit he's done."

I climbed out onto the scaffolding. I needed to make my way down from the penthouse rooftop to the hotel proper. They had to be behind the other rooftop unit, close to the staircase Maggie had climbed.

I pulled out a pocket light and risked flicking it on. I carried it in my teeth, seeking a way down. I spotted a ladder, took a step in that direction, and stopped. How was a one-armed man going to carry a rifle down a ladder?

I jogged in the opposite direction, toward the street, found an access stairway and struggled with a single-hinged door, managing to angle myself through.

"She knows where he is." Panama's voice. "We can make her lead us to him."

"No. We'll find him another way."

"Fuck that. Let's teach her how we do it in the jungle."

"We're not in the jungle."

"I've never given a necktie to a woman."

"This is a homicide detective."

"So?"

"So, we can't bring that kind of heat down on ourselves."

I exited the stairwell and turned toward the hotel's rear.

"What are you talking about? You weren't opposed to killing cops when I nectktied those two in the Cellars."

"This one's well connected."

Maggie had no fear. "Don't be stupid. You touch me, and there'll be no deal. It'll be all-out war."

Panama's voice was full of malice. "That ship done sailed. The war is on."

I stepped into the shadow of the second penthouse unit. Flashlight off. Rifle raised. Eyes peeled. I lifted one shoe and then the other, taking high steps to keep from getting tangled in the vines.

Silence in my earpiece. Mota was mulling his options. I inched my way around a pile of scrap metal, choosing my steps oh-so-carefully. Sweat rolled down my nose, stung my eyes. The corner was close. Almost there.

I moved past, edging my way up to what used to be a mini-courtyard pinned between penthouse units. The staircase leading down sat on the far side. The junk-strewn courtyard was lit by a portable gas lamp sitting on a crate. Maggie faced my direction, her hands raised halfway, like she'd gotten tired of holding them high. Mota and Panama stood opposite Maggie, their weapons drawn, covering both her and the staircase.

Maggie broke the silence. "So what if the war already started. I'm giving you the chance to end it."

"And if we don't?"

"If you don't, my money's on Juno." A lengthy pause followed before she added, "He can be a ruthless son of a bitch."

Damn straight. Exhibit A: I wasn't above shooting two men in the back.

I blinked sweat out of my eyes, told my racing heart to settle down. I held my weapon lefty, finger on the trigger, forestock resting on what was left of my forearm.

I pinned down the trigger. No hesitation. No doubt. Panama was right. This was war.

I swept the weapon left to right, the targeting system firing timed bursts that briefly cast the rooftop in a fiery glow. Panama collapsed first, Mota an instant later, his body falling into a pile of scrap, followed by the sound of breaking glass.

Maggie's body jerked and she let out a startled scream. Her eyes and jaw opened wide. She blinked, her face dotted with blood. Same with her hands and shirt.

I rushed forward, toward the smell of roasted meat. She ducked and went for Panama's weapon, which still sat in his hand.

"It's me." I came out of the shadows, rifle in one hand.

She pulled the weapon from his dead grasp and held it in both hands, her face seized by shock.

"It's me," I repeated. "It's okay."

She lowered the gun. "What did you do?"

I stepped up to Mota's lifeless body, peeled his gun out of his hand. "I ended it."

She stared at the bodies, bewildered.

I watched the spreading pool of blood, his hat getting caught in the flow, blood sponging into the hat's weave.

Maggie looked at her hands, at the spattered blood. She wiped them on her pants.

My feet tickled with pins and needles, sensation slowly coming back. I turned to take another look at Mota, a pane of glass partly trapped under one shoulder, shards radiating outward. His pretty-boy face was pressed into the rooftop, nose squished up, lips pushed into a guppy mouth.

A fist struck my back. "What did you do!"

I winced and arched my back. Another shot landed, this one on the kidney, the heft of her pistol making the blow sink painfully deep. More blows came and I took every one of them. She hit me with words too, a torrent of angry venom: *They were listening to me, asshole. Why did you jump the gun? They were going to take the truce.*

She figured the rest of it soon enough. Words snapped from her lips. *You set me up. You didn't want a truce. You used me as a diversion. You made me an accessory.*

I waited quietly until she was spent, my back getting plenty tenderized.

Tentatively, I turned to face her and bowed my head. "I had to end it. There was no other way."

"Yes, there was, dammit! I was about to make a truce."

"We can't trust Mota's word."

"How do you know? You didn't even try."

I looked into her blood-speckled face. "Some doubts can't be left to chance."

Exasperated, she rubbed her forehead with her free hand. Feeling the blood, she pulled her hand away. "Jesus." She buried her face in her sleeve and tried to wipe it off. "You couldn't do it, could you? Couldn't give up your protection business

like you promised. Now you're eliminating your competition."

"I gave the protection business away."

"Bullshit."

"I did. I gave it to Chicho's bouncer. She and her sister are
going to run it."

Maggie aimed her gaze down at the bodies. A cloud of flies
swirled about. The sound of chittering lizards came from the
shadows, a four-legged army ready to feed. "Why didn't you
tell me what you were going to do?"

"You think you could've convinced them you were on the
up-and-up if you'd known? Would you have even come?"

"I can't believe you. I really can't. What are you going to do
with them?"

"Hide them under some scrap, come back in a few days after the flies and lizards pick them clean to collect the bones."

She closed her eyes. "Christ."

With nothing more to say, we stayed where we were, alone
with our thoughts, me hoping she'd accept the decisions I'd
made, hoping I hadn't driven us permanently apart. The air
hummed with flies. Squawking horns sounded from the street
while sirens sang somewhere in the distance.

I built up the nerve to ask, "Are we okay?"

She kept quiet, seconds stretching by. Finally she spoke. "Are
those sirens coming this way?"

twenty-six

My ears tuned into the whine of sirens. They couldn't be coming for us. *Couldn't be.* We were totally alone. Isolated in this
condemned rooftop courtyard.

Yet they grew in strength, the walls echoing with their wail.

Maggie pulled out her phone. I dropped my rifle and nabbed
the portable light, took off on a dead sprint, crossing the roof,
running for the side that faced the street.

I sped past ventilation fans, weaved around piles of junk,
skidded around a corner and up to the wall. I poked my head
over, into the blare of sirens, the strobe of blue and red lights a
mere block away.

I told myself they weren't coming for us. They were coming
for some other reason. Some kind of coincidence.

Packed traffic slowly parted, cop cars creeping closer, more
coming from the opposite direction. Shit!

I was running again, back the way I'd come, my brain tee-
tering on the brink. Maggie yelled to me, "We gotta go! They're
responding to a call of officer down."

She went partway down the stairs before I could summon
the breath to tell her to stop. "It's too late. They're almost
here. They'll have the alley and the hotel entrance blocked
before we can get down there."

She stopped. All I could see was the back of her head, the
rest of her body hidden by the staircase she'd partially descended.

Her voice sounded distant. Defeated. "Mota has a biomon. He gets wounded and it alerts KOP. Tells them where he is. They've been thinking about making them standard-issue."

"It's okay," I said, as if saying it could make it true. "I'll 'fess up. I'll cop to everything. You had nothing to do with it."

She turned to face me, her voice rigid with stern accusation. "You ruined everything."

"It'll be okay," I pleaded. "You'll be in the clear."

She came up a step. "I'll never see another promotion. You destroyed my career."

"It'll be okay."

Another step. "You made me an accomplice."

"I'll tell th—"

"I never should've associated with you." Step. "What was I thinking?" Step. "You're a selfish prick." Step. "A crazy drunk."

The words struck with such force that I wished she'd just punch me some more. I'd fucked it all up. Fucked it every possible way. I was going down. Hard.

But no way in hell was I going to let her fall with me. She didn't do anything wrong. She was KOP's only chance for a better future. She was family.

I had to keep her clear, but a flurry of logic painted a bleak best case. There'd be a full investigation. She'd have to face inquiries. What was your relationship with cop killer Juno Mozambe? To defend herself, she'd have to vilify Mota. She'd have to sully a dead cop's name. That in itself was a violation of the cop code. Even if she managed to keep her shield, her chances of becoming brass would be destroyed. Rusedski would bump her out of Homicide. She'd never be trusted with a position of leadership.

Cleaning up KOP was Maggie's mission. People like us needed a mission. Without a mission, we were empty shells. Husks of skin and bone.

Without a mission, we were like Niki. We might as well kill ourselves.

Maggie sliced me again with her tongue. "You ruin everything you touch, everything and everybody."

No. I squeezed my hand into a fist, pressed it into my forehead. I wouldn't go down like that. I couldn't. There was always a way. I'd flip this thing on its head. No such thing as a rap I couldn't beat. Nobody could work the angles like me. I was the king of cover-ups. Master of the frame job. Reality didn't mean shit to me. Not when I could create my own.

There was *always* a way.

I closed my eyes, darkness closing around me. I pushed a knuckle into my temple. *Think!*

Darkness cracked, a ray of light shining through. I rode the light. Thoughts dominoed. Random patterns lined up into rows.

I rushed up to Maggie, nose to nose, eye-to-eye. "Lock the gate."

She scrunched up disbelieving brows, but already there was a glint of hope in her eyes. She knew my genius. My gift.

I could feel the fire in my eyes, nerves gone electric. I was a mad scientist. A possessed soul. "Lock the gate. Do it now!"

She ran down the stairs, the power of my insanity impossible to resist.

I knelt next to Mota's body, blood seeping into my pant legs, flies bouncing off my hand, my face, slipping inside my shirt. I didn't let myself think about what I had to do. I grabbed his belt, yanked it free of its prong, and slid it through the buckle. I reached for his pants, grabbed the cloth next to the button, and wrestled it free.

Maggie was back.

I didn't look up. "My rifle. Get rid of it. Heave it onto another roof."

I pulled down the zipper, parted the flaps.

I heard the gate rattle on its hinges. They were here.

I gave instructions, my voice calm and flat. Disassociated. Like it wasn't my voice at all. "Flash your badge. Give orders. Tell them there's no emergency. I need a minute so don't let them break through the gate. Make them get a key. Stay back so they don't see the blood spatter on your clothes."

I reached into his shorts and pulled it out.

Voices echoed up the staircase, Maggie's take-charge attitude silencing them. She was the real deal. Always rose to the occasion. She was going to make a great chief.

I took a moment to study the broken glass that had been trapped under his body when he fell. I selected a long shard, picked it out of the expanding pool of blood.

Maggie returned. "What now?"

I stayed between her and Mota's body. "Did you let them see you?"

"I stayed back far as I could."

"Good. You need to cover the spatter patterns on your clothes. Flip Panama over like you're checking to see if he's alive. Get as much blood on you as you can."

I squeezed the glass shard tight in my hand, felt it dig into my palm. "We were following Lizard-man. He did this. We surprised him before he could finish. He made it down the stairs before we could stop him. He locked us in."

She wrestled with Panama's body, knees slip-sliding in blood as she rolled him over. She rubbed her hands together, wiped them on her shirt.

"That's good enough. Now get down there to greet them."

She hurried for the staircase. I waited until she disappeared from view. Didn't want her to see this.

I pinned it to his stomach with my right, sawed with my left. I was on autopilot. A machine. My soul locked inside a safe.

Cold. Efficient. Utterly ruthless.

The glass cut all the way through. The jingle of keys on a chain sounded nearby. I took my glass shiv by the edges and wiped it back and forth on my pant leg, bloody prints wiping off before carrying it a couple steps to a ventilation fan and dropping it through the grate, hearing it shatter somewhere inside.

The gate creaked open, the sound of shoes on stone stairs. I rushed back to Mota's body. Reached for it, picked it off his stomach.

Unis spilled onto the roof, two, four, six. Flashlights and quiet voices.

I held it in my fist. Had to take it with me. Had to plant it on Lizard-man when I found him. Had to.

I backed away from the body, from the mass of dancing flies. Nothing to see here.

I watched the unis, watched them look at me, at the bodies, back at me. I moved into shadow, leaned against the wall. I took my balled fist and shoved it into a pocket.

Maggie jumped on them. "This is a crime scene, people. We have a dead captain here. Nobody touches anything. Somebody go get me a goddamned towel."

One of the ashen-faced unis leapt at the chance to get away from the corpses. Maggie called to his back, "Get one for Juno too."

More unis arrived, one of them announcing that Lieutenant Rusedski was on his way. I stayed put, felt the cool brick through my shirt, luxuriated in it. A rush came on. The surge of exultant heat made my skin flush. My tingling feet felt like they were floating. I'd done it!

My soul came up from where it hid, body and soul reintegrating. With it, my mood spoiled, the rush going south. My floating feet fell, and my flushed skin broke into a sweat.

Did I really do it? Inside my pocket, I felt it in my fist. God, I had it in my hand. The urge to throw it and run seized me, and rattled nerves brought on a case of the shakes. I tamped it down, forced my hand to let go and pulled my fingers out of my pocket.

I stared at Mota's corpse. His defiled, desecrated corpse. Christ. If there was any justice at all, hell would have a special place reserved for me. They'd build me a whole wing.

The young officer returned with towels and a couple wet cloths. I approached and greedily nabbed a cloth before moving back into the shadows. I wiped my face, rubbed it over my cheeks, my forehead.

Maggie talked as she cleaned up, explaining to no one in particular, "We came here to find the serial who killed Froelich and Wu. I caught a tip from one of my informants. Said she heard from one of her hooker friends who turns tricks downstairs that she'd seen a strange guy hanging around up here. The description was close enough I thought I should check it out. Juno had a run-in with this guy so I brought him with me to see if he could identify him. We were about to plant ourselves in that bar across the way and watch for him to show when we see these two fools head into the alley and up the stairs. We wait a few minutes, unsure what to do, then decide to follow them up."

I wiped the cloth across my neck and forced myself to pay attention. Maggie wasn't really speaking to them. She was talking to me. Getting our story set before Rusedski arrived. Just in case he interviewed us separately.

"We come up those stairs, and this is what we find." She gestured at the bodies. "He must've heard us coming and hid behind that pile of junk there. We come through, and all of a sudden he's racing down the stairs behind us. Juno tried to catch him, but the guy was too quick. He got to the gate at the bottom first and locked us in."

I could feel the bulge in my pocket. I stood totally erect, trying to make my pants hang loose so I wouldn't feel it pressing against my leg.

Maggie unfolded her cloth, put the whole thing over her face and scrubbed it clean, her voice coming through her hands. "We checked to see if they were still alive, but they were long gone. By the time I went for my phone, the sirens were almost here. You must've just missed him. Anybody see a young guy running down the street, big mop of black hair?"

They shook their heads no.

I felt a trickle on my leg. Holy hell. I lifted my knee and sopped up the blood by forcing my pant leg taut.

A gruff voice came from the staircase. Lieutenant Rusedski. "What happened?" Spotting us, he stomped across the tar paper. "What the hell are you two doing here?"

Maggie kept cleaning her hands. "We were—"

He jabbed a finger at her. "I took you off the goddamned case!"

I squirmed in my pants, a blood spot showing right below the bulge.

Rusedski kept his ire on Maggie. "You are so fucking fired. I don't care who your parents are. You went too far this time."

She raised a hand, thumb and index finger almost touching. "We came this close to catching him. Where were you and your precious task force?"

Rusedski leaned in. "You've been holding out on me. Keeping evidence to yourself when you should've turned it over. You're fucking finished, you hear me?"

"I'm not going to listen to this shit. C'mon, Juno, let's go."

I gladly took a step toward the staircase. Toward salvation.

Rusedski put up a hand. "Not so fast, dammit." He motioned us past a pile of junk to where we could talk privately. "Tell me what happened, and you leave anything out, I swear to God I won't just bounce your ass, I'll bring charges."

Maggie huffed, playing the wrongly accused to a *T.* She went into it, same story as before. This time with more detail, more embellishments.

Another day, another place, I would've appreciated her performance, but I had to get out of these pants. God, I couldn't breathe, couldn't keep from checking the blood spot again. I could feel it resting on my leg. I could *feel* it.

Calm down. Pretend it's not there. Concentrate.

The coroner arrived. Not Abdul, dammit. He'd picked a fine time to take a day off.

The forensics wouldn't match. Wouldn't be close. Bronson Carew didn't shoot his victims. He stabbed them. His postmortem mutilations weren't ragged, half-assed cuts. He didn't leave chips of glass in the wounds. Probably wasn't left-handed either.

But Carew was a psycho. An unstable, delusional psycho. Who could say that his MO couldn't change? It wasn't that big a stretch, was it? Rusedski would fall for it. The killer was in a rush. He got interrupted midway. The evidence couldn't be expected to be a perfect match.

It was too big a leap for him to think I could've done this. That I shot two men in the back. That I pulled down Mota's pants, picked up a piece of glass, and did what I did. Too outlandish. Even for me. I wasn't that vicious. Or that desperate. I wasn't that fucked in the head.

Except I was.

Med techs set up lights. The coroner got generous with the fly gel, gunky globs applied to the wounds.

"Who is that?" He pointed at Panama.

Maggie said, "Ask Juno."

Great. Rusedski aimed eagle eyes at me. "Well?"

A fly landed on my pocket. I nervously swiped it away. I cleared my throat to make sure I still had a voice. "He's a Yepala cop, a sheriff."

"You shitting me?"

I shook my head and waved for him to come close, like I didn't want the unis and med techs to overhear. He took an impatient step forward, and I beckoned him closer, hoping that I could bring him in near enough that he'd have no place to put his eyes except my face.

He stayed where he was, his pissed glare telling me I better talk.

"The YOP sheriff was in business with Wu, Froelich, and Mota."

"What kind of business?"

I glanced down. Three flies on my leg. *Fuck.* I stuck my thumb in my pocket, let my fingers hang over the bulge. "They were dealing a new drug. The genie."

"Genie? As in magic lamp?"

I nodded as I struggled to line up the words in my head. *Concentrate.* "It's a date rape drug harvested from genetically engineered snails, but it doesn't put anybody under. It gives you control over them, makes them do anything you want."

He chewed his lip, processing.

I felt a fly on my knuckle, twitched a finger to make it take off. "You give somebody the genie and you get a helluva lot more than three wishes. It puts you in complete control until it wears off."

"How long does that take?"

I gave him an unknowing smirk.

He was silent, gnawing on his lip, wheels turning inside his eyes.

I wiggled my fingers, flies launching and boomeranging straight back. I had to get out of here, needed to fast-forward to the end of this conversation. This charade wouldn't last. Damn flies were going to give me away.

Words spilled out fast, nervous energy impossible to contain. "These assholes unleashed the ultimate rape drug. And the fucker who took my hand was one of its first victims. Bastard got raped, and then he got ignored when he came to the police."

"He came to us?"

"Damn straight. But when Froelich and Wu found out, they swept it under to keep their operation going. They said he was a willing participant, told him he must've enjoyed it. Now he's getting his revenge."

Rusedski kept gnawing that lip. I kept spinning my yarn. "Mota was all over my ass because he was trying to cover his. He and this piece of shit from Yepala necktied Kripsen and Lumbela in an attempt to stop me."

I saw a hint of fear creeping into his eyes. He was beginning to understand that he'd landed in the middle of a big-ass shit storm, and he was already trying to figure a way to keep himself clean. Classic low-level brass. First thought: containment.

I glanced down, my hand dotted with flies. My pants pocket too. I took a hurried step forward and bumped into him. I pulled my hand away from my pocket, put it on his shoulder, and whispered in his ear, "All these killings, it's all about the genie. The public gets word that two of your detectives unleashed this devil, you're going to fall."

Check-fucking-mate. I had all the leverage I needed. *You want containment, you stop riding Maggie. You give her whatever she wants. You make her a star.*

I opened my mouth to drive the point home.

He pulled away from me. "Who is he?"

"Who?"

"Who the fuck do you think? The serial. What's his name?"

"I don't know."

"Don't try that crap on me. He came to the police. He filed a report. What's his name?"

Shit. Shit. Shit. My heart sank into my stomach, my stomach into my intestines, intestines dropping right out of me. My leverage was gone, evaporated. *You said too much, you stupid shit.*

I couldn't let him find Carew. Not until I found him first. I had to plant my evidence. This case had to be closed up tight. And soon. I couldn't let Rusedski's task force mull over all the fucked forensics on this rooftop, couldn't let them think too long or they might pull on one of a thousand loose threads and unravel the fabric of our story.

"You two are done holding out on me." He turned to Maggie. "You think you can steal the glory? You think you can steal my job one day? Well, fuck you. You want to keep your job, you give me that name."

I couldn't tell him. I *had* to find Carew first. What were the odds we could outrace an entire task force? They'd post his pic on the news. Some do-gooder spots him and calls it in, we're done for.

"Tell me," he insisted.

My pocket was hopping with flies. I was out of time. Had to get out of here before he looked down.

He stared at Maggie. Then at me. He had us and he knew it. I'd said too damn much, gave my whole game away. *Idiot.*

"His name is Bronson Carew."

"Where does he live?"

"I don't know. He's been off the grid for months."

He eyed me with intense suspicion. I happily took the heat. All that mattered now was that he kept his gaze above my belt. "Look him up yourself, you don't believe me."

He pulled out his phone. "Don't think I won't."

I took the opportunity to move away, deeper into the darkness, my mini-swarm coming with, my heart rate red-fucking-lined.

I tried to ignore the flies, the thing in my pocket. I watched Rusedski call up a holo-head, black hair, eyes like wildfire. Bronson Carew.

My spine went to ice, visions of that face shifting into the stripe-faced man-eater, steel teeth dug into my flesh. The missing part of my arm tingled, a hollow kind of prickle. Unscratchable. Unsootheable. Unbearable.

I wanted out of these pants. Wanted out of this skin. Out of this nightmare of my own making.

Maggie kept her distance. The look on her face said I better get used to it. I told myself she couldn't cut me out of her life. Shit like this sticks to you. It follows you around for the rest of your life and beyond. She and I were permanently linked. Shackled. Like me and Niki. Me and Paul.

You couldn't ever cut the shackles loose. You just had to learn how to drag it all with you as you walked.

Rusedski put the phone in his pocket and stepped up to Maggie. "Here's how it's going to play. You're going home to clean up and then you're going in to work. You'll sit at your desk until I catch Carew. Day, night, I don't give a shit. You'll stay there until we catch his ass."

She nodded.

"And you're going to keep this genie shit under wraps, absolutely no mention of Froelich or Wu's involvement. Got it?"

"Yes, sir."

"You be a good girl, and I'll keep all this off your record."

The status quo had been reestablished, my checkmate reduced to a draw. I could live with a draw. So could Maggie. But I had to find Carew first.

Or it was game over.

twenty-seven

RUSEDSKI turned his back on us and faced the small crowd of hommy dicks. "The cop killer's name is Bronson Carew. Time for an old-fashioned manhunt. Listen carefully, this guy is dangerous. He killed your brothers in blue. Use any force necessary."

Rusedski's intent was clear. He didn't want a trial, didn't want the truth about his detectives' involvement with the genie to come out. On that score we agreed. The genie had to stay bottled.

But Maggie and I had far more to lose if Carew's story went public. Nobody could ever know that he was nowhere near this rooftop tonight. I couldn't let Rusedski's task force get Carew until I planted my evidence.

Questions came at Rusedski from several directions, his task force members seeking clarification. Maggie gave me a look and headed for the stairs. Good a time as any. I sucked in a deep breath and swept my hand over my pocket. Flies launched. I felt them bounce off my fingers, my shirt. I walked. They pelted me in the face. Buzzed in my ear.

I came out of the shadows, my eyes on Maggie's back, my heart thumping like a pile driver. Flies followed, black dots streaking across my vision.

I moved as fast as I could without drawing attention. I stepped around a junk pile and took one last peek at my handiwork. Mota and Panama, blank eyes staring at the Big Sleep's bleak sky.

I passed behind Rusedski. Flies darted into his circle and scribbled the air with humming flight patterns. I saw him shoo with his hand, as did the detective next to him. I put one foot in front of the other, the stairs only a few steps away. *Don't look. Don't look.*

Maggie was already on the stairs, me and my buzzing entourage approaching fast. I reached the stairs, took my first step down.

"Juno." I stopped at the sound of my name. As did my heart. Slowly, I turned my head, but kept my body facing forward, flies zeroing in on my pocket.

Rusedski's eyes were cold. My nerves turned frigid. "You stay out of our shit, you hear me? You're not a cop anymore."

I gave him the finger and hurried down the stairs.

I stood in the shower, hot water trickling from a caked showerhead. I'd scrubbed my skin clean three times over. Same with my hair, enduring the pain of a scalded scalp. I turned off the water and toweled, wet bandages feeling heavy on the end of my right arm.

I pulled on a fresh set of clothes and exited the bathroom. Two sealed plastic bags sat on the floor. One had my bloody clothes inside. The other leaked water onto the floor. I'd bought a nice piece of fish on ice around the block from the hotel, then found a bathroom, dumped the fish, and emptied the contents of my pocket into the bag of ice.

I suppressed a shiver. I was one demented bastard.

I checked the time. Deluski was supposed to be back by now. I went through the curtain, out to the hall and walked to his room, threw open the curtain.

The room was empty. Dammit. I needed to know what he'd found out about Carew. These last few hours were all the head start I had on Rusedski's task force.

I leaned against the door frame. Time ticked past, every second adding another turn of the wrench that had hold of my gut.

When we'd first left the hotel, Maggie and I walked down the street together for a time. I'd said something stupid, something like, "Close call."

I remembered the way she accelerated her pace. No relieved smile. No acknowledgment of my quick thinking skills. Nothing but double-timing legs trying to put distance between her and me.

The street had been crowded with cars and pedestrians, packed walkways and crammed sidewalk stands. Maggie carved a path for herself, legs pumping, me tagging along, saying things like, "Slow down," and "Hold on a minute."

I tried to tell her she couldn't shut me out. We were partners. She needed to find a way to forgive me. But she wouldn't look at me. Wouldn't stop. Wouldn't listen.

What else could I do but let her go? I had a lase-rifle to retrieve. I needed ice.

Deluski appeared at the end of the hall.

Finally. "What you got?"

He came my direction, with soft steps and worried eyes. "Not much. Nobody I talked to has seen Carew in months. His financials were interesting, though. He lives off a trust fund he got from a charity."

"Let me guess. Hudson Samusaka is a donor."

"And a board member. Carew made several big withdrawals starting about a year ago. The balance is almost zero."

"Probably used most of it to pay the doctor for his work."

He asked the big question: "What happened with Mota?"

"It's done." That was all the detail he'd ever get.

He blew out a breath. "It's really over?"

"You're clear. I want everything you got on Carew, then I

want you to move back home. Get some sleep and get back to work tomorrow."

"You're gonna need my help finding him."

I shook my head no. "He's not our problem anymore. I told Rusedski all about him. There's a whole task force tracking him down. Only a matter of time before they find him."

"You saying we're done?"

For him the answer was yes. I wasn't going to let him get dragged into the mess I'd made of things on that rooftop. Let him think it was Rusedski's game from here on out. "It's really over," I said.

His eyes misted, and he put a hand out to the wall to steady himself. "I can't believe it."

I grabbed his shoulder, squeezed down with my fingers. "You remember this day, you hear me? Fresh starts are hard as hell to come by."

He nodded, gaze aimed at the floor. I held on until he met me eye-to-eye, man to man. "You hear me?"

He nodded a yes.

"What did you get on Carew? I need to pass it along to Rusedski."

"I went down to the south-side docks where he grew up. I asked around but like I said, nobody's seen him, not in a long time. I got some family photos, pictures of when he was young." He handed me a chip.

"Thanks."

With a weak smile, he said, "I stopped at the hospital on my way back to check on Maria's sister."

"And?"

"She got cut up good."

"She'll live?"

"She'll need a lot of work if she wants to keep her job."

"She can work for Maria."

He went into his room to grab his things. I went into my own room, nabbed the bags on the floor, and headed toward the exit, leaving a trail of dripping water. I pushed my way outside into the church courtyard.

I threw the bag with my bloody clothes into the trash bin and made for the stairs to the street. The preacher gave me a wave from the church doorway. "Good-bye now."

"We're out of here," I said over my shoulder. "Thanks for the digs."

"Jesus loves you."

Only because he never met me.

I sat on a park bench, downed the last bite of a 'guana taco, hot sauce running down my wrist. I wiped my mouth with a napkin then set it flat on my lap and rubbed my wrist across it. Some of the simplest shit was such a pain in the ass.

The park was busy for so late: dice rollers and card players, flasks and bottles. People jawed, and loud music swirled in O smoke.

I was alone now. Completely, utterly alone. Didn't see that coming when Paul died. Didn't realize he was just the first to leave me. Niki. My crew. Maggie.

I balled the napkin and tossed it at an overflowing trash can. I sucked on a can of soda, bubbles making my overheated tongue sting. The leaky bag sat by my feet, my shoes in a growing puddle of water. I called to the woman behind the fryer, the one who had prepared my taco. "Got ice?"

She nodded, then stood and opened the cooler she'd been using as a chair.

I untied my bag, brought it over, and held it open so she could dump ice in, held it high so she wouldn't look inside. Finished, I tied it back up and returned to the bench.

I pulled out Deluski's chip from my pocket, pushed it against my temple; photos were picked up by my optic nerve, imagery going straight into my brain.

Bronson Carew as a baby, as a young boy. Always posing alone. A forced smile on his face.

Frustrated, I pulled away the chip. This shit was worthless. A manhunt like this required manpower. Rusedski had a task force. I had me.

Maggie should be helping. Her ass was on the line same as mine. But she was chained to her desk until Carew was caught. Truth was I wasn't sure she would help even if she could. I'd pushed her too far. She had a good heart, and the goodhearted couldn't associate with me, not if they wanted to stay that way.

I'd have to pull our asses out of the fire myself. Plenty fair considering I was the one who struck the match.

I put the chip back to my temple and called up his mother's picture. Silver hair. Brown skin rutted like a sun-baked terracotta rooftop. She seemed too old to have given birth to a nineteen-year-old. Lagartan women weren't prone to gestate their babies in tanks like offworlders. Didn't have the money.

I pulled up a pic of his two older sisters when they were his age. Locked arms and broad smiles.

I pulled away the chip, the sisters' image fading with it. I recognized her. The sister on the right.

Miss Paulina.

New possibilities blew into my mind, a ripple effect of connections and deductions. Sudden understanding gusted at gale force.

Riding a high of explosive comprehension, I stood and grabbed my plastic bag, tossed it over my shoulder, and let the ice chill my back as I walked, a glimmer of imaginary sunlight marking my path.

twenty-eight

THE car I'd been following pulled into a reserved space next to a glass-enclosed office building. I handed a thousand pesos to the cabdriver and climbed out onto the curb.

She was out of her car now, heading toward the building entrance, long legs taking short strides inside an ankle-length tapered skirt.

I did my best to ignore the kink in my back—last night's rooftop hop still exacted a toll—and hustled to catch up. She stepped toward the door, hips wagging, straight black hair moving to and fro. I closed the distance, the bag of ice swinging from my hand.

She heard my approach and glanced over her shoulder.

"Mrs. Samusaka."

She stopped, her hand on the door handle, her face as icy as the diamond studs in her ears. "Are you following me?"

"I need to talk to you."

"You'll need to make an appointment." She pulled open the door.

"I need to talk to you *now*. Walk with me."

"I'll do nothing of the sort." She stepped through and let go of the handle.

I shoved my words through the closing gap, getting the whole sentence out just before the door shut. "I know who killed your son."

She slowly turned around and faced me through the thick

glass. Reflections from the neon signs atop the bank across the street sparkled in the glass, her blank canvas of a face painted with flashing reds and blues.

She cracked the door. "He wasn't murdered."

"He was."

"The police said—"

"The police lied."

"Why would they do that?"

"Because your husband paid them to."

She didn't know what to believe, her face pressed into the slivered door, her eyes swirling pools of confusion. "That's not true. You're a damn liar." Her tone didn't match her words; instead, the accusation limped from her mouth.

"Please, walk with me. You'll never forgive yourself if you don't at least listen to what I have to say."

She took a look around, like she had to remind herself where she was. Then she came out and with a little more coaxing fell in step alongside my clipped wing.

"What do you know?"

The street was late-morning lackadaisical, light traffic and strolling pedestrians. I took weighty steps knowing the revelations I was about to unload.

"Your stepson killed your son."

"I don't have a stepson."

"That's because your husband never told you. His name is Bronson Carew."

She grabbed my arm, nails digging like claws. "Carew? That's Paulina's name."

"Your housekeeper. Yes. Your husband got her pregnant, but he couldn't allow her to raise the child in your house or you'd eventually find out. You'd catch him playing with the boy. Or you'd see the resemblance in the boy's face. One way or another you'd find out, so she sent him to be raised by his grandmother."

She let go of my arm. "She could've quit to raise him."

"But she didn't. Maybe she loved your husband. Or maybe she couldn't face going back to life on the south-side docks. Whatever the reason, she chose to stay in your home and sent her son to be with her mother. She probably convinced herself that the best thing she could do for her son was to keep earning a regular paycheck."

We turned left, this street too narrow for cars, traffic noise fading, the rocking sound of slushing ice taking its place.

"But I don't ever remember her being pregnant."

"Did she ever take a leave of absence?"

"She left us for a few months once. She had to care for her sick father."

"Nineteen years ago?"

Her last objection dashed, Crystal Samusaka stopped in her tracks. "That son of a bitch."

I faced her profile, her lips pinched so tight I could barely see her lipstick. "Has he been unfaithful before?"

She stared straight ahead. "My husband is a selfish man. But he never had a bastard before."

"Why did you stay with him?"

She took a large, overreaching step but the tapered skirt held her back. "I wasn't born rich, Mr. Mozambe." She hiked up her dress to her knees and stormed forward, short strides no longer satisfactory.

I stayed with her. "Your husband paid the police to report your son's death as an overdose. I couldn't understand why he wouldn't want the police to find his son's murderer until I realized he was protecting another son."

"My God, Paulina brought a young boy to the house sometimes. She said he was her nephew. Brownie was his name."

"Could be a nickname for Bronson."

"He was such a strange boy."

"Did he play with your sons?"

"Sometimes, but mostly they picked on him. He couldn't have been more than nine or ten when she stopped bringing him. But I saw him years later when Franz brought him around. Franz said he'd run into Brownie somewhere, and now they were palling around."

I stopped, put the bag down, and pulled Deluski's chip from my pocket, held it to her temple. "That him?"

She jerked her head away. "That's him." Tears came, twin raindrops rolling down her cheeks, her mouth caught in a silent, misshapen cry. She let her skirt fall back down, hands moved to her eyes.

"Why?" she managed to wail. "Why did he kill my boy? Franz tried to be his friend."

I lowered my eyes. "You won't like the answer."

"Tell me!"

"Your son was involved in the gay community. At some point he got sucked into a clique centered around an offworld doctor. This doctor made a new drug called the genie. It makes people extremely susceptible to suggestion. Your son Franz used the drug on Carew. He raped him for several days."

The crying stopped. I expected denial. Refusal to believe. A wall of motherly love that would keep her from seeing the truth about her son. Instead she asked, "Is it a pill?"

"A liquid. It comes from snails."

Her face went white. She wobbled on woozy legs. I reached for her in an attempt to catch her before she went down, but she'd already dropped to a seat on the asphalt. "Snails," she whispered.

I sat next to her. "That's right."

A pair of teenagers walked by, strange looks aimed our way.

"Hudson gave me a snail to eat."

I nodded, not entirely surprised.

"He told me it was a delicacy, fed it to me in a wine sauce. It was his birthday. He took me to bed, undressed me. Th-then he brought out a stranger from the closet. I remember wondering what he was doing in there. Hudson told me he was a friend. He wanted me to have sex with this man while he watched."

The genie was true evil. "And you did it."

"I did. I didn't want to, but I did. I couldn't understand what was wrong with me. I thought I was depraved. I mean, who would do something like that?"

"You were raped."

She pulled at her hair, strands coming out in her fingers. "I fucked him."

"That wasn't you. It was the drug."

"How could I—"

I pulled her hand away from her hair, gave it a pat. "It wasn't you."

"Oh my God, he filmed it. I let him film it."

"When was this?"

"He just had another birthday, so a little over a year ago."

The last tile cemented into place, the Samusakas' dirty mosaic now in full focus. Franz and his pop were quite a pair. Franz the young entrepreneur, selling the doc's plastic surgery and introducing the genie to his gay friends. His father, a man who treated family like possessions. A man who would let his own wife get raped for his pleasure.

Franz must've shared the genie with his father. *Hey, Pop, look what this snail can do. Gee, that's pretty neat, son. I think I'll try that on your mom.*

"Do you remember when your home was broken into?"

She closed her eyes, her hands back in her hair, squeezing down, clumped strands poking through her knuckles like weeds through a fence.

"That was Carew's doing. Paulina let him in, which was why no windows or locks were broken. He wanted Franz's rape vid. He ransacked Franz's room to find it and then he brought it to the police, but the police ignored it. These were the same two detectives who later covered up your son's murder. They said the vid didn't prove he was raped. Looked like he enjoyed it."

She wrung her hair some more.

"Carew killed them."

She moaned.

I kept talking. "Your other son, Ang, was the first to find his brother's room after Carew ransacked it. But instead of reporting the robbery right away, he decided to hit his father's study. He doesn't like his father, does he? I'm guessing Franz was your husband's favorite."

I couldn't tell if her moaning meant I was right or wrong. I plowed ahead anyway. "Ang found your husband's vid, the vid of him feeding you the snail and everything that followed."

She grabbed my arm, nails digging in. "Are you saying my son watched me?"

"Yes. He has the vid. But at first, he let your husband think the burglar took it. It must've taken him a few days to figure out what he wanted to do with it. He's been using it to blackmail your husband ever since. I didn't know what was on the vid until now."

Her moans turned to sobs. Another shattered life. *Welcome to the club.*

"Carew went into hiding after killing Franz. Nobody will admit to seeing him since. Your husband and housekeeper won't talk to me. I came to you hoping you could help me find him."

She wiped her face with a sleeve, fabric streaked with mascara. "How would I know where he is?"

Figured as much. I stood and stretched my aching back. I picked up my bag. It was mostly water now, the ice melting away. Just like my options.

"Brownie ran away one time."

"He did?"

"This was right before Paulina stopped bringing him over. He was gone for two days, hiding in the abandoned boathouse."

"You have a boathouse on your property?"

"It's on the lake. Hudson's father used to fish there. When he died, Hudson stopped maintaining it. He doesn't like to fish."

"Is it still there?"

"It's jungle now."

The boathouse was right where Crystal Samusaka said it would be, cracked stone walls held in place by a sprawl of thick roots that spilled down the sides like a melted scoop of coffee ice cream, ferns sprouting from the crevices.

I sloshed through shallow lake water. I'd given up on the trail, thick jungle making it nearly impassable. I looked back to see if anybody was coming. Stopped and listened.

I'd gotten a helluva scare when I jumped the wall, saw a line of uniforms with flashlights coming right at me. Rusedski's task force had made the Carew–Samusaka connection, and a search of the grounds was under way. Wouldn't be long before they made it here.

Rusedski was probably in the main house right now, grilling Hudson and Miss Paulina, the proud parents of a lizard-man serial.

I climbed onto the twisted dock, turned off my flashlight, and pulled the weapon I'd picked up on the way here, actually stopped by my place to get it. I faced the boathouse, honed in on dim light seeping from the window.

He was here. And time was short.

Dock boards creaked under my shoes. I gripped the weapon tight in my left, plastic bag handles hooked over my right's crooked elbow.

I moved slowly in the dark, approaching the doorway, picking my way through tumbled stone and tangled roots when a loose rock rolled out from under my foot. I caught my balance, plastic bag swinging from my arm, the sound of crinkling plastic. I steadied the bag with my gun hand, breath held in my lungs, silence restored.

Did he hear that? I waited, listening.

Nothing.

I allowed myself to breathe, allowed my foot to take another step when a voice came from inside. "I can hear you."

My soaked pant legs suddenly felt cold, like I'd waded through ice water. I trained my weapon on the doorway, finger sweating on the trigger. *Wait for him to come check on the noise. Just wait him out.*

Time passed, a minute, maybe longer.

"I can see you."

Heartbeats thudded in my chest. *Don't believe him. Stay quiet and force him to come to you.*

"I can see you through a crack in the wall. Whoever you are, you should come in. I don't have a gun."

His voice was calm. Soft. I didn't move, eyes probing the shadows, my finger primed to fry the doorway with fire.

The wall lit with points of light, a bright light poking through a half dozen cracks and holes. I looked down at the constellation of light spots on my chest. Shit.

"See, I could've shot you right then if I had a gun instead of this flashlight. Come inside."

I wanted to run. Wanted to be anywhere but inside that boathouse. But I had no choice. I had to see this through.

I followed my weapon to the doorway—a slanted rectangle of stone—and inched my way inside. The air was scented with formaldehyde. Weak light drooled from a portable light wedged into a cluster of roots that had conquered the rafters. The room was long and narrow. Floor-to-ceiling racks ran up each side with canoes stowed in several bays, one of the shelves converted to a sleeping space, pillow resting on a blanket.

I stood face-to-face with Bronson Carew, arms by his sides, his flashlight aimed at the ground. He glanced down to the missing part of my right arm, an out-of-kilter smile forming. "It's you."

I kept my lase-pistol on his chest, wondering why I hadn't already wasted the bastard.

Black bangs hung over ink-centered eyes. "You can't shoot me. In fact, you're going to give me your gun."

I caressed the trigger, itching to get this over with, but he was unafraid. Confident.

He twisted his neck to look toward the boathouse's back corner. "Come on out, Ang."

From behind one of the canoes came Ang Samusaka. He held a knife to his own throat, trickles of blood running down his neck and sopping into his shirt collar.

Carew reached a hand into his shirt pocket, pulled out an empty snail shell. "I told him if anything happens to me, he should start slicing. Give me your gun."

Shoot him anyway. That was my first instinct. Who gave a shit about the Samusakas' youngest? Punk was a junkie black-mailer. Screw him.

Carew put his index finger into the shell, made it dance like a finger puppet. "Give it or I tell him to do it."

I had to pull the trigger. Kill him and plant my evidence. The Samusaka kid didn't matter. Let him hack through his carotids. Why should I care?

Carew put the shell back in his pocket and held out his hand. "Gimme."

My gaze turned back to Ang, knife held in his fist, blade pressed under his chin. Eyes dead as gravestones. "Ang. Put the knife down."

He didn't budge.

"Don't bother," said Carew. "Keep at him long enough, he might start obeying you. But I've been working him for a whole day now."

Ang was so young. Barely out of school.

Stop thinking that way. He's a junkie and a blackmailer. He was disposable. I couldn't afford to let myself think of him as a victim.

A victim trapped in this hell for a whole day. Victim of a fucked-up home. A domineering asshole of a father.

Just like my father.

And Niki's father.

Like so much of the misery in this world, all of our collective pain and anguish could be traced back to that one simple cause: assholes having babies.

Carew held out his hand. "Give me the gun."

"Ang!" I called. "Put the knife down."

Carew stepped forward, put his hand over my gun's barrel. "Let go."

I didn't want to. This was a time to be hard. Cold. Ruthless. This fucker had to burn. Wu's little girls demanded it.

Yet there was Ang, his death sentence tied to my trigger finger.

A cockeyed grin broke on Carew's face. "Ang, this is your brother. When you hear me reach three, start cutting."

Sweat rolled down the back of my neck, pulse kicking into high gear. *Pull the trigger. Fucking do it.*

"One."

Can't be helped, Ang. Collateral damage. That's what you are.

"Two."

Heartbeats flew by like fence posts at high speed. *You should've grown up faster, Ang. Should've made your life count for something when you had the chance.*

"Th—"

"No!"

His voice stopped short, lips poised to finish the word.

"Fucking take it." Disgusted, I let him twist my gun from clinging fingers. My hand stayed where it was, reluctant to break aim. I glared at the blank-faced Ang. *You better be worth it.*

Carew took a step back and trained the lase-pistol on my head. "Move away from the door."

I complied. Plan B was already formulating. Cops were coming. Soon. All I had to do was keep us alive for another ten minutes. Fifteen, tops. No fucking problem. Son of a bitch like him had to play with his prey before feeding.

"Don't want you running away. Go over to the window. Get on your knees."

I walked to the window, a row of wrought iron bars twisted by a strangle of viny roots. I stole a look out, praying for the sight of approaching flashlights. No luck.

I set my plastic bag on the floor and dropped to my knees next to a short stack of canned goods, Ang little more than a meter away. "Tell him to put the knife down."

Keeping the gun trained on my head, Carew took a seat on a short stool by the door. "Ang, my darling brother, it's time to cut your throat."

Before I could react, Ang dragged the blade across his flesh, plowing a deep red furrow.

I jumped for him, reached too late, caught a warm spray on my hand. "What the fuck!"

Carew laughed, a childlike giggle etching into my eardrums. "You should see the look on your face."

Helpless, I watched Ang fall forward, bumping one of the canoes partly off its shelf before he flopped to the left and hit the floor, a bent-back leg pinned underneath as his blood and life drained into the dirt.

Bile scorched my throat. I'd fucked up royally. *Never give up control. Never!*

The sound of screeching lizards drew my eyes to the wall, a half dozen stripe-faced man-eaters reacting to the ruckus, strings running from a stake in the ground to tiny leather collars around their necks. To their right sat a small terrarium, slimy glass walls dotted with snails.

God, I was such a dumb fuck. I wiped my hand on my pant leg, white linen stained red. Just like my burning cheeks. I should've known better, dammit.

"You should've shot me," he said.

"No fucking kidding." Cops are coming, I told myself. This wasn't over. They'd be here soon. They'd see the light in the window just like I did.

"Who are you?"

"Juno." All I needed was time.

"You a cop?"

"Used to be." Just keep him talking.

"Cops are liars."

"Yes, they are." Time.

"You were in Wu's apartment when I brought back his head."

"I was." Every second my odds got better.

"You saw his wife and daughters."

"I did." *Tick, tick, tick.*

"He killed them all himself, you know. You should've seen it."

I opened my mouth to respond but his words drilled deep. Some suspicions didn't need confirmation. The thought of those poor girls waking up in bed, their father standing over them, a lase-blade in his hand. The confusion. The betrayal. The terror.

I couldn't stand to look at him, had to look away, my eyes landing on Ang's lifeless body.

His gaze followed mine. "Now I regret killing him so soon." He pulled a tube of glue from his pants pocket and gave it a good whiff. "I wasn't done with him. Barely got started. But I couldn't resist fucking with your head."

I turned back to him; his grin was knotted and twisted like the gnarled roots hanging overhead. "He was your brother."

Carew made like he wanted to spit. "He was spoiled. Undeserving."

"Sounds like every rich kid I ever met. What did he ever do to you?"

"He wouldn't respect me. *Me*. His own brother. I'm no street trash." He rapped the gun against his chest. "I'm a Samusaka! He and his asshole brother lived in *my* rightful home. They ate for free. They fucked for free. They got everything they ever wanted, cars and clothes. Money. I deserved to live that life. I'm his son too."

"Did they even know you were their brother?"

He brushed the question away with a wave of the gun. "Why are you here?"

I bit the inside of my cheek, unsure how to play it. Decided I had nothing to lose by playing it straight. "I came here to kill you."

"Ha!" He waved the gun at me. "How did that work out?"

"Not good."

"Why do you want to kill me?"

"You're a monster."

He leveled the lase-pistol. "That's not true. Take it back."

I stared into the barrel, wanting to wilt, wanting to melt

into the dirt. But I had to keep him talking. I fished for courage, summoned enough to look him in the eye. "You kill people for no reason."

"Bullshit! They deserved it. Every one of them deserved to
die."

"Wu's family didn't deserve it."

"Detective Wu was a liar. His wife deserved it for fucking
him. His spawn was tainted."

"Those girls were innocent."

"Don't give me that. I bet you didn't even know them. What
were their names?"

I didn't know.

"You're a fucking idiot. You live in a dream world like all the
other fucking idiots, thinking children are magical little angels. My brothers weren't angels. They stole my whole life. My
father. My home. They took my mother and made her nanny
them instead of me." His tone turned caustic, corrosive. "I was
her son, goddamnit. That was my food she cooked and fed to
them. That was my play time they stole. Those were my smiles
and hugs."

I sharpened my tongue, the only weapon I had left. "That's
because she loved them more than she loved you."

I thought I saw an eye twitch, the only sign that my blow
might've landed.

He stood and walked to his dead brother; the exposed parts
were already covered with flies and geckos. Nearby, the man-
eaters strained at their collars, feet scratching at the dirt, desperate to go in for a feed. "Well, now she'll have no choice
who to love most. Same with my father."

Carew moved the gun to his left hand, kept it and one eye
on me while his right hand shifted into the steel trap that took
my hand. "I'm the only one left."

He opened the jaws wide and reached for his brother's thigh.

I closed my eyes, heard the snap, heard the thump of meat landing in the dirt, the excited squeals of lizards.

Jesus. I rubbed my arm, told myself not to panic. The cops were coming, had to be getting close. When I opened my eyes, he was back on the stool, his hand returned to normal.

Buy time. Keep him talking. "You get that steel trap from Dr. Franklin?"

"I got *two* steel traps." He gave me a wink. "I was getting ready to use my favorite on my dear brother, but now I'll have to use it on you."

A chill came over me, nerves coated in frost.

He startled me by jumping up from his seat. "I want to show you something." He grabbed hold of a low-to-the-ground canoe and pulled it off its shelf to the floor. I heard the sound of clanking glass. "Look."

I raised up on my knees to peer over the canoe's rail. Glass jars gathered at the boat's low point, flesh souvenirs preserved in formaldehyde. Hair stood up on my arms and the back of my neck.

"I'm going to add yours to my collection."

I looked to the door. What the fuck was taking them so long?

"What's in the bag?" he asked.

"Why don't you come see?"

"Nice try. Throw it over here."

I grabbed the plastic handles and tossed it in his direction. He snatched it up and poured the contents out onto the ground, the dirt acting like a sieve, water running into the earth while a few last ice cubes stayed on the surface along with what I'd taken from Mota's corpse.

Carew's face bunched in puzzlement. "What have you brought me?"

"What does it look like?"

He bent down and picked it up. He held it to the light, licked his lips. "I don't understand."

"Consider it a gift."

His dark eyes didn't know what to make of that, but he couldn't resist. He carried it to the far corner, set it on a shelf, and grabbed an empty jar with his now free hand. He raised the jar to his mouth and blew out the dust before setting it on the ground and reaching for a glass jug. He removed the stopper and did a sloppy job of pouring with one hand, formaldehyde splashing and spraying, a rotten pickling smell wafting through the room.

He dropped my "gift" into the jar and sealed it. "We're more alike than I thought."

"We're nothing alike."

A crooked grin. "Whose is it?"

I shook my head, no intention of answering.

"I can make you talk." He stepped to the terrarium and lifted the lid.

No fucking way. I'd make him shoot me first.

He nabbed a snail, tossed it at my feet. "Eat."

I picked up the snail, held it up to study it. "Franz made you eat one of these, didn't he?"

"Franz." He said the name like it was a bitter pill. "He pretended to like me, acted like he was happy to have a new brother. He brought me to the house a few times, introduced me to Ang. Then he invited me to a party at an abandoned house near his old school."

I turned the shell in my fingers.

He shook his head to fling hair out of venomous eyes. "He told me it would get me high, like sniffing glue." His voice choked on emotion, the gun trembling in his hand. "Then he took me upstairs an . . . and he kept me there."

"But you made him pay."

"Damn straight. First I took his weapon." He aimed the lase-pistol at my crotch. "Then I took his life. He learned his lesson. Believe me, he learned his lesson. Now eat."

Fuck that. I threw the snail out the window.

The air exploded with fire. I closed my eyes against the flash of heat, the spray of stone shrapnel and burned moss. I covered my head, lungs choking on smoke.

The smoke cleared and I straightened up, the warmth of hot stone at my back. He shook his head like he was disappointed in me before tossing another snail my way. "Eat."

I reached for the snail, tossed it back at him. "No."

He came at me, the gun trained on my head the whole time. He stepped straight up to me, pressed the lase-pistol's barrel against my left eye like I'd once done to him. I felt wet snail pushing against my lips. I kept my mouth closed, lips pinched tight like steel doors against the pressure.

"Eat!"

No fucking way.

A voice sounded from somewhere outside. I felt the lase-pistol lift off my eye, the snail off my lips. He leaned toward the window.

I didn't hesitate, arms reaching, feet centering underneath me. I had him around the hips, shoulder in his gut, knees extending, legs surging forward. The lase-pistol fired, a sizzling explosion somewhere behind me. I lifted him off the ground and threw him down with all the force I could.

He hit with a thump, a cloud of dirt dusting up. I kicked at the weapon in his hand and made contact with the toe of my shoe. The gun bounced free.

I lunged for the lase-pistol, reached for it with the wrong hand, reached with fingers that weren't fucking there. I switched hands, but he was on me before I could grab hold, the two of us tumbling to the ground, roots jabbing into my shoulder and backbone.

He was on top of me, skin like slate, forked tongue flicking. He punched with his steel trap hand, my jaw taking a brick-like impact. My vision went hazy, my arms and legs weak. A blur of jagged steel came for my throat.

I couldn't stop him, my reflexes soaked in molasses.

The room went bright with lase-fire, shouts all around. I saw double-vision uniforms. Heard garbled voices I couldn't understand.

I closed my eyes and let sleep come on a draft of charred meat.

twenty-nine

WE faced the curtain of strung monitor teeth, light leaking out from Chicho's office. We'd already chased out all the hookers from the lobby. The johns too.

"You ready?" whispered Maria.

I was. Chicho had to be tamed once and for all. Prick thought he could welsh on our deal? Thought a little case of buyer's remorse entitled him to dump me for Mota? This asshole cut up Maria's sister and set me up to die.

But the business wasn't mine anymore. I put my hand on Maria's shoulder. "You need to do this on your own."

She turned her eyes on me, heavily inked lashes and painted lids, little worry lines in the corners.

"You'll do fine. I'll wait right here."

"But—"

"Remember what he did to your sister."

She nodded and erased the fear from her face, the lines becoming deep, angry cuts. She extended the telescoping steel baton in her hand.

"Be strong but stay under control. Never lose control."

She tilted my way to give me a peck on the cheek. I leaned into the kiss, took a welcome shot of perfume up the nose.

She went through the curtain. I listened to the strands of teeth clacking and chattering. I heard him argue. Then a thump. Followed by more thumps. Apart from the yelps and whimpers, it sounded like somebody using a rug beater on a heavy rug. A dirty, filthy, mud-caked rug.

I found a seat and reclined into the cushions. Rug like that might take a while to clean.

thirty

I WATCHED the street, a woman sweeping her sidewalk, another pushing a squeaky-wheeled cart piled with fried dough. Signs of a waking city.

I waited on Maggie's steps just like I had a couple weeks ago. She would come out soon. Almost time for work. I hadn't tried to contact her until now. Keeping my distance seemed like the right thing to do. Let her take time to cool. Let her reason things through.

I looked over my shoulder at the door. Through the crack along the bottom, I could see lights on inside. Wouldn't be much longer.

I decided to keep myself busy. I reached into a pocket and pulled out a small spool of fishing line, the thickest, heaviest line I could buy. Using my leg as a meter stick, I uncoiled a rough ten meters and threaded one end through a sinker. Now how in the hell was I going to tie a knot?

I manipulated the line with one hand, looping and twisting, pulling the knot tight, holding it up, and watched the sinker fall off the end. Damn.

I tried again, used all my powers of concentration. It was a momentary break from a constant rehashing of the last few weeks, my thoughts shadowed by storm clouds, menacing black billows of my own making.

I wished it would end, the nonstop barrage of racing thoughts.

The constant accounting of a lifetime full of mistakes. Failures of courage and pride. Failures of stupidity and hubris.

The door opened behind me, and I heard a weary sigh. I twisted around to see her: pressed blouse and slacks, shined shoes that reflected the porch light.

She looked down at me. "I was wondering when you'd show up."

I took a deep breath, organized the thoughts in my head. "I need you to know I had your best interests at heart from the very beginning."

She came down the first few steps to take a seat. "I know you did."

"Things just went to hell."

"You can say that again."

"Everything I did, I did for the right reasons. I didn't mean to—"

She put a hand on my arm. "You can stop."

Relief blew through my mind like a fresh breeze, stormy skies parting. "So we're okay?"

"I've been thinking about something you asked the last time we talked on these steps. You remember asking what I saw in you when we worked that first case?"

I did.

"Loyalty. That was what stood out. Loyalty to the chief. Your wife. Your people. You're the most fiercely loyal person I've ever seen."

The praise made me uncomfortable. I looked down, fiddled with the still-unattached sinker.

"You were a loyal friend to me until you seized that crew of yours. That was when you started shutting me out, started making decisions without me. Big decisions. All the shit you put me through, that's the thing that bothers me most."

"I was trying to protect you."

"Of course you were." She chuckled to herself. "Always loyal."

We both stewed in the irony, me rolling the sinker in my fingers, her silently rubbing her hands together. "You heard all the cases closed. Mota and the Yepala sheriff. Carew. Wu and Froelich."

I nodded, my voice somber. "Kripsen and Lumbela too."

"Nobody will ever know what really happened on that rooftop."

"Nobody but you and me." I needed confirmation, had to ask again. "So we're good?"

"You done shutting me out?"

"I'm done."

"We do this together?"

"Together," I said. We were partners again. A team. The goal hadn't changed. I still had to take back KOP. Maggie had to become chief. Only this time we'd do it different. We'd do it without a power base centered in criminal activity. This time, we'd do it the *right* way.

"What are you going to do about your arm?"

"I made a doctor's appointment for next week."

"Really?"

I nodded.

"Are you going to have them grow you a new hand or go with something artificial? They can do some amazing stuff, you know."

"I don't want that high-tech shit."

She smiled. "A newly grown hand it is."

"Actually, I was thinking of a hook."

She laughed like I was joking. But I wasn't. I could do some damage with a hook.

The laughter faded, but we stayed where we were, together again. I had to tell her what I had planned. From now on, decisions like this had to be made together.

I cleared my throat. "I've been figuring I should go to Yepala tomorrow and kill the doctor. What do you think?" I almost laughed at how ridiculous it sounded, but there it was. Business partners talking business.

Her body tensed. I could see it in her posture, the way her spine straightened, the way her shoulders crept up. She wrung her hands as if they were a poor substitute for my neck. But she stayed silent. She knew I was right. It was the only way.

She pulled up her legs, dropped her chin onto her knees. "I reported the doctor to the governor's office."

"And?"

"His staffer brushed me off. Thanked me for bringing the issue to their attention and showed me the door."

"Did you expect anything different?"

"No. But I had to try."

"The doctor has to die, Maggie." Simple as that.

"He's an offworlder. You know how many self-defense systems he must have inside him?"

"I made a plan." I held up the sinker. "Help me tie this thing on."

I flicked another gecko off my arm. The little shits kept crawling all over me. The clinic's thatch rooftop was totally infested with geckos and 'guanas. I reminded myself that this was a good thing. It meant there was so much scratching and climbing, nobody would notice if I made some noise.

I remembered the first time I had the chance to kill the doctor, when he was sleeping in Mota's bed. At the time, I didn't know he was an offworlder. Didn't even know there was a man under those curly locks and that petite nose.

Turned out I was lucky as hell that I didn't make the attempt or the doc would've smoked me a dozen different ways. Killing an offworlder wasn't easy. I had to be smart. Careful. Patient.

I'd been up here for more than a day now. Snuck past the guards in the dead of night and climbed the slatted west end of the building. Not as hard a climb as I thought it would be. My right arm still had an elbow, and the slats were spaced plenty wide enough for me to hook my forearm through.

The doctor arrived eleven hours ago. Right on schedule. The guy I'd bribed at the flyer rental company had the time nailed.

I'd watched the flyer land. Watched him check on the snail pen. Watched him walk up to the clinic and disappear under the eaves.

He'd be in bed by now. Sleeping directly underneath me. I'd seen him sleeping once before.

He slept with his mouth open.

I drank down the last of my water and stuffed the canteen back in my pack. I rolled over and peered through a narrow copper pipe I'd inserted through the thatch. I waited for my eye to adjust to the darkness, the room barely lit by an outdoor floodlight. Forms took shape. Pillow. Head. Hair. Mouth.

He was sleeping on his back, but his open mouth was to the right of where I wanted it to be. I pulled the pipe out of the thatch, picked a new spot, and began the tedious effort of working it through the many layers of weather-beaten fronds.

I pushed my way through, cringing at the crinkling, crunching sound of dried leaves. I told myself he wouldn't notice. Mating season was over. It was nesting time, 'guanas all over this roof, gnawing and digging and burrowing.

I put my eye up to the pipe again, waited for my vision to adjust. The stupid bastard had moved.

I kept at it for ten, twenty, thirty minutes until I finally lined it up. I took the fishing line and sinker, dropped the sinker into the pipe, and slowly played out the line, lowering it down centimeter by centimeter. I looked through. Lowered some more. Looked through again.

The sinker dropped slowly, painstakingly, toward that open mouth, farther and farther, straining the limits of my depth perception. I hoped I wouldn't make contact by going too far. I stopped, put the line in my mouth, and gripped it with my teeth. Reaching for my bag, I dropped fingers into the side pocket and pulled out one of the snails I'd five-fingered from the snail pen.

What comes around goes around, Doc.

I set the shell on the thatch and dug the snail out with thumb and index finger. I gripped it in my palm and squeezed, let the juice run off my hand into the shell.

I took the shell and held it to the line, gently poured a drop onto the cord, watched the drop disappear into the pipe. I had to imagine it the rest of the way, a tiny bead of liquid descending from the rafters. A raindrop rolling down a blade of grass. A dewdrop running down a spider silk.

I poured another drop and another and another, the genie on its last magic carpet ride.

I pulled the line back up, stuffed it into my pack along with the short run of pipe. I grabbed the pack, slipped the shoulder straps over my shoulders, and went to the roof's edge, lay face-down with my feet hanging off the edge. Squirming backward with my legs hanging down, my feet found a rafter.

I crouched on a beam of rough-hewn wood. The doctor was awake, sitting up in bed, his light turned on. He was in his underwear, revealing toned legs and sculpted offworld pecs. Styled hair hung to his shoulders.

I kept my voice low, knowing there was at least one guard somewhere downstairs. "Stand up."

He did.

"Come over here and help me down."

Bare feet padded across rippled planks. He reached up and spotted me as I climbed down. I reached the floor and stood face-to-face with him. I looked deep into his eyes. Looked for signs of terror, but I found nothing. His eyes were flat. Unfeeling. I was used to instilling fear, great buckets of it.

This felt so wrong. So unnatural.

"You know what's happening to you, don't you? You're in my control now."

"Yes," he whispered.

"Where's your new nurse?"

"She left. I don't make her stay overnight when I'm here."

"Who else knows how to produce the genie?"

"Nobody. I don't need the competition." His voice was bland. Monotone.

"What about breeders? Who's breeding them?"

"They can't be bred."

"Why not?"

"I wired them to be sterile. That way I was sure to keep my monopoly."

"How do you produce them?"

"I let unmodified snails mate and treat the eggs."

I needed to verify it again. "Nobody knows how to do the procedure?"

"Nobody but me."

"You have a phone in your head?"

"Yes."

"Delete everything."

"What do you mean?"

"Your notes. Your inventions. Delete every fucking thing you've ever done. Delete the backups. Delete it all."

He closed his eyes, his brain jacking into unseen systems.

I reached into my bag, pulled out a few meters of rope, a noose on one end. I picked a rafter near the bed and tossed an end over.

"Call your nurse," I told him. "Tell her you have to leave. Make her come in as soon as she can."

Her holo appeared. I didn't look at her. I didn't look at him. I stayed focused on the rope, tying a well-practiced one-handed knot to keep it attached to the rafter.

"She'll be here in an hour," he said.

I checked my knot, gave the rope a rough tug. I turned around to find him waiting for his next order. His face was as blank as rock, his eyes made of glass.

This was supposed to be a righteous kill. He stole my arm. He created the genie. He experimented on people. Disfigured them beyond belief.

I should be riding a wave of virtuous vengeance. I should be soaring on wings of ruthless victory.

But all I felt was disgust. Disgust for a drug that could erase a person's humanity. A drug that could enslave both the body and the mind.

I went to the door without looking at him again, gave my final order on the way out. "Hang yourself."

I passed the staircase, didn't worry about my creaking footsteps. Some of the patients walked around from time to time. I'd seen it myself.

The sound of rope snapping taut made me pause, the to-and-fro creak of a rafter. It was done.

I went into the circus of horrors that posed as a patient ward. I needed to see them one more time.

I moved from bed to bed telling them not to worry. Their nurse would be here soon. And in the morning aid workers would come to take them away from here. Maggie had anonymously made arrangements.

Bed to bed, I consoled them. *Help is coming.* I pulled up the sheet for one. Straightened the pillow for another.

I stopped at the last bed, his mouth replaced with mandibles that opened and closed. I recognized this one. Took me a second to remember where. The other YOP cop, the one who had confronted me with Panama on the dock, the one I'd brained with a bag of coins.

One of his bug legs reached for me, scraped along my arm. I stood over him, looked into desperate eyes.

"Your nurse will be here soon."

The leg batted my arm.

I knew what he wanted, his eyes speaking words he couldn't say. I pulled a curtain to separate him from the others, then took the pillow from under his head, held it up for him to see. His eyes lit, a tear dripping free, legs clicking excitedly.

I pressed the pillow down. Held it in place until the legs went still.

Hour after hour, I piloted the rented boat downriver. I paid no attention to where I was going, just kept with the flow, knowing all the tributaries eventually led home.

I couldn't think. Didn't want to. I felt numb. So much death. So much suffering. So many enemies with black hearts.

I'd cry if I only knew how. I'd let out giant wails. I'd stomp my feet and throw a fit. I'd pound my chest and scream at the heavens.

If I only knew how.

I looked to the east, where the sky was skirted with the blue and pink of approaching dawn. The Big Sleep was almost over, my world soon to emerge from night and once again know the sun.

I turned off the motor, let the river guide me. I stared at the sky and waited.

Waited for the darkness to lift.

about the author

WARREN HAMMOND works as an instructor in the computer industry where, over the past eighteen years, he has taught thousands of information-technology professionals. An avid traveler, he and his wife have traveled widely on several continents. *KOP Killer* is his third novel, following *KOP* and *Ex-KOP*. He lives in Denver with his wife and two cats. He is working on a new mystery novel.

Find out more at www.warrenhammond.net.